Thorn in My Heart

Thorn in My Heart

LIZ CURTIS HIGGS

Doubleday Large Print Home Library Edition

WATERBROOK
PRESS

This Large Print Edition, prepared especially for Doubleday Large Print Home Library, contains the complete, unabridged text of the original Publisher's Edition.

THORN IN MY HEART
PUBLISHED BY WATERBROOK PRESS
2375 Telstar Drive, Suite 160
Colorado Springs, Colorado 80920
A division of Random House, Inc.

All Scripture quotations are taken from the *King James Version* of the Bible.

The characters and events in this book are fictional, and any resemblance to actual persons or events is coincidental.

ISBN 0-7394-3522-1

Printed in the United States of America

**This Large Print Book carries the
Seal of Approval of N.A.V.H.**

To Sara Fortenberry,
who understands my passion
for writing fiction
better than anyone.
You were there from the first,
from that wintry day years ago
when this wee tale was born.
Thank you for encouraging me,
trusting me, believing in me.
Love you, sis.

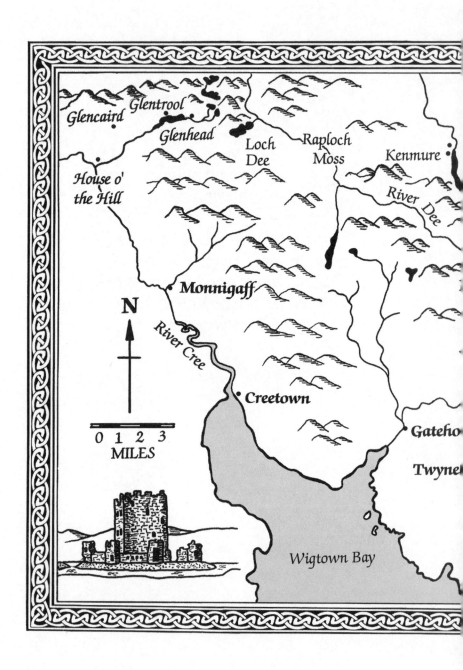

GALLOWAY, Scotland
1788
by Benny Gillies

River Nith

Dumfries

‘llan

‘vay

Urr Water

Milltown

Lochend

Drumcultran

Auchengray

Lowtis Hill

Newabbey

Haugh of Urr

‘reave

Carlinwark Loch

Dalbeaty

Criffell

‘tonhill

Kirkbean

‘cudbright

‘undrennan

Solway Firth

Highlands

Lowlands

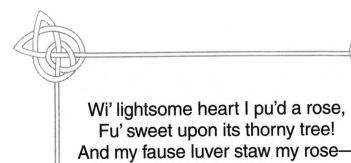

Wi' lightsome heart I pu'd a rose,
Fu' sweet upon its thorny tree!
And my fause luver staw my rose—
But ah! he left the thorn wi' me.

ROBERT BURNS

Prologue

My mother groan'd! my father wept.
Into the dangerous world I leapt.
WILLIAM BLAKE

Glen of Loch Trool
Summer 1764

Breathe not a word of my visit, Jean. Not to a soul."
The midwife merely nodded, opening the *bothy* door wider to receive her unexpected guest. Rowena McKie brushed past her into the cottage, then eased her ungainly body onto a rough bench. Her skirt caught on the splintery wood, and she snatched it free with an impatient yank. Another

ragged seam for Ivy's busy needle and thread to mend. "Tell me the babe's coming soon, Jean. Mr. McKie can't sleep at night for worrying."

Carrying her husband's heir through the long days of a Lowland summer had ground Rowena down like corn at McCracken's mill. Her feet were swollen, her knees ached, and even fresh meadowsweet could not ease the burning in her stomach. Rowena pressed her damp palms against the unfinished oak and took the deepest breath she could. She'd come to the midwife for answers and had no intention of leaving without them.

"Now, now." The older woman leaned over and squeezed Rowena's shoulder, her touch as gentle as her words. "Nothin' *mair* than nerves. Yer first time and all." Jean's eyes were wreathed in wrinkles and blue as forget-me-nots. Her dress was made of striped drugget, the too-snug bodice made for a younger woman. Beneath the ragged hem poked her bare feet, browned by the sun, the nails grass stained but neatly trimmed. "Ye were right to come knockin' on my door. What would folks in the glen be sayin' if I didn't tend to Mr. McKie's firstborn? Yer time is still a month off, but when it comes—"

"A month?" Rowena's eyes widened. "Are you daft, woman? I'll not last a week like this! Can't you see how the child moves within me?" To prove her claim she arched her back, inviting the midwife's inspection. "Look for yourself. Like a wild goat kicking his heels to one side, then the other."

"Mair than one wee goat." Jean smoothed her hands across the fabric of Rowena's dress, measuring the shape of her distended figure with a practiced eye. "*Twa,* I'd say."

Rowena's mouth dropped open. "Twins?"

The midwife nodded thoughtfully. "Boys, I'll wager."

Speechless, Rowena stared down at her belly. Her husband, Alec, had pleaded with the Almighty to bless her barren womb with a son. But two at once? Another kettle of fish, that. She rubbed her aching sides, feeling the child—children, if the midwife was right—moving beneath the gentle pressure of her hands. The walls of Glentrool were built with a large family in mind. Would her aging body be so accommodating?

A swift kick in her abdomen seemed an uncanny answer. "Speak the truth, Jean. This constant commotion, the sharp pains in my ribs. Surely this can't be the usual way of things, even with twins?"

The midwife chewed on her lip, continuing to press and prod Rowena's middle. "Twa *bairns* are always harder on the *mither.* But I fear somethin' is amiss." A note of compassion crept into the older woman's voice. "How *auld* are ye, Mistress McKie?"

"Too old to be having my first, if that's what you mean." The worst of her many worries had come home to roost. "I'll be thirty-eight come November."

Jean made a *st-st* sound against her teeth. "If I weren't so certain this was the Lord's doin', I'd be gatherin' *stanes* for yer burial cairn. But seein' how the Almighty has placed his hand upon yer womb, I'll be usin' these instead." She reached into the money pouch tied at her waist and unfolded her fingers to reveal two silver coins in her palm. "All ready to tuck into their fists. Ye know the custom?"

Rowena nodded, relieved to hear the woman's confident tone. Jean was a woman who feared the Almighty, not a common *wutch*. The silver pieces cast no spell; they were meant for good luck and the blessing of wealth. It seemed Jean expected the children to live. And so, please God, would she.

Rowena rose unsteadily to her feet, hoping the change in position might offer some relief. Instead it yielded another vicious kick from her hidden offspring and a jolt of pain at the base of her spine. Jean's passing comment crept into her bones like a damp mist, chilling her. "You said something is amiss?"

The midwife nodded slowly. "They're twins . . . but not the same. *Verra* different lads. One stronger than the other. By and by, the older will serve the younger."

Rowena's mouth went dry. *Twins but not twins.* A bad omen after all. She would see them baptized by the parish minister at the earliest possible hour. But the older serving the younger? That was not the Scottish way of things. Staring hard at the woman's unblinking blue gaze, Rowena searched her lined face for assurance. "Is this a word from the Almighty?"

"'Tis that, aye." Jean's gray head bobbed slowly up and down. "Time will prove me truthful."

"I've little doubt of that." For the moment she would let the subject rest. Jean Wilson was the finest *howdie* in Galloway. Rowena knew she would be in good hands when the time came. "I'd best be home before Mr. McKie discovers I'm gone and frets himself sick. I slipped out the door without telling him where I was going." She shrugged slightly, knowing Jean would understand. "He's *fash* enough these days, watching my belly grow." Rowena moved toward the door, gathering her light plaid about her shoulders. Summer or not, the evening winds blew a stout breeze across Loch Trool. "Don't stray far, Jean. I'll be sending my maid-servant Ivy Findlay round soon enough. You'll be here when she calls?"

"I've not missed a birthin' in the glen all these years, Mistress McKie."

"Aye. By God's mercy, mine will not be the first."

Bidding her farewell, Rowena left the thatch-roofed cottage behind and picked her way along the winding path toward home. Awkward as she was of late, riding on horseback was impossible and a carriage out of the question, with no proper road and bogs at every turn.

Rowena slowed her steps, more exhausted than she could ever remember. And no wonder. *Twins!* All well and good for Alec, nearing sixty, to pray for an heir. He didn't have the burden of carrying the babes. "Nor the challenge of bearing them," she announced to a wheatear that flew over her shoulder, its black-and-white tail flirting like a lass's fan.

She tilted her head back, taking in the steep slopes rising all around, so different from the rolling hills of east Galloway where she'd spent her girlhood. Mulldonach loomed on the right, where Robert the Bruce had claimed his first victory against the English troops by rolling great boulders down the steep slopes and crushing the army. Ahead rose Buchan Hill, once the hunting ground of Comyn, Earl of Buchan, now covered with McKie flocks. Rough and craggy at the top, the mountains gave way to slender stretches of grass and sparse, piney woods along the meandering loch.

At the heart of the glen stood the granite walls of Glentrool, the only laird's house for miles and her home for the last twenty years. Guests marveled at the imposing tower house with its round turrets and soaring chimneys that stood in the shadow of the Fell of Eschoncan. When asked how it had been constructed in so remote a setting, Alec borrowed a tale from the Bruce and insisted, "The stanes rolled *doon* the mountain, and the *hoose* built itself!"

When Archibald McKie, Alec's father, bartered a bride for his son from the distant parish of Newabbey, Glentrool had welcomed her with pine-scented arms. *Bartered* was not quite the way of it, Rowena reminded herself with a chuckle, but it was not far from the truth. Her brother, Lachlan, had urged her to marry Alec, and she'd agreed sight unseen. It was not merely the vast McKie lands that had appealed to Lachlan's greedy nature. The fine gold bracelets McKie's manservant had slipped around her wrists were enticement as well. "A bonny bride is soon decorated," young Lachlan had whispered in her ear, pocketing the silver McKie's man had pressed into his own hands. "Haste to his side, lass, and let him see what his coin has purchased."

Rowena and Alec were married a fortnight later with their parents' ardent blessings.

How young she'd been! Eighteen, green as Galloway grass in May. What had she known of marriage, of life in the lonely glen, far from village and friend? She'd learned to care for her older, steady-tempered husband, even to love him as the years passed. Respect had not come so easily. Alec gave in too readily to her wishes. He was more wind-bent willow than stalwart oak, good man though he was. Rowena shook her head, thinking of all the times her headstrong nature had overwhelmed his passive one. "Such a *heidie* lass I've brought under my roof!" he would say, then pinch her cheek a bit harder than necessary. Willful she might be, but before summer's end she would present him with not one heir, but two. It was a secret too good to keep, yet too dangerous to tell until the babes were safely tucked in her arms and away from the fairies' grasp.

"*Och!*" Rowena yanked her skirts clear of a prickly blackthorn bush, imagining the seasons to come with two strong-willed young sons. Who would help her raise them when their father grew too old and weak to be of any use? Her parents were gone. And her brother lived in distant Newabbey, separated from her by mountains and moors.

"I'll be needing your help, Lord," she whispered, stepping gingerly along the mossy banks. "If I'm to raise my sons worthy of their father's blessing, I canna do it alone."

*   *   *

Rowena was anything but alone when her time came.

Half a dozen women gathered about her birthing room to witness the birth of the McKie heir. Rowena vaguely recognized their faces through the pain that hung over her like a shroud, yet she could not think of a single one of their names. Was that McTaggart's widow in the stiff gray bonnet? Or one of the McMillans from Glenhead? Every one of her neighbors would later insist that she was present at the birth. Rowena heard the women murmuring, felt their eyes on her. For the moment they offered more gossip than comfort.

She sat propped up in the midst of the enormous bed she shared with Alec, its heavy curtains drawn tightly back. The autumn sun streamed through the casement window and across her pillow, warming the room. In the hearth a fire blazed, to be used for boiling water as needed and for staving off the chill the evening air would bring. For now the heat only added to Rowena's misery. "Jean," she whispered, her mouth parched, her breath coming in gasps. "Thirsty."

The midwife dipped her finger in a cup of cool water and ran it along Rowena's lips to moisten them. "I canna *gie* ye anythin' to drink, Mistress McKie. Later, I promise, ye can have yer fill." Jean put the cup aside, then leaned over her, almost singing in a voice low and rhythmic: "Breathe now. There ye go. And again. That's the way." Jean smoothed Rowena's hair back from her brow and adjusted her pillow, then reached for a blue thread of spun wool stretched out on the bedside table. "Gie me yer ring finger, Mistress McKie."

Rowena obliged, lifting her hand from the sheets bunched around her in a futile attempt at modesty. As instructed, she breathed as deeply as she could while Jean's nimble fingers wound the blue thread around her finger, above her thick silver wedding band.

"Keep her safe from the fever, Almighty God," Jean intoned, tying the string in a neat bow, then squeezing Rowena's fingers against the knot. " 'Twas your mither's and yer *granmither's* thread before that, aye?"

Rowena nodded. Both her foremothers had bravely survived their labor without succumbing to childbed fever—spared, it was thought, by the common blue thread. Rubbing her thumb over the worn wool, Rowena prayed it would bring her good fortune as well. So little about birthing was within a woman's control. Jean had placed the family Bible under her pillow, as custom dictated, and an old nail under her bed for safe measure, lest a changeling be substituted for the healthy babe. God alone knew how the day would end.

The midwife eyed the women gossiping across the room, then leaned closer and whispered in Rowena's ear, "Come midnight we'll see the lads born." The two women had not breathed a word of their expectations to anyone, not even to Alec McKie. What, and bring ill luck knocking at the door? No, indeed.

Rowena studied Jean's face, hungry for more news. "Before midnight? Wednesday then?" The month, the day, the hour—every detail of the birth had a meaning. "Or will it be Thursday?"

"Hush now." Jean reached down and pressed two gnarled fingers to her lips. "The Lord knows, Mistress McKie. Trust him."

Before the hour ended, trust in God was all Rowena had left. Excruciating pain cleft her in two as the twins fought over who would appear first. Day dragged into evening. Eyes bleary, arms drooping at her side like broken wings, Rowena staggered around the room until she could walk no more. Drained of strength, she crouched in the bed, hands clutching her knees, and begged the heavens for mercy. At the end she could do naught but push when Jean demanded it, then fall back in an exhausted stupor, only to push again a moment later.

In desperation, the neighborhood women circled her bed, holding aloft their cherished family Bibles, pleading for the Almighty's enemies to be hurled into the Red Sea. "Help me," Rowena pleaded again and again. It was taking too long; it was all taking much too long.

The starless sky was black as pitch and every candle lit when the midwife finally shouted with glee, "I see a tuft of *bricht* red hair!" A cheer rang about the room, then busy hands hastened to their duties. Everything moved at a faster clip. Drenched in tears and sweat, Rowena made a final effort to end her agony. One floor below, the workings of an ancient clock began to grind loudly, preparing to strike the hour.

A cry split the air first.

"He's here! Yer son is born!" crowed Jean.

One. Two. Three.

Rowena sank into the bed, barely conscious as the distant chimes rang.

Four. Five. Six.

She could hear the babe whimpering as Jean called out, "Och! There's a second child, there is! Close on his brother's heels. Ye'll not be long deliverin' this one."

Rowena felt the urge to push again.

Seven. Eight. Nine.

Jean's voice rang out, louder than the chimes. "One mair push, Mistress McKie, and ye'll have twa bairns lyin' in yer arms."

Ten. Eleven. Twelve.

The whole gathering held its breath until another lusty cry rang out in the crowded bedroom. The clock was silent now, but all else was in an uproar.

"Twa sons, they are! Twins!"

Rowena fell back on her pillow in a faint, while all around the room merry bedlam reigned. Amid the clamor Jean made short work of the cords with a sharp knife, then fed each child a wee spoonful of salt to chase away the fairies and gave them a quick dunking in cool water from the loch to make them strong and healthy. Dazed, Rowena could do nothing but watch as every precaution was taken. A candle fashioned from the root of a fir tree, cut into thin splinters and seeping with turpentine, was carried around her bed three times. Rowan twigs were tossed on the fire. Prayers were said by each woman in turn before passing a dish of oatmeal and water and supping three spoonfuls. With two fragile lives hanging in the balance, this was no time to put aside the old ways.

Jean left the others to their business and tended to Rowena's needs, clucking and fussing as she helped her sit up. She propped a bolster behind her, then firmly pressed a shivering, squalling infant into the crook of each arm, their wet bodies tightly wrapped in newly woven linen. "Nothin' alike, yer lads," Jean murmured, leaning closer as she pushed aside the soiled sheets. "See how the red one wears a hairy cloak, and the other has naught but a bit o' goose down on his head?"

Rowena could not take her eyes off their tiny faces, pinched and wrinkled, their hungry cries piercing her soul. "My sons," she whispered, brushing a light kiss on each head, fighting tears. Afraid to speak the names she'd chosen for them until the lads were baptized, she pressed her cheek to their damp heads and in her heart lifted them to heaven in prayer: *Evan Alexander McKie,* the one with a full head of red hair and a lusty cry. *James Lachlan McKie,* his downy-capped younger brother. "May I love them both the same," she said softly.

"'Twill be a challenge, different as they are," Jean agreed, patting her arm. "Not even born on the same day, these twa. But both McKies, no mistakin' that."

Rowena pulled her attention away from her sons

long enough to meet the midwife's sympathetic gaze. "What do you mean they weren't born on the same day?"

Jean glanced behind her, then crouched down until they were eye to eye. "Did ye notice the clock chimin'?"

"Aye, but . . ." Rowena's limbs suddenly began to shake uncontrollably. "Wh-what . . ."

"Not to worry. To be expected, this chill of yours. 'Twill pass soon enough." Ever efficient, Jean tucked woolen blankets around Rowena's legs and shoulders, then lifted a cup of tepid tea to her lips. "Now then, about the time of birth. This red and *birsie* son of yers was born when Wednesday was on the wane. But this smooth one came after all twelve chimes ushered in Thursday. D'ye see how it is?"

Rowena stared down at their damp heads. "'Wednesday's child is full of woe,'" she whispered, a rhyme spoken by every Scottish mother from time out of mind.

Jean nodded, her jovial expression growing more serious. "Aye, so it is. And 'Thursday's child has far *tae* go.'"

"Oh, but not yet, wee one." Rowena swallowed hard, horrified at the mere thought of the younger, smaller twin being taken from her side. *Jamie.* The look of his sweet, brown-tufted head had already stolen her heart. "Please, not yet."

"Have no fear. Both will live." Jean's voice was low but firm. "The second one, born past midnight, will have the power to see the Spirit o' God abroad in the land. He's gifted, that one. Remember what I told ye the month last? 'The older will serve the younger.' See that ye don't forget when the time comes."

"When might that be?" Rowena's shivering continued as she drew her babies closer still. "How will I know?"

Jean shrugged, not unkindly. "We *niver* know when or where, Mistress McKie. Like any mither, ye must stand at the ready. Almighty God will show ye what's tae be done." Jean squeezed her shoulder with frank affection, then gently touched each infant's head. "And now, mistress, what else may I do for ye this *nicht?*"

A fresh spate of tears rolled down Rowena's face and over her trembling lips. "Tell Mr. McKie . . ." She choked on her words, clutching her babies tight against her swollen breasts. "Tell him his prayers have been answered. God has seen fit to make him a father."

One

And all to leave what with his toil he won,
To that unfeather'd two-legged thing, a son.
JOHN DRYDEN

Glentrool
Autumn 1788

Heaven help us, Jamie. Your father has . . . *Och!* I cannot bear it."

Jamie watched his mother storm about the fading gardens of Glentrool. Up and down she walked, hands waving through the air as she fretted over Alec McKie's latest blunder. After two dozen years beneath her roof Jamie was well acquainted with his mother's theatrics. He simply folded his arms across his blue serge waistcoat and waited.

The forenoon sun lit the grassy paths but did not warm them. A crisp autumn wind rustled through the pines and sent a golden pile of rowan leaves swirling about his buckskin breeches and her billowing gray skirts. Rowena, named for the hallowed tree with its bright red berries, grabbed the fabric of her dress with both hands and shook hard, sending dust and leaves flying. "It's not fair, what the man has done. Not fair at all!"

"I'm sure you're right, Mother." A smile played at the corners of his mouth. Despite her age and agitated state, Rowena McKie still made a *sonsie* sight. In seasons past, reports of her coal-black hair and sparkling dark eyes had traveled from one end of Galloway to the other, from the harbor at Portpatrick to the *vennels* of Dumfries. Covetous men had eyed her at kirk and market alike, giving his father no end of trouble defending her honor and keeping ne'er-do-wells at bay. A bonny wife came at a steep price, Jamie realized, one he did not intend to pay unless the lass was verra bonny indeed.

Rowena gnawed at her bottom lip, her brow furrowed. The news was bad, it seemed. Whatever had taken place since they'd shared breakfast earlier, it was clear his father had outdone himself.

"Are you going to tell me what's happened, Mother, or must I guess?"

"Listen to me, Jamie." A long strand of hair, lately streaked with silver, fell to her neck. She tucked it back in place with graceful fingers, her gaze firmly locked with his. "It's about your brother."

Jamie grimaced. It was always about Evan.

"Your father summoned him. Sent Thomas Findlay out at dawn, as if the man had nothing better to do than scramble his way over the Rig of Stroan looking for your wayward brother. It took Thomas all morning to find him." She leaned toward him and lowered her voice to an urgent whisper. "You should have seen Evan dragging himself through the door in his filthy hunting plaid. That red mane of his was a tangled mess. And his *beard!* I'm ashamed to call him my firstborn."

Jamie merely nodded while his stomach bore the brunt of the news, twisting itself into a hard, painful knot. Rowena McKie might be ashamed of her older son, but Alec McKie doted on Evan, endlessly praising his keen hunter's eye and strong bow arm. "No doubt Evan came straightaway when he heard the news," Jamie grumbled. "He kens which side his bannock's buttered on."

His mother eyed him, one brow arched. "You'd be wise to do the same."

Jamie studied the toe of his boot, not wanting to provoke her displeasure. From nursery days he and his brother had been pitted against each other by their doting mother and father, compared and contrasted, weighed and measured like livestock: "Jamie is taller, aye, but Evan is stronger." "Jamie is clever, aye, but Evan is brave." If such comments were meant to be helpful, the plan had failed miserably. A bitter rivalry for their parents' favor had ensued. Aggravation turned to seething animosity as Alec and Rowena made their preferences all too apparent.

Jamie, less than a minute younger than his twin, had no claim on his father's heart at all. His mother's heart was another matter entirely: Jamie owned the whole of it and Evan not a bit. Such had always been the case, and more so of late. His wayward brother strayed far from Glentrool's boundaries; Jamie stayed closer to home, keeping his mother company and the family ledgers neat. Evan cared little for social discourse; Jamie's manners were impeccable. Evan had married a woman his parents loathed; Jamie had prudently heeded his mother's advice concerning marriage. On three occasions he'd brought a lass home to Glentrool for his mother's assessment, and each time Rowena had whispered, "Not this one."

So be it. With his father's love and attention firmly settled on Evan, Jamie dared not risk losing his mother's favor as well by choosing an ill-suited bride. He had plenty of time to find a wife. For now, the verdant hills and rich flocks of Glentrool were more than enough to satisfy him.

"What sort of reception did Father give Evan?" Jamie asked, knowing the answer.

"He ignored your brother's slovenly appearance and welcomed him with open arms. Not that your father can see well enough to notice how your brother dresses, mind you. Instead, he *blethered* on and on about his two favorite subjects."

"His old age being one of them," Jamie offered, certain she would nod in agreement. "Did Father mention how he's *fey* and nigh to dying? And how his sight wanes by the hour?" Jamie regretted the glib tone of his words the minute he said them. The man was, after all, nearly blind. "So then. The other matter he discussed?"

"Dinner."

"Aye, it would be." Despite his failing eyesight, Alec McKie's appetite for savory meat remained sharp as ever, particularly when served with red currant jelly and roasted potatoes. Evan, skilled hunter that he was, courted their sire's approval with roe deer, hung to a high flavor, and fresh salmon pulled from the Minnoch. Jamie was too impatient for fishing, useless with firearms, worse with a bow. He could handle a sword when necessary or plant his fist in a man's gut if provoked. For the most part, words were his weapon and logic his armor. In the war to please his father, he'd been soundly beaten by Evan.

"Your father sent him off with quiver and bow, bound for the Wood of Cree to hunt wild game. Said he had a taste for venison."

Jamie shrugged, not really caring. Family intrigues held no fascination for him. His mother thrived on them, so he humored her. "Tell me why Evan's hunting concerns you."

Her eyes sparked. "It's your future that concerns me, James Lachlan McKie!" She stepped closer, hands clasped tight about her waist. Her pointed chin, as sharp as his, jutted upward. "Your father's last words to Evan before he left were, 'I want to give you my *blissin* before I die.'"

"His . . . blessing?" Jamie's jaw tightened. Now she had his full attention. The man's blessing was a great deal more than a kind word. His father meant to give his *heirship*—Glentrool and all the land's riches—to Evan. *Evan,* his fool of a brother! Jamie could barely speak the words. "Glentrool will be . . . Evan's?"

"*Wheesht!* Don't even think such a thing! You alone are meant to claim it, Jamie."

She'd said so before, dozens of times. That *he* should be his father's heir. That he was the canny one, who managed the flocks and fields with a prudent eye. That it was the Almighty's will he should rule Glentrool someday. Jamie had believed her because he wanted to, because he loved Glentrool and despised the brother who would inherit property he neither labored over nor deserved.

If his mother was right, Evan would claim Glentrool as his own. All the land, all the goats and sheep, and every room of the house.

"Do you know what this means?" Jamie ground out the words, turning on his heel to pace the ground. "The moment Father is dead, Evan will toss me out on the moors without a single guinea or a second thought."

"Nae! I will not allow it." His mother lunged after him and snatched his sleeve. "Do you hear me, Jamie? Your father did this on his own, without saying a word to me."

He turned to find her eyes bright with unshed tears. "Is that what irks you most, Mother? That he didn't seek your counsel?"

"Nae!" She swung away from him, her cheeks scarlet. He'd nicked her pride too near the bone. A moment later she turned back, her features cooled but her jaw firm. "What irks me most is a father who refuses to credit both his sons equally." Her eyes narrowed. "And a son who's forgotten all the things his mother has done for him."

Jamie had no choice but to nod in acknowledgment. Hadn't she made certain he slept in the largest bedroom and rode *Walloch,* the finest mount in the McKie stables? Wasn't she the one who surrounded him with books, as expensive as they were to come by, and intervened whenever Evan appeared to be getting the upper hand? Gratitude was the least he could offer her, though at times the weight of her favor pressed down on his chest like a gravestone.

"You've done much for me, and I'm grateful." He dipped his head, a gentleman's bow. "What would you have me do in return?"

She slipped her hand through the crook of his elbow and led him farther away from the busy house, apart from listening ears and curious glances and windowpanes that shone down on them like the eyes of the Almighty. She inclined her head toward his and squeezed his arm affectionately. "I have a wee plan, Jamie."

Hearing the warm note of persuasion in her voice, he knew he was doomed to do her bidding.

"Your father will be expecting Evan to serve him alone in the dining room, by his own hand in a week or so, will he not? A *gustie* haunch of venison and the best of our kitchen garden spread about Glentrool's table like gifts for the king. An evening supper to close the day and seal Evan's future, aye?"

Her vivid imagery sharpened Jamie's tongue. "What has this to do with me?"

"Patience, lad." She steered him along the leafy path, crushing rowan berries beneath her best shoes. "While your brother is off hunting south of Trool, you and I will be planning our own fine meal to garner an audience with your father."

He jerked her to a stop. "I'm no hunter, and you ken it well."

She lifted her head to meet his gaze. "You don't hunt for goat meat, Jamie." Her smile creased the corners of her eyes, which shone like polished onyx. "Not with young goats aplenty on Buchan Hill."

"Goats?" He shook his head, uncertain of her meaning. "Do you mean to serve him goat meat instead of venison?"

She brushed her hand through the air, as though plotting and scheming were a simple matter. "'Tis nothing to season one meat to taste like another. Did I not spend a girlhood summer learning cookery in Dumfries? We'll serve your father a noontide meal a few days hence, long before Evan and his roebuck darken Glentrool's kitchen door."

"All well and good to disguise the meat. What of my own hide, Mother?" He glared at her, hoping he might alter the reckless course she'd charted. "I can alter my voice, but have you plans to smother me in spices as well?"

"Not spices, no. But something every bit as fragrant: your brother's plaid." Her smile stretched farther, revealing a row of teeth grown blunt with age. "Your father will not realize what he's done, not until it's too late. Until then, it will be our *saicret,* Jamie." She stroked the fabric of his sleeve with a firm hand. "Yours and mine."

Two

A secret at home is like rocks under tide.
<small>DINAH MARIA MULOCK CRAIK</small>

Newabbey Parish, East Galloway

Was dinner to your liking, Father?"

Leana McBride sat at attention across the table from her father and watched while he dragged the back of his hand across his mouth, ignoring the linen napkin by his plate. His ebony hair, threaded with silver, was pulled back from his broad forehead and tied into a severe tail. The pewter buttons on his coat gleamed in the firelight.

"It was food, and it was eaten." With a surly grunt, he pushed his chair away from the table and

yanked his gray waistcoat into place, not once looking in her direction. Instead, his gaze shifted to the
window and the darkening sky beyond it. "Storm
blowing in from the west. See to it that the ripest
apples are picked, Leana, or we'll lose the best of
them." He waved his hand dismissively. "Go on with
you. I'm expecting a visitor shortly. See that you
don't disturb us."

She stood and dipped a slight curtsy, then
headed for the orchard, gathering up two baskets
at the kitchen door before letting it shut softly
behind her. When Lachlan McBride was in one of
his disagreeable moods, the sooner out of his presence, the better. Twenty years of trying to placate
her father had not softened his bark nor toughened
her skin. If she spoke up, he called her impertinent.
If she remained silent, he pronounced her dull. She
had no choice on such occasions but to seek the
sanctuary of her gardens, knowing he wouldn't
bother to look for her. Little wonder no woman in
Galloway would have her widowed father for a husband. Land and silver alone were not enough to
warm a woman's heart.

The blustery winds plucked at her neatly coiled
braids as Leana made her way toward the family's
meager grove of apple trees east of the house,
where they were protected from the prevailing
southwest winds. Her father's forecast was no
exaggeration; the sun was nowhere to be seen.
Heavy clouds were stacked, one behind the other,
like huge boulders ready to tumble out of the sky.
Against the slate-colored canvas, the round, yellow

fruit shone brighter than usual, ripe and golden, begging to be picked. Leana wasted no time kilting her wool skirts around her legs and climbing the wooden ladder that stood propped against a gnarled trunk. Turning her back to the wind, she began picking all she could grasp, careful not to lose her balance. The pippin apples felt warm and smooth in her hands, the fruit still firm but not too hard for knife or tooth to penetrate. She filled one willow basket, then another, reaching and bending in quick succession, keenly aware of the wind growing colder and the sky more ominous.

The atmosphere suited her unsettled mood. At dawn a knot of apprehension had settled in her stomach, tightening as the morning dragged on. An inkling of something about to occur, something close to home, would not leave her in peace. What it might be, she could not fathom. Perhaps it was naught but a change in the weather.

Spying a few apples just beyond reach, she moved up another rung on her ladder, drinking in the view as she did. Her beloved Auchengray stretched around her, its fields burnished the color of antique gold. Three miles east stood the village of Newabbey with its cozy cottages and parish kirk that greeted the McBrides every Sabbath. The western horizon hung thick with rain that would soon water the elegant walled gardens of Maxwell Park. To the north stretched hilly woods of oak and ash, elm and beech, and, farther still, the bustling streets of Dumfries. Leana knew, without turning around, what loomed behind her: Tannock Hill and, beyond it, Criffell, rising nearly two thousand feet from shore to summit, dominating the Solway coast. Many a sailor claimed to have spied diamonds sparkling among Criffell's rocky crags, but no gemstones had ever been found, as often as the more ambitious among them had searched.

The distant bleating of sheep echoed across the hills, magnified by the hollowness of the air before the coming storm. The low clouds seemed close enough to touch. Leana craned her neck, trying to catch a glimpse of the flocks and her sister, Rose. Overseeing all of Auchengray and its flocks was Duncan Hastings's responsibility. But Rose, who couldn't bear to remain indoors a moment longer than necessary, invariably found some excuse to join the seasoned shepherd at his labors.

Leana, with her pale skin and sensitive eyes, stayed safely inside and away from the sun's glare. She tended her gardens at dawn when fog and mist offered a cloak of protection, then spent the balance of her daylight hours spinning wool or embroidering linen, squinting through her dreadful spectacles. She knew full well that her younger sister thought her overly cautious. "Shame on you for hiding in the house, Leana!" Rose had chided her recently. "You're much too *timorsome* for a McBride." Perhaps she *was* timid, but only compared to the bold and fearless Rose.

There were other differences between the sisters, some less obvious than the color of their eyes or the five years that separated them. Rose disliked routine; Leana thrived on it. Rose found a new interest every week; Leana was content with her gardening season after season. Rose maintained an ever-shifting collection of friends; Leana found quiet companionship among her borrowed books and occasional visits from Jessie Newall, a young married lass from a neighboring farm. Despite their differences, the sisters were as close as two rosebuds on the same thorny stem, bound together with a loyalty born of love and utter trust.

Leana climbed down the rickety ladder, grateful to have her feet on solid ground once more, and lifted the two heavy baskets of apples, pleased at the heft of them. If there were currants and cinnamon enough in the larder, their housekeeper, Neda Hastings, would see to it that fresh pies appeared on tomorrow's table and the next day as well. Leana hurried toward the kitchen door, the first drop of rain stinging her neck. Maybe Rose would help pare the apples or roll out the crust. Or maybe not.

Just beyond the cherry trees, a peal of laughter rang out. Seconds later Rose bounded into view, her thick, black braid bouncing behind her. "Leeeannaaahhh!" she sang, twirling about in the stiff breeze, arms lifted to embrace the coming rain.

As Leana watched Rose gambol about like a lamb finding its footing, she felt a catch in her throat. *Dear, dear Rose.* Even at fifteen she was still a child. Her own child in many ways. A strong need to protect her younger sister swelled inside Leana like the Solway tide rushing to shore. Rose was so impetuous, even careless at times, blind to the dangers of the world beyond Auchengray's whitewashed walls. It was that very innocence that made her utterly charming. And wholly vulnerable.

"I've missed dinner, haven't I?" Rose laughed again, flinging open the back door with abandon, her eyes twinkling. "Naughty Rose, as usual. Father will kill me. Or you might."

Leana grinned and shook her head, carting the harvested fruit over the threshold. "No one would dream of doing such a thing, Rose." As she deposited the apples on the stone floor, she murmured, "Do keep your voice down though. Father's expecting company and will not take kindly to your *roarie* ways."

Rose sniffed dramatically. "No noisier than usual."

"As you say." Leana tugged her sister's braid with genuine affection. "Upstairs with you now. See to your filthy hands and face."

"Mothering me again, are you?"

"My favorite task," Leana assured her, gently prodding her forward. "Every girl needs a mother, Rose. Neda stepped in to mother me years ago and later gave me the happy task of doing the same for you."

"But I don't need—"

"Wheesht!" Leana lifted a finger to her lips in warning. "I hear voices in the spence. Away with you, and not another word." She watched Rose grab her skirts and disappear up the steps, lower lip protruding in a decided pout. Bless the girl, she would recover her good spirits by the time she rounded the bend on the stair.

Leana turned instinctively toward the men's

voices, curiosity drawing her to the closed door. Who'd come to call on such a *weatherful* day? Her father's prudent ways and shrewd manner—bordering on dishonest, some whispered—made him the most successful bonnet laird in the shire, earning him the begrudging respect of the local gentry. A prosperous farmer and landowner, Lachlan had once merely worked the land, as Duncan now did, with a common wool cap known as a Scotch bonnet perched on his head. When Lachlan purchased Auchengray from the heritor some ten years past, his worn bonnet had given way to the three-cornered black hat of a gentleman. A man in his position might welcome anyone into his home, from lowly peasant to Lord Maxwell himself. One such person spoke with her father now . . . but *who?*

She stood outside the door, ears straining to hear. Strong winds whistling between the panes and rattling the shutters nearly drowned out the muted conversation in the spence. The family spent most of their waking hours in the larger living room, while the adjoining spence, a small parlor, was used for entertaining privileged guests. It held the best pieces of furniture, including her father's bed, as was the custom. The only drawback was the room's shallow hearth. When guests arrived, a wee stove with a bit of lighted turf inside served as a footstool, keeping their feet warm if nothing else.

But *which* guest, Leana wanted to know. Giving in to temptation, she leaned her ear against the wood just as the winds subsided and Lachlan McBride's sonorous voice carried through the door.

"My daughter Leana is the backbone of this household."

A warm glow filled her cheeks. Her father seldom spoke so kindly about her.

"Aye, I ken she's a hard worker, Mr. McBride."

A familiar voice. Older. Someone from the next parish, though his name evaded her. And what were they doing discussing her so freely? She pressed closer, straining to hear what else the mysterious neighbor might say.

"I've oft thought of how useful the lass might be at Nethercarse."

Useful? She backed away from the door, stunned. Was she no more than a servant to be hired away at Martinmas? Certainly not. In any case she'd hardly welcome a visit to Nethercarse, a large but dreary farm in Kirkbean parish with a herd of *shilpit* cattle. They'd passed it many a time on the road to the Solway coast, the property poorly marked by a battered sign on a crumbling stone gate.

"But Leana is also useful here at Auchengray." Her father's voice sounded stern, almost defiant. "As it stands, I find your proposal unacceptable."

Her heart fluttered. *Proposal?*

On the other side of the door, Lachlan cleared his throat importantly. "Unless, that is, you truly . . . ah, value her many talents. Do I make myself clear? Come up with a more generous offer, Mr. McDougal, or I canna even consider it."

McDougal. Leana sank to her knees, her right shoulder sagging against the wood.

"You're a canny man, Mr. McBride," she heard the man grumble. "Always thinking of filling your *thrifite,* aren't you?"

"My money box is my business, Mr. McDougal. And so is my daughter."

Fergus McDougal. She'd seen him at market. He was past forty and looked older still—a dried-up, *ill-fashioned* farmer who'd worked his first wife into an early grave, leaving him with a house to manage and three growing children to feed. A widower, like her father. It seemed the men understood each other. Fergus McDougal needed a housekeeper and a governess, but a wife came cheaper. And Lachlan McBride needed silver more than he needed a daughter. Silver that would buy more sheep, expand his holdings, impress his neighbors.

"Make another offer come Monday," her father said. "I'll be expecting you."

Leana touched her hand to her throat, as though holding back all she might say, and felt her pulse pound against her trembling fingers. She was ready to marry, but not like this. A woman should marry for love. Not for money, nor for pride. And not Fergus McDougal. *Please God, no.*

The sudden scrape of chairs against the stone floor startled Leana to her feet. She darted through the living room, hearing the door behind her unlatch at the very moment she turned down the hall toward the kitchen. Breathless with fear and dread, she stumbled into the kitchen and found Neda, head of their household servants, calmly plucking a chicken.

"Neda," Leana managed between gulps of air. "Father is . . . well, he's . . ."

"Talking to Fergus McDougal, I ken." Neda yanked out another fistful of feathers. "Probably seein' if that miserly man will sell him some dairy cows. Mr. McDougal is a man of means, though ye canna tell by the look of him." She dropped the feathers into a basket by her feet, shaking her head as she did. "That *faither* of yers niver tires of makin' a bargain, does he?"

"Nae." Leana groaned, sinking onto a three-legged stool. "He doesn't."

Three

Fathers by their children are undone.
WALTER VON DER VOGELWEIDE

Father will kill me. Or at the least disown me."

"Jamie, *think!*" His mother threw her hands into the air, her patience clearly worn thin from days of pleading her case.

Jamie had done a good deal of thinking. In particular, he'd thought about how angry his father would be when he realized he'd blessed the wrong son—if the plan even succeeded, which he greatly doubted—and how furious his brother would be when he discovered his blessing had been stolen.

His mother's thoughts, on the other hand, were centered on his father's appetite. Standing in Glentrool's great stone kitchen, an apron tied over her good linen dress, Rowena McKie had spent most of the morning doing what she did best: marshaling dinner. Crocks of freshly churned butter and ripe cheese stood at attention. Baskets bearing the season's last harvest of beetroot and peas awaited further orders. Inside the brick oven nestled beside the massive hearth, fresh bread had passed muster and had baked to a crusty, golden brown.

Though Glentrool boasted a cook imported from Marseilles and a bevy of servants, his mother was happiest overseeing important meals herself. As a girl of seventeen, she'd studied the domestic arts in Dumfries, preparing herself for the day when a manor house would be hers to command. Her training was evident; she'd gone to great pains for an ordinary Saturday dinner. But then, Jamie reminded himself, this was no ordinary meal. Before it was over, he would be laird. Or he would be dead. When he mentioned that possibility to his mother, she lost what remained of her fine temper.

"Och! When has Alec McKie ever lifted a finger against his own blood? Never, that's when." She snapped her fingers at the cook's helper, who in turn poked at the meat roasting on the spit. "Is it done, Betty? Seasoned to Mr. McKie's liking?"

Aubert Billaud, their *pernickitie* French cook, had long since abandoned his post in a huff, leaving Betty to fend for herself. Her red hair gathered up in a tidy knot, her face and hands freckled by the sun, the buxom lass kept her opinions to herself and merely nodded.

Rowena left nothing to chance. "A pinch of nutmeg, a pinch of mace, aye?"

"More than a pinch, Mistress McKie."

"Good. I've no further need of you then. Leave me to serve my husband."

Betty's eyes widened. "But, mistress—"

"Away with you! A wife can serve her husband a meal if she takes the notion, can't she?"

Jamie bit his tongue. When his mother boiled hot as Scotch broth, arguing with her was pointless. The girl quit the room without another word, her bare feet soundless on the flagstone floor. He watched the door latch behind her skirts and envied her escape.

"You chose well," his mother commented, nodding at the meat. "Two goats will hardly be missed among five thousand sheep." She moved about the hearth, stirring the various pots that hung over the fire, a self-satisfied smile on her lips. "We've *tatties* and *neeps* to serve with the meat and claret to wash it down. Your father's appetite should be more than sated."

Eying the generous portions, he imagined all the calamities the hour ahead might hold. "Potatoes and turnips won't hide the fact that this is not venison." He stared at her pointedly. "And that I'm Jamie, not Evan."

She met his gaze, then held it. Held it for so long he wondered if she would ever answer his charge.

"If he asks, tell him it was a doe," she said evenly. "A young one. The flavor is milder."

His stomach sank. "Must I tell tales about the meat as well?"

"Aye, you must!" The spoon in her hand hit the edge of the iron pot with a sharp crack. "Are you so daft that you cannot feel disaster nipping at your heels? Your brother's roebuck is already hanging in the meat cellar, cleaned and skinned, hours away from your father's table."

"Mother, I'm—"

"*Hours,* Jamie!" She pointed her spoon toward a pile of green shallots wrapped in a cloth, her hand trembling. "See those? Your brother's wretched wife picked them this morning, then strolled into my kitchen and announced, 'Mr. McKie likes shallots with his venison.' As if I don't know how my own husband likes his game!" Her voice, stretched tight as a hunter's bow, nearly broke. "That *donsie* woman is counting the minutes until her husband is the future laird of Glentrool and she its mistress."

Rowena despised her daughter-in-law. "Inferior English stock," she'd grumbled under her breath on Evan's wedding day. Judith was a Cumberland lass, a Sassenach from the south. That was enough for their mother. The girl was not to be admired or trusted for any reason. Jamie didn't much care for his sister-in-law's simpering, affected manner either but surprised himself by rising to her defense.

"Judith would never do such a thing."

"Now who's telling tales?" His mother exhaled slowly, her shoulders sagging as if she bore a heavy burden. "Son, if you have any regard for me or for Glentrool . . ."

It was a constant refrain. He had no choice but to answer, "You know that I do."

She circled the table, closing the gap between them. "Then you must go through with this, Jamie." She touched his arm, and her features softened. "Would that I'd told your father that *you* were the firstborn from the very beginning and spared this day's deceptions."

"Would that you had," he agreed and meant it. "Too bad the midwife didn't tie a red string round my wrist like that babe in the *Buik*."

"Little help a scarlet thread would've been." She brushed a stubborn clump of hair back from his brow, then patted his cheek. "We'd have lost sight of it in your brother's red locks."

Evan and James. One red and woolly, one dark and smooth. Two brothers cut from altogether separate bolts of cloth. But only one could be hailed as McKie of Glentrool.

He turned to watch her wrestle the meat off the spit and onto a serving platter and knew the time had come to slip into his older brother's identity and spirit away his blessing. It was unthinkable. Unforgivable. Yet do it he would. For his mother's sake, aye, but for his own sake as well. Glentrool was more than land and livestock; it was his lifeblood.

Jamie asked her the one question that had haunted him for days. "How will I ever look Father in the eye again?"

She lifted her chin and offered a rueful smile.

"Your father can't look any of us in the eye, blind as he is. That's why this scheme of mine will work." Glancing briefly at the door to the dining room, she added, "The day is gray and *dreich,* the fire dying, the room smoky with peat. Stay at arm's length, and keep your voice low, like your brother's." She finished arranging the vegetables around the goat meat, then rinsed her hands in a bowl of water and dried them on her apron before she pulled it off and discarded it in a basket of dirty linens. "Your father will smell Evan's hunting plaid on you, reeking of moss and heather, and be thoroughly convinced." She paused to adjust the woolen fabric draped across his shoulder, wrinkling her nose as she did. "When he tastes your seasoned meat, prepared just the way he likes it, your father will know without any doubt whatsoever that you're his beloved heir."

Jamie took a deep breath, wishing he could inhale her confidence, then glanced down at his hands. The hands of a gentleman, not a hunter. A terrible prospect gripped him. "What if Father touches me? My skin is smooth, and Evan's is—"

"Birsie. I remembered that in the dark of the night and nigh to fainted 'til I thought of something. Here." She thrust a small, furry bundle at him. "These should do."

He unfolded a pair of crudely fashioned goatskin gloves and brushed his hands over them in disbelief. "What sort of *swickerie* is this?" The fur was a dingy white, not bright red like the hair that covered Evan's arms and hands, but the color was of no consequence. *Clever woman.* He didn't need to *look* like his brother. He needed to *feel* like him. Though clearly made in haste, the snug gloves fit over his fingers like a second skin. He stuffed the ragged edges inside his cuffs, then stretched out his hands. "Mistress McKie, you amaze me."

She seemed pleased with the results and touched his gloved hands to be sure. "They'll do. You'll see. Once he has eaten your food and blessed your head . . ." A slight shrug of her shoulders finished her thoughts. "He'll not be sorry, Jamie."

"When he discovers I'm not Evan, Father will be more than sorry. He'll be furious. And no wonder." Disgusted with himself, he snatched off the gloves and flung them on the floor. It was wrong, every deceiving bit of it. No matter how much he wanted to claim his father's blessing, he could not steal it and take pleasure in it as well. "He will banish me from Glentrool and curse the day I was born."

Rowena's eyes grew black as midnight. "Then let him curse the woman who bore you."

"Mother! You don't know what you're saying."

"Aye, I most certainly do!" A hint of color moved across her cheeks. "I also knew the will of God when I heard it." She retrieved the gloves with a hasty swipe and pressed them firmly into his hands. "Remember what I've told you all these years?"

He mumbled a phrase she'd repeated more often than bore counting. Words that his mother insisted came from the Almighty himself and not from a mere midwife. *The older will serve the younger.*

How many times had he soothed himself with that promise when Evan sent him to bed with bruises? Or thrown them in Evan's face when his older sibling had bested him at hawking? The time had come to test the prophecy made long ago in the glen of his birth. A glen that would become his inheritance within the hour, if his courage would hold.

"The howdie told me to be ready." Rowena wrapped the warm bread in a cloth and tucked it beneath his arm. "And so I am. The table is set with pewter, glass, and claret. Your father is waiting for his dinner." She lowered her voice to a faint whisper. "You want this, Jamie. I know you do. Now go."

Four

The bow is bent, the arrow flies,
The winged shaft of fate.
IRA ALDRIDGE

Jamie gripped the platter of meat and strode toward the dining room door with his brother's plaid tightly pinned to his shoulder and his hands covered with the skin of an innocent goat. His mother knew him far too well. Right or wrong, he *did* want Glentrool. Would lie for it. Steal for it. Beg for it, if it came to that.

His mother opened the door enough for him to slide past, then latched it securely behind him without a word. No going back. Only forward, toward his father, seated in the place of honor at the head of the long table. Jamie paused for a moment, letting his eyes adjust after the bright firelight of the kitchen. The room was square, the beams darkened by peat smoke, the walls covered with dingy portraits of McKie ancestors from decades past. One shuttered window offered a meager light, guiding him forward, closer to the man whose name he bore.

The patriarch's gray head hung low, his chin resting on his once broad chest, now sunken with age. Slender fingers gripped the arms of his chair. His elbows jutted out, as though any minute he might rise to his feet. His clothes were clean though long out of fashion, the plaid wrapped around his bony shoulders faded and worn. The old man waited, unmoving, for his dinner.

Jamie swallowed whatever pride he had left.

"Father?"

Alec McKie's head shot up, his unseeing eyes searching the room nonetheless. "Who is it?"

"It's . . . Evan. Your firstborn." Jamie nearly choked on the bitter lie, then forced himself to speak again, keeping his voice low and gruff like his brother's. "I've brought the venison you asked for. So . . . so that you'll bless me, as you promised."

Och! What a fool he was, blurting it out like that. Goat meat or venison, it no longer mattered. He'd given himself away with his too-eager words. Standing at the far end of the table, he gripped the heavy platter and waited for the inevitable. The mantel clock ticked loudly in the silent room, matching each heartbeat thumping in his chest.

His father cleared his throat with a gurgling cough. "You mean to tell me you've managed to hunt this deer, clean it, skin it, gut it, and hang it to a high flavor, all in so few days? How is that possible, my son?"

Jamie closed his eyes. It was useless to pray. He would seek mercy later. "The Almighty guided my bow."

"Is that so?" His father lifted his head, squinting at him in the dim light, his rheumy eyes unfocused.

Between the gray mist curling through the cracks around the window and the thickening peat smoke, even Jamie couldn't see clearly. He studied his father's features as best he could. Was the old man suspicious or merely curious? Before Jamie could decide, his father urged him forward with a feeble wave.

"Come closer, Son. Let me touch the hands of a hunter."

Heat rushed to Jamie's face. *Evan's hands, he means.* He put the platter aside and moved toward his father, balling his gloved fists in agony. Why on earth had he listened to his mother? He should have let *her* make a fool of herself, let *her* risk everything. Such regrets were useless now. He was standing before his father, and he was still Evan, if only for a moment longer. He bent over and rested his fingers on his father's sleeve, holding his breath as the man lightly patted the top of his hairy glove.

"I must confess, lad, your voice sounds more like young Jamie. But these are Evan's hands, no doubt of that."

Jamie nearly groaned with relief. *No doubt.* He rose, quickly withdrawing his touch.

"A pity to be so blind that I cannot see my own blessed son." His father's tone was gruffly teasing when he added, "You *are* Evan, aren't you?"

Jamie closed his eyes in shame. "I am."

The man nodded, as though satisfied. "Enough of this chatter. Bring me your venison. I've been tormented by the fine smell long enough."

Jamie turned to reclaim the platter from the sideboard, then placed the steaming meat on the table. He watched, teeth gritted, as his father leaned forward and hung his prominent nose over the offering. Surely the smell would be his undoing. His father would realize it was goat meat and guess the rest. But the old man said nothing as he stabbed at the food with his fork and poked it into his mouth with eager anticipation.

His father chewed several bites in a row, then shook his head. "Something is missing," he muttered, piercing yet another hunk of meat.

"M-missing?"

His father clinked at his empty glass with the blade of his horn-handled knife. "Something for an old man to drink. Or were you hoping I might choke to death on this roebuck of yours?"

"Sorry, Father." With a less than steady hand, Jamie poured a glass of the claret that his mother had opened earlier. His own dry throat longed for a taste of the dark red liquid. Instead he dutifully sat in a straight-backed chair by the door and let his father eat in peace, as was the man's custom, the silence punctuated by an occasional grunted request for more of this or that.

When Alec McKie unwrapped the kitchen cloth to discover fresh bread waiting for him, he grinned like a child just served syllabub. "Bread to celebrate, is it?" he crowed, tearing the loaf in two with glee. The McKie household was unaccustomed to bread, wheat being scarce in Scotland. Oatcakes or barley bannocks were the usual fare. His father's gnarled hands worked the soft bread through the meat juices, then tucked the sopping mess into his mouth with obvious delight.

Jamie fingered Evan's plaid through his gloves, grateful to draw a deep breath for the first time in nearly a week. It grieved him to admit it, but his mother's plan was working. She'd insisted her husband's appetite would overrule his common sense and all his other senses as well. And she'd been right.

Jamie reminded himself that it was not the first time he'd served a meal with less than honorable intent. As a lad of fourteen, he'd been about to eat a hearty bowl of barley broth when his brother staggered into the house, famished from a long afternoon of stretching arrows across his bow. Evan demanded his bowl of broth, and Jamie struck a bargain with his hungry brother: "Swear that I'm the older, and you can have my broth."

"Who cares who's older?" Evan fumed. "Just give me your broth before I starve to death."

Jamie circled the bowl with his arms, as though guarding it. "Swear first."

Evan spat out an oath, then threw himself into a chair and pulled up to the table, thrusting out his hands with an ugly sneer. "Give it to me, and be quick about it."

Jamie remembered serving the broth with fresh bannocks and a victor's smile. Nothing tasted better than beating his brother, whatever the game. In those days Evan didn't care who inherited Glentrool. Perhaps his brother's foolish bargain of a decade past would prove useful on this grim day. Jamie would take any favor providence might care to bestow. The ruse was not quite finished. He had yet to get what he came for.

His father leaned back in his chair with a satisfied belch. "A gustie fine meal, that." He threw out his arms in a welcoming embrace. "Come now, Son. You've done your part. Time I did mine."

Jamie scrambled to his feet, uncertain of what was expected of him. "Sir?"

"Kiss my cheek, then let me give you my blissin."

Ignoring the uneasy knot in his stomach, Jamie knelt beside his father's chair and leaned into his embrace, pressing his lips against the man's dry, leathery cheek. Suddenly the mantel clock began to chime the hour. *One. Two. Three.* Startled, Jamie yanked his head back as a shiver of fear skipped along his spine. His brother's voice and hands were deception enough. A false kiss went beyond the pale.

His father, oblivious to all but what he chose to believe, squeezed the aromatic plaid around Jamie's shoulders. "Aye, this is my beloved heir.

Smelling like the moors and mountains of Glentrool, which Almighty God made long before the first McKie fought to claim it. God himself knew that one day it would all be yours, my son." His father's eyes filled with tears as he laid his wizened hand on Jamie's head.

The weight of it nearly crushed him. He longed to cry out the truth, to be spared the guilt growing inside him. *No, Father! It's Jamie. Look and see before it's too late!*

It was already too late. Alec McKie had risen to his feet, using his other hand to steady his tottering legs. His voice was surprisingly strong, his words utterly sure. "May Almighty God bless you, my son. May he bless your land with rain and sun, your flocks and herds with abundant grazing. May your brother be subject to you and all Glentrool look to you as their laird. Cursed be anyone who curses you. And blessed be all who bless you."

Jamie trembled beneath the man's touch, letting the words he'd waited a lifetime to hear sink deep into his soul. Never mind that they were his by proxy. They were his, forever. His father had blessed him, had deemed him worthy to bear the hallowed name *McKie*.

"Thank you, Father," he whispered in response, straightening to look into his father's face, praying his sire might know the truth after all. The eyes were open but unseeing, the face smiling yet aimed at some distant point across the room.

It was then Jamie heard voices coming from outside the house. Evan. Judith. His mother, sounding frantic. Had they been there long? This much was clear: They were headed in his direction.

"I must go." Jamie tried to sound calm, bolting to his feet and gathering the remains of dinner with little grace. "I . . . I will do my best to honor your blessing." Plate and silver in hand, he hurried to the door that led to the kitchen. To freedom, he hoped. To escape. At the last he turned to watch his father drop back into his chair, confusion etched on the patriarch's features. Jamie called across the room, neglecting to lower his voice. "Forgive me, Father. Forgive me for . . . leaving so quickly."

Jamie yanked open the door, pressing his armful of dishes against the borrowed plaid, soiling it further. The kitchen was blessedly empty. He discarded the remains of dinner and tossed the musty plaid aside, his mind racing.

Two rooms away familiar voices drew closer, and the front door shut with a sharp bang.

Five

The sky is changed!—and such a change! O night,
And storm, and darkness, ye are wondrous strong.
GEORGE GORDON, LORD BYRON

A loud crack of thunder rumbled through Rose
McBride's open bedroom window, rattling the
panes and her nerves as well. Throwing aside her
woolen coverlet, she swung her legs over the side
of the bed and hurried barefoot across the room. To
her dismay, the rain had already drenched the curtains. "Och! What a nuisance!" She thrust one arm
into the downpour and yanked the casement sash
closed.

Patting herself dry with the hem of her nightgown, Rose shivered in the darkness as she

watched the rain pelt against the glass at a sharp angle. Sheep bleated in the distance, a pitiful sound like lost children calling for their mother. "Hush now, wee ones." Rose peered out into the inky night, knowing they were safe yet worrying nonetheless. Auchengray's flocks were accustomed to copious amounts of wet Scottish weather, but thunder and lightning were another matter. There was naught to be done but wait for the storm to run its noisy course and hope the morning would bring a warm October sun and drier skies.

Rose gathered her damp nightgown around her and climbed back into her box bed, grateful for its cozy warmth. Built into the wall, the enclosed bed had three solid sides and a fourth that opened into the room. She closed her bed curtains, then burrowed deep into the folds of wool, already feeling sleepy again, when a second thunderclap stopped her heart for a full beat. *"Hoot!"* she fumed, slapping her hands on the covers. Would she never get a decent night's rest?

Her ears perked up at the sound of soft footsteps in the hall outside her door. Someone else was awake. *Leana.* A gentle knock on the door followed.

"Come in," Rose whispered, loud enough so her sister might hear but their father would not. Lachlan McBride did not take kindly to midnight disturbances.

The door creaked as she opened the bed curtains. Leana glided in, bearing a candle that lit her womanly features, now decorated with a smile. "I knew you couldn't sleep through such a clamor."

"You're right, as always." Rose patted the edge of her bed, making room for company. "Sit you down," she said, which Leana did, easing onto the heather mattress.

Five years older and many shades paler, Leana was in some ways her mirror image, in others her complete opposite. They were the same unremarkable shape and size. Not too tall, not too short, not too round, not too thin. The same wavy hair fell down to their elbows, more sparse than they both liked but easily dressed. The same slender hands and feet graced their limbs.

By the light of day, those similarities shrank to nothing. Only their striking differences caught the eyes of their neighbors. Her shiny black mane and Leana's colorless one. Her dark eyes, which every man noticed, and Leana's grayish blue ones, which nigh to vanished in a certain light. Her rosy lips and Leana's full but wan smile. The two sisters were sunlight and shadow, summer and winter. As one blossomed, the other seemed to wither. Rose could no more explain it than she could take credit for it.

Leana glanced at the rain-streaked window. "The sheep will be fine, won't they?"

"You know they will."

"And what of you, my little sister?" Leana leaned closer, examining her. "Rose, you look unwell."

She jerked her chin, embarrassed by such scrutiny. She'd been feeling a bit feverish all day, but what of it? "A good night's sleep will cure whatever ails me. No need to concern yourself."

Leana regarded her evenly. "Is that a hint you're dropping?"

"I'm saying I don't need you to fuss over me, Leana."

Her older sister abruptly stood. "And so I shan't."

"Come now, Leana. No need to get all *kittlie.*" The woman was too sensitive by half, and Rose knew all her tender spots. She tugged on the sleeve of Leana's nightgown. "Stay with me until the storm passes."

Leana settled onto the bed, her face pointed toward the window. Neither spoke for a full minute, listening to the tempest raging outside Auchengray's whitewashed walls.

In the flickering candlelight, Rose studied her sister's profile and was struck anew by how much older Leana looked now than at the start of summer. A woman through and through, ready for marriage and motherhood. More than ready. Their father had yet to find a suitor worthy of Leana, or so he said. Rose saw through his subterfuge. With no wife under his roof and no more guineas in his ledger for yet another housemaid, their father wanted efficient Leana to himself. To tend the kitchen garden and spin the coarse wool from their blackface sheep and stir prunes into his cock-a-leekie soup.

Rose feared it might be the same for her in a few years. Auchengray needed her skilled hands with the flocks, her gentle touch with the horses. Most of the local gentry made certain their daughters were engaged in more genteel pursuits—painting on glass, making wax flowers, writing letters, and playing whist—but not their father. He saw no reason for his daughters to lead a life of leisure when their able hands spared him from hiring more servants. If either of the girls ever married, their husbands would be forced to pay handsomely, Rose was certain of that.

Let some son of a Galloway farmer steal one of his daughters for a song? Not Lachlan McBride. Not this year. Not any year.

"It wasn't the thunder that woke me," Leana finally confessed, fingers picking absently at a loose thread on her sleeve. "I haven't slept a wink."

"You?" She was dumbfounded. Leana was the soundest of sleepers.

"I couldn't help it, dearie." Leana didn't meet her gaze, staring instead at the window as lightning tore a ragged gash in the night sky. "Remember, our father had a visitor *yestreen.*"

Not just any visitor it seemed. "Do you mean a . . . suitor?"

When Leana shrugged at the question, Rose touched her hand in silent support. Courtship was no longer a topic for easy discussion. Not when so many young men of late had crossed Auchengray's threshold hoping to catch a glimpse of *her* instead of seeking out Leana.

"Not a suitor," Leana finally admitted with a lengthy sigh. "Merely an interested party."

"Ah." Rose grinned in anticipation. Nicholas Copland probably. Hadn't he cast an admiring glance at Leana on the Sabbath last? A studious sort, good with words. She watched Leana's face, hoping she was right. "Does this interested party of yours have a name?"

Another wave of thunder rumbled through the room as Leana's gaze met hers. "Fergus McDougal."

"*What?* That horrid old farmer from Kirkbean?"

"The very one."

Rose shot to her feet. "Under no circumstances are you to marry that man!"

"If they come to some agreement, I'll have no choice." Leana rose and stood next to her, folding her arms tightly against her gown as though suddenly chilled. "I dare not go against Father's wishes on so serious a matter."

"Och! Never mind about Father. What are *your* wishes, Leana?"

"Daft as it sounds, I've always dreamed of marrying a man who loves me." She wandered toward the darkened windows, staring out at the stormy night sky. "A man who would choose me above all others and love me for who I am." Leana released a lengthy sigh, then turned toward Rose. "Aye, but this courting has nothing to do with love."

"And everything to do with money." Rose clenched her fists as bitter, angry tears tightened her throat. "Fergus McDougal, of all people! How dare Father even consider such a match?"

"Because he wants something from the man. Grazing land, silver coin, dairy cows—only heaven knows." Leana sighed heavily, clearly resigned to her fate. "You know what Father says: 'The older daughter must marry first.'"

"Where is that written, I'd like to know."

Leana pressed a finger to her lips and guided Rose away from the door. "Hush, dearie, or you'll wake him." She leaned closer and added, "I'd rather not confess how I learned about McDougal's offer."

"Confess it to *me* at least." She couldn't resist scolding her. "And shame on you for keeping such *ugsome* news to yourself all day." While her sister described the conversation she'd overheard outside the spence, Rose fought to keep her temper in check. Fergus McDougal! What *was* their father thinking? When her own wedding day came—and that would be many years hence, for she had no intentions of throwing her youth away on marriage and motherhood—Rose meant to marry the wealthiest, bonniest lad in Galloway, whether her father approved of the man or not.

"Nothing is decided yet," Leana concluded, her features lined with concern. "Do mention me in your prayers, Rose."

"You know I will." Overcome, Rose threw her arms around her and hugged her tight. Her only sibling, her dearest friend. She pressed her warm cheek against Leana's cooler one. "No one matters more to me than you do, dear sister."

Six

Envy is born in a man from the start.
HERODOTUS

Your brother means to kill you, Jamie." His mother clutched his forearm, pulling him closer. "Ivy overheard him threatening to do so this very night. Just do what I say—"

"Haven't I done that one time too many?" Jamie yanked his sleeve free and turned to face the hearth. The scent of roasted meat dripping with spicy herbs still lingered about the kitchen, filling his nostrils with the stench of his deceit.

"Come now, lad." His mother's voice took on a cajoling tone. "There's a remedy for everything, even those things that don't turn out the way we'd planned."

"It was *your* plan, Mother, not mine." By sheer luck he'd slipped away only moments before Evan had marched into the kitchen with his own plans in mind. Plans to serve an evening meal of venison to their father. Plans to hear a blessing spoken over his head. Plans to subdue his younger brother for good. Plans which, Jamie knew, had gone terribly awry.

"Are you going to tell me what happened after I left?"

His mother gestured wildly as she spoke, clearly agitated. "I told Evan and Judith the discarded dishes were yours, that you'd eaten alone and left. They roasted the roebuck together, and I . . . well, I helped them. To make sure the meat was seasoned properly. And to give you time to . . . to . . ."

He grimaced. "Escape."

"Aye. After Judith went upstairs to bed, Evan served your father himself. I listened at the door, of course—"

"Of course."

"And as soon as Evan spoke, your father demanded to know who he was. When Evan told him . . ." She gulped, her eyes wet with tears. "Oh, Jamie. Your father was so angry his voice shook."

Jamie's stomach turned to stone. "What of Evan?"

"He . . ." She bit her lip, avoiding his gaze. "He cried out, loud as the *deid* bell at a funeral. Begged your father to bless him, too. Not once, but three times." Her shoulders drooped, and her chin fell to her chest. "It was an awful thing to hear, Jamie."

"Father blamed me, not you, didn't he?" Jamie watched her head nod ever so slightly. "And Evan the same?" A second nod. "Did Father give him any sort of blessing?"

As she lifted her head to answer him, the outer kitchen door banged open, and a rain-soaked wind blew into the room. Jamie turned around slowly, knowing what he would find: a lone figure wrapped in a sodden plaid, glaring at him with hate-filled eyes.

"These were in the stables." Evan flung a familiar pair of goatskin gloves, which slapped against Jamie's legs and fell to the floor. "Care to explain yourself, Brother?"

Rowena answered instead, her voice trembling. "Bide a wee while, lad. Hand me your—"

"Haven't you taken enough out of my hands this day, Mother?" Evan's words, sharp as their father's broadsword, cut through the air, clearly wounding her.

Jamie's back stiffened. Their mother had played a part in the deception, but Jamie wouldn't see her punished for it. Not when he'd willingly knelt by their father for the family blessing, as sacred a thing as any signed parchment. Not when he'd kissed the laird's cheek. *Like the kiss of Judas.*

Certain of his duty, Jamie took one step toward his brother. "If you've words to say, Evan McKie, say them to me."

"Aye, I will. More words than you'll be wanting to

hear." His brother's eyes matched the granite of Cairnsmore. Cold, hard, brooding. "You've planned this for ten years, haven't you, Brother?"

"Ten . . . ? What are you getting at?" Jamie didn't dare take his eyes off Evan, yet he longed to see what story his mother's face might tell. Had the woman planned this *cantrip* all along? Had he agreed without knowing it?

Evan spat on the floor like the coarsest of men. "Ten years ago you made me pay for a dish of barley broth with my birthright, remember?" His eyes narrowed to slits. "You were practicing even then for the day you'd make it stick."

"Come now, Evan." Jamie shrugged nonchalantly, hoping to appease him. "We were naught but lads—"

"Aye," Evan growled. "And now we're men and hardly brothers."

"Evan, I—"

"Father blessed me, too, you know." He brushed back a handful of red hair matted down by the rain, revealing a fierce scowl. "He promised I would live by the blade of my sword. And answer to you." He snorted as he said it, curling his lips in disgust. "As to the second, I will never bow to my thieving younger brother. And as to the first, my dirk is sufficient for you." Evan threw off his plaid and hurled himself across the room, his short dagger unsheathed and shining with a murderous gleam.

"Jamie!"

Their mother's scream was drowned out by their own war cries. Jamie lunged at Evan, and both brothers landed hard on the unforgiving floor. Back and forth they rolled, hurling insults as brutal as their blows. Evan overpowered him, pressing the flat of his blade against Jamie's chin, proving he meant business. Jamie bucked and shoved, trying to escape the weight of his sibling, who was stouter by a stone and stronger by far. The flagstones chilled his neck, and he tasted blood in his mouth.

Evan stared down at him, eyes wild, his breathing heavy and thick with whisky. "I mean to kill you, Jamie!"

Jamie wiped a trickle of blood from his chin. "I don't doubt you, Brother." Heaving Evan aside, he rose to his knees, then tore into him with his bare hands while their mother, hysterical by now, begged them to stop.

"Lads, no more! Evan, you're hurting him!"

Ignoring her, they staggered to their feet, then plowed into the table, sending the cook's best pottery crashing to the floor in a noisy, shattered heap. Fists flew, brutally connecting with flesh and bone. Curses echoed through the once-quiet house. When the blade of Evan's dirk caught the firelight, Jamie lunged forward to knock it free, cutting his hand but sparing himself a deadlier blow. The dagger clattered across the floor and landed at the feet of a newcomer to the terrible scene.

Father.

Jamie saw him first and tried to blurt out his name between blows. Evan, oblivious, hammered away at Jamie with a meaty fist until he finally glanced up and froze.

Alec McKie stood over the two of them tangled in a bloody knot. His gray eyes watered more than usual while he worked his mouth, clearing his throat as he did. "Rowena."

His wife moved toward him, visibly shaken as she stepped over the remains of her kitchen. "Alec . . . oh, Alec. I can explain."

Jamie watched his father slowly lift one hand to silence her. When the man spoke, Jamie wished he had not.

"You have brought shame to Glentrool this day, James McKie."

A dull heat coursed through Jamie's limbs as he shoved Evan aside, then used the overturned table to pull himself to his feet. Every part of him had taken a beating, not the least of which was his pride. He swallowed a mouthful of bloody spit, then forced out the words. "I'm sorry, Father."

"Sorry? Bah! You should be more than sorry for taking advantage of a *shooglie* old man." He leaned on his cane, as though to prove his weak and tottery condition. "You know very well I can't see. And my hearing of late has me nigh to shouting at your poor, innocent mother."

Innocent? Jamie closed his eyes as the truth sank in: Father knew nothing of his mother's role in their deception. Meaning his father would never forgive him. Meaning Evan would indeed see him dead, and soon.

"It's your brother who needs to hear your apology, Jamie." Alec nodded at Evan, then turned back toward the front room, mumbling over his shoulder.

"See that the two of you come to some peaceful agreement, aye?"

Jamie hung his head. What was their father thinking? There'd never been peace between the brothers, least of all now.

Evan stood close behind him, his sour breath hot on his neck. "I've business to attend to elsewhere. And no interest in making amends, Jamie." His voice was a low hiss in Jamie's ear, the words meant for him alone. "Watch your back, man. I'll plant my dirk in it the minute Father's in his grave." Evan slung his plaid over his broad shoulders without ceremony and stormed through the doorway into the wild, rain-swept night.

Seven

Guilt's a terrible thing.
BEN JONSON

Jamie, nothing is gained by heaping guilt on your-self."

He shot his mother a withering look. "Who should I blame then? You? Almighty God?" Jamie wrapped his bleeding hand with a clean rag, shaking his head in frustration. "I'm guilty as sin. And a dead man as well."

"Keep your voice down, lad." His mother pulled him farther away from the door to the parlor, where his father sat nursing his disappointment with a thimbleful of whisky. "I'll speak to your father. He'll come round by and by. Meanwhile, I intend to keep you safely away from Evan's blade. I have a wee plan."

"Not another—"

"Aye!" she hissed. "'Twill secure what we both want."

"Och!" He threw the blood-soaked cloth to the floor. "What *you* want, you mean."

"Not me, Jamie. You."

"Is that so?" He thrust his face in front of her and ground out the words. "How can you possibly know what I want?"

"Wheesht!" She lifted her hand, but he was too fast for her. Grasping her wrist in midair, he held it for a moment while his pounding heart slowed and his anger cooled. He met her hard-eyed gaze, noting the grim line of her mouth, then slowly pulled her hand toward his face. Ever so gently he pressed his cheek against her palm in silent appeal.

It had exactly the effect he'd hoped for. Her eyes softened, and her jutting chin relaxed. "I'm sorry, Jamie."

"Not as sorry as I am," he confessed. "I know you only want what's best for me."

"And what's best for Glentrool," she added, dropping her hand and taking a step backward. "Which is why you must do as I say."

"Which is . . ."

"Flee at once to my brother, Lachlan, at Auchengray."

"Uncle Lachlan? I barely know the man!"

"Even so, he's kin. Lachlan will see to your bed and supper long enough for Evan to forget what you did to him—"

"What *I* did? What *we* did, you mean."

She brushed away his protest like so much dust. "We both know your brother's ill temper never lasts longer than a fortnight. I'll send word for your return the minute I'm certain you'll be welcome again at Glentrool." Letting out a lengthy sigh, she picked up the discarded rag and studied the stains, her eyes downcast. "Tonight, seeing you and your brother tear each other apart, I thought I might lose both of you."

He took the bloody cloth from her hands with a gentle tug. "You worry too much. It's not Evan who concerns me. It's Father." He met her gaze, measuring her mood. "Will you make things right between us?"

She lifted her shoulders in a light shrug. "He's always known you were meant to inherit the land, Jamie. Haven't I told him so a thousand times? Now's the time to remind him." She turned and knocked softly on the door as she pushed it open, clearly certain that her husband would not refuse her company. "Alec?" Rowena left the door open and swept into the room where the laird of Glentrool sat, his head hanging low over his empty glass, waiting for someone to tell him it had all been a ghastly nightmare.

"Alec, we must talk." She eased gracefully into a chair and scooted it closer to his, reaching out to brush her tapered fingers across his arthritic ones.

The hour was late, the fire in the grate reduced to a dull glow from the dying embers. "This . . . this creature that Evan took for his wife is driving me mad with her demands and complaints."

Jamie watched from the doorway, incredulous. Why was she discussing Judith, of all people? Weren't the disastrous events of the day sufficient without bringing up old news?

Across the room his father merely nodded in agreement. "What would you have me do, Rowena? She's from the south, aye, and a sharp-tongued, contentious young woman. But she's still our daughter-in-law."

"You're right, of course." His mother's smooth words gave away nothing. "Not much to be done there. All the more reason we must be very certain Jamie doesn't make the same mistake."

"Jamie," his father grumbled, shaking his head. "Always young Jamie. You think of no one else in this household, do you, woman?"

At the mention of his name, Jamie's pulse quickened. His father had yet to notice him hovering in the wings, so poor was the man's eyesight. Would his mother wave him into the room? Include him in the conversation? Jamie quietly took a step closer, his ears straining to catch every word.

"I'm thinking only of you, Alec," she crooned, patting his hand. "Of your future grandsons and the future of Glentrool. You know as well as I do that Almighty God himself promised this land to your children's children. *Jamie's* children, Alec. Not Evan's. Don't you see?"

"Nae, I can't see!" he answered gruffly, the corners of his mouth turned down. "My eyes failed me miserably today, which is how Jamie managed to steal an old man's pride and an older brother's blessing with a single plate of food."

"Several plates," she teased him, "judging by how little came back to the kitchen." She fiddled with a frayed edge of his plaid, no doubt choosing her next words for best effect. Despite the tension in the room, Jamie couldn't help but marvel at his mother's ability to turn things in her favor. A worthy advocate, Rowena McKie. And a formidable foe, as his father surely knew.

"Alec, your blessing was not stolen." Her tone remained warm but firm. "It was rightfully claimed, no matter what Evan says. Leave such choices to the Almighty, dear husband, and we'll do what we can to help Jamie prepare for the future. I think it best he leave Glentrool at once. See a bit of Galloway before he settles down. Find a bride worthy to bear you a grandson."

Jamie nearly swallowed his tongue. *A bride?* She hadn't said a word about marriage. When had that become part of their plan?

His father's brow creased with concern. "I have no taste for matchmaking, if that's what you're thinking."

"How well I know your dread of courting!" A sly smile decorated her features. "Didn't your father send a manservant to explore east Galloway and seek a wife on your behalf?"

"Aye, and a fine one he found," he admitted.

"Though I wish I'd been the one to first clap eyes on you that day by the loch near Auchengray."

"You saw me soon enough, riding into Glentrool in search of my new husband."

He nodded slowly. "A bonny queen of Scotland you were, astride your chestnut mare. I'd gone out that evening to *pit the brain asteep,* as my mother would say."

"My dear Alec." She smoothed a hand across his weathered cheek. "Meditating on the hills like a *halie* man."

Alec chuckled, a gurgling sort of laugh. "Not holy at all, merely trying to put my thoughts aright. Then who should appear in the gloaming but my betrothed and her maids, descending from *heiven* like angels amid the heather."

Jamie's cheeks heated at their sentimental murmurings. He'd heard the story of his parents' unusual courtship many times. But not like this. Not in a poet's words from an old man's lips. He edged toward the kitchen, longing to escape, when his mother looked up and caught his eye, motioning him to wait.

She shifted her gaze back to her husband and leaned closer. "Alec . . ." Her manner was innocence itself. "Another bonny lass lives at Auchengray now. A suitable wife for your heir." Rowena's tone grew more persuasive. "My brother, Lachlan, the young man who accepted your father's generous bride price and who sent me to you so long ago, has two grown daughters of his own: Leana and Rose. Remember?"

"So he does." Alec nodded slowly, grimacing as he did. "Poor fellow raised the twa lassies all these years without a mother. They'd be of a marrying age now, I ken."

"Aye," she murmured, "they would."

Jamie stared at the two of them plotting his future, and his anger rekindled. Gone from bad to worse, this wretched day. Now he was required not only to steal away under the cover of night, but to find a wife and produce an heir as well. His desperate thoughts tumbled over one another, entangled with a dim memory of two wee cousins he'd met on a trip east with his parents a dozen years past. One pale, one dark. But so young! Round-faced children, not brides.

"Leana has seen no more than twenty summers and Rose fewer still, with many years of childbearing ahead of them. Both are bonny, Lachlan tells me in his letters." Rowena's teeth gleamed in the candlelight. "And neither one is English."

"Well then!" Alec McKie was clearly convinced. Pounding the arm of his chair with a shaky fist, he declared, "Find Jamie. Let us make our peace with each other before we send the lad off hunting for a bride."

"Find Jamie, you say?" His mother winked at him across the room. "I know just where to look."

Eight

And then comes a mist and a weeping rain,
And life is never the same again.
GEORGE MACDONALD

Keep your horse to the path," Rowena had cautioned him. "And beware the bogs." Useless words when the hoary mist was so thick Jamie could barely see past his gelding's nose. The night air crawled about like a living thing, nearly smothering him. His damp shirt clung to his skin, and hair sprang from beneath the brim of his tricornered hat in unruly waves. No wonder Evan returned from hunting looking so *frichtsome*. A gentleman's grooming was no match for Galloway's wild autumn weather.

Jamie squinted into the mist, straining to see what might lie ahead. The narrow track along the Water of Trool would lead him west to his first night's lodging at House o' the Hill Inn. An hour earlier he'd copied a map from his father's atlas, the crude rendering now safely tucked inside his small traveling pouch. Two new cambric shirts and a fistful of coins rested beside the map and a brief but vital letter from Rowena to her brother, Lachlan McBride, giving the McKie blessing on the marriage. He'd also packed bannocks and hard cheese to last a day or two. Not that he'd likely need them. After a short night's sleep, he would break his fast and turn south to Monnigaff and Creetown, veer east to Gatehouse and Carlinwark, then press on to Newabbey and his uncle's farm a few days hence. It was the long way but by far the most traveled. Coaching inns and taverns awaited him at every junction. Let his brother sleep on the moors and hunt for his supper. Jamie intended to rest his head on a pillow and dine from a pewter plate.

Plodding on through the mist, he consulted the watch hidden in his waistcoat pocket and groaned. Midnight, and already his legs ached. Please God, by week's end he would be settled at Auchengray. Odd to think of living anywhere but Glentrool, even for a few weeks. Already he itched to get back to his ledgers with their long columns of neat and orderly numbers. Though his father had sent him to university to be trained for the kirk, it was managing land and breeding sheep that stirred Jamie's soul. He'd returned from Edinburgh to become overseer of the

McKie flocks. Henry Stewart, Glentrool's head shepherd, had taught Jamie everything his books had not.

Did his uncle have sheep at Auchengray or only fields of grain and two daughters? Jamie tried again to picture how his cousins must look, grown as they were, but only vague images came to mind. Would Leana or Rose be the one to bear the name McKie? At least there were two to choose from; he'd have some say in the matter.

Jamie flexed his hand, trying to ease the pain of the dagger wound that scraped across his palm, when a twig snapped close behind him. He held perfectly still, senses on full alert. Had Evan followed him, intent on planting a blade in his back? Ever so slowly Jamie lowered his right hand to the dirk firmly nestled in his boot. The feel of the hilt in his grip gave him a fresh measure of confidence. He straightened and jerked Walloch's reins, abruptly swinging the horse's head around, then called out into the swirling mist. "Show yourself, man."

Neither sight nor sound greeted him. Only the sensation of an unseen presence permeated the foggy air. Jamie swallowed his fear and spoke again, louder this time and with more conviction. "If you've come to finish what you started, Evan, I'm prepared to do the same." He pressed his long legs against the horse's sides, urging Walloch forward. "Come out where I can see you."

Silence.

Apprehension, like an icy finger, trailed down Jamie's spine. If not his brother, then who? Jamie had no enemies, no outstanding debts, no quarrel with neighbor or kin. Gypsy traveling folk, a common sight across Galloway, seldom ventured far from the main roads. Who else might trail him across the boggy ground at night, and why? He waited, listening for a footfall, the jingle of a harness, another snapping twig. No sounds met his ears except that of the water gently lapping on the banks of the Trool and the sheep bleating on the *braes*. Feeling foolish, he turned west again, determined to think no more of his red-haired brother. He would do as his father had oft instructed: "Pray to God and walk forward."

Soon the rushing waters ahead grew louder, plunging over steep linns and swirling around granite boulders. The Minnoch, icy cold from its journey through the Merrick range, would soon meet with the Trool, a treacherous crossing to navigate in the best of weather; in the dead of night, in heavy fog, it could be lethal. Walloch knew the fording spot well and boldly plunged into the water, carrying them both across without incident, other than soaking Jamie's breeches. No matter. The patrons at House o' the Hill would hardly notice or care. It was a rough place, favored by smugglers heading east from Portpatrick. A bowl of hot stew and a heather mattress were all he required.

"There's a welcome sight," Jamie murmured, patting the horse's neck with relief as the inn came into view at the crest of a hill, its four small windows aglow from the hearth. He pointed Walloch toward the cluster of stables situated downwind. The stock pens were crowded with packhorses belonging to the *lingtowmen,* named for the coil of rope, or *ling-tow,* which they wore around their shoulders as they transported smuggled goods inland. Jamie was grateful he had only one leather pouch to carry. His shoulders and legs ached, his seat was numb, and all his thoughts had dwindled to one: sleep.

A scruffy lad in a tattered shirt hurried out to greet him. The boy eyed his horse, then flashed a mouthful of crooked teeth. "Will ye be spendin' the nicht, sir?"

"Aye, I will." Jamie dropped to his feet with a muffled grunt. The mere mention of rest, however thin the mattress, had him digging for a copper penny to pay the lad for his horse's keep. "I'll be off at first light. You'll have him groomed, fed, and saddled, will you?"

The boy winked, slipping the coin into his pocket. "I'll no' fail ye, sir."

"And your name, lad?"

The young man ducked his head. Shy, embarrassed, or half-asleep—Jamie wasn't sure which. "George," he finally confessed.

"Like the king himself, is it? Well done, George. I'll give you another coin like that one in the morning when I see his coat gleaming. Are we agreed?"

The toothy young smile returned. "We are. What d'ye call him, sir?"

"Walloch."

The lad eyed the horse's hooves. "Dances, does he?"

"Aye. Off with you now. With any luck I've an empty bed waiting for me."

Convinced Walloch was in good hands, Jamie slung his pouch over his shoulder and trudged back uphill toward the inn, its whinstone walls promising dry shelter at the least. He'd passed the place dozens of times, shared a flagon or two with friends there, but never slept beneath its pitched roof. Strange to be lodging so close to home. Jamie pushed open the weathered oak door, pausing to let his eyes adjust to the murky interior. Few souls inside the low-beamed room even looked up, so intent was their conversation. Narrow benches stretched along roughly hewn tables stained by flagons past and present. Mismatched but sturdy-looking chairs huddled close to the blazing fire in the far corner where a stew cooked unattended. Along the wall a battered wooden sideboard displayed a row of pewter plates and bowls, one of which, Jamie hoped, would soon contain his belated supper.

He stepped further inside, searching the two adjoining rooms for a suitable place to land, when his gaze halted abruptly. A familiar head of hair, red as hot coals, poked above the crowd. *Evan.* His brother sat there, plain as day, with his chair pulled up to the fire and his broad, plaid-covered back to the door. Jamie edged into a shadowy corner, his heart slamming against his chest. What was Evan doing at House o' the Hill? Jamie hadn't breathed a word of his lodging plans to anyone. Had Evan followed him after all? Or was it ill luck and nothing more?

A male voice bellowed across the room, "McKie! Where've you been?"

Instinctively Jamie swiveled in that direction. So did Evan. In a half-second his brother would turn and discover him—alone and poorly armed. Jamie lunged for the door, yanked it open, then pulled it shut behind him with a muffled bang, his breath ragged, his face hot. Had Evan seen him? Would he come roaring outside with his dubious friends in tow? Jamie quickly pulled his dirk from his boot, his gaze glued to the inn door as he backed down the hill toward the stables. Glentrool was his, and Evan could do nothing to change that.

Except kill him.

Nine

To that dark inn, the Grave!
SIR WALTER SCOTT

Sir, was there somethin' wrong with Meg's barley stew?"

Jamie whirled around to find the stable lad edging toward him, confusion on his grimy features.

"I had some o' that stew meself and *thocht* it right *guid*—"

"Never mind the stew!" Jamie hissed. "Where's my horse?"

The boy fixed his gaze on Jamie's unsheathed knife and shifted from one foot to the other. "S-sir, I've b-barely started rubbin' him down. Pardon me sayin', but afore ye take him out again he needs a proper feedin'—"

"All right."

"He's drippin' wet, sir—"

"All right, I said!" Jamie shoved the blade inside his boot with a groan of frustration. Either Evan hadn't seen him, or his brother was deliberately waiting inside the inn and making him suffer.

"Pay me no mind, young George," Jamie muttered, starting to pace. "By all means, care for the horse. That's what I paid you good copper to do." He waved the boy back to his labors, wanting time to think, to plan the hours ahead. Though he needed to eat, he had food enough in his pouch. And though he needed to sleep, he'd not catch a wink in the rafters of House o' the Hill, knowing Evan lurked just below him. Worse, he'd have to get past Evan and his cronies first, and the odds were not in his favor.

Jamie turned toward the stable hand, who'd gone to work brushing Walloch's black coat with long, sure strokes. "Tell me, lad, have you a plaid you might loan me for the night?"

"A plaid?" His brow tightened. "What would ye be wantin' that for?"

"Warmth," Jamie snapped and produced another coin. "For your trouble."

"N-no trouble." The boy disappeared into one of the stalls and returned with a tattered length of wool. "Will this do?"

"'Twill have to." Jamie tucked the worn plaid under his arm. "Under no circumstances is anyone to walk off with my horse, no matter what manner of tale or how many shillings he offers. Do you understand?"

George nodded. "Yer mount will be here 'til ye come to claim him yerself."

"Clever lad." Jamie impulsively ruffled the boy's hair. "See you at dawn."

With plaid and pouch firmly in place, Jamie turned to face the road, peering down one direction, then the other, weighing his options. Evan would expect him to ride south toward Monnigaff, the very route he'd planned. Jamie would head north, if only for the night, toward their Uncle Patrick's estate of Glencaird. It was the last place Evan would look for him and for a very good reason: Two cairns—burial chambers from the dawn of history—dotted Glencaird's grazing lands, and Evan was exceedingly superstitious. Who knew what evil spirits one might still find among the hallowed stones? "The deid are not to be trifled with, Jamie," his brother had once warned him, eyes wide with horror. "Mark my words."

"Consider them marked, Brother," Jamie announced to the misty night air, lengthening his stride as he reached the bottom of the hill. To the nearby cairn he'd go. A slab of rock would make a fair bed, sparing him the unhealthy dampness of the ground. He scrambled over the *dry stane dyke* that bordered Uncle Patrick's land and aimed for a grove of rowan trees standing guard near the ceremonial site, keenly aware of an uneasiness growing inside him.

He slowed his steps across the uneven ground until his boot struck one of the rounded stones encircling the cairn. Older than King David of Scotland, older than King David of the Bible, the ancient ruin had lost many of its stones over the centuries, exposing a long chamber lined with split boulders. Across the top was a massive slab of granite too heavy to be carted off by a local farmer in need of building materials. Beneath it were buried the remains of men lost to history, their bones long since turned to dust. Jamie swallowed hard, his gaze taking in the desolate scene. By day, a cairn was naught but a pile of rocks. At night, the stones whispered of mysteries untold and dreams forgotten.

Mustering all his courage, he moved toward the tomb. Even if Evan did discover him asleep, his brother wouldn't have the nerve to step inside the sacred circle. Jamie shook out the musty plaid, preparing to spread it across the stone slab, when his boots brushed against a cluster of berries hanging from stout, purplish stems. The flowers had faded, but the profusion of glossy black fruit remained. Something to add to his meager bedtime meal perhaps? He reached down and plucked the good-sized berries and brought them to his lips, then cringed at their disagreeable taste and spewed them out. "Stick to your bannocks," he muttered, tossing the berries aside and brushing off his hands. He settled onto the plaid and made do with the provisions in his sack, trying not to think of the flagon of ale he might have had at House o' the Hill nor the soft heather mattress in the rafters. Nor the rocky grave beneath him.

He thought instead of the terrible day's events, of his father's face when he'd served the old man goat meat for venison. Before they parted, son and sire had forged a tenuous truce, and his father had extended a second blessing on him—this time on purpose. But all the grand words in the world could not erase the ones spoken earlier: "You have brought shame to Glentrool this day, James McKie." Even now, that shame pressed on Jamie's chest like an enemy's shield, forcing him to his knees.

He would not presume to pray. How could he possibly ask Almighty God to listen to the prayer of a sinner such as he? Yet another burning coal to add to his head: There'd been no hour of family worship that night, not after his brother and he had turned the kitchen into a battleground. Every night but this one the supper table would be cleared and the family Bible lifted from its timeworn box by the hearth. "Let us worship God," the elder McKie would say, his tone solemn, his intentions clear. The household servants would join them, quietly taking their seats on wooden benches along the far wall. When his father lined out a psalm with a tuneless voice, they'd respond in unison with the familiar words from the Psalter: "Happy is he that hath the God of Jacob for his help, whose hope is in the Lord his God."

Hope. Jamie had little hope left. Evan's threat was not an idle one. His brother longed to kill him and soon—before Jamie could marry and produce a son who would inherit Glentrool in his stead. Leaving was a necessity, and so was a hasty marriage.

The LORD *of hosts is with us.* His father's favorite prayer from Psalms echoed in Jamie's heart. *The God of Jacob is our refuge.*

Refuge. Hiding among stones, running for his life. An odd place for the laird's newly blessed son to find himself. There was naught to be done but sleep and hope the *morn's morn* might bring some relief from his guilt. Jamie unbuttoned his waistcoat and tucked his traveling pouch inside his voluminous shirt for safekeeping, then wrapped himself in the plaid, his cocked hat put aside for the night. He would sleep only a short while, intending to leave before dawn.

Unless Evan found him first.

With a stone beneath his head and a tawny owl hooting *too-whit, too-whit* from a neighboring tree, Jamie shifted on the granite slab until he felt reasonably comfortable. "Let me sleep the sleep of the dead," he murmured as his eyes drifted shut and his body relaxed into slumber. Beyond the dark circle of stones, a rowan twig snapped in two.

Ten

And yet, as angels in some brighter dreams
Call to the soul when man doth sleep,
So some strange thoughts transcend
our wonted dreams,
And into glory peep.
HENRY VAUGHAN

God help me!" Jamie bolted to his feet, awake in an instant, his pulse racing. He pressed a hand to his chest, willing his heart to calm and his shallow breaths to lengthen. What had awakened him with such a start? A dream, he decided, struggling to recapture the last threads of it.

The morning sun had yet to show its face above the eastern hills, but already the air was clear.

Jamie rubbed the grit from his eyes and shook his head, trying to loosen the strange vision's grip on his imagination. But the dream—if it *had* been a dream—refused to be dislodged. A staircase figured into it somehow, taller than any mountain in Galloway. Not a mahogany stair, like the one at Glentrool, this one was bright and shining as a full moon in a midnight sky. Winged creatures moved up and down the stair. And the voice he'd heard! It had rumbled like thunder and roared like the sea.

Even now Jamie's insides trembled as he recalled the vivid images and the words that were spoken: "The land you sleep upon, to you will I give it, and to your seed." It was true; all the McKie lands would be his someday, even that of Uncle Patrick, who had no heir. But what of his own seed, the children he and his lady cousin—he knew not which one—would someday bear? Was this his father's blessing, revisited in the night, or was it something more?

A light breeze lifted the hair off his neck, sending a chill down his back, waking him further. In a moment the dream would be gone for good. He hastily closed his eyes and washed clean his thoughts. Like a snippet of a song, a spoken promise came to mind, the words as solid and true as any written on a page: "Behold, I am with you wherever you go, and will bring you again into this land. I will never leave you."

Who would be with him? Was that Alec McKie's voice he heard echoing through his dreams? *Nae.* The words were different and the voice like none he had ever heard before. Slowly opening his eyes again, Jamie lifted his gaze to Merrick's peaks and the sky above it, washed with stars. "Who is it?" he whispered to the heavens. "Who is the one who will never leave me?"

Not his father, doomed to leave this world only too soon.

Not his mother, nearly forty years his senior and aging by the hour.

Not his brother, who would leave him for dead if he could.

Who? Who would never forsake him?

And then Jamie knew. And knowing, he fell to his knees on the hard rock. This was no ordinary dream. The Almighty, the Holy One, had come to him in the dark of night. In a prayer, in a dream, in no more than a vapor, the Maker of heaven and earth had come to his rocky bedside. Had come to watch over him—*him,* James Lachlan McKie—to bless and protect an ungrateful son who'd deceived his father and stolen his brother's blessing.

Jamie's mind reeled, his eyes stinging with tears. How was it possible? No one deserved God's favor less than he did. *No one.* Undone, he ran his hands across the stone slab, trying to grasp the astounding truth: Almighty God still cared for his wretched soul. The Father of mercy and God of all consolation had not punished him for his sins. Instead, he had stood by him in the night and offered him hope for the future.

"*Bethankit!*" Jamie whispered to the ancient stones. "God be thanked."

And he *was* grateful. Grateful to be spared his brother's vengeance, to have lived through the night to see another day. Could he put his thanks into words? Speak to the One who'd spoken to him in the night? Jamie sat back on his heels and began as though Thomas Findlay or some other friendly soul were sitting across from him at Glentrool's dining table. "If it please you, be with me, merciful Father. Show me the way to Auchengray and the way home. Give me bread for each day and clothes to cover my back."

Jamie's face grew warm as he realized he'd not prayed in such a manner before, right and good as it seemed that Sabbath morning. Dare he ask for provisions so boldly, without making some promise in return? He grabbed the loose rock that had served as his pillow and held it aloft. "May this stone be my witness. If you do as I've asked, a portion of all that I have now and in years to come will belong to you." With a new and unfamiliar sense of reverence, he placed the rock on top of the cairn and rose to his feet, brushing the dust off his hands.

Around him the air was growing lighter and the sky more dove gray than dark blue. As if he were just now waking and seeing things for the first time, he noticed his borrowed plaid in a *slitterie* heap near his feet, apparently discarded during his restless slumber. His gelding Walloch waited elsewhere for him, boarded with the stable lad at House o' the Hill. At least he'd not dreamed of losing his mount while he slept among the plants and rocks. He rubbed a berry-stained hand across his stubbly face. "You were a tired man, Jamie McKie, to claim a stone for a pillow."

"Aye," a gruff male voice behind him answered. "And a fool as well."

Jamie spun on his boot heel and reached down for his dirk, then froze, his dream forgotten, his hand gripping nothing but air.

"Missing somethin', lad?" An old Gypsy stood a stone's throw away, his arms folded over his chest, a wry grin stretched across his craggy features. "Have ye naught in yer boot but breeches and stockings?"

Jamie straightened, his peaceful thoughts gone, his face hot. Bad enough that he hadn't heard the man approach. He'd also missed the deft fingers that had lifted the dirk from his boot as he slept. Jamie made certain that his words, at least, bore a sharp edge. "I suppose you know the whereabouts of my blade."

The elderly man's face darkened beneath the brim of his cap. "Nae, I do not. All I know is that on my way to Monnigaff I came upon a daft young man talking to himself while standing on an auld grave. And a rude lad at that, accusing me of stealing his dirk." The Gypsy lowered his arms with a certain swagger, taking his time about it, and shortened the distance between them with two firm steps. He was broadly built and short in the legs, his strength apparent from the thickness of his arms. Though his clothes were plain, the silver on his boots shone. So did the fiendish gleam in his eye. "Only a fool would speak so boldly when he has no dagger, no horse, and no friend in sight."

Jamie realized his mistake and none too soon. "I'm afraid I've misjudged you." He couldn't bring himself to add "sir." Not to a weather-beaten tinkler, the traveling sort who lived in a mean tent by the roadside, tinkering and trading. Jamie could flatter the man though. "You have a knack for hammering tin and sharpening blades, do you not? Surely a man wouldn't bother to steal what he could better fashion himself."

"Aye, I make a fine knife when I put my mind to it." As if by magic, a slim dagger appeared in the Gypsy's hand. His dark eyes, trained on the deadly blade, no longer met Jamie's gaze. It was some time before the traveler spoke again, his voice low but far from sinister. "I'll not cut ye down, lad. I'm a tinkler, not a murderer." He sliced the blade through the air, smiling faintly as he did. "Seeing how fate has stolen yer dirk, ye'll be needin' a new one." All at once the Gypsy pinched the blade between his thumb and forefinger and extended the carved bone handle toward Jamie, an unexpected gesture of trust. "Have ye a shilling to spare?"

Jamie nodded immediately, weak with relief. "Aye, I do." If it came to it, he'd buy back his own knife to be rid of the man and his foreign ways. "Right here in my leather pouch." He patted his shirt, surprised when his hand touched nothing but cambric and skin. "Och, it must be wrapped in my plaid." He bent down to shake the length of wool, chagrined to see nothing fly out but blades of grass and bits of dirt. Had the pouch fallen among the rocks while he tossed and turned in his dreams? Cold dread knotted in the pit of his stomach as he began to search. It had to be there. It *must* be. He jammed his hands down one crevice after another, avoiding the truth as long as possible.

"Ye've not lost yer purse, have ye?"

Jamie finally stood, biting back an oath. "So it appears." Furious, he kicked the stone slab, then ignored the pain that shot through his foot. No use denying it: The leather pouch was nowhere to be found. His shirts and bannocks could be spared, but without coin or banknote, his journey was over before it had begun. And to think, he'd promised a portion of it to God! Let the Almighty find his own silver. As to his midnight blessing, God could do with it as he pleased. Clearly his words had not improved Jamie's lot one bit. In mere hours he'd gone from being laird of all the land to a penniless vagrant.

The missing purse no longer of interest, the tinkler squinted at Jamie's stony bed. "Tell me ye didn't sleep among those berries?"

Jamie was in no mood for Gypsy lore. "What of it?" he growled.

"Don't ye know the plant, man? That's belladonna."

"Bell *what?*"

"What a stupid lot ye gentry are!" The Gypsy threw up his hands and stamped about the stony ground like a man possessed. "Ye wrapped yerself up for the night in a patch of plants meant to kill ye."

"Kill me?" Jamie stepped back, eying the crushed berries on his plaid.

"Ye're lucky ye didn't lose more than yer silver." The Gypsy, still huffing, came to a halt in front of him. "Let me see yer eyes. Come along; I won't hurt ye. Haven't I already offered ye a blade, and me without one in the other hand ready to cut ye?"

Reluctantly Jamie let the man jerk down his chin and peer into his eyes, ignoring the reek of onions on the Gypsy's breath and the grime on his hands. "What are you looking for, man?"

"Just what I've found. The centers of yer eyes are black as pitch. In a moment, when the sun is brighter, ye'll be squeezin' 'em shut from the pain. I'm surprised ye can even talk. Most times the voice is gone."

"The voice?" Jamie jerked his chin out of the man's grasp. "What are you saying?"

"Have ye not heard of deadly nightshade?"

Jamie had heard of it all right. Though he was not an expert in plant lore, Scottish history was another matter. "The soldiers of Macbeth poisoned a whole army of Danes with it. Chaucer called it *dwale*."

"Aye, but the Scots call it something else: Jacob's ladder." Bending over the offensive plant, the tinkler poked at it with his dirk. "They say, the auld wives do, that men who taste the berries of belladonna— or nightshade or dwale or whatever name ye choose—will sleep the sleep of the dead. No wonder ye didn't feel your dirk and pouch slip away." The Gypsy looked up, his face lit with curiosity.

"They also say the berries give a man ferocious dreams. Was that the way of it?"

Jamie slowly nodded, noticing for the first time that morning how lightheaded and wobbly kneed he felt. Last night's dream—the light, the voice, the words, the angels, the tall, bright *thing* he'd seen— had it merely been the leafy spell of Jacob's ladder addling his sleepy brain? How real it had seemed! And how grieved he was to think it might not be. "I dreamed . . . ," he began, hearing a slight quaver in his voice. "I dreamed I talked to God."

"Almighty God talkin' to the likes of ye? Ha!" The Gypsy spun in a circle, cackling like an old crone, arms flung out wide. The polished tin buttons on his coat caught the first full rays of the sun. "Did no one ever warn ye, lad?" he shouted, delighted with himself. "Ye should never tell a lie on the Sabbath."

Eleven

Can wealth give happiness? look round and see
What gay distress! what splendid misery!
EDWARD YOUNG

Leana frowned at her reflection in the one decent looking glass in the house, a mirror with half the silvering worn off, mounted over her dressing table. *Serviceable* was the only word one could use to describe her hat. It was the same hat she'd worn every Sunday for four years, and it had not improved with age.

Too many earthly possessions turned the mind toward temporal desires and away from eternal truths, or so the Reverend John Gordon said. That explained why the collection box sat on a table inside the kirk door rather than being thrust in front of the parishioners during the worship service by an elder bearing a long pole, as in bygone days. Better not to speak of money and God in the same breath, the minister cautioned. "Since I'm off to a worship service," Leana murmured, straightening the brim, "*serviceable* will have to do."

"What a dreary thought!" Rose appeared in the doorway, her hands folded around a flowered reticule, her rosy mouth in a petulant pout. "That old gown of Mother's again?"

Leana looked down at the faded blue linen and shrugged. "It was this or the gray serge."

"Och! That horrible thing? I thought Neda cut that up for rags." Rose swept into the room, still shaking her head. The scent of heather, which Leana stitched into her sister's hems and cuffs, wafted around her. "We simply must ask Father for something from the household account. You help Duncan keep Auchengray's books in order, Leana. Isn't there a *bittie* to spare for new Sunday gowns and hats for both of us?"

"That would require Father to unlock his wooden thrifite. A most unlikely event." The key to the revered money box hung round his neck for safekeeping. According to Duncan, Lachlan wanted the key close to his heart: "Ye ken what the Buik says, Leana: For *whaur* yer treasure lies, *thar* yer heart *wull* be. Yer faither's heart is naught but cold silver, lass." Duncan understood his master's miserly ways, and so did she. Lachlan was not about to spend an extra guinea dressing his two daughters.

Leana shrugged. "Not this month, I'm afraid, dearie."

"Ah, well. No harm asking." Rose giggled, her good humor already returned. "Guess what Susanne Elliot told me Sunday last?" Rose made certain to arrive at kirk early and linger late. The weekly exchange of neighborhood news in the kirk-yard was the highlight of her week. "Susanne said a woman in Dumfries on the High Street makes the loveliest hats. One has an enormous brim . . ." Rose put aside her drawstring purse to create an imaginary hat with her hands. "It circles round the head, sticking out especially far front and back. The crown is flat—all the fashion now in London, Susanne says—and it's wrapped in silk ribbons that trail down the back. You tie it under your chin with a ribbon as well, a nice wide one in a big, pretty bow. Doesn't it sound heavenly?"

"Heavenly," Leana agreed. "And expensive. Father would never allow it."

"Hoot!" Rose snatched up her reticule with a noisy huff. "All the man thinks about is how much things cost."

"A cruel necessity of life, Rose. We're rich in land but poor in silver. Remember when you were nine and we had such a terrible harvest?"

"Terrible." Rose sighed dramatically. "No meal, no flour."

"Aye, and no bannocks, no bread, no oats, and no barley for our broth."

Rose leaned forward and added in a conspirator's whisper, "Lady Maxwell confessed to me she had pies on her table that winter that weren't meant to be cut. They were only to keep up appearances."

"Because they were made of clay." Leana nodded soberly. Even the gentry of Galloway struggled to put food on the table that season, including their wealthy neighbors, the Maxwells. "It was a dreadful year. People nigh starved to death. Our father doesn't easily forget such things. That's why he's prudent. Another famine could come without warning." When her sister's eyes widened, Leana quickly added, "Oh, Rose, don't fret. We're prepared, truly we are. Neda has enough pickled mutton and smoked herring in the cellar to feed us for a whole year." She stood and lightly hugged her sister, tipping her head to the side to avoid knocking both their sorry bonnets on the floor. "What we don't have is silver for luxuries like pretty clothes and fancy hats."

Rose wiggled out of her grasp. "And I won't let you earn that money by marrying that decrepit old farmer. Promise you'll say no. Promise?"

"I promise I'll try." Whether or not Father would listen was another matter completely.

Appeased, her sister gathered up her gloves and reticule. "I'm going down the stair to steal one of your apples and see if I can't think of a much better suitor for you than Fergus the Haggis."

"Rose!"

"Well he *does* have a paunch that would do a sheep proud." Rose floated out the door, waving her hand over her shoulder, a bemused expression on her face.

Leana watched her sister descend the stone staircase that angled through the center of the house, her footsteps light, her spirits blithe as ever. Rose deserved a good scolding for her impertinent words, but Leana knew she'd never be the one to punish her. From childhood, Rose had held sway over everyone she met. Over Neda and Duncan Hastings, who should have known better. Over Lady Maxwell of late. And over her, the older sister who adored her. Only their father put the fear of God into Rose, and then only for an hour of family worship each evening. Every other hour Rose bloomed with an artless charm few could resist.

"Leeeannaaahhh!"

"Coming." She pressed a handkerchief to her damp forehead and cheeks, then tucked it in her sleeve and hurried down the stair. A day at kirk would be the very thing to put aside her worries about Fergus McDougal. He would be miles away, worshiping in his own parish of Kirkbean. Tomorrow would bring troubles enough; this day belonged to God. Leana reached the bottom step and discovered the usual morning bustle under way as the servants gathered for the long hours ahead. The table had already been laid for that night's supper, the food having been prepared the day before and the house made spotless. Sabbath was reserved for worship, not for work. Half a dozen domestic servants stood in a solemn row for their employer's inspection, their best clothes pressed, their faces washed.

Leaving her father to his duties, Leana ventured

out into the blue-sky morning to find Rose waiting for her at the edge of the road, tapping her foot, arms akimbo. Leana lifted the brim of her hat to meet her sister's gaze. "The others may be a while, and Father will follow in the chaise. Suppose we go on ahead of them."

Rose took off at a brisk walk, her full skirt swinging with each step, her petticoats rustling beneath them. Hoops were not permitted in the McBride household—"vain contraptions," their father called them—so the sisters and Neda did the best they could with layers of starched fabric. Leana didn't mind, but Rose did.

"I'll be wilted by noon," Rose fussed as they hurried along the road heading east. "Look how my skirts are already drooping!"

"But, dearie, you'll take up less room in the pew," Leana murmured, keeping her sensitive eyes to the ground and away from the sun. It took less than an hour to reach the parish kirk. Longer if Rose stopped to chat with neighbors along the way. At the moment they were alone on the country road, still a bit muddy from Saturday night's storm. Both sisters held their skirts above the worst of it and left Auchengray and its orchards behind, heading downhill past meadowlands studded with rocks and verdant pastures dotted with sheep. Leana never wearied of the journey to Newabbey, for the view changed with the seasons: wildflowers in spring, yellow whin in summer, scarlet rowan trees in autumn, holly berries in winter. Scotch pines, green all year, appeared on both sides of the road now—

a few trees at first, then a whole forest, dark and cool, with a lush bed of brown pine needles blanketing the ground beneath their branches.

Leana pointed to the piney carpet. "Remember playing leapfrog there?"

"Aye." Rose slowed long enough to survey the familiar spot before continuing her breathless pace. "And I remember picking needles out of my hair for two days."

Leana tugged on her sister's braid when it bounced within reach. "Your memory fails you, little sister. I was the one who plucked those pine needles out while Neda lectured us on proper games for young lassies."

"Lectured *you* is more like it," Rose tossed over her shoulder. "I was the innocent party."

Leana heard the smile in her sister's voice. Rose *was* innocent in so many ways. The dear girl marveled at London fashions she'd not seen, paid no mind to the village lads who gazed at her with lovesick glances, and thought Lady Maxwell considered her a peer. In truth, naive Rose merely amused the gentlewoman. Leana fretted each time her sister visited the red sandstone elegance of Maxwell Park, knowing she'd come home dreaming of riches that stretched far beyond Auchengray's dry stane dykes.

"Nearly there," Rose sang out.

Leana put aside her concerns to feast her eyes on the lush green meadow beside them. Newabbey Pow, with her sparkling clear waters, meandered through the sunlit expanse, shadowed by the hills that gathered around Criffell's feet. The grimy walls of a snuff mill appeared—the scourge of the neighborhood, by their father's measure—then another sparse forest of evergreens enveloped the sisters in a piney bower again. When at last they reached the village, both sisters were flushed and thirsty. Guarding their skirts, they crouched by the meandering *burn* to drink their fill.

Leana had just scooped up another handful of the cool water and brought it to her lips when a male voice behind her so startled her that she splashed it down the front of her dress instead.

"Miss McBride?"

She stood in haste, nearly losing her balance, then spun around to discover Fergus McDougal seated on a horse-drawn cart. She was grateful their kirk was so near, or the bonnet laird might have insisted they both join him on the narrow seat. Neither the horse nor the cart had much to recommend it. As to the farmer in his Sunday attire, she noticed only his wide brown eyes focused intently on her. "Mr. . . . . McDougal I believe?"

"Aye." When he smiled, she saw that his teeth matched his eyes. "The verra one."

"Wh-what a surprise to find you in Newabbey this Sabbath morning." She brushed her hand across her dress as though the spilled water might sweep off like birch leaves. Or cornmeal. Or pine needles. Where *was* Rose?

"Mr. McDougal," her sister chimed in, stepping close beside her, "hadn't you best be getting on to Kirkbean? To your own parish?"

His smile broadened. "*Mebbe* 'twill be your sister's parish before long." He tipped his hat, ignoring Rose altogether. "I've always favored a woman with fair hair and a strong back."

Leana stared at his blond mare and nodded. "I see."

He leaned across his knee with some effort and winked, as though such a gesture might bring her into his confidence. "I've an appointment with your father in the morning, Miss McBride. I'd be obliged if you made that discussion a matter of prayer at kirk this morning."

"Oh, aye," Leana assured him, her mouth dry as oats. "I'll pray most fervently."

"So will I, lass." He straightened, nodding confidently, then shook the reins. The cart jerked forward. "So will I."

Twelve

Does the road wind up-hill all the way?
Yes, to the very end.
CHRISTINA ROSSETTI

Jamie stood along the banks of Black Burn, shaking the cold water off his unshaven face. He missed his valet this morning and, in particular, the man's way with a razor. Drying his hands on the plaid, he pulled on his hat and started up the steep slope toward House o' the Hill stables, where he knew his horse waited for him. Did his brother wait as well, dirk in hand? Nothing would surprise him, not after the strangest of dreams and a most rude awakening. The sly-tongued Gypsy tinkler had continued south, leaving the future heir of Glentrool to face the day without money or map. Jamie had regained his wits though and intended to use them.

The pungent smell of peat smoke tinged the chilly air as the inn came in sight, its stock fences sheltered by an old stand of sycamores, protecting the beasts from the elements. He felt a twinge of guilt, thinking of young George. Last night he'd promised the stable lad a second coin for brushing down Walloch's filthy coat. He'd paid a fair wage, yet he'd promised more, a promise he could no longer keep. Jamie paused long enough to shake out the borrowed plaid with a vigorous snap, then folded it carefully to conceal the berry stains.

Judging by the sun, still low in the eastern sky, and by his growling stomach, it was nearing eight o'clock. A quick glance at the watch in his pocket confirmed it. The lingtowmen and their packhorses, laden with contraband, had no doubt departed the inn hours earlier under cover of darkness, eager to get their smuggled goods safely over the moors before the Sabbath dawn—or an overzealous exciseman—put a stop to their activities. Even the righteous Alec McKie availed himself of their goods when the price was favorable, which it always was. Salt and tea for the larder, candles and linens to store in the spence, printed silks to please Rowena—all found their way through the doors of Glentrool, courtesy of Thomas Findlay's shrewd bargaining.

Home. Jamie trudged up the hill, chagrined to realize how much he already missed Glentrool and its odd assortment of characters. Ivy Findlay, with her pinched features and tightly drawn brown hair, ruled the household staff with a piercing gaze. Ivy's husband, Thomas, factor to the McKies, had taught Jamie all there was to know of balancing ledgers. Aubert Billaud, of the high forehead and long nose, called Marseilles his true home and Glentrool's kitchen his domain. Jamie imagined them pressed and dressed by now, prepared for the long journey south to the kirk at Monnigaff. Six horses carrying six riders: Alec and Rowena, Evan and Judith, Thomas and Ivy.

In agreeable weather the rest of the household walked to the kirk with Henry Stewart, Glentrool's head shepherd, leading the way. When winter's worst kept everyone home, Alec led them in worship around the hearth. Jamie, seated at the elder McKie's feet, sometimes caught a glimmer of his father's zeal for God. His grasp on it vanished the next moment, but he couldn't deny what he saw and felt during those Sabbath hours at home.

"Guid Lord's Day to ye, sir!"

Jamie looked up with a start and found George bounding out to greet him, the wiry lad's clothes appearing even more threadbare by the light of day. Jamie handed him the plaid with a hasty apology. "Beg pardon for returning with your plaid but not, alas, with your coin."

The boy's cheerful countenance fell. "I'd hoped to put it in the collection box this mornin'. For the *puir,* ye ken."

Jamie's neck grew warm. "I'm sorry, George. Truly I am. You see, I . . . I *lost* my traveling pouch."

What was he to do? Confess to a child that he'd been robbed while he slept? "When I find it, I'll be certain to pay you what I promised."

"I'm sure ye will, sir." George studied him closely, his grubby fingers wrapped around the plaid. "Are ye not the laird's son?"

The heat in Jamie's neck spread to his face. "Aye."

"A McKie without coins in his pockets?" The boy shook his head in wonder. "Niver heard of *sic* a thing."

"Well, now you have." Jamie marched past him toward the stable, anger and shame fighting for the upper hand. "Saddle my horse, and I'll be on my way."

George scrambled to catch up with him. "Home to Glentrool is it, sir?"

Jamie ignored the question, slowing as he approached his tethered mount. *Home?* Walloch was all he had left of home. He ducked beneath the crudely thatched roof laid with branches and bracken and lowered his voice. "Morning, boy." The gelding lifted its sleek ebony head and whinnied in greeting. All at once Jamie felt calmer. *Speak quietly. Move slowly.* Glentrool's stable master had taught him well. Jamie stroked the horse's neck, putting them both at ease.

"Ye've got a fine animal there," the stable lad said softly. "Already been fed and watered. I'll have ye saddled in a blink, Mr. McKie." The lad was good as his word. Moments later Jamie was riding over the crest of the hill with the Cree Valley behind him and the glistening Trool before him. He brought Walloch to a gentle halt and gazed down at the familiar landscape. *Home to Glentrool, is it?* And then what? Ask for more money, draw another map? Or admit defeat and beg his brother for mercy? Having no money in his pockets meant no lodging at inns along the way, no evening meals at friendly tables. A plaid on rocky ground and stale bannocks from a pouch were good enough for one night but a poor prospect for several nights in a row, even if he still had such things in his possession, which he did not.

Behold, I am with you.

The hairs on the back of his neck rose to attention. A remnant from his troubled sleep perhaps. Or the lingering taste of Jacob's ladder. It was decidedly *not* the God of Abraham and Isaac, not the God of his grandfather Archibald and his father, Alec. Only a dream at the end of a wretched day. He was alone and must fend for himself, without silver or copper, without map or compass. Taking hold of the horse's reins, Jamie descended into the glen, toward the opposite side of the loch from Glentrool. He would head due east through the mountains. Not the longer, more civilized route south, then east through *clachans* and burghs, as he'd planned. Rather, the shorter, wilderness trek toward the Rhinns of Kells and across Raploch Moss, with only his horse and the rising sun to guide him.

It was rough going, dodging boulders as he threaded through the ancient forest of oak and hazel. An occasional break in the trees gave him a last look at Glentrool. He slowed, finding it hard to bid farewell to the place he'd called home. There was the island he and Evan had paddled out to as lads. The steep falls of Buchan Burn, whose rushing waters had lulled him to sleep on warm summer nights. By day the twins had often shoved each other into the Buchan's turbulent linns, arriving home cut, bruised, and laughing. Whatever brotherly relationship they'd once had, it was gone by the time they were grown, ruined by greed, pride, envy, anger—he no longer knew which to blame.

Jamie rode across the meadows beyond the loch, pausing at Glenhead for a final backward glance before resolutely turning east, swallowing hard as he rode. The sun arced across the sky at an autumn angle, its warmth a welcome hedge against the stiff winds blowing down from the Merrick range. Now and again he spied a fox darting through the undergrowth though nothing edible crossed his path. Walloch was well satisfied with the bubbling water of Glenhead Burn and the abundance of grass along its banks. Jamie's stomach was not so easily appeased. As the day wore on, it ceased growling and merely ached. He scoured the ground for berries and searched the sparse woodlands for a wild apple tree. Thoughts of food consumed him.

The woods gave way to stark moors and rocky fells. Above him, brown-and-white goats perched on craggy shelves no wider than their hooves, looking down at the intruder on horseback. Their staccato bleating sounded as if they were laughing at his plight. *Ha-ha-ha-ha-ha-ha.* Across the vast track of moorland, the distant call of red grouse taunted him. *Go-back, go-back, go-back.* The hours dragged on, gray and colorless as the landscape. His seat ached from riding, his hands from gripping the reins. By late afternoon when a shepherd's bothy came into view, Jamie offered up a grateful prayer and urged Walloch forward toward the low cottage. The walls were made of rough stone without mortar, the roof thatched with heather. A bright-eyed shepherd came out to greet him, bearing a brimless Scotch bonnet on his head and a kind smile on his weathered face.

"D'ye ken whaur ye're goin', lad?"

Jamie waved vaguely toward the moors. "East to New Galloway, then south along the banks of the Ken."

The older man appraised horse and rider, eyebrows arched. "Not a path the *gentrice* usually favor."

Jamie only shrugged in agreement, hoping to discourage any further questions.

"Name's Gordie Briggs," the shepherd offered, jerking his head toward the cottage. "Join me for a bit o' supper? 'Tis naught but broth and barley, hardly what ye're used to eatin', but—"

"Aye." Jamie had already dismounted, not caring how eager he appeared. "Much obliged, Gordie." He followed him inside, noting the freshly swept earthen floor and the stone flags round the hearth, the tidy shelf of provisions, and the peat fire as warm and inviting as Gordie himself.

Within minutes Jamie was busy tucking away a

generous serving of thick broth with bannocks as hard as Walloch's hooves, grateful for both. In return, he served the shepherd a plateful of neighborhood gossip, knowing the tales would travel far beyond the peat-blackened walls of the bothy. In the lonely glens, a shepherd spread news more efficiently than the *London Chronicle.* Jamie mentioned nothing of consequence, keeping an eye on the open door and the fading sunset beyond it. An hour at the most and darkness would descend on the hills like a shroud.

"Ye sure ye won't spend the night, lad?" Gordie peered at him by the flickering light of a fir candle. "'Twill do ye good to sleep near a warm hearth 'stead of *oot* on the moors on a moonless night." A faint smile, more gums than teeth, decorated his wizened face. "I've ne'er seen a more *wabbit* soul in all me days."

"Aye." Jamie's shoulders sank at the admission. "I'm weary, no denying it."

The shepherd's eyes held no judgment, only compassion. "Seems ye're in a hurry to put a *meikle* mountain or two between yerself and whatever it is ye're runnin' from."

Jamie's mouth grew dry. "B-beg your pardon?"

"I'm thinkin' this journey east was not of yer *ain* doin'." The shepherd met his gaze and held it, then slowly rose and moved about the bothy, tidying up after their meal. "Ye'll be safe here, lad. No one bothers Gordie Briggs. Find a spot by the hearth, and I'll throw a plaid o'er yer back."

Jamie was too tired to argue. He did as he was

told, yanking off his boots, then stretching his long frame across a sheepskin spread over the flagstones and using his forearm for a pillow. "I'm much obliged, Gordie," he mumbled as a plaid was dropped over him. The familiar scent of the peat burning on the grate warmed him from head to foot, and he soon sank into an untroubled sleep.

When Gordie shook his shoulder, startling him awake, Jamie was distressed to find the sun filling the forenoon sky. He'd given his brother more than enough time to catch up with him. Jamie made short work of straightening his clothes and washing his face with the wet cloth Gordie offered, rubbing the cold rag over his rough cheeks.

"Ye'll not leave without a dish o' *brose,*" the shepherd insisted, his tone firm as he handed Jamie a bowl and a horn spoon. Too famished to refuse, Jamie bolted down the watery oatmeal mixed with salt and butter while the shepherd chattered on about the fine weather, praising God and quoting Thomson like a scholar: "'Thy bounty shines in Autumn unconfined, and spreads a common feast for all that lives.' Isn't that the way of it this mornin', lad?"

Incredulous, Jamie paused, the spoon halfway to his mouth. "You've read *The Seasons*?"

The shepherd grinned like a *brownie,* his merry eyes dancing. "Ye're lookin' at this wee hovel o' mine and thinkin' I've not been schooled."

Jamie shoved the spoon in his mouth rather than admit that was exactly what he'd been thinking.

"Me mither taught me to read from the pages of

the Buik sixty-odd summers ago." Gordie pointed to a thick Bible next to the cottage's only window. "When I'm on the hills mindin' the flocks, I read this." He pulled a battered volume of poetry from his shirt, holding it up long enough for Jamie to see the title, then tucked it back inside. "Belonged to my father," he explained. "The sheep seem to like the sound of me voice." His gaze grew wistful as it aimed toward the door. "And I like sayin' the words. They roll round yer mouth like fresh-picked *blae-berries,* hard and sweet."

"So they do, Gordie Briggs." Jamie regarded the man with newfound respect. "I'll wager your flocks are longing for a line or two of verse this morning." He stood, putting the bowl aside to brush the dirt off his breeches. "You've been more than hospitable. It's time I saddled Walloch and made my way to New Galloway."

The shepherd followed him outside, eying his mount without blanket or pouch. "Have ye no plaid?" Gordie asked. "Or are ye stayin' at the coach inn?"

"I'm . . . not sure yet." Jamie couldn't bring himself to confess the truth.

The shepherd disappeared into the dark confines of his bothy once more and emerged bearing a parting gift. "Best take this, lad. The night wind blows hard o'er the Black Craig of Dee."

The stout plaid that had served as his bedding was thrust into his arms. Jamie accepted it with a duck of his head, humbled by the man's generosity. Gordie Briggs, a shepherd with little to his name, gave freely. Jamie, inheritor of a vast estate, had nothing to give but thanks, and that came with some effort. The shepherd pointed out the best route to the distant village, then sent Jamie on his way with a block of hard cheese wrapped in cloth and a squeeze from his sturdy hand.

The going was slow along the shores of Loch Dee, shadowed by the rugged heights of Cairngarroch with its rocking stone, an enormous boulder so precariously balanced that even the slightest breeze tilted it back and forth. His late breakfast carried him through the day, and the shepherd's cheese served as a fitting supper. On the Sabbath he'd prayed for daily bread and a place for his head; he could not deny his needs had been met.

He emerged from the hills to face the bleakest part of his journey later than he'd hoped. The setting sun grew cooler on his back while the moon rose above the far eastern hills. Before him stretched nothing but moors, desolate and uninhabited, rife with bottomless mossy patches that could swallow man and beast in one black, gurgling gulp. He trained his eyes on the slow-moving stream called Clatterinshaws Lane and eased his grip on the reins, trusting Walloch's instincts to choose the safest passage through the watery, dark bog.

Behold, I am with you. The words, whatever their source, pounded inside him. *I will never leave you.* Comfort indeed when he felt so alone. With each breath the air grew colder, moistened by the peaty ground of Raploch Moss. He threw the plaid over his shoulders and tucked its ragged ends inside his coat, his spirits lifted by thoughts of the helpful shepherd. He would need another meal tomorrow. For now, solid ground and a safe spot for tethering Walloch would be sufficient.

"Soon," he whispered into his mount's ear, his eyes straining to see ahead. The gloaming had nearly faded into night when Jamie felt Walloch's hooves strike the packed dirt surface of the Edinburgh road. Sheer relief made him giddy. "Ride, boy!" he cried, not caring who heard him. The horse needed no further urging, lengthening its gait into a full gallop. Jamie grinned as the night wind blew past his ears. The rhythm of Walloch's hooves pounding the road matched the merry beat of his heart.

When it grew too dark to ride so recklessly, Jamie slowed to a trot and looked for a proper hiding place for the night. Before long he spotted an inviting grove of pines by the wayside and guided the horse toward the tall evergreens, then dismounted. Walloch stepped cautiously over the soft carpet of pine needles, and Jamie did the same, confident it was dry and sleepworthy. He unbuckled the girth and lifted off the saddle with a grunt, then used the shepherd's plaid to brush the worst of the debris from Walloch's coat. "You'll be missing young George tonight," he murmured, doing his best to make his mount comfortable. "Things will be better once we get to Auchengray, I promise you that."

Jamie perched his hat on a fallen log, then wrapped the plaid around him. He knelt down in a thick pile of needles, sinking into them with a weary sigh. Three long, anxious days had taken their toll. He would sleep soundly, knowing Walloch would whinny at the slightest threat or disturbance.

Closing his eyes, Jamie fell asleep in mere moments. If he dreamed, he did not remember it. It was black as midnight when a coarse, guttural voice woke him with a start and the thud of a heavy branch on the back of his neck sent him sprawling across the ground.

Thirteen

Heaven from all creatures
hides the book of fate.
ALEXANDER POPE

Leana plunged her hands into the loamy soil of her garden and breathed in the fresh morning air. Fergus McDougal was expected any moment, and by noon her fate might be decided. Until then, she would enjoy the last of her blooms and pretend Mr. McDougal was a handsome lad of four-and-twenty with a fine set of teeth, copious hair, and a penchant for books. "And flowers," she whispered, drinking in her surroundings.

Purple spikes of betony delighted the eye, even in October, and French marigolds still shone like tiny suns against the dark green leaves. A stand of rosebay willowherb prepared to release its snowy shower of white seeds. In the next row the kitchen garden had a different appeal: It made her mouth water. Yellow turnips with their purplish tops fairly begged to be mashed with butter and salt. Dutch parsnips and cabbage, already plucked from the ground, would someday find themselves nestled in mutton stew, while leafy kale waited for the first frost to bring out its spicy flavor in a well-seasoned broth.

Not to be outdone, her physic garden rivaled that of any howdie or healer, the tender plants providing a soothing balm for her neighbors when illness struck. Each plant was carefully marked and planted in the same spot each year. "Heaven help me if I gave someone henbane instead of hearts-ease!" she'd once explained to a visitor. Prepared with caution in her stillroom, henbane healed the worst of headaches. In larger doses, it was, like its herbal cousin Jacob's ladder, a deadly poison.

Leana stood and brushed the soil off her hands, then pulled out a paring knife and snipped some lavender petals drying on their stems. A nagging tension had settled into her shoulders, tightening as the misty-moisty air crept up her spine. Perhaps an infusion of lavender would ease the pain. She slipped the petals into her pocket and walked the length of the physic garden, past meadowsweet and chamomile, hart's-tongue and pearlwort, stonecrop and valerian.

Finally Leana reached the plot of ground that

pleased her most: her mother's rose garden. It was planted the year Agness McBride arrived at Auchengray as a new bride full of good intentions. She'd chosen delicate colors, which suited her genteel nature—Maiden's Blush, Rosa Mundi, and fragrant white Musk climbing the dry stane dyke. Leana's few memories of her mother were rooted in this garden, where she'd sat at her mother's feet, pulling out tufts of grass while her mother sang to her roses. "Pruning and crooning," her mother called it. "A lullaby for the *flooers* I like and for the wee daughter I love."

But her mother's healthy spirit dwelt in an unwell body. After losing Randall, Lachlan's only son, at birth, her mother had a difficult time bearing Leana, then breathed her last giving birth to Rose. Agness McBride's dying wish was that her infant daughter be named for her favorite flower. Her husband complied, though it would be Leana who carefully tended her mother's plantings. Ever since Rose first toddled into the garden, the girl had no use for the sharp thorns and pernickitie nature of her namesake flowers. "Too hard to grow, too painful to touch," her sister later confessed. "But they bloom with one glance from you, Leana. Our mother should have named *you* Rose, not me."

Mother. Leana thought of her daily, missed her always, but especially when she worked amid the gentlewoman's roses. The mild climate of east Galloway, tempered by the warm ocean currents that swirled across the Atlantic and through the Irish Sea, meant that even now, well into autumn, a few stubborn blooms remained. Leana carefully lifted one fading Damask rose to her face and sank into its silken center, inhaling the sweet perfume.

"Mind the thorns!"

Startled from her reverie, Leana turned, grasping the flower too tightly and pricking her forefinger. "Ouch!" She dropped the bloom and pressed her bleeding fingertip to her lips as her younger sister hurried toward her.

"Poor thing, are you hurt? Let me look." Rose examined the tiny puncture, making appropriately sympathetic remarks as she did. "Those naughty flowers! You really should wear gloves."

Leana pressed her thumb against her finger to stanch the blood before it stained her dress. "But then I can't feel the soil between my fingers."

Rose wrinkled her nose. "Exactly."

Amused, Leana knew gardening was the last subject on Rose's mind. "Now then, what did you come bounding out here to tell me?"

"Goodness, I almost forgot! It's Mr. McDougal. He's *here,* talking to Father in the spence."

"Oh dear." Leana dropped her hands to her side and took a deep, steadying breath, her sore fingertip forgotten. "That means Father will call for me any minute and expect me to look presentable." A quick glance at her nails, embedded with soil, sent her flying toward her bedroom with Rose close on her heels, offering advice.

"Let me dress your hair," Rose insisted, breathlessly trailing her up the steps. "Neda braids it too severely to my way of thinking. And for heaven's sake, take off your apron." They paused at the landing, and Rose eyed her nails with horror. "And those *hands!* Come, we'll hide in my room until Father bellows for you."

Leana surrendered to her sister's ministrations, grateful for her skill with brush, comb, and powder. Neither her loom nor her garden cared what Leana looked like, but Lachlan very much cared and would punish her severely if she did not look her best. In minutes Rose had worked several minor miracles, scrubbing Leana's dirty hands until they were pink and clean, turning her tightly woven braids into softer, looser ones neatly gathered on top of her head like a yellow spring bonnet.

"If only you'd cut one of those pink roses," Rose murmured, continuing to poke stray hairs into place. "It would sit like a bonny bird in a nest, it would."

"And lay an egg, no doubt." Leana pressed her hand to her mouth as a nervous laugh slipped out. "Imagine Father's face if—"

"Leana!" A sharp knock at the door brought both sisters to their feet. "You are to join Mr. McBride in the spence at once."

"Aye, Neda. I'm coming." Leana's hands shook as she brushed them over her skirt. Silly to be so timorsome. She hugged her sister, taking care not to undo her handiwork. "Whisper a prayer for me, Rose. Mr. McDougal may yet change his mind."

Rose nodded, biting her lip.

Leana found Neda waiting for her on the landing, the housekeeper's features somber. "Come quickly, lass." Leana did as she was told, following the woman's plain drugget skirt as it swished around the corner and through the house to the closed spence door.

Neda knocked, much more lightly this time. "She's here, sir."

Lachlan McBride swung open the door, took Leana's elbow, and guided her into the room. "This way, Daughter. That will be all, Neda." The woman curtsied and was gone. Behind Leana the latch fell into place with a decisive click.

Her father's voice was smooth, persuasive, yet his gray eyes were cold. "Leana, I believe you've met our neighbor from the next parish, Mr. McDougal. *Yestermorn* on the road to kirk, I'm told."

Speak o' the de'il, and he'll appear. She gazed at the man seated in Auchengray's second best chair—her father, as always, claiming the best for himself. Fergus McDougal's ample form spoke well of his larder but not of his labor. Like her father, he was probably accustomed to giving orders and letting others do the hard work of farming his land. She curtsied, though none too deeply. "Mr. McDougal." She would not pretend to flatter him by commenting on their Sabbath meeting. His frank stare would see right through her duplicity.

"Miss McBride, 'tis a pleasure to share your company once again."

He looked worse when he smiled. She averted her eyes, staring instead at the clock ticking on the chimneypiece. "Aye," she said, hoping it would suffice. She thought of Rose's name for him and put it out of mind just as quickly. Tasty a dish as it was, boiled haggis did not a bonny sight make.

"I've been discussing a certain proposal with Mr. McBride." Fergus leaned back in his chair, pushing his stomach against the buttons of his coat, straining them further. "We've come to a place in our . . . ah, negotiations where it seems prudent to include you."

Her father's thrifite caught her eye, displayed rather than hidden, its wooden lid slightly ajar. She kept her voice steady and her face blank. "Here I am, at your bidding."

"Sit," her father commanded her. "Next to Mr. McDougal. Do try to smile, Leana."

She couldn't stop herself. "So he can see whether or not I have all my teeth?"

"Leana!"

She dipped her head, shocked at her own heidie behavior, then looked up when Mr. McDougal of all people came to her rescue.

"Now, now, Mr. McBride. Your daughter is merely more headstrong than I'd *jaloused.*" He reached over and patted her arm. "You ken how the old saying goes: 'Bitin' and scratchin' are Scotch folks' wooin'.' If she'll promise not to scratch, I'll promise not to bite."

"Of my two daughters, Leana is by far the gentler one." Her father's eyes bored into hers. "She'll lift nary a finger nor a word against you, McDougal. I'll see to that."

"Will you now?" Mr. McDougal pivoted in his chair and studied her more closely than he should have, appraising her from head to toe, his unblinking gaze finally settling on her face. "Eyes seem a bit weak," he murmured. Then raising his voice as though she had hearing problems as well, he asked, "Can you see clearly, Miss McBride? Won't do to have a blind woman caring for my bairns."

"I can see perfectly well," she said evenly. Well enough to know that Fergus McDougal was an ill-mannered buffoon. "Though bright sunlight hurts my eyes, I am fully capable of caring for children and managing a home. And I've spectacles to wear when I stitch."

Her father swept his hand through the air, indicating the various needlework samplers displayed on the spence walls and the wool rug beneath his feet. "As you can tell by her handiwork, she is skilled with both needle and spinning wheel."

"Aye, so she is," Mr. McDougal agreed, patting her arm again and finishing with a firm, meaty squeeze that made her feel faint.

Lachlan eyed them both. "We've not discussed it, but if you have any concerns, might a handfast be wiser?"

"A *handfast?* Father!" Leana touched a hand to her cheek, expecting the heat to singe her finger. Before the Reformation it was common in Scotland for lads and lasses to live under the same roof for one year and one day as though they were husband and wife. At the end they could part company with no loss of honor for either party. The kirk had put an end to the immoral practice long ago.

"Nae," Mr. McDougal protested, to her great

relief, "I've no time for a handfast. And neither, I think, does Miss McBride."

"What of Gretna Green then?" Lachlan stroked his chin. "Many a lad has escorted his bride to that wee village for a hasty wedding. Not with a real minister, of course, but legal enough for us Scotsmen. It's not forty miles to the Dumfriesshire border. You'd be married on the spot and in bed that night."

"Father!" Leana knew she was crimson, a most unbecoming color.

"It seems your daughter is too proper for such conduct, much to her credit. The lass must be wooed." Mr. McDougal turned to her, eyes gleaming. "When shall we commence to courting, Miss McBride? Would Wednesday be too soon?"

"Wednesday?" Leana's heart sank. *"This* Wednesday?"

The gentleman farmer shrugged, waving his blunt fingers. "Not to worry, Miss McBride. The banns are far from being read. I'll court you properly for . . . shall we say a month? By Martinmas, I wager, you'll be well won."

"She is won already." Her father's sharp tone brooked no argument. "Court her all you like, McDougal, but know that your offer has been accepted."

"Glad to hear it." The farmer rose with some difficulty, then yanked his coat into place. Watching him, Leana wondered absently if his buttonholes sighed with relief when he undressed at night.

Long ago Leana had accepted that she would not marry a wealthy man or a handsome one. Such things mattered not one whit. Instead she prayed that her future husband would be a man whose faith in God made him trustworthy. A man who was always loving and kind by intent. A man nothing at all like her father.

More than once working in her garden she'd closed her eyes and imagined a fine husband fathering six *cantie* children happily gathered round her skirts. *Nae, seven.* A full quiver. Fergus McDougal came with three children of his own and would no doubt expect her to bear him many more. The children she would quickly grow to love; the husband she would not. Leana stared at the man's hunched back as her father steered him toward the front door, one hand squeezing the farmer's fleshy shoulder, and knew all hope was lost.

Fourteen

Behind the dim unknown,
standeth God within the shadow,
keeping watch above his own.
JAMES RUSSELL LOWELL

His watch was lost. His hat was ruined. His beloved mount was gone for good.

"A horse, a horse," Jamie recited with a weary groan, trudging along the Edinburgh road. "My kingdom for a horse." Not just any horse. *Walloch.* A finer beast could not be bought or borrowed—or stolen—in all of Scotland. The pilfered pouch, map, and coin were easily remedied. Not immediately, but eventually. Walloch was irreplaceable and, that morning in particular, woefully missed. Jamie hadn't seen the faces of the miscreants who'd knocked him unconscious and taken off with his mount. Highwaymen, he guessed, gingerly rubbing the back of his neck and wincing at the pain.

Naught to be done but press on to New Galloway as planned, although miserably on foot. The miles to Uncle Lachlan's house stretched endlessly before him. It was Tuesday. Would he arrive by Wednesday? Thursday, at the latest. Never, if he continued to sulk and drag his feet. Grateful for what he had—dry weather and comfortable boots—Jamie drew a deep breath and lengthened his stride. He was a McKie. The world had not yet devised a scheme that could defeat such men.

Head held high, crowned with his much-battered hat, Jamie surveyed his hilly surroundings as he walked. It was a mild morning. The sky, a watery shade of blue, was dotted with sharp-edged clouds, as if cut from sailcloth and pasted in place. Ling heather blanketed the autumn moors with dusky purple. Thickets of evergreen whin sprang up here and there across the rough, grassy hills. Among the whin hopped a flock of chaffinches pecking at the ground for breakfast, each one singing a loud *chwink* as it flew off.

Jamie climbed steadily while his groaning stomach reminded him how many hours had passed since he'd shared the shepherd's brose. Heaven alone knew when he would find such hospitality again. Fate had been kind in one respect: Jamie had been tightly wrapped in the shepherd's plaid when the highwaymen appeared, so they'd left it behind. He adjusted the fabric over his shoulder, momentarily distracted by the memory of Evan and his musty hunting plaid. This one gave off a similar aroma. At least he'd be dry and warm when night-time came again.

Flocks of blackface sheep stood about on both sides of the road, heads bent to the ground, horns curved about their ears. They were evenly scattered as though carefully placed by a shepherd making good use of his master's grazing land. Out of habit Jamie weighed and measured them by sight, guessing what they might earn at market, noticing which ones were ready for mutton stew, which ewes looked best for lambing. The landowner would be bringing the *tups* in shortly, breeding his flocks for next Easter's lambs. Poor, innocent ewes knew nothing of what was to come.

Jamie halted in his tracks. *Like his cousins, Leana and Rose.*

They, too, waited—unaware that he was headed in their direction. Not knowing that he intended to choose one of them for his wife, to bed her well and breed a son. How else could he be certain that Glentrool would always belong to him and to his seed? Rowena's hastily written letter to her brother, Lachlan, was meant to open the doors of Auchengray and convince his uncle that his daughter's marriage to Jamie came with the McKie blessing . . . and the McKie lands.

But the letter was gone. Gone with his traveling pouch and all its contents. Why hadn't he remembered it until now?

Furious with himself, Jamie kicked at a clump of heather by the road, sending the tiny flowers flying. What a fool he would look, showing up on his uncle's doorstep after all these years, hat in hand. "And a sorry specimen of a hat it is," Jamie muttered, yanking it off his head. The thing had been trampled beyond recognition by the thieving brigands who'd stolen his horse. He pressed his fist into all three corners, doing what he could to reshape it, then jammed it back on his head. A gentleman wore a hat, however *dashelt* it might be.

Jamie walked on, his jaw leading the way. No point bemoaning the loss of his mother's letter. He had more than enough time to come up with a plausible story about his unexpected visit to Auchengray. In any case these were his relations. Lachlan's nephew—Rowena's favorite son—would surely be welcome anytime for any reason.

Jamie patted at his pockets until he remembered his watch was gone. Without it he could only guess at the time. He tipped his head back to gaze at the sun, gauging its position. Noon perhaps. The dinner hour for common folk. Not far ahead stood the royal burgh of New Galloway, known for its weekly markets and quarterly fairs. The town boasted inns and alehouses enough for any traveler but none that served patrons without penny or purse.

He crested the hill and approached the outskirts of the prosperous village, a stopping place for drovers herding cattle to Dumfries and travelers riding northeast to Edinburgh. Even though it wasn't market day, the High Street, lined with houses, was far from empty. Irish servant girls, their bright hair bound in tidy knots, swept the steps and shook out rugs, calling to one another as they worked, their musical voices like birdsong. A troupe of Gypsies ambled by with all their worldly goods strapped on their backs. Jamie studied their swarthy faces carefully, looking for the man who'd come upon him at the cairn. The tinkler had sworn he was not the one who robbed him. Jamie remained unconvinced. After many minutes he realized that all the tinklers had the man's same luminous dark eyes, yet none matched the Gypsy he'd seen at Glencaird.

"Were ye meanin' to catch the noon ferry?"

Jamie turned to find a tall, gangly fellow not much older than he staring at him with an earnest expression on his freckled features. He was a tradesman of some sort. A weaver, judging by the skeins of wool stuffed in the satchel that hung from his bony shoulder.

"Forgive me for speakin' *sae* boldly, sir." The man's cheeks colored, and he ducked his chin. "But if ye don't mind me sayin', ye look a mite *taigled.*"

"Confused, am I?" Jamie chuckled at his honest appraisal. "Aye, I could use a bit of information."

The tradesman straightened with a firm nod. "I'm yer man, sir. Ben McGill's the name. Born in New Galloway, I was." A shock of auburn hair fell across his forehead, which he flicked aside. "Ye bein' a visitor and all, I thocht ye might be needin' the ferry to carry ye 'cross the Ken. She's too deep to ford, even if ye had a horse, which it seems ye don't."

"Nae," Jamie agreed, sobered by the reminder. "I

don't." He also didn't have money for the ferry. "Mr. McGill, I'm bound for Newabbey. Will this road—"

"Och!" the man exclaimed, nodding vigorously. "Newabbey is a fine village."

"So should I—"

"Not sae big as me own nor sae bonny," he continued, as though Jamie hadn't made a sound. "But friendly enough to gentlemen like yerself. Twa alehouses, ye ken."

"I see—"

"Now, the abbey's in ruins but an impressive pile o' rubble even so. Sweetheart, they call it. Meikle history round that parish." Ben McGill peered at him more closely. "Have ye family there?"

"Aye." Jamie edged down the street a step. "I'd best be heading south now."

"Nae, lad!" The weaver took a step as well. "Ye'd be much better off turnin' north and takin' the ferry, like I said. Ye can follow the moor road east through Balmaclellan to Dumfries or head south along this side of the Ken." He gestured expansively, the satchel of wool forgotten. "'Tis a *loosome* stretch o' water, Loch Ken. Grand, it is."

"Yes, I've seen it. I—"

"Spent *mony* a day fishin' on that loch. Pike and perch aplenty. The pike are of a monstrous size, mind ye. They've got the head o' one hangin' at Kenmure's castle. Fish weighed fifty-seven pounds, it did."

Jamie's mouth gaped. "It did?"

"If pike's not yer fancy, the Ken is famous for trout and salmon. Aye, and fresh eel. Me wife refuses to cook it, though there's nothin' to fryin' up a plateful. A slab o' butter, a handful o' salt from the Solway—"

"Sounds delicious, Ben." Jamie extended his hand, struggling to keep a grin from taking over his features. "I'll be sure to try my hand at catching eel."

The man's eyes widened. "But ye've no basket for the task, lad! And no boat!"

Ben McGill was still sputtering as Jamie took off downhill through the center of town, calling over his shoulder, "This road leads to Carlinwark, does it not?"

"'Tis the *lang* way round," the weaver warned, his volume climbing. "Are ye sure *aboot* the ferry?"

Jamie lifted a hand in farewell, not daring to turn around. "I'm sure," he managed to say before swallowing a loud guffaw. For a young man who'd lost everything, Jamie found himself in good spirits that day.

Behold, I am with you.

"Better the Almighty than Ben McGill," he whispered, allowing his grin free rein. He nodded happily at each person as he passed, no matter their rank, startling more than one servant and causing many a maiden to blush. He was halfway through the village when a sign in the window of one of the town's inns caught his eye: *Post Office.*

An idea took shape as he made his way through the jostling crowd of patrons gathered inside the open doorway. He sought out the innkeeper, a portly sort wrapped in a soiled apron handing out pints of ale in a noisy, low-beamed dining hall. "If ye're needin' a room, lad, we're full at the moment."

Jamie held up his hands, palms out. "Not a room, nor a meal. It's the post I'm after."

The man turned a weary eye on the clock hanging over the door. "Ye're just in time, if ye've got the thing written. The postboy ought to be ridin' up any minute. In fair weather he arrives at noon, four days a week."

Jamie couldn't believe his good fortune. "Have you a pen? And a sheet of writing paper that I might . . . well, might borrow?"

"*Borrow?*" The innkeeper smirked. "Only if ye have a coin to . . . um, *lend* me first."

Jamie let out a heavy sigh. "In truth, I don't, good fellow. I'll sign a note for it, if you like. Send along the money the minute I arrive—"

"Enough with yer fine words!" The innkeeper reached beneath a desk that was old and battered when George I was crowned. "Ye gentrice are all alike, expectin' favors." He slapped a piece of inferior writing paper on the desktop, staining the edges with his fingers, then shoved an inkwell in Jamie's direction, spilling the contents as he did.

Black ink slowly pooled in a knot in the wood. Jamie took care to keep his sleeve out of it and wrote as quickly as the ill-used pen would allow.

To Lachlan McBride, Esquire
Tuesday, 7 October 1788

My dear uncle,

I bring you greetings from your sister, Rowena McKie, and her husband, Alec McKie of Glentrool. You will remember me as their son and your namesake, James Lachlan McKie.

To the matter at hand. I am to inherit Glentrool at my father's death—please God, that will not be for some time—and am seeking to marry a woman of proper upbringing. It was my parents' stated desire that I choose one of your two fine daughters. Forgive me, but my mother's letter to that effect has been . . .

Jamie paused. What to write? *Stolen?* Lachlan would think him a weakling. *Lost?* Inept, if not worse. *Misdirected?* A complete lie. The sound of hoofbeats nearing the door forced him to finish without further contemplation, haste making his bold script nearly illegible.

. . . delayed. I, however, am not detained in the least and will present myself at Auchengray this very week. I would request the pleasure of your generous hospitality for a few weeks at most, until all necessary arrangements can be made.

A bleary-eyed postboy appeared at his elbow. "Time I was leavin', sir. The post waits for no man, not even a gentleman."

Jamie groaned as any persuasive thoughts flew straight away. "A final word, then it's yours to take."

I trust this forthcoming union of our families will meet with your approval.

Your grateful nephew,
James Lachlan McKie of Glentrool

He signed his name with a flourish, sprinkling a bit of sand on the page to dry the ink, then waved the paper about until he was certain it would not smear. Custom dictated that the recipient pay for the post, though Jamie regretted not having the smallest coin to share with the postboy. He quickly folded the paper, then tipped a candle over the seam, and sealed it with a dollop of wax, pressed down with a grimy thumb.

"If you please, sir." The postboy held out his hand. "The letter."

Fifteen

Go, little letter, apace, apace,
Fly.
ALFRED, LORD TENNYSON

Rose opened the letter, breathless with excitement, nearly tearing the gilt-edged notepaper in the process. Her gaze skimmed over the lines, her pulse quickening with each one.

"Oh, Neda!" She waltzed about the kitchen, fluttering the letter like an elegant fan. "I can't believe it! The most wonderful news I could possibly imagine. Truly it is."

The older woman put her hands on her hips, the berry juice from her fingers dyeing her worn apron a vibrant hue. "Will ye be sharin' that *ferlie* news, lass, or makin' me guess?"

"Sharing it, of course. I can't bear to keep it to myself." Rose read the brief missive aloud, adding a bit of drama here, a dash of inflection there. "What do you think, Neda?" she asked when she finished, carefully refolding the letter. "Shall I say yes?"

"What would stop ye, I'd like tae know?"

"Leana, of course." Rose sighed, her elation fading like the sun disappearing behind a cloud. "It doesn't seem fair for me to enjoy such an outing and leave her behind at Auchengray."

Neda tugged the letter from her hands. "Mind if I read it again? Mebbe there's a way yer sister could be included."

Torn between her own delight and Leana's certain disappointment, Rose dropped onto the stool next to the basket of berries. "Read it aloud if you like, but I'm afraid it's hopeless."

Neda, proud to be one of the few servants at Auchengray who could read and write, jumped at every opportunity to demonstrate her abilities. She cleared her throat and held the paper at arm's length, trying not to squint.

To Miss Rose McBride
Tuesday, 7 October 1788

Dearest neighbor,

I hope this letter finds you in good health and cheerful as ever.

It has come to my attention that, although you have been a guest at Maxwell Park on several occasions, none of those visits included sharing a pot of tea with a gathering of my close friends. I intend to remedy that at once.

"Tea with Lady Maxwell, is it?" Neda lifted her brows appreciatively. "Young Rose is coming up in the world."

Unless your duties at Auchengray require you to be otherwise engaged, I shall expect you promptly at four o'clock this afternoon.

Fond regards,
Lady Maxwell
Maxwell Park

"Curious business, this. And ye're quite right," Neda agreed, handing back the note. "You canna include yer sister without offendin' Lady Maxwell, seein' as her ladyship wrote only to ye."

Rose bit hard on her lower lip, trying to sort out her feelings. "I fear I can't risk that."

"Indeed not."

"Risk what?" a third voice asked.

Both women turned to find Leana standing inside the open back door. Her arms were brimming with roses on the cusp of losing their bloom; her face was filled with sisterly concern. "Who might be risking what?" Leana asked again, easing the drooping flowers into a pail of water left behind by forgetful

Annabel. Her gaze landed on the letter. "Is it bad news, Rose?"

"Not . . . not bad news, no." Rose patted the letter against her skirts, debating the best way to handle things. She couldn't bear to see her sister wounded. Yet how could she celebrate her own good fortune without suffering pangs of guilt? Of course, *she* was not the one who had made the decision to exclude Leana. If it was not her choice, how could it be her fault?

"One of Lady Maxwell's servants brought this letter to our door," she explained, wanting to prepare her.

Leana slowly held out her hand. "May I read it?"

Rose watched her sister's face as she read in silence, amazed when Leana's mouth popped open in astonishment and then bloomed into a smile.

"Rose, this is quite something!" Leana stepped forward and pressed a warm cheek against hers. "A pot of tea with her ladyship, and you the daughter of a bonnet laird. Remarkable, I'd say." Leana stood back and pressed the note into Rose's hands, her eyes twinkling. "You must promise to describe everything in detail the minute you get home." Leana turned to wink at their housekeeper. "Mustn't she, Neda?"

"Aye." Neda glanced at Rose's gown and dirty bare feet. "It seems we've a few details of our ain to take care of. Put a pail of water on to boil, Leana, while I see to Miss Rose McBride's dress."

Relief washed over Rose like the water that soon would wash her feet. It seemed that Leana understood. No, more than that, she was happy for her, genuinely so. The hours passed quickly as Leana and Neda pressed her best blue dress, combed and beribboned her waist-length black curls, then touched a bit of powder on her freshly scrubbed cheeks.

Rose waited until the last possible moment to present herself to her father. Too late for him to protest her visit or ask many questions.

"Pride goeth before destruction," he cautioned, adding weight to his words by pointing to the wooden box where the family Bible was stored. "Don't be aiming above your station, Rose. The Maxwells are too powerful to be trusted, and papist besides." Lachlan McBride had an uneasy regard for nobility. Bonnet lairds and tradesmen were one thing, lords and ladies quite another, and Catholics frichtsome.

She gave a quick curtsy, then hurried toward the stables where Willie, Auchengray's *orraman,* waited for her with the two-wheeled chaise. A kind and quiet man in his early sixties, Willie handled all the odd jobs that fell under no one else's jurisdiction— tasks like escorting her to Maxwell Park. She gaped at the carriage, seldom used except on Sundays, its polished leather seat gleaming in the afternoon sun. "Not old Bess with a sidesaddle?"

"Not today." His wrinkled skin wreathed the grin of a much younger man. "Not for a visit with Lady Maxwell. I'll be drivin' you meself. Can't have your hands gettin' soiled and smellin' like leather." Willie nodded at her white silk gloves.

Rose glanced down, extending her fingers to admire the treasured gloves she'd borrowed from Leana, gloves that had once belonged to their mother. Leana wore them only on the most special occasions. The rest of the time she kept them wrapped in linen, taking them out now and again to run her fingers along the fragile seams.

"You are most thoughtful, Willie," Rose murmured, squeezing her hands tight to hold her emotions in check. "We'd better get on with it. I mustn't be late."

"No indeed. Come, let me help keep yer skirts oot o' the mud."

Rose climbed nimbly into the chaise, her mind already two miles away, her heart beating with anticipation.

Sixteen

A good jack boot with double sole he made,
To roam the woods, or through the rivers wade.
GIUSEPPE GIUSTI

Jamie did not need to ask a stranger for directions; he knew where he was going and precisely how to get there. Hadn't he copied a map from the *Geographiae Scotiae* on his father's desk? True, he no longer had the map, but he'd *drawn* the thing. He remembered that the road from New Galloway led southeast along Loch Ken and the River Dee toward Carlinwark. Short of being swallowed whole by one of Ben McGill's monstrous pikes leaping out of the Ken, he'd reach his destination by suppertime.

He trudged on, the glassy blue surface of the loch to his left, an endless afternoon of walking before him. The mere thought of food was all it took to set his stomach groaning. "Wheesht!" he hissed as it grew louder, grateful he had the road to himself for the moment. He'd borrowed a handful of apples from the fertile orchards of Kenmure, certain the landowner wouldn't miss them. Now the tart juices gurgled in protest, souring his insides.

Jamie emerged from the shadows cast by a densely wooded rise of tall conifers and spied a family of barefooted peasants ambling toward him. The father pulled a *ricklie* two-wheeled cart filled with baskets of dirt-caked tatties and two wee sons, their faces brown as the potatoes. Alongside them walked a woman who could only be their mother, so loving was her expression as she sang a lilting tune:

> Kenmure's on and awa, Willie!
> Kenmure's on and awa;
> Kenmure's lord is the bonniest lord
> That ever Galloway saw.

No doubt they were tenants on Kenmure's estate, singing the praises of the unfortunate viscount who'd lost his head in the rebellion of '15. All of Galloway knew the story of William's brave march on Preston, his capture and trial for treason, his beheading at London's Tower. A gruesome affair, hardly fit to be set to music and sung to children.

"Guid day to ye, sir," the peasant said, tipping his cap.

Jamie, unshaven and disheveled, was relieved to find his standing in society still apparent. It was his boots that marked him as a gentleman—Italian leather, finely tooled and well fitted, if a bit mud splattered. Jamie greeted the stranger with a perfunctory nod. "How much farther to Carlinwark?"

The man looked over his shoulder as though the distance were signposted. "Eh . . . twelve miles, I'd say. Could be fourteen." He turned back to study Jamie. "Ye'll make it by the gloamin' if ye put a bit o' *smeddum* in yer step."

Jamie bristled at the peasant's impudence. Surely the man understood he was accustomed to traveling on horseback, not on foot like a commoner. If it took him longer, so be it.

"Follow the banks o' the Dee past Balmaghie," the man continued, inclining his head to indicate the route. "Ye'll come to the castle they call Threave. Hundreds o' years auld and prime full o' woe." The peasant lowered the handles of his tipcart, oblivious to his sons' distress at toppling among the vegetables, and used both hands to point the way. "Cross the bridge, then turn north and follow the road into the village of Carlinwark, past the Three Thorns. Ye'll be wantin' to watch for Gypsies, lad, travelin' alone as ye are."

"So I shall." Not that he had anything left worth stealing. Jamie thanked the man, then strode past him, grimacing as he heard the peasant's wife peck away at her husband like a hen come upon fresh grain. Her sharp scolding reminded him of his mother. Rowena McKie's words might be more refined, but the tone of voice was quite the same. Jamie shook his head as he walked, wondering how his father Alec had endured his wife's constant belittling. Whichever one of his cousins he claimed for a bride, Jamie intended to make very sure her nature was gentle and her words seasoned with sugar, not salt.

The miles and hours passed without incident as he put one booted foot in front of the other, always keeping the meandering Dee in sight. Occasional herds of black cattle rumbled by, sending him scrambling to higher ground for safety. The beasts were purchased the day before at Keltonhill on the first market day in October, or so he'd learned from a local farmer with an incredulous look reserved for travelers foolish enough not to know that simple fact. Jamie merely shrugged, keenly aware of being what the Buik called "a stranger in a strange land." This Galloway was not *his* Galloway. The rugged hills and glens of home had disappeared, replaced by lush farmland and wide, flat meadows. Bonny as the landscape might be, he could not return to Glentrool soon enough.

Above him the pale gray skies had grown darker, the clouds thicker. Such a changeable sky could revert to sunshine without a moment's notice or usher in a fierce autumn storm and drench him to the bone. The rain did not concern him, but the brooding sky did. It bore down on him in silent warning, as though it knew something he did not. Jamie refused to acknowledge his discomfort, training his gaze on the hedgerows instead, ignoring the ominous heavens, even as a memory from three nights past haunted him: Had he truly conversed with the Almighty in his dreams?

A low rumble of thunder overhead sent Jamie's thoughts bolting elsewhere.

He quickened his steps, matching the hasty rhythm of his heartbeat, and eyed the countryside for a safe haven from the coming storm. An hour passed, then a second. The rain threatened, nothing more, nor did the sun reappear. When a massive square tower rose in the distance, gray and foreboding as the clouds themselves, Jamie stopped to gape at it. On an island in the Dee stood the remains of Threave castle, embrasures for archers' bows piercing the tower walls like eyes narrowed into menacing slits.

A flock of goldeneye flew across the gloomy hills, the whistling of their wings swallowed up by the stark landscape that was once home to the Black Douglases. The earls were gone now, but their spirits seemed to hover over the land, holding sway even from the grave. Unnerved by the deserted fortress, Jamie began walking again, faster now. When another rumble of thunder rolled over him, he fairly ran along the marshy riverside, past the eerie castle, craning his neck for a place to cross the Dee, for cross it he must. By the time he arrived at the old bridge—short of breath, his blistered heels crying out for mercy—Jamie knew he must attend to his wounds without delay. He would reach Auchengray tomorrow, but only if he first found some relief for his swollen, bleeding feet.

Jamie dropped onto the bridge with a weary grunt, not minding the damp stones under his breeches. He grasped one filthy boot and tugged with all his might. It came off abruptly, sending him sprawling backward. The second one came more easily. He parked his boots next to him, dangled his legs over the edge of the bridge, and let loose a noisy, satisfied groan, despite his empty stomach. How good the cool air felt on his swollen feet! The fast-moving waters of the Dee tumbled over the rocks far below—inviting but too far away to be of much use to him.

As the threat of a storm passed and twilight fell, the insect world struck up its familiar chorus. Jamie leaned back on his elbows, content to simply breathe and listen. It was then he heard the muffled sound of wagon wheels coming down the road, coming closer. Low male voices, children singing, the music of a woman's throaty laugh, tin pans banging against a wooden brace—all floated past like leaves from a nearby ash tree. He sat up, wincing as he scraped an elbow on the rough stone. Tinklers. Gypsies, he'd wager.

Round the bend came a wagon pulled by two shelties, broad backs straining against the load of kettles and pots, crockery and horns. Fore and aft walked Gypsies of all ages, dressed in ill-matched if colorful garb, whispering and giggling among themselves until they spied Jamie and fell silent, averting their eyes.

He struggled to stand, ashamed to be caught without his boots on his feet, sore and bleeding as they were. The dozen or so Gypsies busied themselves with their cartful of goods, speaking in a musical cant. Were they Marshalls or MacMillans? Watsons or Wilsons? The roads of Galloway were thick with such families—foreigners and nomads drawn to a land where smuggling and cattle *reiving* constituted a way of life, where most folk looked the other way when His Majesty's laws were bent in two.

None of the wary travelers would meet his gaze save one. He appeared to be the oldest, the patriarch, who stepped forward, then broadened his stance and folded his arms with a familiar swagger. "We meet again, lad."

Jamie blinked, trusting neither his eyes nor his memory. "We've crossed paths before?"

"Aye, ye know we have." From behind the Gypsy rose a chorus of soft chuckling. "Near a certain cairn in a certain parish, name o' Monnigaff."

Jamie peered at the man more closely. It *was* him. Sporting a different coat on his back but nonetheless the same traveler who'd found him last Sabbath morning waking from a most curious dream. "So it *is* you," Jamie murmured, at a loss for what else to say. He counted four younger men behind him and a passel of women and children unpacking their cart by the roadside. The odds were very much against him. "What . . . ah, what shall I call you?"

The Gypsy's dark eyes brightened. "Ye shall call me for supper!" he crowed, and the others laughed more boldly, sneaking glances at the gentleman with his torn clothes and foolish questions. Sobering slightly, the Gypsy nodded his head, though he did not offer his hand in polite greeting. "Me name's Marshall, and that's all ye need to know."

"James Lachlan McKie of Glentrool," Jamie said with as much bravado as he could muster, locking his hands behind him. Conversing with tinklers in the gloaming was a strange business. Cutpurses who helped themselves to others' pockets and pouches were a common occurrence and no threat to him since he had naught worth stealing. A cutthroat was another matter, sticking a knife in a man's gullet for no reason other than he didn't care for the look of him.

As though reading his mind, the Gypsy produced a slender blade—Jamie had seen that before as well—and the man carved it through the evening air. "Have ye found some new silver ye might share with a poor family of travelers?"

Jamie lifted his chin, determined to stand his ground. "I have not."

The Gypsy pretended to search the bridge high and low, eyes wide in mock astonishment. "And where's yer *grye,* man? Have you no mount to carry ye?"

"No horse," Jamie said, his jaw tightening. "Not since yestermorn."

"Why then, ye're one o' us!" the Gypsy cried, throwing out his arms. The knife mysteriously disappeared and with it any threat. "Ye sleep by the road, eat what the Almighty sees fit to feed ye, and greet every man as an equal." His grin revealed a misaligned mouthful of teeth. "Only yer *strods* tell the world ye're a man o' means."

"My what?"

"Strods." The gypsy pointed to Jamie's feet. "Yer boots, man."

Both men stared at the empty boots, which were precariously perched on the edge of the bridge. Jamie suddenly wished they were on his feet. The Gypsy spoke to the others in a cant all their own, gesturing as he did.

Presently a young boy stepped forward with a carved walking stick in his hand and a gleam in his elfin eye. "Now, sir?"

"Aye, now," the old Gypsy said.

The boy marched up to the boots and promptly pushed one off the bridge with his stick, sending the boot splashing into the water below.

"You!" Jamie lunged for him, but the boy was too quick, darting back to his mother, who wrapped him in a blanket of arms and skirts. "How dare—*och!*" Jamie threw himself onto the bridge, leaning over from the waist, grasping in vain at the boot far below. It lodged itself among the rocks temporarily, then broke free and sailed along with the current, disappearing under the bridge. With a muttered oath, he scrambled to his feet and ran to the other side, only to see the boot emerge and continue bobbing downstream, farther beyond his reach. It would fill with water soon enough and sink to the murky bottom, useless to anyone.

"Why?" He turned on the Gypsy, his face flaming. "Why would you discard one boot when you could have stolen them both and sold them?"

The Gypsy's smile was warm, not sly as before. "Because then we'd be thieves, just as ye expect. We're tinklers, tradesmen, and *horners.* Not thieves."

"But—"

"D'ye know why the world thinks ill o' the Gypsy race?" The man's animated features grew still. "They say that a Gypsy blacksmith forged the nails for the cross. True or not, we've been condemned to wander the earth forever, a people with no home." His shoulders sagged as he said the words. "May it ne'er be said of a Marshall that he did not honor God's chosen one."

Jamie's heart stuttered. *Behold, I am with you.* Had God really chosen to bless him, then stripped him of everything that made him a McKie? Jamie stared at the man, at a loss for answers. None of it made sense, especially not this thieving Gypsy. With grim fascination Jamie watched the man's jaw work as though chewing over what to do with him.

At last the Gypsy spoke. "One o' yer strods has disappeared. The other is worth nothing to ye." He nodded at the young boy, who slipped from his mother's grasp long enough to retrieve the lone boot and place it in the Gypsy's gnarled hands. "It'd make mony a useful purse. Or shoes for a half-dozen barefoot *chauvies,*" he murmured, caressing the leather, his dark eyes intent, his dry lips pursed. "So, James McKie, will ye sell me yer fine boot?"

Jamie's mouth dropped open. "*Sell* it to you?"

"Not for coin," the old man quickly added. "We've none o' that in our tents. But we've food enough for any Scotsman. Are ye hungry, lad? Will ye sell me yer strod for a bowl o' Gypsy stew and a walking stick for your journey? Seems a fair bargain."

Jamie shook his head, dazed at the turn of events, then agreed that a meal would be a fine trade. After all, a useless boot was hardly a sacrifice, and the carved stick could be of some value. Within moments one of the Gypsy women presented him with a crockery bowl brimming with thick, fragrant stew and a carved horn spoon. Jamie scooped up the stew, bringing it to his lips, then abruptly stopped. Might it be tainted on purpose? A simple ploy meant to do away with famished travelers and rob them of their worldly goods?

The man named Marshall eyed him evenly. "A horn spoon holds nae poison, Mr. McKie. Had I the notion to kill ye, I'd have done it on that rock in Monnigaff."

Ashamed of himself, Jamie shoved the spoon in his mouth, gulping down the lukewarm stew with a grateful nod. Half an hour later he finished a second bowl and stood to take his leave, reveling at the sensation of a full stomach, when he saw the young Gypsy boy, soaking wet, come trotting up to the encampment.

On the child's face was a look of triumph. In his hands he held Jamie's other boot. Muddy and drenched, but his boot nonetheless.

"What's this?" the old Gypsy exclaimed, blinking

his eyes dramatically. "A strod to match the one I just bought? Lucky day for me, I'd say." Agile for his age, the man yanked off his shoes and pulled on the boots, struggling a bit with the wet one, but soon standing to model them for his appreciative clan. "Why, I look like a fine gentleman!"

"And I look like a fool," Jamie fumed, stabbing his walking stick into the ground and stamping off with as much dignity as he could muster while marching in bare feet with blisters.

"Aye, but ye're a fool full o' stew," the Gypsy called after him. "Not so bad a trade, eh? God speed ye, lad. Yer feet will carry ye home."

Seventeen

But, oh! what mighty magician can assuage
A woman's envy?
GEORGE GRANVILLE, LORD LANSDOWNE

Leana pressed an armful of freshly laundered linens against her face, breathing in the crisp October air captured in their folds. The clatter of cooking pots drifted in from the kitchen next door. Neda was taking her time preparing supper, stalling until Rose and Willie made their appearance. If they tarried much longer, Lachlan McBride could be counted on to raise his voice in protest. At Auchengray the evening meal was served at seven. "No visit with royalty is going to interfere with my supper," her father had announced when Rose had left for

Maxwell Park earlier that afternoon. Royalty and nobility were not one and the same, but Leana saw no need to mention it and risk his ire.

The laundry door was propped open to usher in the fading sunlight. She stood near a warm patch of it as she matched the linen corners, pressing the fabric flat between her fingers. Mary had worked so hard to scrub the tablecloths clean, the least Leana could do was fold them. After being laid out to dry on a patch of grass where the flocks wouldn't trample them, the linens would still need to be ironed, a thankless task only a seasoned laundry maid like Mary could handle. Some cold December day perhaps, when the cumbersome business of washing was out of the question.

Grateful that winter was two months away, Leana breathed in the rich scent of herbs wafting through the doorway. Basil, clovelike and peppery, tickled her nose. Aromatic thyme, useful for chasing away an occasional nightmare, tinged the evening air. Fragrant pennyroyal piqued her thirst for a steaming cup of tea.

And what of the tea being poured at Maxwell Park?

Leana released a lengthy sigh, her thirst forgotten. She was pleased for Rose and her sister's growing relationship with Lady Maxwell. Yet something tugged inside her, pulling her this way and that: pride in the gentlewoman's attentions, yet concern for her possible motives; joy in Rose's newfound confidence, yet fear of where it all might lead. "You fret too much," Leana said, catching a glimpse of her reflection in the window. Worry wrinkled her brow and pinched her lips into a tight, unattractive line. She forced herself to smile, then laughed at her foolishness. *Enough.*

Leana quit the stuffy laundry room and escaped to the vegetable garden to dig up some neeps for dinner and bury her misgivings. The sun was low in the sky by the time her skirts were filled with firm yellow turnips. She stood, gripping the corners of her apron to keep the root vegetables from tumbling out of her *by-pit* basket, then nearly dropped the entire harvest when Willie and Rose came riding up the drive and startled her, whistling and calling her name.

"We're home, Leana. We're home!" Rose sang out, waving gaily. Willie had barely pulled the chaise to a full stop when Rose scrambled out of it, her manners forgotten so eager was she to reach Leana's side. Once there, she eyed the dirty turnips, then wrinkled her nose, taking a step backward to avoid soiling her blue dress. "At least I'm not late for supper."

"And a good thing you're not," Leana scolded her gently. "I was worried about you."

"No need to be," Rose insisted, looking over her shoulder at Auchengray's most diligent servant. "Willie saw to an errand while we chatted, then brought me safely home."

Leana smiled at them both. "I see he did." It was hard to remain cross with her sister; she'd clearly had a fine afternoon. "So, was your time with Lady Maxwell everything you expected?"

"Oo aye!" Rose dissolved into a girlish giggle before she composed herself, her face aglow, her dark eyes sparkling. "Neda serves a cup of tea with naught but a biscuit. But at Maxwell Park, her ladyship's mahogany table is covered with fruit tarts and fresh shortbread and . . ."

Rose went on describing the fragrant black tea, the delicately painted bone china, and the glowing tapers in silver candlesticks. Leana listened and nodded and tried her best not to be envious. She'd seen the fabled interior of Maxwell Park as a child of four, with her mother. But she'd never sat at Lady Maxwell's table.

Would an invitation to his lordship's Hogmanay Ball be next for Rose? The last day of the year—Hogmanay—was a cause for celebration in every Scottish home, Maxwell Park especially. Eligible gentlemen from half a dozen parishes brought their menservants and their purses to Lord Maxwell's door at December's end, dancing in the new year and shopping for a bride. Might Rose be included on the guestlist this year?

A slender vine of envy curled around Leana's heart like bindweed.

A wealthy suitor for Rose. Fergus McDougal for me.

Appalled at her selfish thoughts, she searched in vain for a suitable comment. "I'm so happy for you, Rose." And she was, truly she was. She would allow nothing—least of all their future marriage prospects—to drive a wedge between them. She would *not.*

"Do you know what Lady Maxwell said of us?" Rose tipped her chin up, assuming the gentlewoman's haughty air. "'You and your sister are hardly *kintra* folk, my dear. Your father is laird of his own land, and Auchengray is a perfectly respectable property.' That's what she said, Leana! Isn't it wonderful?"

"Aye," she murmured, "wonderful." Leana bit her tongue to keep from asking if Lady Maxwell noticed how the poorest among their neighbors truly lived. Huddled in rough stone cottages, their windowless walls blackened with peat smoke, their cupboards bare, the hardworking kintra folk could only dream of drinking tea at all, let alone at Maxwell Park.

Rose still held her chin aloft, an imaginary saucer in her hand. "Then her ladyship said, 'You would do well to appreciate what your family has accomplished. It is that spirit of improvement that most impresses me about you, Miss McBride.' *Och!* Isn't that grand, Leana?"

"Grand." Her apron was growing heavy and her heart heavier still. "Come, lass. Neda is waiting for these vegetables. Neeps may not be the usual fare at Maxwell Park, but they'll fill our table well enough."

Her sister groaned and rolled her eyes as she followed Leana into the kitchen. "None for me, thank you."

Neda stood at the hearth giving orders while two scullery maids, Annabel and Eliza, wisely obeyed. "See that ye slice those carrots thin as reeds, otherwise Mr. McBride will toss them to the dogs and ye along with them." Neda softened her words with a broad wink. "And don't be slippin' a bittie in your cheek when ye think I'm not lookin'. We've no rabbits in this hoose needing to be fed. Only the quiet one in the cookin' pot."

Leana poured the turnips from her apron onto a cutting table and nodded at Rose. "Look what I found in the garden."

Neda gave the sisters her full attention as she poked a lock of copper-colored hair beneath her plain cap. "If it isn't Miss Rose McBride, home from an afternoon with the gentrice." A wry grin stretched across her ruddy face, the skin freckled yet unlined despite her fifty-odd years. "Will ye be having supper with your family, or is Auchengray too common for ye now?"

Rose brushed off her comments with an airy hand. "I'm quite full at the moment, though I'll surely be famished by the time supper is served." She swept through the cluttered room, holding her skirts above the floor as though the surface were hard-packed dirt and lime instead of good, clean brick. "I'll be back to help in the kitchen as soon as I finish cleaning my shoes."

Leana watched her sister move toward the stone stair, skirts still in hand, certain Rose would not appear again until the supper bell rang. Which she didn't.

Not a word was said about Maxwell Park that night. After their supper of stewed rabbit seasoned with onions, surrounded by Leana's freshly picked vegetables, the table was wiped clean and the family Bible placed in front of Lachlan. "Let us worship the Almighty," he intoned, opening the thick book. His voice reminded her of Reverend Gordon, who scowled when he spoke and growled when he preached. Neda and the other servants sat about the room on rough benches, the rushlights above them doing little to dispel the evening gloom.

"From the Seventy-eighth Psalm," the laird of the house announced, his sharp eyes regarding his congregants closely. "Repeat each line after me. 'Give ear, O my people, to my law: incline your ears to the words of my mouth.'"

Leana recited the familiar verse, struggling to incline her ears and master her emotions. What vexed her so? Was it Rose's bright future . . . or her gloomy one? Her father's even gaze met hers. The line of his mouth was grim. Had he guessed her feelings?

He read again, then paused, keeping a close eye on her. "I will open my mouth in a parable: I will utter dark sayings of old: Which we have heard and known, and our fathers have told us."

Our Father. Her eyes wandered to the hearth as her thoughts drifted. Did God the Father resemble Lachlan the father? Often cross, sometimes cruel, waiting for her to make a mistake?

"Pay attention, Leana!"

Her head snapped in his direction. "Y-yes sir."

"Now then. The fourth verse." Lachlan's eyes narrowed. "Do not miss the meaning of this one, daughter. 'We will not hide them from their children, shewing to the generation to come the praises of the Lord, and his strength, and his wonderful works that he hath done.'" When they'd all responded in unison, he reminded them, "That is my responsibility. To teach my household, servants and daughters alike, that we are to fear God."

Leana thought back over the words and did not remember *fear* being among them. Not in that verse. Words like *praise* and *strength* and *wonderful* were the ones that caught her attention, while her father rushed over such words, dwelling on those more sobering.

He continued reading about fathers teaching their children the commandments of God, even as the patriarch Jacob had taught his own sons. It was Leana's turn to watch closely and see if memories of *his* only son, dead at birth, might cloud Lachlan's eyes or muddle his words. They did not. His voice was stern as ever, despite the promise he gave from the Scriptures: "They might set their hope in God."

Hope. Leana's gaze drifted to the front window, black with night. She'd not lost hope in God, not yet. But hope was waning nonetheless. In a year or two Rose would be married and gone, sharing a new life with some Galloway gentleman, leaving Leana with a meager choice: Stand in the parish kirk with Fergus McDougal by her side or remain at Auchengray as a *stayed lass,* unmarried and unloved, while her father grew old and gray and his bitter tongue sharpened with age.

Even lemon balm from her garden couldn't ease the painful knot inside her.

"Let us pray," her father declared, closing the Bible with a soft thud.

Leana squeezed her eyes shut, praying more fervently than she could ever remember. She loved Rose dearly and did not wish her sister ill, not for a moment. She only longed for a small measure of happiness for herself. A hope and a future. With a young husband who loved her for all the right reasons.

Please, God. Please. Her silent prayer took shape and form, sculpted by her imagination. Let him be a *braw* man of twenty-odd years, not a stout man of forty. Let his kind eyes and ready smile warm the air around him. Let his head rise well above hers and his smooth brow conceal a fine mind. *Please, God.* If such a man existed, let him come to Auchengray before it was too late.

Eighteen

The man is coming, and the hour,
The shaft is on the wing.
HENRY INGLIS

I beg your pardon, lass, but how far is it to Auchengray?"

The dairymaid, not ten steps ahead of Jamie, halted her wooden pails in midswing and eyed him over her shoulder, a shy smile playing across her features. "Sir, if ye shot an arrow o'er Lowtis Hill, ye'd pierce the verra heart of Auchengray."

Jamie's pulse quickened. "Might you tell me how to find it?"

"Oo aye!" She turned to face him, putting down her heavy milk buckets with a slight grunt. "Ye'll go past Drumcultran—that's the auld tower up this road, d'ye ken?—and then doon the hill. Ye'll be fordin' a burn as wide as ye are tall, aiming all the while for Lowtis Hill. See it there?" She pointed one stubby finger toward a steep rise covered in the hazy blue mist of late morning, its heathery slopes dressed in a velvet patchwork of muted purple and russet brown.

"*Whan* you come to Lowtis," she continued, "follow the road round the north of it, past the Maxwell place. At Lochend ye're not two miles from Auchengray, just doon the same road on the left."

He would arrive within the hour. From habit, Jamie reached for his watch, then exhaled with irritation when his fingers found naught in the pocket but lint. "Have you some idea of the time, lass?"

She shrugged. "Didn't I just come from Mistress Chalmer's hoose this Wednesday mornin' and her wantin' mair milk than *ane* lass can carry? 'Twas ten o'clock by her *wag-at-the-wa'*. Pendulum swingin' steady as could be." Her frank gaze wandered from his unshaven face to his unshod feet. "Will the folk at Auchengray be expectin' ye, sir?"

"Perhaps," he said, not sure of the answer. Had his letter found its way into Uncle Lachlan's hands? If so, he'd be happily received, even in such a wretched state. If not, he'd quickly explain his predicament—omitting certain details—and throw himself at his uncle's mercy. With any luck, Lachlan McBride was a compassionate sort.

"I'm much obliged, lass." Jamie reached up to tip his hat before remembering he'd traded the sorry thing for a night's sleep on a cold barn floor north of Carlinwark and two hard bannocks for breakfast. Dropping his hand, he strode past her without further ado, noting she wore the rough country shoes and stockings of her class. He was an educated gentleman and she, a poor milkmaid, unaccustomed to men doffing their hats at her. What did it matter how he treated her?

Jamie slowed his steps, his conscience stirring. It *did* matter. The Buik clearly said, "In lowliness of mind let each esteem other better than themselves." His mother had not taught him that, nor had his schooling. It was a lesson learned at his father's feet on a wintry Sabbath morning at Glentrool. He could still hear Alec McKie's strong voice filling the room: "Before honor is humility, lad. Mind your pride."

Chastened by the memory, Jamie turned and called out to her retreating back, "A good day to you, miss!" and bowed properly. Though his head and feet were bare, at least he'd done the honorable thing.

The sky above was a cloudy Galloway gray—neither dark nor light, stormy nor bright—yet around the edges a fringe of watery blue touched the hilltops. A faded linen cap trimmed in blue lace. Would his lady cousins, Leana and Rose, wear such caps when they greeted him at their doorstep? "Leana," he said aloud, trying the name on his tongue. He softened all the vowels in Lowland fashion and was pleased with the sound of it. *Leh-ah-nah.* "And Rose," he said, drawing out the *O* with some relish. A bonny flower in any garden. "But not without its thorns," he reminded himself.

The brilliant hues of a male pheasant caught his eye as it skittered beside the dry stane dyke, long tail smartly cocked, brown and red feathers gleaming. "Would that I had such a fine suit of clothes," he mused, ashamed of what the lasses might think of their cousin from the west. He would bathe in Lochend and wash off what he could. Soon enough one of Auchengray's servants would take a razor to his face, but until then his beard was hopeless.

Jamie shifted his gaze from the road ahead long enough to assess the granite walls of Drumcultran towering over his left shoulder. The fortified house with its parapet walk stood amid a noisy farmstead of hens and chicks, ducks and geese, all clucking and quacking at once, paying him no mind. He returned the favor, increasing his pace to escape the din, and tried to ignore the sharp stones that pierced the soles of his feet with every step. Following the dairymaid's instructions, he soon crossed the narrow burn, pausing to soothe his feet in the cool stream before shaking off the water and pressing on.

Not much longer now.

The closer he came to Lowtis Hill, the more massive it appeared until the thickly wooded mound was all he could see. He circled around to the north, past the estate the lass had said belonged to a Maxwell. Nothing unusual; Galloway was thick with Maxwells, many of noble birth. The house was impressive, an elegant country estate surrounded by tidy outbuildings and a walled garden that invited closer inspection. Someday he might call upon them, though he'd not be in the neighborhood long.

Vague memories of his first and only visit to Auchengray stirred inside him. He'd been a lad of twelve then, not prone to notice his surroundings. Yet the curve of the road looked familiar, and the gentle roll of the land offered a pleasant welcome. Almost like a homecoming. It was here his father had stopped the carriage and pointed ahead to Lochend, where his grandfather's servant had found Rowena drawing water for Auchengray's flocks long ago. She must have made a very bonny sight, because the servant quickly dressed her in gold bracelets and proposed on Alec's behalf.

Jamie could still remember his father's telling his young sons that day by the loch, "A marriage by proxy is full of surprises."

"Perhaps so, Father," Jamie murmured now, his voice lost in the rustling of the leaves beneath his feet. "But I intend to see my betrothed before I agree to marry her." He grinned, knowing he would see both his bridal prospects, and very soon.

The loch's smooth surface glistened between the trees. No more than half a mile long, it would serve nicely—not for a trysting spot with his future wife, but rather for a much-needed bath. He walked the length of it until he reached the head of the loch where a copse of trees offered sufficient cover. After tossing his filthy coat, waistcoat, and breeches over the lower branches of an accommo-dating pine, he stepped into the water with care, not certain how steep its banks might be, using his walking stick to prod the floor of the loch. It was cold, colder than the shallow stream had been. He found a likely spot and planted his stick in it, then sank into the water up to his neck, shivering as he dipped back to soak the grime from his hair. And to think he'd considered wearing a wig to impress his cousins! It wouldn't have lasted past Raploch Moss.

He ran his fingers through his thick hair, disgusted to find twigs and stems tangled among the badly knotted strands, then straightened to see what could be done for the stains on his shirt. As he scrubbed with his bare hands, he took in his quiet surroundings. The far shore of Lochend boasted fine, gentle hills dotted with heather and whin. Moorhens with bright red bills paddled about the surface, keeping a safe distance from the long-legged newcomer. When the slippery scales of a fish moved past his shins, Jamie leaped with a startled shout, then peered down into the clear water. A long-snouted pike glided by, then vanished.

"Fancy that, Ben McGill!" Jamie announced to the moorhens, picturing the look of astonishment on the face of the *bletherie* New Galloway weaver. "I've not caught an eel, but I've found a meikle pike—"

"Who's Ben McGill?" a male voice demanded.

Jamie turned too quickly, thrashing his arms through the water to keep his balance. A trio of young men draped in shepherds' plaids looked on with obvious amusement.

"Can I help ye, sir?" one cried, playfully offering

his wooden crook. The others eyed the discarded clothes dangling from the pine boughs, plainly curious.

"He's a gentleman from the look of his coat."

"Aye, but a poor one from the lack of his boots."

Jamie managed to climb out of the water after several awkward attempts and stood before them, his shirt and drawers drenched, his blistered heels and fiercest scowl both on display. "Have I properly entertained you, lads, or must I dance to a hornpipe?"

"Och! No need for that," the oldest looking of the three assured him. "It's clear ye've had a long journey, sir. Call me Rab Murray, if ye like." He offered his hand and introduced the others while Jamie squeezed water from the hem of his linen shirt.

"What parish is home for you lads?" If they hailed from neighboring farms, their friendship might prove useful.

"Newabbey," they replied in unison.

"Is that so?" Jamie grinned back at the three of them. "Do you know Lachlan McBride, by chance? Grandson of Neil McBride?"

"Aye." The three exchanged a look Jamie couldn't decipher.

Jamie wiped his dripping chin with his forearm, regarding the young men with some concern. Perhaps his uncle suffered from some malady or—*God be about us!*—was already dead and gone. "Is he . . . is he well, this Lachlan McBride?"

"He is well, aye," the youngest of the three said. "Matter o' fact, if ye stay right whaur ye are, ye'll be sure to see one o' McBride's daughters come walkin' by anytime." The lad craned his neck down the shady lane. "We passed her a bit ago, headed off to tend her faither's sheep. Aye . . . aye, I'm sure that's her. Comin' now, she is."

"Now?" Jamie grabbed his breeches, trying in vain to swallow while his heart pounded in his throat. "Are you certain, lad?" He shook the fabric to loosen the worst of the dirt, then shoved one leg inside the tight-fitting buckskin breeches before he realized his legs were still dripping wet.

"I'm verra sure," the young shepherd answered, grinning. "A beauty, that one."

Nineteen

I slept and dreamed that life was Beauty;
I woke, and found that life was Duty.
ELLEN STURGIS HOOPER

Leana saw him from a distance, walking up the road to Auchengray. Her hands gripped the gate, chilled at the prospect of seeing him again. Bad enough that last night she'd dreamed of him, dreamed of Fergus McDougal, of his thick, eager fingers plucking at her gown. Today she would be alone with him.

"It's only a wee stroll over Auchengray Hill," Rose called from her perch atop the dry stane dyke. "Not more than an hour or two, Father said, and with Willie not far behind you. He'll see to it the man behaves himself. And I'll be near as well, tending the sheep for Duncan. You've nothing to fear."

"I pray you are right." Leana moved closer to her sister, one hand nervously tugging at her dress bodice, pulling it toward her chin. "Mr. McDougal is also joining us for dinner. Whatever will we talk about?" she murmured, watching the man draw near. "He's almost as old as Father."

"Not *that* old, though past forty, I'd say." Rose, swinging her feet like a child at play, smiled mischievously. "Could be if you'd mention his age . . . oh, every few minutes or so, he'll see what a terrible mistake he's making."

"But they've struck a bargain, the two of them," Leana fretted, keeping her voice low as Mary, the laundry maid from Newabbey village, strode past Mr. McDougal and through the gate, headed for the house. "Good day to you, Mary," Leana called after her. No need to consult a watch; Mary arrived every Wednesday morning at precisely ten o'clock, no matter the weather. "Father has spoken to Mr. McDougal," Leana hissed as he drew near. "It's been decided."

Rose turned her back toward the approaching farmer, then cupped her hands around her mouth to guard her words. "Fear not, Leana. All is not lost." Her sister jumped down, landing right in front of her. "Not until you say, 'I do.'"

"If you say so." Leana hugged her sister and motioned her off toward the grazing pastures. *Dear, contrary, adorable Rose.* Filling her with envy one moment, plying her with encouragement the next.

Leana smiled a little and swung open the gate. "Mr. McDougal." She sketched him a brief curtsy. "You've come for our walk, I see."

"That I have, lass. Quit my cart and horse at the corn mill in Newabbey." He glanced in that direction, yanking on his snug waistcoat as he did. "The cart was so heavy with grain I'd be bouncing all over this rutted road of yours."

The road to Kirkbean is no better, she wanted to say but held her tongue. "You were wise to walk those miles then. Shall you stop and refresh yourself before we—"

"Aye. Believe I shall." He strode toward the house while she hurried to keep up with him. Despite his girth, he kept a good pace, though he seemed winded by the time they reached the door. Neda greeted them and led them to the spence, her eyes regarding Leana with something uncomfortably close to pity.

Her father waited in his customary chair, standing only long enough to greet his guest and order Neda to bring libations before resuming his seat. "So then, McDougal, what news from Mr. Craik? Have you been to see him at Arbigland since we last met?"

"I have not, though I'm told the society will be meeting in a fortnight. You'll be joining us, of course?"

Leana listened halfheartedly as they sipped their drams and discussed her father's favorite subject: increasing the value of Auchengray's fields and flocks. The renowned Mr. Craik was president of the

Society for the Encouragement of Agriculture, a group of landowners dedicated to improving their holdings. Arbigland, the Craik estate on the Solway coast, was a monument to his beliefs: Four hundred acres of water-clogged clay had been transformed into fertile farmland. Fergus McDougal's house of worship in Kirkbean had also been designed by the elderly Mr. Craik, a man much admired and respected by all of Galloway.

His daughter, Helen, was renowned for a different reason entirely.

Leana had not met Helen Craik, but she knew the tragic story. The cherished daughter of a wealthy man, Helen had thrown convention aside and fallen in love with a young groom at Arbigland named Dunn. Those who knew him declared the lad a brave and braw young man. Dunn's lifeless body was found near the gates of the estate, felled by a single shot. By his own hand, insisted Mr. Craik, and the sheriff agreed. By Helen's hot-tempered brother, the servants said, and the neighbors agreed.

Helen Craik had departed for England immediately, never to return. Her beloved's spirit still remained at the crossroads, or so the gossips reported. Leana shuddered at the thought of the poor young man's wraith wandering the parish roads very near the farm of Fergus McDougal.

"Is it my company that chills you, lass?"

Startled from her reverie, Leana clasped her hands in her lap to keep from shivering again, so real in her mind was the apparition. "Nae, not at all."

She abruptly stood, taking a deep breath to steady her nerves. "Perhaps if we took our walk now, the sun might warm me."

McDougal rose with a grunt, and her father quickly did the same, stepping from the room to summon Willie to serve as escort. The laird of Nethercarse waited until her father's voice faded down the hallway before angling his head toward hers. He reached for her elbow and tugged her closer, brushing his parched lips against her ear. "By Hogmanay, I'll be the one to warm you." His breath was hot, his whisper thick with her father's best whisky. "Sooner, if you like."

"Let me find my wrap," Leana stammered, bolting from the room, tears stinging her eyes. Like a bird trapped in a cage, she flew from one room to the next, frantically looking for Neda, for Rose, for someone to set her free and release her from such a thankless duty.

Neda appeared moments later bearing the woolen wrap and a grim expression. "Mr. McDougal is waiting for you in the garden and none too patiently. I thought you might be needing this." She tucked the wool around Leana's shoulders, smoothing her hair as she did. "Show him your mother's roses, why don't you?" Neda added softly. "'Twill help the man forget you fled from his touch."

Leana gasped. "How did—"

"Come, lass." Neda chuckled, slipping an arm around her waist and guiding her down the hall. "'Tis the only reason a proper young lady runs from a suitor." Her voice softened. "He's not the man I would have chosen for you, Leana, but he is the man your father has chosen. You must honor them both with all your heart and honor God in the bargain. Remember what I taught you? Submit yerself unto yer ain husband, as unto the Lord. 'Tis your Christian duty as a wife and a daughter. Aye, Leana?"

"Aye." She stood at the threshold of the back door, watching Fergus McDougal bend down to bury his bulbous nose in her white Damask roses. *'Tis.*

Twenty

To what happy accident is it
that we owe so unexpected a visit?
OLIVER GOLDSMITH

Rose fairly flew across Auchengray's pastures, aiming for the hills, the sheep, Lochend—anywhere but home. She'd never felt such a need to run, to put as much distance as she could between her sister's misery and her own joy.

Poor Leana! Doomed to marry such a *hatesome* man. Rose felt miserable, truly she did. It was unfair and unjust that her older sister must marry, while she, five years younger, had all the time in the world to find a suitably rich husband. Not that she was in any hurry to do so. By no means.

Rose picked up her skirts and leaped over the dry stane dyke, built only high enough to keep the sheep from wandering off to another pasture. Without Duncan to direct them, they might not move at all until the forage plants were gone and the grass turned to mud. While the shepherd was busy elsewhere this morning, she would inspect several of the flocks and see to the collies as well.

She reached the summit of Auchengray Hill and drank in the fresh southwesterly winds that lifted the tendrils of hair around her face, tickling her skin. The distant trees, dressed in a faint autumn haze, looked like a watercolor landscape with milk spilled over the canvas, muting the colors. Fine farms stretched in all directions—Troston to the north, Glensone to the west—and Lowtis Hill seemed close enough to touch, though it was two miles away. Leana and Fergus would be climbing in her direction soon. My, but her sister was kittlie this morning! Marriage might be the best thing for Leana. Give her some confidence, ease her sensitive nature. Mr. McDougal, however, was *not* the man to manage it.

Rose attended to her duties, counting the sheep in each pasture—only so many per hilly Scots acre—examining their legs for lameness, their sides for bloat. Duncan handled the less pleasant tasks of shepherding when diseases appeared among the flocks. Now that it was October, Duncan had purchased Auchengray's tups for the season and would herd the rams home from Jock Bell's farm later that day. A week, two at most, and the rams would be about their business, introduced to the willing ewes, one by one. Rose cherished the lambs that came during Eastertide but found the breeding process unpleasant. She kept her distance during those weeks and pitied the ewes who had no choice in the matter.

All at once she thought of Leana, and her heart skipped a beat. Leana also had no choice. Would *she* have one when the time came?

Rose put such melancholy thoughts aside and finished with all but her last pasture for the day, calling a farewell to the dogs, which guarded the flocks as well as any shepherd. Her work done for the moment, she took off, gamboling over Glensone Hill like a four-day-old lamb.

"Ro-sieeee!" A male voice carried across the hilltops, borne by the wind. "Rosie McBride!"

She shook her head in exasperation and headed for the road below. No need to guess who that might be, shouting her name so boldly. Rab Murray was the only lad in the parish who called her *Rosie,* knowing how she hated the childish nickname.

"Robert Murray," she scolded him, catching sight of his red hair and checked plaid. "I'll call you *Rabbie* and see how you like it."

The shepherd, a year older than she, merely grinned as she approached, elbowing the two lads with him. "Ye may call me whate'er you like, Miss McBride, if ye'll call me yer ain dear laddie."

"I'll do no such thing!" she said, rolling her eyes. She was not being *flindrikin,* not at all. Merely taunting him. "Why are you not with your flocks?" She narrowed her eyes playfully. "Are the three of you up to no good?"

"No good whatsoever." Rab gave her a broad wink. "Care to join us, lass? We're headed to Lochend for a bit o' fishin'. Fresh pike makes a fine supper when it's stuffed and baked in a savory sauce."

"It does," she agreed, gazing up at the sun to gauge the time. "I might come in a bit. Just to keep you lads company, you ken." Fishing was hardly a lady's pastime. She gazed down the road toward Lochbank Farm and Maxwell Park beyond it. She could not risk her ladyship seeing her in such a disheveled state—muddy old shoes, drugget dress, her hair barely tamed by an unruly braid. Still, Lady Maxwell seldom ventured across the open park grounds, preferring instead her walled garden. Rose would hardly be likely to meet anyone of quality by the loch.

"Go on with you, lads." She sent the shepherds off with a broad wink. "I'll join you soon enough." As they disappeared over the hill, she made her way to Auchengray's last holding, approaching the flock as Duncan had taught her. It was no good hurrying around sheep or raising her voice. A gentle word, a familiar scent, and the sheep remained calm, allowing her to run her hands along their woolly coats, grown thick again after the June shearing.

She was dismayed to discover the cumbersome water trough on its side. It would take several strong backs to turn it upright before she could fill it with fresh water from the loch. Perhaps the shepherds would help. "I'll see to it you have something to drink before the day is over," she promised the sheep, moving among them with ease, taking note of the brightness of their eyes, the healthy color of their gums when she pulled back their lips. Rose sang to them as she worked, watching their ears twitch with amusement. "I'm not the songbird my sister is," she confessed to a gap-toothed ewe. "But I sing a bonnier tune than *you* do, old girl."

Rose finished at last and hurried down to the road, shaking the tendrils of wool from her skirt. She would go to the loch as promised and see what sort of fish the lads had caught. Within minutes she spied Rab and the other two shepherds standing by the roadside, hands on their hips, looking straight at her. Even from a distance it was clear they boasted smiles from ear to ear. Suddenly they shifted their attention to the loch—not to the water, she realized, but to a person. Someone else was with them. Someone they found very amusing indeed. Their low-pitched laughter floated toward her, arousing her curiosity, drawing her closer, quickening her steps to a full run.

"Have the three of you gone daft?" she called, nearly out of breath by the time she reached them. "Come now, that can't be a pike you're talking to, lads."

"'Tis a big fish, all right." A grinning Rab stepped forward as though to block her view, and the others quickly flanked him. "Bigger than any pike I've seen in Galloway." He glanced over his shoulder, then looked back at her. From behind the three of them came the sounds of pine boughs thrashing and a male voice, deeper than theirs, grumbling rather loudly. Rab hastened to explain, "Our catch is ... not suitably dressed for ... ah, a proper lady's eyes just now. Mebbe if ye—"

"Suitably dressed? A *fish?* Rab Murray!" She stepped closer, and they tightened ranks. "Fish do not talk, nor do they blush."

He laughed softly. "This one might."

"Hoot!" Rose struggled to see over their shoulders, then stamped her foot. "I've had quite enough of your foolishness—"

"Begging your pardon, Miss McBride."

The shepherds parted, bowing to the unseen visitor who'd spoken.

The dark-haired stranger stepped forward. "You'll find I am neither fish nor fowl," he said, his mouth on the verge of a smile. "Though I'm wet from head to toe, and my wardrobe is most foul."

Rose tried not to stare. "Indeed, sir." His clever speech marked him as someone of quality; his appearance did not. Though fashionably cut, the man's clothes were a disgrace—stained with mud and covered with damp spots. His feet were unshod—a gentleman, barefoot! Fine for country lasses and male servants but not for the gentry. And his *hair.* Soaking wet and clinging about his shoulders. When she realized her mouth was hanging open, she snapped it shut.

He inclined his head toward the shepherds. "I believe you lads have some flocks that need tending."

They disappeared like pipits on the wing. Rose did not even notice which direction they went, so shaken was she by this shameless gentleman with the too-familiar smile. Almost like her father's, though that was hardly possible.

"So, lass." He moved toward her. She sensed the warmth of him even from a few steps away. "Tell me, are you Leana? Or are you Rose?"

Twenty-One

Journeys end in lovers meeting,
Every wise man's son doth know.
WILLIAM SHAKESPEARE

I'm Rose." Her eyes narrowed. "Have we met?"

Jamie fought a smile. "Aye, we have."

Twelve years earlier a pink-cheeked cherub had climbed into his lap, tugging at his locks. "Cousin Jamie," the black-haired child had said, eyes twinkling. "I'm Rose!" That same lass stood before him now, grown into womanhood, a creature as lovely as her name. *Rose.*

"Who *are* you?" she demanded petulantly.

"You weren't expecting me?"

"Nae!" She colored, though not with embarrassment. Irritation maybe. "Kindly introduce yourself, sir."

The letter hadn't arrived after all. She didn't know who he was or why he'd come. He closed his eyes for a moment, marshaling his courage, then took a steadying breath. "I'm your cousin."

"My *cousin?*" Her brows lifted into two graceful arches. "But my cousins are two fine gentlemen in Glentrool. And you . . ." The truth slowly dawned in her eyes. "Surely you're not . . ." Mouth agape, Rose studied his hair, then his face, then the whole of him before letting out a faint gasp. "Are you . . . my own cousin? James Lachlan McKie?"

"Aye, dear Rose." He held out his arms. "I am."

"Jamie!" She squealed and leaped into his embrace, three years old again. "It's you, it's you!" Pressing her warm cheek against his damp, bearded face, she sighed in his ear. "Cousin Jamie, come all the way from Glentrool."

Jamie swallowed hard and blinked harder. He'd done it. Without compass or coin he'd traveled the length of Galloway and found his family. On foot. Alone. *Do you see, Father?*

Rose suddenly pulled away from him, her skin more pink than ever. "Forgive me, Cousin. I shouldn't . . . Well, we haven't . . ." She demurely folded her hands behind her back and turned to watch a moorhen gliding along the loch surface, her black braid brushing her fingertips.

"Nothing to apologize for, Miss McBride." He spoke in his most mannerly tone, as though they were at a society gathering dressed in their best attire and not two *tattie-bogles* standing in the middle of a country road, one of them covered with bits of wool, the other dripping with water from the loch. "If I had a hat, I would gladly sweep it to the ground. Unfortunately I have no hat."

"So I see." Rose shifted her gaze toward him again, amusement sketched across her features. "Nor do you have a horse." She glanced down, her dimples deepening. "Nor boots."

"Cousin, the list of goods that are no longer in my possession grows by the hour."

She laughed, tipping her head back as she did. "Poor Jamie." Her sweet laughter filled the air like lilting notes from a wooden flute. "Father will be pleased to see you, whatever your sad state."

"I hope that's true." He would need a ready explanation of some sort, enough to open the doors of Auchengray. Why hadn't he planned what he might say to Lachlan long before now? Jamie brushed his hands over his sullied coat, disgusted with his appearance. "As you can see, I'm hardly fit to sleep indoors, let alone dine at my uncle's table."

"Wheesht!" Rose turned and slipped her hand through the crook of his elbow. "Such foolish talk, Cousin. You've had a hard journey is all." She tugged him forward. "We'll hasten home to a tasty dinner of oyster pie. Our housekeeper Neda is quite the cook." She chatted away in a cheerful babble, her conversation filled with people he didn't know and places he hadn't been. "Your cousin Leana and Mr. Fergus McDougal of Nethercarse will be there. Won't Leana be shocked to see *you?*"

He was content to let her talk, slowing his steps while he considered what he might tell Lachlan. True, his father had sent him off to seek a wife, but how would Jamie account for his hasty departure? His brother threatening to kill him was sufficient reason, but Lachlan would want to know what had fueled Evan's anger. Alec's decision to name his younger son heir to Glentrool explained much, but how had such a turnabout occurred? Every detail raised fresh questions that begged for answers.

Jamie discarded one fabrication after another, arriving at an unpleasant conclusion: He would tell his uncle the truth about what had happened at Glentrool. The Almighty had promised to bless him; let him bless an honest confession then.

"Jamie McKie, you've not heard one word I've said."

He stopped to smile down at his bonny cousin. Sunlight filtered through the oak-leafed canopy above, lighting her face like a candle. "Aren't you the canny one, Rose? You've caught me thinking about what I'll say to your father."

Her animated features grew still. When she spoke, he no longer heard music in her voice. "Tell him only what will satisfy him. 'Tis the safest way."

"I see." What he saw was a shadow of fear lingering over the young woman's face. "Thank you for . . . ah, warning me."

She shrugged and looked straight ahead. "Auchengray is not an easy roof to live under."

Wanting to hear her laugh again, Jamie arched

his brows in mock disdain. "'Tis a heidie thing for a lass to be saying about her own father."

"Och!" She jerked her chin at him, but a smile tugged at the corners of her mouth. "I'll thank you to keep my headstrong words to yourself. And your opinions as well." She quickened her steps, pulling on his sleeve. "Come, I've something to show you, Cousin."

He climbed over the dry stane dyke, then followed her up a steep hill, headed toward a knot of blackface sheep. "These are my father's flocks." She swung her arm in a proud arc. "Aren't they a fine lot?"

Jamie nodded, already assessing the animals' conformation. Straight backs. Strong chests. Solid legs, widely set. "Aye, fine indeed. Healthy coats, too." He approached one of the older ewes and lightly ran his fingers over the long, coarse wool. "Good texture. Have you been checking their feet?"

"What kind of shepherdess do you take me for?" She bristled, her dark eyes snapping. "You can be sure I keep an eye on their feet and all else."

"It's clear that you do." Jamie could not keep the admiration from his voice or the delight from his face. "Have you many more like these?"

"Hundreds." She planted her hands on her hips, measuring him in rather the same way he'd studied her flock. "Are you bent on progress and improvement, like my father? Always with an eye to better breeding?"

"That I am. Breeding is of utmost importance." He

matched her bold stance and regarded her with such keen interest that her cheeks turned as rosy as her name. "Tell me, lass, have you found a worthy ram?"

"Th-that's Duncan's duty," she stammered. "Duncan Hastings, our overseer. He's to bring the tups to Auchengray this afternoon." She looked about, as though seeking a way of escape, when a wry smile suddenly lit her face, and she pointed across the pasture. "In the meantime perhaps you could turn my watering trough aright."

The old trough was enormous, built of solid oak. It was clear she didn't think him strong enough for the task. Indeed, four men might not be able to manage it. He marched over to the massive trough, determined to prove himself. Grasping the rough edges, he ignored the splinters piercing his skin and heaved the trough with all his might. It barely moved as he strained against the weight. His face grew hot, and his knees threatened to buckle. At last, as though helped by an unseen hand, Jamie turned it upright, dropping it into place with a noisy thud as the sheep trotted over, bleating loudly.

"They'll be needing water," he said, plucking the worst of the splinters from his palms. "Hand me those buckets."

She did so, her eyes wide with frank admiration. "I've not seen a gentleman do such a thing before."

"Well, now you have." He left her standing there and made his way back to the loch, filling both wooden buckets to the brim and lugging them up the hill. It took several trips—him hauling, her watching—before the trough was full. He refused to grumble about the weight of the buckets or complain about the hill, which grew steeper with each round. He was strong as any man and would earn her admiration by the sweat of his brow if necessary. Hadn't he turned over a trough only the Almighty himself could have budged?

When he finished, Rose arched her back, stretching out her arms as though she had dragged all those heavy buckets of water herself. A coy smile decorated her features. "The sheep are too stupid to be grateful. But I am, ever so."

Only then did Jamie notice what he should have seen at once: Rose McBride was the very image of her Aunt Rowena. The same womanly shape blooming from a small waist, the same dark hair and sparkling eyes, the same persuasive charm. No wonder he felt at ease with her; no wonder he thought her bonny. His father had sent him on a journey to find a wife. Who could have known he would find a young Rowena—a loosome Rose— waiting for him at journey's end?

Jamie stood before her, still breathing hard from his labors. "Are you truly grateful, lass?"

"Aye, truly." She moved one step closer, her chin almost brushing his chest, and gazed up at him, the picture of innocence. Though her black braid was windblown and tangled, her bright eyes shone like jewels. And though her cheeks were brushed with dirt, her rosebud mouth formed a perfect bow. "Oh,

Jamie," she said, her voice soft as a sleeping baby's sigh, "I'm glad you've come."

"So am I, Cousin." He bent his head and lightly kissed her, surprising them both. Tears stung the back of his throat. "So am I."

Twenty-Two

In life there are meetings which seem
Like a fate.
EDWARD ROBERT BULWER, LORD LYTTON

If Fergus kissed her that afternoon—if he dared even try—Leana would bolt from the man's side and run the rest of the way home.

"Mr. McDougal, you must be famished by now." Leana slipped her hand from his arm and lengthened her stride as much as her heavy skirts would allow. "Neda will have dinner waiting. My sister, Rose, should be along shortly." She glanced over her shoulder, grateful to see Willie keeping a close watch on them. The manservant nodded at her, his expression filled with compassion. *Dear Willie.* He disapproved of the match. Only her father saw its benefits and only because they benefited him.

"Why the haste, Miss McBride?" Fergus caught up with her effortlessly. "Dinner will wait. Although I must confess, my hunger is seldom sated." He drew her hand back and firmly placed it on his arm. "We've climbed two wee hills, and already you're eager to return to Auchengray." He leaned closer, ignoring Willie's throat-clearing noises behind them. "Am I to gather you do not favor my suit?"

Leana could not meet his gaze, certain the truth would be reflected in her eyes. "Not at all," she answered, knowing her words carried two meanings and he would hear the one that suited him. By dodging deceit and keeping Fergus appeased, she hoped to avoid her father's wrath and the Almighty's displeasure as well. It was an exhausting game more suited for a juggler at court.

"It's the brightness of the sun," she explained, tapping her wide-brimmed hat. Her long sleeves and linen gloves protected her fair skin, but her tender eyes longed for relief. "I prefer shade over sunlight, Mr. McDougal, and a cool, dark room over a brightly lit hill."

"Well then," he said with a low chuckle, "I'll see to it we spend many happy hours in cool, dark rooms."

She refused to acknowledge his comment, pressing a hand against her stomach to keep it from turning over in protest. The last half-mile passed with blessed swiftness, his attention distracted by a pair of herd dogs snarling and snapping at each other a short distance ahead. "A regular *collieshangle,*" he said, quickening his pace to keep up with them. Not Auchengray dogs, she noted, grateful for small mercies.

By the time they arrived at the house, Leana was overheated and thirsty, though with no appetite for oyster pie. She excused herself in the hall, then hurried to her room to repair her appearance and have a moment to herself before the ordeal of dinner began. When she removed her hat, she discovered her hair in shambles. She combed and braided it again, pinning the braids in place with limited success, bathed her hands and face at her washstand, then slipped down the stair to the dining room, hoping no one noticed her delay.

Her father's stern greeting proved otherwise. "Why have you kept Mr. McDougal waiting?"

"Sorry, Father." She ducked her head and took her seat posthaste. Lachlan sat at the head of the table, with Mr. McDougal on his right, then Leana. Across the table her sister's chair was conspicuously empty. Leana carefully drained her voice of any emotion, lest she spark her father's temper. "Rose should be here any moment, Father. Might we bide a wee while?"

"And watch Neda's savory meal grow cold? I should say not. Let us pray."

Heads bowed, hands folded, they offered thanks to God for the meal before them and for a goodly number of other things before finally sinking their forks into the flaky crust. Well-seasoned oysters, beef, bacon, and shallots vied for her approval, but Leana could barely swallow a bite. When she saw a look of concern crease Neda's brow, she hastened to explain. "It's delicious, Neda, truly it is. No claret for me though."

Their meal dragged on, the conversation stilted and one-sided, her father expounding on topics only another bonnet laird could appreciate. Fergus McDougal nodded, apparently listening, but his brown eyes focused solely on her. She felt his gaze moving over her features, almost tasting her, as though she were the main course. Maybe she was. He ate everything on his plate and asked for more, smacking his lips appreciatively, complimenting Neda each time she appeared with another dish. He would be an easy man to please at the dinner table. Leana could not bear to think of pleasing him in any other way.

The servant girls were lifting the last of the dinner plates when the front door nearly burst off its hinges and a flushed and flustered Rose appeared at the dining room door.

"Father! We have a visitor." Rose's anxious gaze moved back and forth between those gathered around the table and their unseen guest beyond the front door.

"Who is it, dearie?" Leana asked, grateful for any diversion.

Rose's reply came out on a squeak. "Our cousin James from Glentrool!"

Jamie McKie. Leana searched her mind for some memory of him. A bothersome lad of twelve tugging at her braids, whining for his supper, and bragging about Glentrool as though it were the only place worth calling home.

Lachlan shot to his feet, tossing his napkin aside. "Rowena's son? Is my sister with him?"

"Nae, Father, but *he's* here." Rose was all but hopping from one foot to another, bidding them join her. "Do come and greet him." She lowered her voice, though the note of excitement remained. "You must forgive his attire, Father. Jamie met with several mishaps on his journey."

Lachlan dismissed Rose with a curt nod, sending her flying back out the door, then turned to their dinner guest. "Pardon me, Mr. McDougal, while I attend to my nephew." His gaze shifted to Leana, narrowing slightly. "Stay where you are, Leana. See that you engage our visitor with your wittiest discourse." Her father disappeared, leaving her at a loss for words.

"Mr. McDougal, I'm not . . ."

"No need to be witty for my sake, Miss McBride," the laird of Nethercarse assured her, sipping the last of his claret. "I have no need of a clever woman. Merely a compliant one."

Compliant. Aye, she'd spent a lifetime learning to be submissive. Rose had never spent one day of her life doing so. Which was why her sister was happily outside, making their cousin welcome, while *she* was stuck in the dining room with Fergus McDougal, making herself miserable.

Enough, Leana. Self-pity made a poor dessert.

She clasped her hands in her lap and forced herself to smile. "Mr. McDougal, tell me about your children."

"Och!" He waved his fork, splattering gravy on the fresh linen tablecloth. "Three more *ill-deedie* children could not be found in Galloway."

"I am sure they're not so bad as—"

"Nae, they're worse!" He abruptly waved at Annabel, hovering in the corner, and pointed at his empty glass. "My oldest son, Dougie, is seven years of age and the instigator of most of the mischief around Nethercarse. His brother, Harry, is five and does whatever Dougie tells him to do. A verra dangerous business. And Martha, the three-year-old, cries for her mother all the livelong day."

"Poor child," Leana murmured, compassion for the girl crowding out her concerns for herself. "I know what it's like to grow up without a mother."

Fergus swallowed a mouthful of claret and wet his lips, staining them a bit. "So you do, lass. Which is why I thought you might be of use to me . . . ah, to my children."

"Of *use,*" she repeated softly.

"Aye. Useful. To me. To my household." His brow darkened, and a frown creased his thick face. "It isn't love you're wanting, is it, Miss McBride?" He lowered his voice and leaned forward. "There are certain . . . ah, *needs* a man brings to a marriage, and I expect those to be met. As to love . . . well, I thought surely a woman of your age . . . with your . . . ah, particular . . ."

Leana stood. She could not bear to hear another word. "I understand. Completely. Mr. McDougal, might I kindly have your permission to greet my cousin?"

He looked perturbed. "Go, if you must, and tell your father I gave my leave." He glanced at the dessert Annabel had set before him moments ago, and his frown faded. "I can amuse myself for quite some time with this tempting burnt cream."

Leana curtsied and glided out the door, biting her lip to hold her tears at bay. What did her sister call him? A "horrid old farmer." *Aye, Rose, he is.* She hurried toward the conversation coming from the front garden. Two familiar voices and a third, not quite so deep as her father's but warmer and laced with good humor, floated in her direction. She ducked around an overgrown hazel, then slowed to a stop, amazed at what she saw.

Lachlan McBride, usually sparing with his affection, held a tall, shabbily dressed gentleman in a loose embrace. "My own flesh and blood!" her father said with obvious fondness, tousling the younger man's already tangled hair. "My sister's son, my own nephew," he added, pressing him to his chest.

"Father, let him breathe!" Rose cried.

Leana caught her breath as well, the ordeal at the dinner table already forgotten. *James Lachlan McBride.* Her cousin. No longer a rough-and-tumble lad, he was a grown man, taller than her father.

"Cousin James."

He turned at her voice. Recognition dawned in his mossy green eyes. "Leana!" He held out a hand to her. "Come let me have a look at you." A warm smile stretched across his bearded cheeks. "How grown you are. A woman now, not a lass."

"So she is." Lachlan's tone was sharp, his cordial manner gone. "A woman who was told to keep our dinner guest amused."

Heat rose from the neck of her gown, quickly reaching her hairline. "He . . . gave me leave to greet my cousin." She held out her hand, wishing it were more steady. "Welcome, James."

"Jamie," he amended with a playful wink directed only at her. "Still just Jamie." He'd noticed her embarrassment—how could he not?—and intervened with a bit of levity. The kindness in his eyes was genuine. Taking her offered hand, he bent over it, dark waves of damp hair falling forward, and planted a light kiss on her fingers, his lips barely grazing her skin. When Jamie straightened and brushed the locks from his brow, their gazes locked.

For one moment Leana thought something passed between them. A slight frisson, the slenderest thread of understanding. It warmed her soul yet cooled her skin so that she shivered in the October sunshine. No one else noticed, perhaps not even he. But she was certain of it. Somehow he had looked inside her heart and approved of what he found.

"Come, come." Lachlan interrupted her reverie, tugging on Jamie's tattered sleeve. "We must clothe you, lad, and see that your stomach is filled." He slung one arm across Jamie's broad shoulders and guided him toward the house, waving the other arm expansively, describing his holdings.

Left to fend for themselves, Leana and Rose followed some distance behind, exchanging glances.

"What do you think of him?" Rose whispered, her voice high as a child's.

"I think Jamie's in desperate need of a hot soak and a good night's sleep." Leana watched Lachlan's broad gestures and overeager words. "Father, however, will insist on learning the purpose of our cousin's visit first."

"Oh, *that!*" Rose giggled. "I already know why Jamie's here."

Leana's breathing stilled. "You do?"

Twenty-Three

How happy could I be with either,
Were t'other dear charmer away!
But while ye thus tease me together,
To neither a word will I say.
JOHN GAY

Well, not exactly," Rose quickly amended, ducking her head. "I mean, Cousin Jamie hasn't *told* me why he's come, not in so many words." She couldn't lie to her older sister. Not because it was unseemly, but because it was *impossible.* Leana's wide, pale eyes missed nothing.

Jamie had *not* come to Auchengray intending to kiss her. Of that Rose was very sure. It was only a friendly kiss between cousins. Over as soon as it began, though it scared her a little. Perhaps she shouldn't have permitted him to do such a thing. Not that he'd asked. Still, it was not why he'd come. Whatever the reason, it was something else altogether.

"I *think* I know why he's traveled east," Rose said, hedging again. "That is, I have an *idea . . .*"

"I see." Leana's lips were pursed, as though she was trying not to laugh. "So you met Jamie while you were out tending the sheep?"

"Aye, near Lochend." The sisters tarried near the front door, their voices low. Rose knew they were expected inside but couldn't bear to keep her news to herself. "Rab Murray discovered him first," she whispered, "bathing in the loch. By the time I saw him, Cousin Jamie was dressed but still dripping wet. No boots, no hat, and a poor traveler's walking stick."

Leana smiled at the picture she painted. "What did you two chat about on the walk home? Was it—"

"Daughters!" Lachlan McBride loomed over them from the open doorway, his brow a thundercloud. "Leana, find your place in the dining room at once. Rose, see that you spend a moment at the washstand in the spence, then haste to join us. Our invited guest has kept his own company long enough."

Rose blushed, Leana nodded. "Aye, Father," they said in unison. Both did as they were told and soon took their seats across from one another at the table—she in her worn drugget dress and Leana in her gray serge. Rose had insisted her sister wear the dreary gown, hoping it might discourage Fergus the Haggis from pursuing things further. *Poor Leana!*

The laird of Nethercarse sat before his empty dish, a stray daub of custard on his waistcoat, a faint scowl on his face. "I met your young cousin, Miss McBride, if only for an instant. Your father wisely sent him up the stair to see to his appearance. 'Twill take a great deal more than soap and water to make that lad presentable."

Rose flew to Jamie's defense. "He traveled nearly fifty miles, much of it on foot."

"The gentleman addressed your sister, not you, Rose." Father's reprimands were a staple at dinner. "Kindly let her respond."

"What you say is true, Mr. McDougal." Leana's slight smile may have fooled Fergus, but Rose could see how it grieved her sister to be polite to the man. "Our cousin Jamie had a long and arduous journey across Galloway. We're grateful he's arrived unharmed."

"However undressed. And unexpected." Fergus almost *looked* like a haggis, so tightly was his mouth drawn between his fat cheeks. "Not the usual manner of things at Auchengray, is it, Mr. McBride?"

"Ah . . . it is not. No."

Rose had seldom seen her father shamed to silence. She stared at her plate, served hot from the kitchen, and hoped someone would say *something*. What an *unco* day it was and only half over!

"Eat your dinner, Rose." Her father's words did

not bite so sharply this time. "Jamie will join us before long."

She plunged her fork into the oyster pie, suddenly famished. Had she eaten breakfast? Supper, yestreen? While the two men conversed and Leana listened, Rose made short work of her dinner. "Is there any burnt cream left?" she whispered to Neda, who soon placed not one but two small dishes before her.

A male voice floated across the room. "My wee cousin has quite an appetite, I see."

Rose looked up and swallowed her first spoonful of custard with some difficulty. "Cousin . . . Jamie?"

"Aye." He stood in the doorway and laughed, a warm, rumbling sort of chuckle. "I'm much altered, thanks to your father's generosity."

Altered fell short of the mark. His hair was pulled back into a sleek tail, no longer a dark, matted mess. In the afternoon light it shone a rich brown. His smooth chin, freed from its bearded bristle, jutted out handsomely, a subtle dare. Even wearing her father's old suit of clothes, Jamie was a braw sight, standing to attention like a gentleman soldier waiting for his marching orders.

"Sit, Nephew."

Jamie claimed the remaining chair next to hers, smiling at her as he sat. "Forgive me for arriving at such an awkward hour, Uncle."

"Och!" Lachlan motioned to Neda and Eliza, who came bearing dishes heaped with food. "Nothing awkward about feeding a starving man at any hour."

Lachlan stood to his feet and inclined his head toward their well-fed guest, who heaved himself out of his chair as well. "Begging your pardon, Nephew. Mr. McDougal and I must retire to the spence for a bit of business. Your cousins will keep you suitably entertained while you dine. Won't you, ladies?"

Rose exchanged glances with her sister, who answered for them. "Aye, Father. Between the two of us, Jamie will be well cared for."

Fergus McDougal moved toward the door, delivering a parting message over his hunched shoulder. "Make your cousin welcome, Miss McBride, but not *too* welcome, if you ken my meaning." He turned and winked at Leana—how perfectly dreadful!—then added, "I'll see you again next Wednesday, when our dinner will not be so *ramstam* interrupted."

"Wednesday," was all Leana said, her voice as cool as the water in Lochend.

Jamie seemed too busy with his meal to notice the drama unfolding around him. His table manners, though, were impeccable, like Leana's. He brought each bite of food to his mouth, instead of bending over the plate and shoveling it in like a plowman. "While I enjoy the best meal I've eaten in a week, might one of you kindly tell me the way of things at Auchengray?"

"Oh, Cousin!" Rose groaned at such a gloomy topic. "As you can see for yourself, Auchengray is the dreariest place imaginable. A bothy compared to Maxwell Park. I visited with Lady Maxwell yestreen, did I tell you? Aye? A grand house with painted paper walls and corniced ceilings and *car-*

pets. Imagine that! Our house is naught but three floors of cramped rooms with uneven stone floors, rough beams"—she waved her hand overhead—"and too few candles. The chimneys won't draw properly, and the casement windows—"

"I didn't mean the house, lass." His reproof was so gentle she almost missed it. "I meant the people. Tell me who lives here at Auchengray. Who are the servants? What sort of property does your father own, and how does he use it?"

Her shoulders sank under such weighty questions. "Ah . . . Leana?"

Her sister lifted her chin and smiled across the table at Jamie. Not the pretend smile she gave Mr. McDougal. This one was genuine, with teeth. "I'd be pleased to tell you about Auchengray, Cousin. Though our house is modest, the lands are well managed and prosperous."

Jamie beamed his approval, continuing to eat while Leana, well versed in household ledgers, filled their cousin's bonny head with names and numbers: Duncan Hastings, the overseer, and his wife, Neda, the housekeeper; so many acres of oats and so many of hay; this many milk cows and that many sheep. Rose was content to nibble on her burnt cream and watch the two of them warm to one another. Jamie not only listened to Leana, he looked at her intently with eyes the color of gray alder leaves in spring, plying her with questions, then nodding thoughtfully at her answers.

Her sister's features, plain as whey, grew almost animated when their discussion turned to vegetable crops. "Perhaps when you've had a chance to rest, you might care to see my gardens," Leana suggested, then lowered her gaze, as though she'd been too forward.

Jamie quietly responded, "I would like that very much, Cousin Leana."

Rose pressed her spoon against her lips, holding back her growing sense of delight. She had no talent for ledgers, but she knew an answer to prayer when she saw one: Jamie McKie was a much better match for her sister than old Fergus the Haggis. Oo aye, he was! They were close in age, both a bit serious minded, and practical to the point of dullness. A perfect couple.

Rose was so caught up in her mental matchmaking, she didn't notice when the conversation dwindled into a comfortable silence and Jamie shifted in his chair to look at her. "Rose, you had much more to say when I watered your sheep."

Across the table the light in Leana's face dimmed. "She did?"

"She needed my help with a watering trough. Isn't that right, Rose?" Jamie continued to gaze down at her, seated next to him.

"Aye," she said, blinking. "The flock was most grateful. And so was I." *Grateful enough to let him kiss you, silly girl.*

Now Jamie was studying her as he'd studied Leana, frankly curious, with the unguarded look of a cousin who has no fear of being rebuffed. "Shall we tell Leana what else transpired this afternoon?"

"We shall not," Rose said firmly, leaning back in

her chair to distance herself. She had plans for Jamie McKie, and they did not include his kissing her, not ever again. She glanced at the plates scraped clean by his fork. "Since you've emptied the table of all our provisions, Cousin, why not start with your departure from Glentrool and describe your journey east?"

"Aye, please do." Leana's features brightened again. "Spare us no details, for my sister and I are eager for news of all you've seen and heard this week."

"Jamie will have to tell Father again later," Rose reminded her. "You won't mind telling tales twice, will you, Jamie?"

A shadow crossed his face. "Nae. I can tell my uncle . . . later."

"Good." Rose stood, glad to stretch her legs. "Come, we'll pull our chairs up to the hearth. A man who's lost his boots has more than one story to share."

The three of them gathered in a half circle facing the warm glow of the peat. Jamie sat in the middle, with a sister seated on each side, their knees almost touching. Servants came and went, clearing the dinner table and trimming the wicks, a pleasant murmur of sound behind them. Jamie rested his elbows on the arms of his chair and sank back. "Shall I begin with the first night, when I slept on a grave older than King David?"

Rose clapped her hands. "Aye, do. What an adventure!"

"Some might call it that." The corners of his

mouth twitched. "'Twas an education far removed from the schooling I had in Edinburgh." He stared up at the ceiling as though collecting his thoughts from between the beams, then dropped his chin and smiled at them both. "George, the stable lad at House o' the Hill. Aye, we'll begin with him."

Leana drank in every word the man said, as though committing each to memory. Rose listened, but she watched, too. Watched her sister's eyes widen with horror at his description of the cairn and heard her gasp with concern when Jamie described the purplish berries.

"Not Jacob's ladder!" Leana touched his arm. "Oh, my dear cousin, you might have died."

"Aye." Jamie nodded grimly. "So the Gypsy told me."

"Gypsy?" Rose couldn't keep the excitement out of her voice. "Never mind the berries, Jamie. Tell us about the tinkler. Did he hold a blade to your throat?"

Jamie chuckled. More stories followed—a missing pouch, a generous shepherd, Raploch Moss in the gloaming, a stolen horse. "When I got to New Galloway, I sent your father a letter, alerting him to my arrival." Jamie glanced at each sister in turn. "Did either of you read it?"

Rose did not need to look at Leana's face to answer for both of them. They never kept secrets from each other. "Nae, Father didn't show us your letter. Perhaps it has yet to come."

"Perhaps." Jamie resumed his journey, introducing them to a talkative weaver, a man with a cart full of tatties, and a clever Gypsy boy who tipped his boot into the Dee. As he spoke, his attentive gaze moved back and forth, from Leana to Rose and back again. Jamie seemed to be measuring them, first one sister, then the other, as though he were a tailor fitting them for new dresses or Duncan at a horse sale on the Whitesands of Dumfries choosing between two broodmares.

A curious sensation, being compared so equally with her sister. Men usually looked at Leana, then at her, and never turned away again. *No matter.* Rose had already measured Jamie McKie against Fergus McDougal and made the obvious choice. It was Jamie who should marry her sister, though Leana might need some convincing, and Father much more so.

A month, Rose decided. She could manage it in a month.

Jamie suddenly yawned and slumped deep into his chair. "My sweet cousins, I must confess I have not slept well in a week. Would you think me terribly rude if I crawled up the stair for a short nap?"

"We are the ones who've been rude," Leana corrected him, touching his arm again. Rose had counted half a dozen such touches in the last hour, smiling at each one. "Forgive us for insisting you entertain us with your stories when *we* were the ones who were asked to entertain *you.*"

"Ah, but you did." Jamie stood, a bit wobbly on his feet in a pair of boots that looked too small for him. He smiled down at them both. "'Twas a most engaging afternoon, ladies."

He bowed and was gone, leaving the two sisters to regard each other in the fading light of late afternoon.

"So." Leana folded her hands and pressed them down into her skirts. "What do you make of our cousin?"

"Make of Jamie?" Rose tried not to smile, but it was useless. *I will make him your husband, dear sister!* She would not tip her hand though. Not for the moment. Leana was too skittish, too uncertain of herself. Rose would simply keep to the wings for once and let Jamie and Leana take center stage.

"Do you find him . . ." Leana wet her lips. "Ah . . . that is . . ."

The poor woman couldn't bring herself to say the word. "Handsome?" Rose offered. "Aye, I do. And so do you, it seems."

Leana's cheeks grew pink. "He is . . . fine, isn't he? Intelligent. And well read, I think."

Rose resisted the urge to roll her eyes. *Well read!* As if such a thing mattered when so much was at stake. He was young, braw, and *not* Fergus the Haggis. No other credentials were needed.

"Rose." Leana stood, slowly pacing before the dying glow of the peat fire. "You said you might know why Jamie is here. Do you?"

"Aye." Rose kept her features perfectly still. "Sheep."

Leana gasped. *"Sheep?"*

"He talked of nothing else all the way home. Ewes and tups. Lambing and shearing."

"How odd." Leana's brow knotted. "Perhaps he thought *you* were fond of sheep, Rose."

"Nae, it was not for my sake." Rose joined her sister by the hearth, linking arms with her, lowering her voice lest Father or Fergus come barreling into the room without warning and overhear. "I think our cousin is here on family business. Perhaps to purchase some of Auchengray's flocks to breed with those at Glentrool."

"Did he say as much?"

Rose shrugged. "He did mention breeding." At least *that* was an honest answer. "Very progressive, our Jamie. Like Father, he favors improvement."

"Aye." Leana glanced at the closed door to the spence. "Improvement. How long might he stay, did he say?"

Rose shook her head. *Long enough, please God.*

Twenty-Four

An honest man's the noblest work of God.
ALEXANDER POPE

Jamie buttered his bannock, then put it aside, anxious to get things out in the open without further delay. "I must be honest with you, Uncle Lachlan, else I cannot live with myself or with you."

"Finish your breakfast, lad. Time enough for truth telling when your belly is full."

Jamie had thought to have this discussion yestreen after supper. By the time he'd discarded his itchy, borrowed clothes and bathed in hot water hauled into one of the bedrooms by a manservant, he'd fallen into bed in a stupor, not waking until the cock's crow startled him from his dreams at dawn.

The morning light cast its bright beams across the dining room table. Jamie watched the two sisters out of the corner of his eye. Seated across from him, side by side, they made a pretty picture: Leana in a light blue gown that matched her eyes, Rose in a printed dress the color of a Galloway sunset in summer, all purples and pinks. He'd awakened to discover he'd claimed one of their rooms, decorated as it was for a lady's taste. But which cousin? Quiet Leana, with her pale skin and graceful gait? Or young Rose, with her dark features and *speeritie* ways? Both had a musical lilt to their voices, both came to just below his chin. They were, in every other regard, two entirely different women.

"Did you sleep well, Cousin?" Rose's dark eyes twinkled. "It's a very comfortable mattress, don't you think?"

"Aye." He'd slept in Rose's bed then. "Forgive me for turning you out of your own room."

Her laugh was like birdsong. "'Tis not as if I had to sleep in the *byre,* Cousin. I shared a box bed with my sister, who never lows like the cattle do and bears a far sweeter scent."

"Now, Rose." Leana's tone was demure, not scolding. "Our guest does not need the details of our sleeping arrangements." She shifted her gaze to Jamie and smiled warmly. "It's only important that he be made welcome and comfortable."

"Rest assured, I am both." And he was. All that remained was to decide which McBride he would claim for his wife.

He'd soaked in his evening bath until the chilly

water wrinkled his skin, counting on each hand his cousins' pleasing qualities. Leana had a gentle tongue, a keen mind, the necessary skills to manage a large household, a gracious manner, and a pleasant face.

Pleasant was a generous word. Leana McBride, with her fair hair braided and coiled about her head, was plain. Nigh to invisible, next to her sister. Perhaps alone in a room she would cast a satisfactory glow. Certainly she was old enough to marry and bear him a son. It was unclear what the McDougal fellow's claim on Leana might be. If the man was a serious suitor, Jamie could encounter a problem pursuing the older of his two cousins.

Or he could pursue the younger one instead. *Rose.*

Jamie glanced at her now over his tea saucer. Yestreen he'd thought Rose bonny when she was covered with dirt and tattered clothing. This morning, scrubbed clean, with her hair freshly dressed and her gown neatly pressed, she was a vision. Skin like cream, lips like fresh berries. Jamie smiled in his tea. Never mind marrying the girl; he wanted her for breakfast.

But she was young. *Very young.* Fifteen, she'd told him. A willful child. Unafraid of standing up to her father, she would no doubt give a husband an earful as well. Hadn't he seen the misery his father endured, married to a beautiful, headstrong younger woman? Rose was also clearly enamored of wealth and all it offered. After seeing Maxwell

Park, would Glentrool be enough for Rose McBride? Would he?

Last night he'd fallen into an uneasy sleep, hoping he might awaken and find the decision made for him. Another dream, another heavenly visit, *something.* He had no time to spare; marriage and an heir must follow in quick succession. If his mother were there, she would name his bride without a moment's hesitation. But *whom* would she choose? Leana or Rose? The older or the younger? Pale or dark? Intelligent or charming?

Och! Jamie put down his saucer harder than he meant to, and it clinked on the table, catching Lachlan's sharp gaze.

"Nephew." Lachlan settled back in his chair. "You've yet to tell us why you've come east."

Jamie glanced at his cousins, who were suddenly more attentive, then turned toward his uncle. "Sir, that might be best shared in confidence." When the lasses' countenances fell, Jamie hastened to add, "I promise, you will know the answer soon enough, dear cousins." *But not until I do.*

Lachlan sent the lasses off to their morning chores, brooking no argument despite their long faces. "We'll move to the spence," he said, pointing the way. "The servants will be wanting to clean the table properly after our meal." They were soon settled in the cozy room, a morning dram before each of them. His uncle took a sip, then licked his lips. "Something tells me I'm not going to approve of what you're about to tell me."

Jamie swallowed more whisky than he intended and felt it burning all the way down to his gut. "Possibly not," he admitted when he could breathe enough to speak. "But I'd prefer to be honest from the start rather than fear what you might discover later."

Lachlan raised his eyebrows slightly. "Prudent."

Jamie pushed aside the whisky, prepared for a long and difficult morning. "Are you familiar with the counsel my mother received from a midwife before my brother and I were born?"

Lachlan nodded slowly, his jaw working on some remaining bit of gristle. "Aye, she told me in great detail years ago, during your first visit to Auchengray. 'The older will serve the younger,' or some such blether."

"Not nonsense, sir." Jamie was amazed at his own conviction. "She believed it to be a word from the Almighty. And so do I."

His uncle's jaw stilled. "Go on."

Jamie fashioned his life story like a master weaver, careful to select the right colors to catch Lachlan's eye and divert his attention from less seemly threads. It was the truth, every word of it—*his* truth, the way he saw things. He described the father who chose Evan as his favorite, the mother who chose Jamie. The bowl of barley broth sold for a birthright. Evan, the lone hunter. Jamie, the overseer of lands and flocks.

That last bit of news made his uncle sit up straighter. "You say you're an expert at husbandry, at managing your flocks to best advantage?"

"Aye, both my parents would agree that I am. My father sent me to university to be educated for the kirk." Jamie paused, not certain how his admission might be received. Other than the slight lift of an eyebrow, his uncle showed neither pleasure nor dismay, so Jamie continued, relieved. "Instead, I studied all that I could about agriculture, then came home to learn the practical side of things under our head shepherd's tutelage."

"Henry Stewart?"

"Aye, Stew," Jamie said, not ashamed of the fondness that crept into his voice at the mention of his old friend. "He taught me more about breeding, lambing, and shearing than I could learn from a lifetime of reading. Did Mother mention him in her letters?"

"Aye, she did." Lachlan glanced at the clock on the chimneypiece, clearly growing impatient. "You've told me many a colorful story, young James, but you've yet to explain why you've come to Auchengray."

Jamie steeled himself. "Here's the way of it, Uncle. The last week of September my father announced to Evan that the time had come to bestow the family blessing. You . . . you do understand how the McKies handle such things?"

"Of course," Lachlan murmured, brushing the question away as if it were unworthy of him. "You were saying?"

Jamie spilled out the truth like fennel seed, sensing Lachlan's fertile mind sifting through the details.

"Father called for his favorite meal to be served by his favorite son—"

"Your brother."

"Aye." Jamie swallowed. The truth of his father's preference still stuck in his throat like a fish bone. "Before Evan's venison could hang to a high flavor, my mother prepared two goats, and I served my father first."

"Rowena offered him *goat* meat for venison?" His uncle laughed. "My older sister always was a clever lass. Then what happened?"

Jamie stumbled over his words, trying to soften the sharp edges of his appalling betrayal and failing miserably. "Father . . . thought I was Evan. And so he . . . blessed me."

Lachlan rubbed his hand across his mouth. "Did he honestly mistake you for Evan?"

"So it appears, sir." The unanswered question. He would never truly know.

"I thought your brother was more solid in his build and shorter. Not to mention that bright red hair my sister was always bemoaning. Why couldn't Alec McKie tell the difference between his own two sons?"

"Because my father is nearly blind." Jamie sighed. "Or because he couldn't bear to see the truth."

Lachlan nodded slowly, biting his lip as though contemplating something. "You've still not told me what brings you here, Jamie. After Alec gave you his blessing, why didn't you remain at Glentrool to tally your heirship and make your brother miserable?"

"Evan threatened to kill me."

Lachlan wrinkled his brow. "Is he so much stronger that you would fear him? That you would flee his presence rather than face his wrath?"

Until that moment Jamie hadn't realized how cowardly it sounded. "Aye . . . he is stronger, Uncle. Cruel. Prone to violence."

"I see." Lachlan saw only too well, Jamie realized. "You would rather reason your way through life than wield a pistol. Or clothe your intentions in a borrowed plaid instead of boldly claiming what is rightly yours."

Jamie shifted in his chair, avoiding his uncle's hard stare by gazing at the intricate needlework pattern on the bedcovers. He wondered absently which of his cousins might have stitched it with such care.

"I did as I was told," Jamie finally said, hating the defeat in his voice. "My mother and father deemed it best I leave Glentrool for a season."

Lachlan snorted. "I suppose Alec McKie invoked the name of the Most High and declared it God's sovereign will that you should run for your life, eh?"

"He blessed me, aye. But so did Almighty God." With some reluctance, Jamie described his heavenly vision at the cairn, doing his best not to sound like a madman. He mentioned neither the berries nor the Gypsy, relating only what he saw and heard in the dark of night.

Lachlan's eyes widened. "Am I to understand you stole your brother's heirship and your father's trust, then dreamed that Almighty God blessed you for it?"

"Aye, sir." Jamie hung his head. "Although I've come to believe that God blessed me, not because of what I did, but in spite of it."

Lachlan regarded him at length. "You may be right, lad." He tipped his head back, as though weighing his words. "If all you say is true, God has favored you from before you were born. Such an undeserved blessing is not to be taken lightly." Slowly his uncle's knitted brow grew smooth. His constant frown disappeared, and when he dropped his head once more to look at Jamie, his eyes gleamed like polished chestnuts. "So you have come to Auchengray to bide a wee while your brother licks his wounds. Is that all that brings you here?"

Heat crept into Jamie's cheeks.

"Hoot!" Lachlan pounced like a cat on a mouse's tail. "You have another purpose, and I ken what it might be. You plan to steal one of my daughters."

"Not *steal,* Uncle!" Jamie protested, bolting to his feet. The man was too shrewd to be borne. "Had you received the letter I sent from New Galloway, you would know that I'm here at my parents' bidding. Not to steal or deceive in any manner, but to choose one of your daughters as my bride. With your permission, of course. I have . . . I have much to offer."

"Oh, I ken all about the riches of Glentrool. The five thousand sheep on the hills, a fine stone manor house by Galloway's bonniest loch. 'Tis a goodly inheritance, to be sure." He waved his hand at the chair Jamie had abandoned. "Sit back down, dear nephew. If Alec McKie bids it done, so it will be. I can see that my daughter will be well cared for, though farther from my side than I like." Lachlan sighed expansively. "I'd always hoped both my daughters would marry men from the neighborhood and raise my grandchildren where I might see them, have some influence on them."

Jamie remained standing, preferring the advantage it gave him. "You'd be most welcome at Glentrool anytime."

"I've not visited in all these forty-odd years, Jamie. Not likely I will in the future." Lachlan looked up, a question in his eyes. Jamie guessed what it might be. "Which of my daughters do you favor, or is it too soon to tell?"

Too soon. It was all too soon. Jamie gazed at the clock and felt his life ticking away. Should he waste another week, another month, getting to know his cousins? Or was it best to make a decision quickly, then live with the consequences?

"Come now, Jamie. A bright lad like you should know his own mind." Lachlan's tone, sharp and accusing only minutes before, had turned to butter fresh from the churn. Such a man required careful watching. "Which daughter might it be, Nephew? Do you not have a preference?"

Jamie closed his eyes for a moment, thinking of his lists from yestreen, picturing his cousins at the table this morning, hearing their sweet voices. If he was honest with himself, he did have a preference. He smiled at the thought of her. *Aye, I do.*

"I'll not tell a soul," his uncle prompted him.

"It is not your knowing that concerns me, sir. It is *her* knowing." He would be kind to them both and careful of their feelings. Weren't they both his cousins, however different they might be? "I prefer to woo the lass first and be sure of her heart before I ask for her hand."

Lachlan shrugged. "Heart or hand, they're yours for the taking."

Jamie was relieved it was so easily settled. "But they must not be told, Uncle. Must not know that I've been charged by my parents to marry one of them. A woman likes to think a man pursues her for love, not duty."

"Aren't you the canny lad, to ken the ways of women?" Lachlan's sly grin reminded him of his mother. "Come, if you already favor one of my daughters, speak her name to me. But do whisper, lest the servants catch wind of it. Might it be Leana . . . or Rose?"

Jamie leaned over to tell him, savoring the taste of her name in his mouth.

Lachlan's eyebrows shot up. "You surprise me, lad."

"Aye." Jamie felt his face grow warm as a grin stretched across it. "Sometimes I surprise myself."

Twenty-Five

You ought to make welcome the present guest,
and send forth the one who wishes to go.

HOMER

Best be on your way, Rose, or Susanne will wonder what's become of you." Leana gently pushed her sister over the threshold and into the mild October morning, squeezing her shoulders as she did. "Remember, the sun will be gone by six o'clock. Father won't have to scold you about being late for supper again, will he, Rose?"

Rose shrugged off her hands. "Nae, he will not, *Mother,*" she said in a saucy voice, then hurried off to spend a Saturday with the Elliot household in Newabbey.

Leana smiled, shaking her head. Ever a child, her Rose. She quietly closed the door, offering a prayer for her sister's safety as always, then glanced down at her hands. *Och!* They were badly stained from her early-morning gardening, without a lemon in the kitchen to be spared. She hid her hands among her skirts and bustled through the house, hoping Cousin Jamie was not looking for her yet. She'd promised to make him a new shirt but couldn't bear to think of fitting him while he eyed the faint brown creases along her palms and fingers.

Silly to be so vain. Especially after Jamie had shown a marked interest in her gardens. The two of them had spent Friday morning walking up and down the rows of plants while he hovered over her shoulder, offering his opinion and asking astute questions. In the afternoon he and Rose had walked the pastures together—counting sheep, Rose said—returning for supper wet from the mist and laughing at their sorry appearance. It was thoughtful of Jamie to spend time with both cousins. No word yet why he'd come to Auchengray. Father knew, but the rest of the household, for a change, did not.

She found Neda sorting out her spice chest in the stillroom. The drawers, no bigger than Father's hands, were stacked about the worn kitchen table. "Oh, dear, Neda. Has Annabel put currants in the cinnamon drawer again?"

The housekeeper nodded, pressing a finger to her lips, then pointing toward the adjoining scullery.

The sounds of clanging pans and splashing water meant Annabel was hard at work and well within earshot. The maid had not been taught to read before coming to Auchengray, her first place of service. While storing Neda's precious spices, she often guessed at the labels, confusing clay sugar with sugar candy, isinglass with arrowroot. "Thank goodness the drawers were empty," Neda whispered. "They needed cleaning oot anyway."

How like Neda to find a way to be kind.

"Speaking of cleaning, have you something for these?" Leana held out her hands, frowning at her blunt nails and soiled skin.

Neda frowned as well. "Yer sister took the last lemon from the cellar this mornin' to scrub her own hands. Promised she'd only use a wee slice, though where the lass hid the rest of it, I canna guess. I meant to use it on the flounder for dinner, so we're both missin' that yellow fruit." Neda wiped her hands on her apron, her lips pursed. "Eh . . . see if Mary doesn't keep a bit of lime powder stored in the laundry. Use it with care. Not a *drap* on yer good dress, mind ye."

Leana scrubbed her hands with the harsh white powder, plunging them in a bucket of water as though she were bleaching linen, pleased to see the grass and soil stains disappear. When she finished, her hands were pinker than she liked and smelled frightful, but at least they were clean. She would soak them in fragrant lavender water, seek out her sewing kit, and find her cousin, in that order.

Jamie might not pay attention to her hands after all, but a gentlewoman should look her best, even if no one noticed.

She walked back through the kitchen, greeting Annabel in passing and touching Neda's shoulder to thank her. When Leana entered the hall, the sound of a man's footsteps traveled down the stair. Too lively to be her father, too confident to be Willie, too loud to be Duncan in his worn leather shoes. *Jamie.*

He reached the bottom step as she turned the corner.

Leana quickly stepped back. "Good day to you, Cousin." She tucked her hands behind her and bobbed politely, still uncertain whether a curtsy was called for or if Jamie should be treated like any other member of the household.

"Cousin Leana," he said formally and reached for her hand.

She clasped her fingers tightly behind her, surprised at how cold they suddenly felt. "If you'll kindly wait by the hearth, my sewing kit is in my room." Ducking past him, she managed two steps before he turned and caught her elbow, smiling as he did.

"There's no need for haste. We have all morning." He tugged on her elbow playfully, trying to look behind her. "Are you hiding something?"

"H-hiding?" Leana could no more hide the smell of laundry lime than she could mask the heat blooming in her cheeks. "Nae. Nae." She was a terrible liar. "Let me . . . ah . . ."

"Let me bid you a proper good morning." Despite her protestations, Jamie drew her hand forward and lightly kissed her fingers. "Ah." He sniffed appreciatively. "Cleanliness is next to godliness."

"Aye," she groaned. "John Wesley."

"Nae," he insisted. "Ivy Findlay, our housekeeper at Glentrool." He grinned and released her hand, then glanced toward the front room. "I'll be waiting by the hearth whenever it suits you. You are more than kind to sew me a new shirt, lass. I'll forever be in your debt."

"Have your guineas ready, sir." She curtsied this time, as low as the steps would allow without losing her balance, then turned and fled up the stair. Whatever was she doing? Such flindrikin behavior! Fine for innocent young Rose, but for her, a woman of marriageable age, being coy with her bachelor cousin was not at all seemly.

Leana had composed herself by the time she headed back down the stair, her arms draped with fabric, her thoughts on the business at hand. She'd noticed how poorly her father's shirts fit Jamie—too tight in the neck, too short in the sleeves—so she'd cut the linen to a larger pattern. All that remained was pinning and stitching. And fitting.

Jamie stood by the hearth, waiting for her, his coat already tossed aside onto a chair. He stretched out his arms on each side. "I am yours to command, Leana."

She bit back a smile. It was Jamie who commanded the room with his wide stance and regal stature. His hands, graceful for a man, yet muscular, reached well past the end of his borrowed shirt-sleeves, and his waistcoat fell woefully short of his waist. Though she'd sewn shirts for her father and Duncan, fitting a braw lad like Jamie was a different matter altogether.

Gathering a handful of pins from her sewing kit, she spread them across the top of the hearthside table. If she poked them between her teeth as usual, then she couldn't speak to Jamie as she worked, which would be most rude. "You must stand perfectly still," she cautioned. "I don't want to stab you by accident."

His mouth twitched. "Might you do so on purpose?"

"Certainly not." Smiling, she smoothed the linen over his shoulders and along his arms, skimming her hands along the fabric, barely touching him as she slipped pins in place to mark the seams. Despite her precautions, it was impossible not to feel the warmth of him through his clothing, not to notice the scent of heather clinging to his freshly shaved chin. Seldom had she stood this close to any man, let alone a man of twenty-four. She willed her hands not to shake and her mind not to wander.

Perhaps if she pretended he were Fergus McDougal . . .

Nae. That would be no help at all; she'd run from the room.

The two men could not look more different. Jamie with his smooth brow, and Fergus with his furrowed one; Jamie with his green eyes set well apart to allow for his strong nose, and Fergus with his brown cow eyes and bulbous nose; Jamie with his half smile, as though he knew a secret worth keeping, and Fergus with his vulgar leer.

Naught in common, not one thing.

Jamie chuckled, startling her. "You've done well thus far. I've not been stuck with a pin yet."

"Aye, but it's trying to keep from pinning your *new* shirt to the one you're wearing—that's what's truly difficult." She slid her fingers beneath the fabric where a cuff would soon be attached, then said without thinking, "It would be much easier if you removed your shirt." She froze, mortified. "Not that I would ever suggest such a thing."

Jamie started to speak, then pressed his lips together. A gentleman, through and through.

Leana could barely say the words. "I . . . beg your pardon."

"An innocent remark, Leana." His tone was kindness itself. "Think nothing of it."

Leana forced herself to continue, silently berating herself for being so careless. Whatever must her cousin think of her now? Swallowing her shame, she started on the side seams, which ran nearly to his knees, and pretended not to notice the doeskin breeches beneath her fingers. She worked her way along one shirt seam, pinning as she went, then bent down to add a final pin at the hem. Without looking up, she held out the fabric to show him how much remained. "Do you prefer a generous hem, Cousin, or a longer shirt?"

"Whatever pleases you."

You please me, Cousin. There, the truth of it.

She rose, keeping her gaze to the floor. Jamie *was* pleasing—to look at, to talk to, to spend time with. But he was not courting her; Fergus McDougal was. "Perhaps a longer hem is best," she murmured, moving behind him where she would be less distracted. Her hands flew along the second seam until she finished, then she stepped back to judge the fit.

"Will I do, Cousin?" Jamie slowly turned around, still holding his arms away from his sides. "As a shirt model?"

She nodded, not trusting herself to say more, and gathered up the rest of the pins. "You'll be relieved to know I won't ever put you through such misery again. I can simply pattern any new shirts after this one."

"What a clever woman you are."

Leana ventured the smallest of smiles. "Now it's your turn to be clever and lift that new shirt over your head without sticking yourself." He did so with remarkable ease, handing it over with a gallant sweep. "Well done." She nodded at his discarded coat. "Do dress yourself, Cousin, for I have reason to expect visitors shortly."

"Someone to see you?" He slipped on the coat, which was also too small. If Jamie was planning to stay at Auchengray for very long, something would need to be done about his wardrobe.

"Indeed not. To see *you*." She watched him button his blue coat. 'Twas a fine color with his brown hair. "Duncan crossed paths with one of the shepherds from Troston Hill yestreen and shared the news of Auchengray's visitor. Your arrival will soon be the favorite topic of conversation in the parish."

"I see." His gaze narrowed. "Will they want to know why I've come?"

She chose her words carefully. "Is it so odd a question?"

"Nae. 'Tis the most natural question in the world. I'll tell anyone who asks that I've come to meet my Newabbey cousins before they marry and *flit.*" He inclined his head. "Is either of you in danger of doing so . . . anytime soon?"

"I'm afraid—*ouch!*" Surprised by a sharp knock at the door, Leana instinctively pulled the unfinished shirt tight against her and stuck herself in several places. She ran her hands over her skin, feeling foolish. "Do forgive me."

Jamie looked genuinely distressed. "Cousin, there is nothing to apologize for." He gently touched her neck, then showed her the spot of scarlet on his fingertip.

"Och!" She held out the shirt, horrified. "Bloodstains are the very worst to get out."

Another sharp knock sounded at the door, which Jamie ignored. "Never mind the shirt, lass. Are you in pain?"

Neda hurried by, eying Leana as she passed.

"Truly, I'll be fine, Jamie." She patted her neck, checking for other wounds. "If you might have a handkerchief . . ."

He produced a worn square of cotton and pressed it against her neck. "I'm sorry, Leana."

A woman's merry laugh floated across the room.

"I'm not sorry in the least, for I would not have missed seeing this for all the world."

Jamie abruptly stepped back, and Leana turned toward the door, relieved to see her dearest friend. "What is it you think you've seen, Jessie Newall?"

The red-haired young woman strolled into the room, a round-cheeked babe on her hip, a toothy smile on her face. "I've seen a bonny sight: Leana McBride talking to a man her own age."

"Ah." Leana smiled. "That." She nodded at her cousin, who bowed from his waist as she introduced her neighbors. "Mistress Jessie Newall of Troston Hill and Miss Annie, kindly meet my cousin, James McKie of Glentrool." Pleasantries were exchanged, though Jamie did not kiss Jessie's hand in greeting, Leana noted with the tiniest bit of satisfaction. "Jessie and her husband, Alan, have the farm on top of Troston Hill."

"Herds or crops?" Jamie asked politely, at which both women laughed and the baby squealed.

"Och, Mr. McKie, if you could see the property!" Jessie shook her head. "Naught but rocks and gorse and the roughest farmland in Galloway. We've a good pasture for blackface sheep, and I've a garden or two, but you'll not find us pushing a plow at harvest time."

Leana remembered her manners. "Cousin Jamie, might you kindly ask Neda to bring us some tea?" He nodded and was gone, looking a bit relieved, she thought. Perhaps he did not care for children.

"Tea would be lovely." Jessie sighed and put her

babe down on the slate floor with care. "Annie gets heavier by the day but refuses to start walking."

Leana dropped to her knees in front of the child, smoothing a hand over Annie's curly head of hair, as red as her mother's. "When Annie is ready, nothing will stop her. Isn't that so, dearie?" Annie waved her arms and blurted out a long, nonsensical sentence, which Leana understood perfectly. "And I'm happy to see you again as well, wee girl. May I hold you for a bittie?"

Jessie shook her head. "You'll be sorry, for she'll ne'er let go. Be calling you Mither before you know it."

Leana scooped up the child and held her close, cooing in her ear and nuzzling her soft head. Her throat tightened. "I can think of nothing finer than having a child call me *Mother.*" She closed her eyes to stem her tears and drank in Annie's sweet baby scent. Soap behind the ears. Milk in the folds of her tiny neck. "Dear Annie," she whispered, cradling the child against her, humming a lullaby. "Baloo, baloo, my wee, wee thing." The two of them stayed that way for some time until Annie stirred and Leana slowly opened her eyes.

Her cousin stood motionless in the doorway, his solemn gaze riveted to her and the babe in her arms.

Jamie.

In the hearth a corner of the peat broke free and tumbled down into the grate. "Look at that, will you!" Jessie crowed. "You ken what the old gossips say,

Leana. 'Fire bodes a marriage.' There'll be a wedding in this house before the year is out." Jessie turned toward the gentleman she'd just met and dipped a curtsy in his direction. "Begging your pardon, Mr. McKie. Have you given any thought to taking a wife?"

Twenty-Six

Love gilds the scene, and women guide the plot.
RICHARD BRINSLEY SHERIDAN

So *that* was why Jamie had come to Auchengray!

Rose pressed the letter to her fast-beating heart, but only for a moment. No point being dramatic when there was nary a soul to appreciate her performance. She needed to get home; she had to tell Leana. *Och!* The mere thought of it quickened her steps along the country lane, her skirts sweeping aside the brightly colored leaves in her path. In less than an hour she would be whispering in Leana's ear, telling her sister a secret too good to keep to herself.

What a grand ending to an ordinary day. She'd

spent several hours with dear Susanne, helping in her father's grocery, taking Susanne's youngest brother for a walk along the Newabbey Pow. *Elliot,* they'd named the boy—*Elliot Elliot!* Rose laughed every time she said it. Whatever were they thinking, giving their poor child a double name? Pray God, the lad would not grow up to resent it.

Later that afternoon the busy grocer had remembered a letter for her father, left in his care by the postboy from Dumfries. "But, Mr. Elliot, I have no coins to pay for it," Rose had fretted, stealing a quick glance at the letter with the boldly scrawled address:

Lachlan McBride, Esquire
    Auchengray
    Newabbey

"Fair maidens wear nae purses," Mr. Elliot had said, pressing the letter into her hands. His head was as round as the cabbages he sold, his body stouter than the ox that pulled his cart to Dumfries on market days, yet Newabbey thought him a most amiable grocer. "You've been a good help today, Rose. Suppose we let your labors pay for your father's post. Now run along."

Run she had, like the wind, all down the winding street full of gossiping villagers. It wasn't until she reached the bridge leading home that she'd stopped to examine the letter more closely. The paper was not of good quality, nor was the waxy thumbprint that sealed it. But above the seal, in the same bold hand, was the name of the one who had sent it: *James McKie of Glentrool.*

Jamie's letter had arrived after all. Too late to matter to her father, too late to be of use to her cousin. Dare she break the seal and read it while she walked? Her mind was adamant: She would *not* open a letter addressed to her father. Very risky. But her heart was lenient: Her father would never know. What harm could it do? With Jamie already at Auchengray, Lachlan would no doubt toss the letter out unread. A pity to waste the cost of a post, even if it was earned by her own labors.

Rose had fingered the coarse paper as she walked, the fading sunlight casting long, slanted shadows across the dirt road. After many minutes of deliberation she'd opened the letter, sliding her thumbnail under the wax to keep it intact, taking great pains not to tear the paper. One never knew when a letter might need to be sealed shut again. She'd read the contents and reveled in her sister's good fortune.

Now, half an hour later, Rose couldn't bear it. She had to read the letter again, though she'd already committed the best parts to memory. Holding the letter before her, she smoothed out the creases and read the words once more.

I am to inherit Glentrool at my father's death . . .

Jamie, the second son, awarded his father's heirship! Curious that he'd never mentioned it.

>   ... and am
seeking to marry a woman of proper upbringing.

With such a vast property to his name, no wonder he intended to marry well. "Aye, but not just any
woman, Jamie." Rose smiled at the paper as
though it might smile back at her. The next line was
her favorite.

>   It was my parents'
stated desire that I choose one of your two fine
daughters.

Well said, for Leana McBride was very fine
indeed. Although Jamie's letter stated that *he* would
choose, Rose knew better. Only one daughter had
marriage in mind, and it was decidedly *not* the
younger one.

> I would request the pleasure of your generous
hospitality for a few weeks at most, until all
necessary arrangements can be made.

"Necessary arrangements," indeed. Rose had
hoped to have a full month to convince Leana and
Jamie of their mutual affection and chase old Fergus away. It seemed she might have that much time
and more.

She grinned as she carefully refolded the letter.
Except for the loosened wax, the post appeared
unopened. Leana, fearing discovery, would no

doubt want it tossed in the fire and the ashes strewn about her garden. Rose had no intention of letting so vital a paper be destroyed. She would hide it safely in their room for a day, many years hence, when Leana would delight at seeing the letter that had changed her too-quiet life.

Rose hastened up and down the gentle hills as the sun sank lower in the sky, staining the horizon crimson. Cultivated fields gave way to more rugged land, with gnarled old trees and outcroppings of rocks the size of cows. Past the dark fell that rose to her left, the road straightened for the last mile home, much of it uphill. The orchards of Auchengray came into view first, then the whitewashed stone house, built some distance from the road. As a child, Rose had feared the many-paned windows across the front because they reminded her of eyes, unblinking and unkind. Leana had cured her of that notion soon enough, telling her to think of them as a row of teeth and the chimneys at each end of the house as the corners of a smile.

"Then what is that frichtsome gray slate roof?" Rose recalled demanding.

"A jolly man's mustache," was her sister's wise answer.

The only jolly man who lived at Auchengray was Duncan and only when a term day didn't loom over him, demanding that his ledgers be in order and his workers satisfied enough to stay with the farm another term. In a month, come Martinmas, Duncan Hastings would not be jolly at all.

Aye, but Leana might be!

Rose knew her broad smile would give her away. How could she possibly contain her excitement with such a letter tucked in the hanging pocket beneath her dress? She flew up the drive to the front door, bursting across the threshold like water over a linn.

"Leana!"

Her sister called to her from the hearth, "In here, dearie."

Rose found her sister sitting close to the fire, two candles on a nearby table barely providing enough light for sewing. Even wearing her spectacles, Leana had to hold the fabric close to her eyes, squinting at her tiny needle weaving in and out of the seam, her mouth firmly pinched into a frown.

Rose was aghast at the wretched scene. In the darkened room, with her face and hair colorless in the firelight, Leana looked like an old woman. Older than Fergus McDougal. Much too old for their braw cousin. Had Jamie seen her like this? He would not soon forget it if he had. Something must be done and quickly.

"Enough sewing for tonight," Rose announced, gently pulling the linen from her sister's hands. "It's too dark, Leana. You'll go blind trying to stitch like that."

"Too late." Leana gave a weary sigh and put aside the shirt. "You are right. I mustn't strain my eyes more than necessary." She slipped off her small spectacles and rubbed the bridge of her nose. "Jamie's shirt can wait until Monday, I suppose."

"Did he . . . see you?" Rose dreaded the answer. "Working on his shirt, I mean?"

"Of course." Leana flexed her slender fingers, no doubt cramped from a long afternoon with her needle. "In fact, he was sitting with me here by the fire until a few minutes ago when he asked to meet with Father before supper." She gestured toward the closed spence door. "Perhaps we'll finally learn why Jamie is here."

Rose closed her eyes, seeing her hopes for her sister dashed against the cliffs like the Solway at high tide. At that very moment, Jamie was probably telling their father that he could not marry weak-eyed Leana, with her plain face and dull ways. That, although he must marry a McBride lass, it would not be the older daughter he would claim for his wife.

It would be the younger one.

Nae! Rose felt her limbs trembling. She was not ready. Not ready to leave Newabbey, not ready to settle down in a lonely glen far from her friends, not ready to marry a man she did not know, not ready to manage his household, not ready to bear his sons, not ready to have children crawling about her skirts. *Nae!* She fell into a chair like a sack of coal landing on a doorstep. "I know why Jamie is here."

Leana stared at her. "How could you know when you've been gone all day?"

Her sister sounded wary. *Nae, hurt.* Rose would show her the letter. Leana would see the sad news for herself. Jamie would make his choice, just as

Fergus had made his. None of their lives would ever be the same. Rose reached in her hanging pocket and pulled out the letter, her fingers suddenly as stiff as elm twigs.

"Who is that letter addressed to?" Leana sounded suspicious.

Rose handed her the post, unwilling to read it again, ashamed to confess her sin.

"Rose!" Leana's hoarse whisper did not hide the fear in her voice. "This was meant for Father." Leana turned her back toward the spence door, then held a candle close to the paper, peering at the words, her mouth slowly opening to an astonished *O*. "Rose . . . what does this mean?"

"You know what it means, Leana." She snatched the letter from her sister's hand and thrust it into the flickering candle. The edge of the paper ignited at once, burning black across the page, eating Jamie's words whole. Rose held it as long as she could, then tossed the letter into the peat fire, afraid it might singe her fingers. "We did not read this," she said grimly. "We do not know why Jamie is here."

Leana reached for her hand. "But, Rose—"

The door to the spence flew open, and Jamie walked into the room as though he'd just signed the deed to Auchengray. "Rose!" A warm smile bloomed on his face. "Welcome home."

Both sisters stood as one, deftly closing the gap between them to block Jamie's view of the hearth. Behind them, the remains of the letter lay in the grate, smoldering. He seemed not to notice.

"Cousin Jamie," Rose said, forcing a smile to her face. "I trust you've spent an agreeable day?"

"Very agreeable." He nodded at Leana. "Your sister is sewing me a new shirt, and Neda is making cock-a-leekie soup for supper."

Rose lifted her brows. "Chicken and leeks. This makes you happy?"

"Aye, lass, it does. My uncle is pleased as well." He stepped closer, and they moved toward him, like a country dance without a fiddler.

"Careful, Cousin," Rose warned. "You'll find your soup brimming with prunes. Father's favorite." Rose longed to glance over her shoulder and see if the letter had turned to soot. But she could not. She could only pray and stand guard, knowing they looked as guilty as they were.

Jamie slowly shifted his gaze from one sister to the other. She felt inspected, like oysters at the market, and knew Leana must as well. "I will see you both at seven," he finally said, striding from the room without looking back. Without seeing the last of his letter succumb to the fire.

The sisters sank into their chairs and sighed in tandem.

Rose spoke first. "Mr. Elliot gave me the letter for Father."

"And you read it."

"Aye." Rose glanced over and watched a dozen emotions move across her sister's features. "For good or for ill, now we know why Jamie is here."

"Who will do the choosing? Father or Jamie?"

"Jamie, of course."

Leana's cheeks lost what natural color they possessed. "Then it will be an easy decision, won't it?"

Rose swallowed. "It will?"

"Aye. No choice at all really." Leana turned toward her, sorrow moving across her features like a cloud blocking the sun. "I'm to marry Mr. McDougal, remember? It's already been arranged. Which means you shall marry Cousin Jamie."

"At fifteen? I couldn't possibly!" By law, she could. By preference, she could also wait a very long time. "Besides, nothing has been decided. Jamie has a choice, Leana, and he might choose you."

Must choose you.

"Might he?" Hope filled Leana's face, and Rose realized her sister's feelings already ran deeper than she had suspected.

Perhaps it was not too late then. She would help Leana win Jamie. She *would.* What had she told her sister on Wednesday last? "All is not lost . . . not until you say, 'I do.'" Those words had yet to be spoken to Mr. McDougal. It was not too late.

She clasped Leana's cool hands. "It would please you, wouldn't it, to make a life at Glentrool with our cousin and his family?" Rose warmed her words with a hint of persuasion. "You two would make a handsome pair."

"Wheesht! You mustn't say such things."

"Why, Leana, you're the color of a Provence rose!" She giggled, her old self again. "I'll say anything I like and whisper whatever words need whispering." Rose pulled her closer and lowered her voice further still. "Promise me you want this match, or I'll not proceed."

Leana nodded, slowly at first, then with more certainty. "I do want it, very much. Jamie is . . . well, everything Fergus McDougal is not." She pinched her trembling lips together and clasped her hands in a tight knot. "Forgive me if that sounds heartless, Rose."

"Not heartless. Honest."

"Jamie is intelligent, educated, and knows something of the world. Mr. McDougal is—"

"A dolt."

Even Leana laughed a little. "As you say, Rose. Jamie is also polite, thoughtful, and a fine gentleman in every sense of the word. And Fergus . . . I mean, Mr. McDougal is . . ."

"None of those things," Rose finished for her. "Any woman would choose Jamie over such an ugsome man."

"Aye. But I have no idea if Jamie would choose . . . that is, if he would find me . . ." Leana pressed her forehead against Rose's shoulder, clearly struggling for every word. "Oh, Rose. All is lost if Father won't change his mind. Yet, if he *would* allow Jamie to court me instead of insisting I marry Mr. McDougal—"

"Say no more. We will pray for that very thing."

"I must confess, I've already done so." Leana gently pulled back from her embrace, eyes glistening with unshed tears. "Rose, the night before Jamie arrived I prayed that God might provide a husband for me. A braw man of twenty-odd years with kind eyes and a ready smile whose head rose well above mine and whose smooth brow concealed a fine mind."

Rose gasped. "Our own Jamie!"

"Aye, Jamie." Leana bit her lip, then whispered, "I believe God has chosen him for my husband."

Rose nodded, a burst of energy rushing through her. All was *not* lost. No, indeed. "You will sit by Jamie at kirk in the morn's morn, and I will make certain the other lasses do not set their caps for him."

Leana pressed a damp cheek against hers. "You are generous to help me, Rose. But you've not shared your own heart. Is Jamie the husband you've always longed for? Has he hinted of his interest in any way?"

"Don't be *sully!* I'm too young to think of marriage. And when I do, I want a whole roomful of choices."

Leana's gaze searched hers. "You're certain?"

"Very much so." Rose nodded as emphatically as she could.

"Aye, then." Leana smoothed her hands across her skirt, her gaze fixed on the door to the spence. "There's only one *tickler* we haven't considered: What if Jamie falls in love with *you?*"

Twenty-Seven

Alas! to seize the moment
When heart inclines to heart,
And press a suit with passion,
Is not a woman's part.
WILLIAM CULLEN BRYANT

Jamie, the choice is yours."

He shrugged. "One is as good as another, Uncle."

"Here then." Lachlan handed him a badly frayed coat. "The one you're wearing will do for the Sabbath, and let the other suffice for the rest of the week."

Jamie thanked him and folded the unfashionable coat over his arm, a grim reminder of his empty pockets. "Uncle Lachlan, it distresses me to have arrived at your doorstep without gold or silver to my name."

"You've silver to your name, lad," Lachlan corrected him. His smile was brief and a bit forced. "It's simply not in your hand."

Jamie was all too aware of that. It was an awkward way to commence with his future father-in-law, borrowing the man's wardrobe and drinking his claret without offering anything more substantial than a promise to marry one of his daughters. "Shall I write to my father, ask him to send a promissory note?"

"You could." His uncle paused, one hand on the oak clothes press, the other stroking his closely shaved chin. "I know you're fash, and rightly so, to be robbed twice and left for dead. 'Tis a hard thing for a McKie to admit he's been routed."

Jamie bristled. "Hard for any man."

"Aye, you may be right." Lachlan's gaze wandered to the side, as though he were weighing the merit of some unspoken plan. The ticking of the clock on the chimneypiece filled the weighty silence until he said, "We'll speak of this again after services. See to my manservant's brush and comb, lad. The chaise is waiting."

Jamie returned to his lodgings on the second floor and finished his morning ablutions in Rose's bedroom. Though she'd been moved next door to share her older sister's box bed, her scent remained, like ling heather fresh from the moors. He took a deep breath, filling his head with her fragrance, his thoughts with her loosome form and face. He'd tried, truly he had, to give both sisters equal consideration. Leana was generous and good but stirred nothing in him. Rose was goodness defined and beauty captured. She stirred everything inside him until his mind spun at the sight of her.

His head was whirring with dreams for Auchengray as well. Duncan and Lachlan had tramped the marches with him, inspecting the fields and flocks, discussing plans for growth and improvement. His clever uncle asked more questions than he answered, yet Jamie couldn't help but share his enthusiasm. The nearby shores of the Solway beckoned any man with a bent to trade fine Scottish wool abroad. Though the house itself was plain and the grounds around it cluttered with too many garden plots, Auchengray was well positioned for expansion, benefiting future generations.

Lachlan had no son, no male heir. McBride's first grandson would inherit everything. *My son.* Yestreen, seeing Leana holding the neighbor's wee babe, he'd realized his heir would be laird of *two* fine Galloway estates someday. Naturally, the child would need to be born first and his parents married before that. Aye, he had much to accomplish. The sooner to kirk today, the sooner to courting tomorrow.

His face scrubbed and neatly shaven, his hair and attire as tidy as the manservant could make them, Jamie thundered down the stair in borrowed boots and joined his uncle aboard the jostling chaise with its ancient springs. What he wouldn't give for Walloch's steady gait this gray morning. A cool stillness in the air whispered of rain. Against the dull sky, the treetops blazed red and gold, leaves poised for the next stiff breeze to send them spiraling to the ground. Newabbey was a tamer landscape than his home parish of Monnigaff, with its wild mountains and moors, but it was pleasant to the eye and soothing to the soul. Or—he smiled at the realization—perhaps he was thinking of Rose.

His uncle broke into his thoughts as though he'd read them. "Have you advised my daughter of your interest?"

"I have not." Jamie settled his gaze on the bend in the road, leaning into the turn as they veered sharply to the right. *Not in words.* If his intentions were not clear to Rose, it was only because she refused to notice them.

Every moment they spent together confirmed his first opinion of her, though such occasions had been too few to please him. She'd barely met his gaze across their porridge bowls that morning, but he could read her maidenly blush: It seemed she found him appealing and would not reject his proposal when the time came.

Lachlan tapped Jamie's knee with the butt of his whip. "You'd be wise to proceed slowly with my daughter. She is young and impetuous, yet innocent in the ways of men. I would have her remain so until her wedding day." His uncle's gaze narrowed. "Do we have an understanding?"

"We do, sir."

They rode in silence, passing a cluster of Auchengray servants on foot, then overtaking Rose and Leana at the village bridge, not far from the kirk. Jamie brightened when he saw their heads— one light, one dark beneath their hat brims—bent in tandem over the stream, deep in conversation. Lachlan brought the chaise to a stop. "Why don't you accompany the lasses to the kirk, lad? I'm sure they'd welcome your company."

Both sisters turned and blushed prettily as Jamie climbed down and brushed the dust from his breeches and boots. "I'd be honored, Uncle." He extended both elbows, and each sister slipped a hand through—Rose on his right, Leana on his left. "Lead the way, fair cousins." The threesome got off to a clumsy start when Jamie tripped on Leana's skirt, then accidentally jabbed Rose in the ribs when he tried to right himself. "I'm making a mess of things, I'm afraid."

"Easily solved," Rose said, untangling herself. "You two walk on together while I run ahead and find Susanne Elliot." Rose took off before either of them could protest, her black braid bouncing merrily behind her.

"Well." Jamie stood, watching her disappear around a curve in the village street. "I'm afraid you're saddled with me, Miss McBride."

"And you with me, Cousin Jamie."

The plaintive note in her voice touched him. Had his disappointment been so obvious? To make up for it, Jamie gave her his full attention, and she responded, tipping her face up, displaying a tentative smile. Her wide eyes, the color of a midwinter sky, revealed her feelings, perhaps more than she knew. *Poor Leana.* A good woman, but not the one he would choose.

He gestured toward the road leading to the parish kirk. "Walk with me, Cousin." The kirk bell rang the hour as they took off, more smoothly this time, with only two strides to match. "I'm eager to see if Newabbey observes the Sabbath in the same manner as we do in Monnigaff."

"The next bell announces the start of the first service," she explained. "Then after dinner, there is an afternoon service as well." Her skirts swayed gracefully next to his battered but well-polished boots. Too narrow for his feet, they pinched his heels as he walked. He would ride in the chaise rather than walk home to Auchengray, for certain.

When Leana didn't speak again, he hurried to fill the uneasy silence. "Tell me, what do you think of your minister? Reverend Gordon, isn't it?"

"John Gordon, aye." Leana shrugged, her smile fading. "Father considers him the finest preacher in all the ten parishes."

"And you find him . . ."

"Dour and dull, serious to a fault. He's a great slave to the paper, reading his sermon as though the ink were still fresh." She dropped her voice, eying the villagers who were assembling in the street and moving toward the kirkyard. "Don't tell Father I said so."

"Fear not." He lightly touched her arm. "Your saicret is safe with me."

Her pointed gaze met his, a light piercing his darkness. "I'd like to think I can trust you completely, Jamie." Her cheeks colored as she said the words, as though they held some deeper meaning he should have grasped but didn't.

"I hope you do. Trust me, I mean." Jamie bit his lip, trying to sort it out. Had she heard about his deception in Glentrool? Or was this something else entirely?

He only knew his cousin Leana was a puzzle—friendly one moment, shy the next, ever blushing, stealing glances at him when she thought he might not notice her. To hear the servants tell it, the woman was practically betrothed to that ill-fashioned farmer he'd met briefly on Wednesday last. 'Twas unkind of Lachlan to approve such a poor match.

"Will your bonnet laird be sitting with us?" he asked, then wished he hadn't.

"He is not from our parish." The corners of her mouth turned downward. "And he is not 'my' laird."

"Oh. I thought you—"

"Not yet," she stammered. Under her breath she added, "Not ever, I hope."

Another puzzle begging to be solved, though he hadn't the patience for it. He could do naught but apologize. "Leana, I fear I've offended you."

"You could never offend me." She stopped and turned toward him, her misery all too apparent. "Please understand, I do not care for Mr. McDougal. But my father doesn't trouble himself with such *fouterie* matters." He watched her swallow, the lump in her slender throat moving up and down. "What say you, Jamie? Is a woman's heart so trivial a thing as to be sold to the highest bidder?"

"Leana, I . . . don't know what to say." Which was the truth. Growing up without sisters and with a mother who was spirited and forthright—quite the opposite of Leana McBride—he had no idea how to answer her. "Forgive me if I seem uncaring." He briefly looked down at her, staring at the faint cleft in her chin rather than at her transparent eyes. "Your father must have his reasons for wanting you to marry Mr. McDougal."

"Reasons? Aye, he has those." Leana slowly turned and resumed walking, her arm loosely linked with his.

Pressing his lips together in a firm line of defense, Jamie had no choice but to follow. He would not be dragged into family squabbles. Let Uncle Lachlan do as he pleased with his older daughter, cruel as that decision might be. It was the younger one whose future concerned him.

As they approached the kirk door, Jamie leaned back to take in the red sandstone remains of an ancient abbey. No roof remained, only tall, sweeping arches that looked down on the kirk like a mother eying her child. What had the weaver called the abbey? "Sweetheart," he murmured.

Leana spun her head in his direction, a hopeful look on her face.

"Sweetheart?" he said again, pointing to the ruined nave.

Her arched brows fell back into place. "Aye,

Sweetheart Abbey the monks called it. Quite a story, that. Lady Devorgilla, the widow of John Balliol, built the abbey to honor her husband. She carried his embalmed heart in a wee casket made of ivory and silver."

Jamie grimaced. "Whatever made her do that?"

"Love." Leana dropped her hand. The crook of his elbow grew cool at once. "She's buried in the choir of the abbey, along with her husband's heart." They'd reached the kirk door and were about to step inside the dim interior when a familiar voice called their names.

"Jamie! Leana!" Rose came bounding up like a collie grateful to see its master. "Susanne will join us shortly. As usual, my friend is fairly brimming with news."

"News?" Leana gently shook her head. "Tittle-tattle, you mean."

"Aye, but gossip you'll be interested to hear, my sister." Rose winked at Jamie, then poked her chin beneath Leana's hat, speaking loudly enough for him to hear as well. "Nicholas Copland has quit the parish, bound for university."

"Edinburgh?"

"Nae, farther still. Aberdeen."

"Is that so?" Leana's tone of voice gave no hint of how she felt about the lad's sudden departure.

"A friend of the family?" Jamie inquired, eager to engage Rose in conversation.

"A friend of Leana's in particular." Rose straightened. An enigmatic smile graced her features. "Had our father permitted it, young Mr. Copland might have become my sister's next suitor." She sighed dramatically. "Alas, it is not to be. Perhaps another suitor will take his place."

"Perhaps," Jamie echoed, wanting to sound agreeable.

The sisters exchanged a glance he couldn't hope to decipher, then Rose turned and motioned to a ruddy-faced lass. "Susanne! Come and meet my cousin from Glentrool."

The girl scurried over, frank curiosity in her small features. With her dark, round eyes, pointy nose, and auburn hair severely knotted at the nape of her neck, she so nearly resembled a red squirrel that Jamie bit his lip to keep from laughing.

Rose made the proper introductions while Jamie bowed and Susanne dipped a shy curtsy. "Sus . . . ah, Miss Elliot is one of my dearest friends," Rose explained, squeezing the girl's elbow. "Her father is Mr. Colin Elliot, the grocer. He goes to market in Dumfries every Friday to buy provisions for his store here in the village. Mr. Elliot carts home the very freshest meats—"

"And the juiciest gossip!" Susanne interjected, blushing and giggling like a silly country maid. Jamie watched her bring both gloved hands to her mouth as if to hide her crooked teeth. Had she held an acorn in her grasp, the picture would have been complete. "Most times Father takes me with him," Miss Elliot confided. "I know all the streets by name."

Jamie, suddenly ashamed of his cruel assessment of the girl, pretended to be impressed. "Quite an accomplishment, that." From the corner of his eye he noted two more young women drawing near, ears cocked like sheep alert to a stranger's voice in the pasture.

"It seems more of your neighbors wish to speak to you, Rose."

"You know better than that, Jamie lad. They want to meet *you.* And so they shall." Rose motioned the girls closer. One was as tall as a Maypole, with a figure to match; the other was a bonny, black-haired girl even younger than Rose. Introductions were made amid much giggling on Rose's part. A charming quality, though he hoped she might temper it a bit in the days ahead. A young bride was one thing; a child bride made him uncomfortable.

When the bell tolled the half-hour, their girlish laughter ceased as quickly as a candle being snuffed out. Rose held up a cautionary finger. "You've looked your fill, ladies. Our cousin has *not* come to Newabbey parish seeking a bride. Have you, Jamie?"

He stared at her. What did she mean, baiting him like that? Her dimpled smile told him nothing. Leana was smiling as well. For that matter, they were *all* smiling. He had no choice but to smile back broadly, as though he understood some secret jest and could barely contain his laughter. "As you say, Rose."

Leana came to his rescue, guiding him through the narrow doorway of the kirk, her hand barely touching his arm, her voice low. "This way, Cousin. Our family pew awaits."

Twenty-Eight

He who lives on hope has a slender diet.
SCOTTISH PROVERB

Leana stared at her bowl of breakfast porridge, wondering where she might find the appetite to eat a single spoonful.

Yestreen at kirk had been utterly embarrassing from the moment they filed into the family pew. Father had been waiting for them and entered first, followed by Rose. When Leana prepared to take her usual place next to her sister, Jamie had stepped around her, making a frightful commotion and disrupting the precentor's gathering psalm. *Och!* The raised eyebrows, the furtive whispers. The congregation had barely composed themselves enough to rise for prayer before Reverend Gordon climbed into the pulpit and bowed to the Stewarts seated in the north loft.

Leana had not known how or what to pray, so torn were her emotions. All through the service Jamie stood, then sat, then stood again, too close for comfort, his arm brushing against her shoulder. The warmth of him was like the foot stove in Auchengray's spence, heating everything around it, especially her. She dared not catch his eye, knowing she'd made a fool of herself that morning. Her improper comments about a woman's heart, about being sold at auction—what must her cousin think of her, blethering on as she did? It seemed he did not think of her at all, so little did he notice her throughout the long service.

She, on the other hand, could not help but see what close attention Jamie gave the reading of the Scriptures. He'd blanched when Reverend Gordon read from Proverbs, "Deceive not with thy lips." Oddly, during the next verse, her father leaned forward and stared at Jamie with a look of sudden inspiration as the minister read, "I will render to the man according to his work." Both men seemed most engaged by Reverend Gordon's morning sermon, dry as it was.

After the first service, they'd had their dinner in the pew. Neda had packed cold chicken and hard cheese, most of which Jamie ate before he realized how many mouths were meant to be fed from one small basket. Two of the Elliot boys recited Scripture verses and answered questions from the

Shorter Catechism. Then came the afternoon service, which began at two and ended at four and included another sternly worded sermon. After so much sitting, Leana and her sister were grateful for a leisurely walk home while Jamie and their father rode ahead in the chaise.

Had they chatted about Jamie's future? Had her name even been mentioned?

"Leana, your brow is tied in such a knot it will take a *gavelock* to pry it open."

"Sorry, Father." She lifted her gaze from the porridge bowl and touched her forehead as though to smooth it by hand. "I was thinking of the Sabbath sermon." *There.* That should appease him.

Her father, seated at the head of the table, nodded his approval. "And what was it that you learned, lass?"

"I learned . . ." Her gaze shifted from Jamie to Rose to Lachlan, each of whom waited with porridge spoon put aside and hands folded. "I learned that any man who will not work . . ."

"Neither should he eat." Her father's smile was broad as an axe and twice as lethal. "An excellent message and timely, don't you think?"

Jamie abruptly returned to his porridge, cold and tasteless as it was. She and Rose followed suit, eating with some haste, while Lachlan took his time buttering his floury bap, making a show of it with his knife in one hand, the yeast roll in the other, covering it with butter as if the entire churn belonged to him. Which, Leana reminded herself, it did.

Jamie cleared his throat. "Uncle, I have made a decision."

Both sisters nearly dropped their spoons. They glanced furtively at each other, then at Jamie, whose face was a mottled shade of red.

"Ah." Lachlan held up his buttered bap, as though proposing a toast. "Go on."

"With your permission I would like to spend a month at Auchengray . . . working." Jamie exhaled, obviously relieved. *Work* was a word not usually spoken by a gentleman. "With the tups in hand, Duncan will be needing help with the ewes."

"A special talent of yours, I understand."

"Aye. Stew taught me well."

"Then your knowledge and experience will be most welcome." Lachlan sank his teeth into the roll, smearing butter on his nose as he did.

Leana quickly looked down, lest she laugh at her father and ruin everything. Jamie staying a month! Long enough for her to win his affections. Surely if Jamie asked for her hand, Father would put aside Fergus McDougal's offer. Jamie was wealthier by far, young enough to produce many grandsons, and, above all, he was Lachlan's nephew. Jamie was also braw and a pleasure to look upon, though that counted only in the smallest degree.

Jamie's jaw was firm with resolution. "Until Martinmas then?"

Lachlan merely nodded, his mouth too busy chewing.

November the eleventh. The date was already

written on her heart. While the two men discussed husbandry matters in tiresome detail, Leana and Rose finished their meal, sharing sidelong glances as they did. Jamie under their roof for an entire month? Who could have imagined so swift an answer to prayer? Since Rose had made it clear she had no interest in marriage, Leana had no fear of hurting her sister. But she had other matters of great concern, Wednesday's dinner with Fergus McDougal among them.

Breakfast concluded and the servants rung for, Jamie excused himself to meet with Duncan. "Ladies," he said, bowing to them both. "Uncle, I shall see you at dinner, unless you have need of me sooner." He disappeared into the hall, though Leana could still hear his warm baritone greeting the servants by name. She smiled at the sound of it. A wise fellow, to have made himself at home so quickly.

Sunday's thick gray clouds had lingered over eastern Galloway another day, emptying their buckets on land and sea in a torrent of hard, blowing rain. The ill weather suited their chore for the day— polishing silver by the light of the hearth—so the sisters willingly donned the aprons Neda brought them and went about their duties while their father finished the last of his tea.

"Too dreich a day for me *granbairns* to come callin'." The housekeeper sighed heavily, frowning at the window. "I've not seen their wee faces in a month." Two of Neda's grown daughters lived with their families south of Dalbeaty, only nine miles away, but far enough in poor weather to keep the bairns safely tucked in their cradles.

"Make good use of the time then," Lachlan murmured, never looking up from his saucer.

Heads bent over their spoons, the sisters rolled their eyes. Did their father think of nothing but work? The task at hand was not hard, only tedious. A bowl of warm water with a sliver of soap made from bracken ashes, an old cotton cloth, and tireless fingers were all that was needed to polish the family's treasured collection of silver teaspoons, knives, and two-pronged forks. Rubbing each piece to a high sheen, Leana had just finished the last of the tortoiseshell-handled knives when an unexpected knock sounded at the dining room door.

"Enter!" Lachlan barked.

A meek Annabel ventured her linen-capped head around the door. "Letter for you, sir. From Maxwell Park." At his command she brought it to him, bobbing her head all the while, then darted from the room.

Maxwell Park? Did her sister know of this? Leana glanced at Rose, whose look of astonishment answered her question. She did not know. Or perhaps her sister was thinking of another letter. One that never reached its destination, reduced to ashes in the grate.

Their father shook out the gilt-edged notepaper and held it as far away as his arm would allow, eyes narrowing as he read the letter aloud.

To Lachlan McBride, Esquire
Monday, 13 October 1788

My kind neighbor,

I trust you and your family are all in good health and anticipating a fruitful harvest this season.

"Not as fruitful as his," Lachlan muttered, mostly for his own benefit.

My wife, Lady Maxwell, has taken a great interest in your young daughter, Rose. Lady Maxwell believes that Rose would greatly benefit from a proper introduction to Galloway society and that our Hogmanay Ball might be the ideal setting for such a debut.

A debut! Beneath the table, the sisters clasped hands and squeezed them tight.

"A debut?" Lachlan practically spat the word onto his plate. "And whose pockets will be emptied for such a *spendrif* occasion?"

Naturally, Mr. McBride, it will be my honor and privilege to provide all that might be required for the occasion, in honor of my wife's affection for her.

"How generous," Leana murmured, genuinely delighted for her sister. "Only the Almighty could bestow such a blessing."

"You see, Father?" Rose's voice floated through the air on a whisper of hope. "'Twill cost our family neither penny nor pound."

> If you will kindly allow a visit from me Thursday morning, I would very much like to discuss my wife's plans in detail and procure your blessing. She is, as you can imagine, most eager to proceed with gown fittings and so forth.

"Eager, is she?" Lachlan smacked the paper with the back of his hand, grinding his teeth as he read the last line.

> Unless Thursday will not suit, expect me promptly at ten o'clock.
>
>   Robert, Lord Maxwell
>   Maxwell Park

Lachlan's voice did not float through the air like his daughter's. It sliced like a dagger, aimed straight at Rose's heart. "How long have you known about this?"

Leana gripped her sister's hand more tightly. If Rose knew, she'd never breathed a word of it to her.

"I knew . . . nothing." It was all Rose could squeeze out, but it was enough to send their father's fist crashing onto the table with an awful bang.

"A likely tale! Nearly a week since your visit to Maxwell Park, and you've said nary a word to me."

Rose's eyes filled with tears. "Father, Lady

Maxwell never mentioned this . . . this debut to me. Not the slightest hint."

"*Och.* I see the way of it. *She* did not mention it, but perhaps *you* mentioned it to her."

He stared at the hearth as though he could not bear to look at her, his chin jutting out like the prow of a ship bound for a dark harbor. "My proud daughter makes plans with the gentry, certain her poor, lowly father will agree to them."

"Nae!" Rose shrank back in her chair. Leana had never seen the girl so frightened. "It was not my idea, Father. Not a bit of it."

Leana could bear it no longer. "Father," she said softly, "it is clear that Rose is telling the truth, for this is the first I've heard of it as well. I believe this was Lady Maxwell's idea altogether. And a very thoughtful one."

"Aye, it is that." Rose sat up a bit straighter. "Perhaps we might consider the benefit to our household, Father. A means to provide—"

"*Provide?*" He stood so quickly his chair nearly tipped into the peat fire. "That is *my* responsibility, daughter. To provide food and shelter for my household and suitors for my daughters. I hardly need assistance with such important matters, do I? Not from either one of you," he added, glaring at Leana as well.

"Nae, Father," they responded in unison, sounding like chastised schoolgirls.

Rose hung on to Leana's hand for dear life. "Will you . . . receive Lord Maxwell on Thursday?"

"And waste his lordship's time? Indeed I will not. A letter will be sent to Maxwell Park at once."

"Nae, Father!" Rose stood, shaking all over. Fear or rage, Leana knew not which. She could only pray for her sister, who'd been offered a great kindness just to have it torn away from her an instant later.

"You dare to stand up to me?" Lachlan roughly shoved his chair aside.

"I stand up . . . for . . . myself." Rose choked on her words while Leana fought tears, knowing what it cost her sister to say such things. "If my . . . my disappointment means nothing to you, Father, then think of the . . . the disgrace this will bring to Auchengray." Rose sniffed, dabbing at her nose with her sleeve. "Think of how it will hurt my . . . future."

"Your *future* is precisely what I am thinking about!" he roared. Leana sensed he had much more to say, but he bit off his words instead, clenching his teeth like an angry man biting on a pipe. "'Tis not the man's offer that most disturbs me, Daughter. 'Tis thinking you kept it from me; that's the rub. There are to be no saicrets in this household. Understood?"

"It is no secret that you do not love me, Father." Rose bravely stood her ground. Though she spoke more evenly, her voice was low, and her heart was clearly broken. "And you do not care what becomes of me." Rose fled from the room, leaving Leana and her father in a room still as death.

Muttering to himself, Lachlan crumpled the letter in his hand and tossed it neatly into the grate. The paper smoldered and sparked, the gilt edges becoming black, then turning to ashes as he strode from the room without another word to Leana, heading for the spence and his writing desk.

Leana sat in stunned silence, watching the paper burn, thinking of Saturday's letter among the ashes as well. Eliza tiptoed into the room to collect the polished silver, with Neda right behind her, a look of concern etched on her freckled features. "Lass, is there anythin' I can do for ye? Or for Miss Rose?"

"Something is wrong, Neda." Leana gazed at the closed spence door. "Father should be dancing a jig at Lord Maxwell's offer. It might have meant a wealthy husband for Rose and silver for his thrifite."

Neda hung her head with a weary shake. "I gave up sortin' oot your sire's thoughts a lang time ago."

"You're a wise one, Neda." Leana pursed her lips, absently rubbing her thumb on the tines of a dinner fork. Something was afoot, of that she was certain. For a household meant to have no secrets, Auchengray had more than its stone walls could hold.

Twenty-Nine

Some friendships are made by nature,
some by contract,
some by interest, and some by souls.
JEREMY TAYLOR

Amonth of hard labor.

Jamie was amazed he'd agreed—no, *offered*—to endure such humiliation. Still, sending a letter to Glentrool and begging for a promissory note had even less appeal. If working like a commoner meant enjoying his uncle's hospitality without guilt or obligation, it would be worth the cuts and bruises, the sweat and toil of sheep farming. Besides, he'd poured enough knowledge into his head. The time had come to use his hands.

His woolen bonnet kept the worst of the rain off his head, but the rest of him was soon drenched to the skin as he strode toward the steading that stood at the center of Auchengray. Let Lachlan have his fine house. The farm buildings were Duncan Hastings's domain, and a fine place of business it was. Jamie passed the *doocot* filled with cooing doves, then a henhouse where Eliza gathered eggs before breakfast. Next came the granary and the barn, then a stable for the horses and a byre for the cows, efficiently milked hours earlier by a dairymaid whose name he had yet to learn. At the end of the U-shaped steading stood lodging for the laborers who came and went by season—crowded bothies, poorly furnished. The workers built their fires on dirt floors and ignored the pungent smell of the dunghill seeping around the hinges of the four-paned window.

Duncan had his quarters with Neda on the third floor of the house, though Jamie suspected the man spent little time there. Hastings was overseer to the flocks and fields but also to the family. His workday was endless. The forenoon hour meant the man was long done with his morning rounds of guiding the sheep up to the hilltops and looking for those that were lame or sick. Jamie would find him with the tups, no doubt, seeing that they were well fed and rested, ready for the work ahead. For it *was* work—thirty ewes for each ram, sixty days of breeding. Work for the shepherd, too, keeping the tups from injuring one another with all their fighting and head butting. Jamie headed for the separate paddock, hoping Duncan would take him on for a month and teach him the Auchengray way of doing things.

Despite the rain, Jamie enjoyed striding across the pastures, feeling his muscles stretch and his limbs grow loose. His strenuous journey east had taught him the value of breathing fresh air, of braving the elements and surviving whatever man or nature threw across his path. He was not the same Jamie McKie who'd quit Glentrool—a man on the run, full of fear and shame. His fears were all but banished. Now he must rid himself of the shame of his deceptions by giving to others instead of taking, working hard instead of hiding behind the clothes of a gentleman.

When he saw Duncan in the paddock ahead inspecting the tups, he thought of Henry Stewart, and a lump caught in his throat. Stew would be doing the very same thing today, readying the rams. So would Gordie Briggs, the shepherd who'd fed him a bowl of stew and wrapped him in a plaid—was that only a week ago? All over Galloway, shepherds were about their work. Soon he would be counted among them.

Duncan nodded to him, then straightened, releasing the ram's curved horns with care. "Come to help, lad, or just to visit? Not that I wouldn't welcome it. They say the shortest road's where the company's good."

"I'd like to offer more than company, Duncan." Jamie shook the water off his tam. "I've come to be of some assistance. If you'll allow me, that is."

"I might." The man's blue eyes were two bright spots on a gloomy morning. "Not without testin' ye though. Tell me what ye've learned about . . . och, start with shearin'. What d'ye ken about sheep shearin'?"

Jamie thought a moment, then rattled off the most important facts. "Start as early in the day as possible. Drive the flocks quietly into the sheepfolds, over the barest ground."

"Aye, guid. And?"

"Two men are needed: one to clip the wool, one to roll the fleece."

"And if you cut the skin?"

"Treat it immediately with balsam and sulfur."

Duncan's slight smile was his only response. "Go on."

Jamie searched his mind for something that might impress the seasoned shepherd. "Sheep will teach you their habits if you'll inspect the pads of their feet."

"Will they now? Studied that at *scuil,* did you?"

"Nae. Henry Stewart, our head shepherd, showed me how."

"Then show me." Duncan stood back and waved Jamie forward.

Jamie brushed his hands over the nearest ram, calming him with his voice and bending closer to examine the animal's forefoot. "A healthy tup, this one. You've led him across some stony ground of late, but it looks as if he's been feeding in a grassy pasture all of his two years."

Duncan slapped him on the back, nearly knocking him on top of the ram. "Right ye are, lad! Well done. Now then, why d'ye think I might be worried about my flocks this year mair than most?"

Jamie watched the man's face twitch with amusement and took an educated guess. "Might it be because the old shepherds say, 'A leap year is never a good sheep year'?"

"Och! Ye're too *cliver* for me, young Jamie. And what d'ye know of breedin'?"

"Nothing, sir," he said with a solemn face. "I'm a bachelor."

The shepherd cackled like an old woman, slapping his leg so hard he frightened the tups, which bounded away from him. "I'll enjoy havin' yer company, lad, and that's a fact. It gets lonely, this work. How lang will ye be staying at Auchengray?"

"A month," Jamie said. "Long enough to help with the breeding." Long enough to earn Lachlan's trust. Long enough to win Rose's heart.

"Until Martinmas, ye say? Lucky for me. D'ye raise blackface up in Glentrool?"

"Aye, we do. Only one lamb per ewe, due to the hills, but healthy ones."

"And how d'ye ken when a ewe is ready to lamb?" Duncan was testing him again.

Jamie smiled. "Her udder drops."

"Should ye move a ewe once she starts in?"

"Nae sir, you should not. Move the ewe, and she'll tarry with her lambing."

"Aye, that she will." Duncan's grin was ear to ear. "That she will." He filled a trough with fresh feed, whistling to himself as he did, then turned to reach for another sack. "So tell me, Mr. McKie, is Lachlan McBride payin' ye for yer labors these lang thirty days?"

"Food and lodging is all. Salary enough for a young man who appears at his uncle's gate unannounced with only the clothes on his back and those in tatters."

Duncan eyed him, the smile still in place. "I ken a canny man when I meet him. You'll get mair from yer uncle than bannocks for breakfast and a pair of auld boots, or my name is not Duncan Hastings. I think ye might have in mind claiming his most valuable possession. Am I right, lad?"

"Perhaps." Jamie looked away before the man saw the truth in his eyes. "Time will tell."

Duncan squeezed his arm with a gruff tenderness. "Aye, I believe it will. Come, we've rams to feed, rain or no. Woe to the shepherd that leaveth the flock, eh, Jamie?"

They worked side by side, the veteran shepherd and the *hauflin,* as Duncan called him. A half-grown lad, green and untested. For once it felt good to be younger, to be the new hand on the farm. He was learning the hard way, learning by doing. Duncan was patient with his mistakes and generous with praise. When Jamie moved too quickly, Duncan held out a steadying hand. When Jamie spoke too loudly, Duncan's index finger, pressed to his pursed lips, said all that needed to be said. The two quickly grew comfortable with each other, exchanging herd lore.

Other shepherds came by as they worked,

observing the tups, offering their opinions on which animal would produce the most lambs come Eastertide. One feisty lad, no more than a dozen years old, declared with certainty, "The best rams are the ones with a twin brother."

"And who told ye that rot?" Duncan demanded.

"You did, sir."

"Aye, and I was right. Twins make the best rams." He winked at Jamie. "Ye've a twin *brither* back at Glentrool, d'ye not?"

Jamie's neck grew warm. "Aye, I do." What had Lachlan told his overseer about Evan? "But not a true twin. Sired by the same father but of different seed."

The young lad piped up, "Who was born first then?"

"It depends," Jamie said, busying himself with a sack of oats.

The boy persisted. "Depends on what?"

"On whom you ask. My mother will tell you I'm the older."

Duncan laughed, and the others joined in. "Who better to ken sic a thing? If yer mither says ye're the firstborn, lad, believe it with all yer heart."

Not only his mother. *God said so.* That's what Rowena McKie had told him. From the beginning of Jamie's life, the Almighty had placed his hand on the lad, his mother said. Held it there still, if Jamie's strange dream proved true. When Alec McKie had laid his gnarled fingers on Jamie's head that last night at Glentrool, Jamie sensed that it was more than a father's touching his son; it was God's blessing flowing through the patriarch's fingers. Odd that he should think of that today, standing up to his ankles in mud and sheep dung, shepherding a flock not his own.

"Whaur is yer head, lad?" Duncan punched his shoulder with a gentle fist, rousing him from his reverie. "Time to clean up for supper. We'll work tomorrow and Wednesday mornin', but then ye've a fine dinner to dress for."

"A dinner?"

"Aye. Mr. McDougal is coming to pitch his woo at Miss Leana." Duncan's eyes had a mischievous twinkle. "If ye ask me, I dinna think the lass is holdin' out her hands to catch it."

Thirty

Joy comes and goes, hope ebbs and flows
Like the wave;
Change doth unknit the tranquil strength of men.
MATTHEW ARNOLD

Leana was present at the dinner table, and yet she was not. Her hand moved, lifting the glass to her lips. Her head bobbed in deference to her father, to Mr. McDougal, to Cousin Jamie. Her mouth curved into a smile when Rose served up diverting anecdotes like they were date pudding. Leana swallowed when necessary, spoke only when spoken to, and clenched her toes to keep from weeping.

Neda, watching over the elaborate dinner service, eyed her with particular curiosity. She had no way of knowing how Leana suffered in silence, grieved by the sight of that lecherous farmer—that hatesome man!—seated across the table from her. Regardless of her misery, dinner proceeded on schedule, all five of them playing their roles like marionettes on a Paris stage. Serving platters came and went, covered with fish, then flesh, then fowl: trout from the nearby River Nith, smothered in cream; *reested* mutton, salty and smoky; and roasted duck in a rich gooseberry sauce. Carrots from her summer garden, prudently stored in the cellar, added color to the overflowing plates. Leana ate what she could, which was very little.

Willie, scrubbed and dressed like a proper house servant, faithfully stood behind her chair, offering her a spoonful of this, a slice of that, but she repeatedly shook her head. It was not food she hungered for; it was freedom. The freedom to choose for herself a man who could make her happy, a husband whom she might please for the rest of her days. That man was seated across from her, though not directly so. On Mr. McDougal's right sat the one she'd placed her hopes upon. *Jamie.*

All at once her cousin's gaze found hers. "A shilling for your thoughts, Leana."

Her mouth fell open. She closed it just as quickly while gripping the napkin in her lap. "Cousin James—"

"You know better," he chided her gently. "Call me Jamie."

"Aye, Jamie. My thoughts, you say? I was . . . thinking of . . ."

"Ewes!" Rose smiled as she said it. "Tell us about your work with the tups, Jamie."

He cleared his throat, the slight shake of his head a tender reproach. "Hardly a topic of dinner conversation, Rose."

"How wrong you are, lad." Lachlan, playing the merry host, beamed at his nephew and winked at his guest. "Mr. McDougal and I would be delighted to hear the details."

Jamie warmed to his subject, though Leana noticed he worded things with great care to avoid sending his lady cousins ducking under the table in red-faced embarrassment. The older men, despite all their farming experience, seemed fascinated by Jamie's astute observations. Leana and Rose stared at their plates and pushed the food around with their forks until, blessedly, Jamie was done discussing his morning hours with the tups.

"Something of interest to the lasses now," Jamie suggested. "Rose?"

Lachlan interrupted before she could answer. "Women care about only two things: husbands and bairns."

"Not so!" Rose jerked her chin, clearly miffed. "Many things occupy a woman's mind. Gardens. Poetry. Music. And food." She aimed a pointed gaze at their plates. "Something which men find of great interest."

"Hear! Hear!" Mr. McDougal banged the handle of his knife on the table in agreement, grinning all the while at Leana. "What sort of cook is your sister, Miss McBride?"

"Leana is a fine cook, sir, and an even better seamstress. She's skilled with a spinning wheel and gifted at making things grow." Rose turned toward her, love and compassion shining in her eyes. "But my sister's mind is her greatest asset. Wise is the man who appreciates it."

Leana marveled at her brave sister speaking in her defense. If only she could be so bold herself. Fergus McDougal did not affirm her sister's heidie comments, but Jamie nodded ever so slightly, as though he might secretly agree—or not. It was difficult to be sure.

"That's quite enough, Rose." Lachlan trained a stern eye on her. "No need to praise your sister's merits. They are only of interest to one man at this table, and he is already quite convinced. Am I right, sir?"

"Aye." Fergus leered at Leana.

Jamie gazed at Rose. Only Rose.

Nae. Leana looked down at her plate, refusing to see what was plainly written on Jamie's face. *Nae.* Rose would never let such a thing happen, even though the lost Maxwell debut had struck a terrible blow.

After moping around the house all yestreen, Rose had awakened as her usual, buoyant self. Before breakfast, bundled in their cozy box bed, the two sisters had revealed their deepest secrets: Leana admitted to caring more for Jamie than might be proper. Rose confessed that, soon after Jamie arrived, he'd kissed her—briefly—standing in the middle of their sheep pasture.

Leana was shocked. "He . . . *kissed* you?"

"It was nothing. Like the kiss of an older brother or an uncle," Rose assured her in a whisper. "Now we must see that he kisses *you,* and not like a relative!" They'd stifled their laughter in their pillows. "Aren't we a pair?" A pair determined to see Jamie choose the right sister for his bride. Unless it was too late. Unless he had already chosen.

"Miss McBride." Fergus McDougal's voice brought Leana's head up with a snap. "Your sister declares you a good cook, yet you've no appetite." His brown eyes studied her across the table. "Are your thoughts . . . elsewhere?"

"Nae sir." She managed a faint smile. "They are very much centered on a certain gentleman at this table." He would think her coy; she spoke naught but truth.

"I'm glad to hear it." He looked pleased with himself and exchanged nods with her father.

Her clever comment was not so clever after all. If she wasn't careful, Fergus McDougal would end their meal with a formal proposal of marriage. He'd made his intentions quite clear. Once their promises were made, sealed with the pressing together of their thumbs and an exchange of gifts, there would be no turning back.

But she had no gift for Fergus, least of all the gift of herself.

She could not let it happen. Not today. Not ever. *Please, God!*

Leana could not bear to look at the man seated across from her, yet if her gaze strayed toward

Jamie, her own intentions would be obvious. She would address her father then and make certain Jamie was in her line of sight. "Father, tell us your plans for Martinmas."

He shrugged. "The same as Mr. McDougal's, I suspect." Her father outlined their November outing to Dumfries while Leana took in the firm line of Jamie's chin, the curve of his high cheekbones, and the heat of his gaze, pointed in one direction: *Rose.*

Her father's voice faded. Leana felt the room pull away from her, as though she were looking at it through Reverend Gordon's new telescope and adjusting the lens. Her perspective changed. She could no longer refuse to see what was clearly before her.

She had been deceived. By no one but herself.

Leana pressed her lips so tightly together she feared she might pierce the skin with her teeth. Despite what she'd foolishly believed, her father would not be dissuaded regarding Fergus McDougal. That was painfully obvious. Yet there were delusions greater than that one, lies she'd whispered into her pillow every night since Jamie had arrived.

She'd told herself that Jamie, a handsome, intelligent young man, would choose a plain woman over a beautiful one.

She'd convinced herself that when he smiled at her, it meant he cared for her. That when he'd caught her elbow on the stair, it was because he wanted to touch her.

She'd assumed that if she let him see her heart, he would want it for his own.

But Jamie wanted Rose. She saw that now, in the warm glow of his eyes as he gazed at her sister, in the curve of his mouth when Rose said his name.

Jamie.

He wasn't looking for a woman to cook or stitch or spin wool or plant a garden. He wanted Rose, a bonny young lass who could not help but learn to love him.

I would love you, Jamie. The pain in her chest was unbearable. *I would, I would.*

"I would like to make an announcement, if I may." Fergus McDougal's voice pierced her thoughts, pulling her back to the table, back to the present with its cold, hard truth. He smiled at her with his stained teeth and his knowing gaze and his sagging jowls. "What I am about to say will be a surprise to no one at this table."

Leana was on her feet before she realized it. "I . . . forgive me, Father." She ran from the room, nearly knocking over Willie and his tall glasses of syllabub, then flung herself out the front door. Looking wildly about, she stumbled down the grassy path toward the road to Newabbey, stopping halfway, bent in two with pain.

Please, God.

Jamie was the man she had prayed for. Not Fergus.

She wiped the back of her hand across her eyes, ashamed of the stubborn tears that would not stop, and wandered aimlessly toward the orchard. Perhaps she would lose herself among the trees. What she would *not* do was go back and sit across the table from three men who neither knew nor loved her. Fergus saw only her useful parts—her hands, her body—but not her heart. Her father saw her as livestock, to be traded or sold as needed. And Jamie saw her not at all.

Leana hid inside a cherry tree's woody embrace and waited for who knew what. Would it be her father storming out the door, breathing threats? Her sister, knowing all too well the situation, anxious to dry her tears? Or her suitor—the word felt like a cherry pit in her mouth—demanding an apology for something he couldn't possibly comprehend?

The front door opened quietly. It was Jamie.

He walked directly toward the orchard, as though he knew where to find her, his steps quickening until he reached her side. Softly he touched her hand, eyes filled with sympathy. "Leana." His voice was like a shepherd's comforting a newborn lamb. "Leana, I'm sorry."

"Sorry?" She turned away to hide her tears. Jamie had done nothing to hurt her, not on purpose. "Why are *you* sorry?"

"Because I . . ." He sighed heavily. "Because."

She felt a lightness in her chest, a tiny flicker of hope. Might he care after all? Did he regret favoring Rose with his attentions? Leana turned toward him, lifting her chin, hiding nothing. "Jamie, I thought . . ." She swallowed hard. "I'd hoped . . ."

But there was no hope in his eyes. It was more like pity. "I truly am sorry, Leana."

"Jamie . . ." Overcome, she fell forward, her head pressed against his shoulder. "Oh, Jamie!"

She felt his hand touch the back of her head, smoothing her hair, and could not stop herself from pressing against his palm. "Why did they send *you* to find me?" she whispered.

"They didn't send me." Jamie shifted his hands to her arms, holding her steady as he leaned back a bit to look at her. His mouth hinted at a smile. "I just move faster."

The front door exploded open. Lachlan. Fergus. Angry shouts flew toward the orchard like two carrion crows on the wing railing at each other with their deep, hoarse calls.

Leana stepped away from Jamie's innocent embrace, but it was too late.

"Do you see?" Fergus shouted, waving his dinner napkin like a flag as he marched toward them. "Do you see your daughter in another man's arms?"

"He is her cousin," Lachlan barked, close on the man's heels. "Nothing more."

Both men reached her side and stood a handbreadth apart, their faces the color of beets. They had not come to blows, but it appeared they'd considered it. Their eyes bored into hers, their fury aimed in a fresh direction.

She sensed Jamie behind her, closing the gap. A wall of support. He spoke first. "Gentlemen, I found my cousin weeping in the orchard. My uncle is right: I meant only to comfort her. Surely you can see—"

"I see a woman who has thoroughly rejected my proposal of marriage." Fergus McDougal's eyes protruded more than usual, and he spewed spittle when he spoke. "Three times I've called on you,

Miss McBride, and three times I've been less than warmly received." He yanked on his waistcoat, his hands shaking with rage. "Nae, three times I've been made to feel a *fool.*"

Leana lowered her gaze. She could not argue with a man who spoke the truth.

As he gathered steam, his neck seemed to thicken. "You have no regard for me and even less for your father's wishes. Did he not assure me you were the agreeable sort? Aye, he did! The very words he said were, 'She'll lift nary a finger nor a word against you.' Yet you rudely abandoned me at this table on two occasions, the last to consort with your lover in the orchard—"

"*Nae!* He is not my . . ." She could not even say the word. "Please, you must not think that of me or of my cousin."

Fergus ignored her, shaking his fists over his head in a fit of exasperation. "What . . . what sort of example would you set for my children?"

Before she could answer, he threw his napkin to the ground. "I will *not* have it!" His voice was at a fever pitch. "I'll not have *you,* Miss McBride. I withdraw my offer of marriage. You have been unfaithful to me before our vows were even spoken." The laird of Nethercarse spun on his heel and addressed her father, who'd waited through it all with a chilling lack of response. "My factor will see my silver returned without delay. Good day to you, sir."

Fergus marched toward the stables. The silence in his wake was thunderous.

When Leana tried to speak, Lachlan lifted his

hand to quell her, then hissed through clenched teeth, "Silence!"

She had never in her twenty years seen her father so livid. Behind her, Jamie whispered, "Shall I stay?"

Her father answered for her, his voice low and even. "You shall not, Nephew. None of this concerns you. Leana, you will follow me."

The warmth of Jamie's presence faded as she moved away from him and hurried after her father, whose belligerent stride carried him swiftly across the lawn, through the house, and into the spence.

He paced around the small room, clenching his hands, then releasing them, not even looking in her direction. The minutes dragged on while she locked her knees to keep from crumpling to the floor. Finally her father stood before her, his face a stone fortress. Gray, menacing, grim.

"Do you ken what your careless behavior has cost me, Leana?"

She did not know, not fully. He'd never shared the terms of his arrangement with Fergus McDougal. She offered the safest response she could think of. "Too much."

"Aye, a good deal too much." He splayed the fingers of his left hand and counted his losses for her. "Silver coin and black cattle. The friendship of a fellow landowner. The respect of my servants. The regard of our neighbors most of all."

Her father's temper could not always be explained. But this time she understood. "You have every reason to be furious with me, Father."

"Be sure of it, I am." His voice was low, but the intensity of it made her tremble. "You! My *bowsome,* obedient daughter. I might have expected such shameless behavior from your sister. But never from you, Leana." He gripped her shoulders, shaking her slightly, forcing her to meet his hard gaze. "You, who favor your mother in so many ways, God rest her soul. Agness McBride would ne'er have treated me so ill."

He'd cut her to the quick. "I'm sorry, Father."

"As well you should be." He dropped his hands, his gaze shifting to the window that faced the road to Newabbey. "Before the sun sets, the whole parish will be blethering about Lachlan's daughter being put aside for . . . improprieties."

"Oh, Father." A tear slipped out. Without meaning to, she'd put in motion a dreadful turn of events. "What . . . what will become of me?"

He shook his head, his back still toward her. "I cannot say. But I fear you will not like it."

"You *do* know, Father, that nothing . . . that Jamie . . ."

"Aye." He grunted. "It's clear where his affections lie, and they are not with you."

She shuddered at the truth spoken so coldly.

"Jamie is a foolish young man with much to learn." He sighed, his frustration clear. "As long as he is under my roof, the burden of teaching him falls on my shoulders."

Leana sank into a chair. And what lessons had she learned that bitter morning? That her eyes were weak, but her heart was blind, seeing only what it wanted to see. That desire and duty were two very different things. And that a single careless action could ruin everything. *Not everything, Leana. You.* It was true; she was ruined. Her body was still pure, but her reputation would soon be soiled by Fergus McDougal.

God, help me.

All at once she saw what she must do. She reached for her father's hand as a drowning woman grasps at reeds. "Father," she whispered, squeezing his fingers, "will you help me?"

Perhaps the strain in her voice caught his ear. When he turned to look at her once more, his stony features softened ever so slightly. "Now, now, Leana. After a time the gossips will find another morsel to chew on."

"And in the meantime?"

"In the meantime, lass, you will quietly go about your days and do as I ask, knowing I have your best interests in mind. Aye?"

"Aye," she agreed, though she feared he had only his interests in mind. Still, the dreadful possibility of marriage to Fergus McDougal was no more. If she could not have Jamie, at least she would not have Fergus.

"'Tis my responsibility, Leana, to see that you're wed. I'll not shirk my duties. When the time comes, see that you don't shirk yours."

"Choose whom you will to woo me, Father." She blinked away a stray tear and offered a tentative smile. "I'll not disappoint you again."

Dismissed with an abrupt gesture, Leana

released his hand and headed for her room, anxious to be alone with her thoughts. Neda met her at the landing, her face covered with concern. "Rose is off helpin' Duncan with the sheep. She bade me give ye this." Neda pressed a paper into her hands, then hastened down the stair.

Leana waited until she was safely curled up in her reading chair before unfolding the sealed note. Penned in Rose's flowery handwriting, it contained four brief phrases: "You have not said, 'I do.' Nor have I. All is not lost. Wait and see."

Thirty-One

In Heaven's happy bowers
There blossom two flowers;
One with fiery glow
And one as white as snow;
While lo! before them stands,
With pale and trembling hands,
A spirit who must choose
One, and one refuse.
RICHARD WATSON GILDER

The thought of wooing a woman made Jamie's mouth go dry and his hands turn as cold as the rushing waters of Buchan Burn.

He had danced with women, shared formal dinners and sunlit walks across the moors with them, stolen kisses from them. Ladies noticed him more often than he paid attention to them, so wooing and winning a woman had never been a tickler. Until now, until Rose McBride, whose innocence required that he be the one to risk all and make his intentions clear.

He thought he'd made them abundantly clear, but her actions piped another tune. If anything, Leana had been more attentive than Rose, without any encouragement from him. Aye, he'd gone to look for Leana in the orchard—someone had to—and had offered his support when her father and her betrothed did their best to destroy her. An ugly scene. It had ended badly, especially for his cousin. His uncle would have a devil of a time finding someone to marry her if the gossips had their way.

But that was Lachlan's concern, not his.

It was Rose he intended to marry and Rose's heart that must be wooed.

If only his mother were at Auchengray. Rowena McKie would have known the ideal spot, the right word, the proper touch. With his mother's guidance, Rose would be won in an afternoon. "A rich man's wooing is seldom long o' doing," his mother had once told him. Longer than a week, it seemed. However many days or weeks it took, he had no doubt he would succeed.

Sensing a servant's quiet presence in the room, Jamie glanced over his shoulder to find Hugh, his uncle's valet of many years, waiting patiently in the doorway. "Come, man, do something with this unruly hair of mine. Perhaps a fresh shave would be in order."

"Aye, sir. Yer beard's a stubborn one. If ye've wooin' in mind, ye best have a smooth cheek."

Jamie merely nodded. No point pretending things were otherwise. As at Glentrool, the servants at Auchengray missed nary an intrigue beneath their laird's roof. He removed his waistcoat, cravat, and shirt, then seated himself at Rose's feminine dressing table, feeling slightly ridiculous. "Get on with it, man. I have much to accomplish."

"Aye." Hugh had come prepared. Emptying his pockets, then making use of the pitcher of hot water he'd brought with him, he efficiently lathered Jamie's face with a heath-scented soap and began his ministrations with a sharp razor and a steady hand. Minutes later Jamie smoothed a hand over his jaw, pleased with the results, while Hugh made quick work with a comb, gathering Jamie's dark brown hair in a sleek tail behind his neck and tying it in place with a narrow bit of silk.

"Time for yer shirt, sir." Hugh dressed him with minimal fuss, brushing off the last crumbs of dinner from his breeches and giving his much-worn waistcoat a tidy look. "Now to your neckcloth." The manservant tied the cravat with nimble fingers, pressed it in place, then stepped back to view his handiwork. His smile was more affirming than any looking glass. "The lady will be won from the first, Mr. McKie. Have no fear of it."

Jamie dismissed him with a word of thanks, then gathered his wits about him before setting out to find Rose. She'd spent a good deal of time sequestered in Leana's room since the debacle. Comforting her sister, no doubt. He would knock on their nearby door in passing, then proceed through the house and gardens until he found her. Stepping into the upstairs hall, he was relieved to find it deserted. The servants had gleaned enough gossip for the day.

"Rose?" He knocked on her door, gently at first, then with a firmer knuckle. No answer. He hurried down the stair, listening for her lilting voice. She was not at the hearth nor in the spence. The kitchen was a noisy din of servants cleaning up after the meal but no Rose among them. Neda caught his eye and inclined her head toward the gardens. He nodded his thanks, then headed out through the front door rather than soil his clothes going through the scullery.

It was a fine day, the colors bright and shimmering against the blue sky. Not that it would last; good weather in Scotland never did. Perhaps Rose was enjoying a walk in the countryside while the sun blessed Galloway with its warm presence. He strolled through the empty orchard and around the east side of the house, watching for the striped gown he'd seen her wearing earlier. He'd almost turned the corner of the house when he heard girlish laughter floating on the autumn air, coming from the direction of the rose garden. An ideal spot for wooing. His stride lengthened as he caught sight of

the two sisters among the thorny stalks, surrounded by blooms once fresh, now bent and
bruised, petals scattered to the winds.

"The two finest flowers in the garden," Jamie
announced, relieved to find them both free of tears,
even smiling a bit after the ordeal. "Surely you
aren't cutting roses for the hall table? They're long
past their prime." He watched their smiles fade and
knew he'd said something wrong. "Or have you
found one still blooming?"

"Two." Leana held them aloft, a profusion of
petals surrounded by dark, almost blue leaves.
"See?"

He bent over to inspect them. Palest pink on the
outside, the color deepened near the center where
the stamen winked at him among the petals like a
tiny green eye. A pleasant fragrance tickled his
nose. "Lovely." He straightened to look at his
intended bride. *The right word.* "Lovely," he said
again, and her face quickly matched the blossom.
He turned and winked at Leana. "What do you call
this breed?"

"Breed?" Leana laughed. "They're roses, Jamie,
not sheep. One plants them, prunes them, feeds
them—"

"And breeds them. Roses are hybrids, cultivated
by . . . ah, breeders, aye?"

Cousin Leana was now the color of the flower in
question as well. "Aye, but we usually call them a
variety of rose. Or a species. Or a type."

He nodded, always willing to learn. "And the
name of this variety?"

The sisters looked at each other, then burst into laughter while Leana managed to say, "Maiden's Blush."

"Ah."

Leana patted her cheeks as though to cool them. "This species seldom blooms so late in the season, but these two surprised us."

Jamie tipped his head, regarding them both. "Just as you two have certainly surprised me."

"Really?" A sudden curiosity shone in Rose's dark eyes. "What did Aunt Rowena tell you about us? We wrote her now and then over the years. Did she tell you what we might be like?"

He bit his lip, hoping the truth wouldn't offend. "She didn't often make mention of your family while I was growing up. And when . . . when it was necessary for me to leave, there wasn't time. I hastened away, knowing only that I would find two cousins at the end of my journey. One dark, one fair, both bonny. That was all I remembered." His smile was genuine and meant to charm. "Believe me, it was enough. Enough to bring me nigh to fifty miles with little food and no silver."

"Are you glad you came?" Rose asked softly, locking gazes with him. "Was it . . . worth your journey?"

His heart swelled with longing, and his voice grew thick. "You know that it was."

Jamie had almost forgotten that Leana was still standing there, holding two fragrant blooms on thorn-covered stems. He turned to her now, wanting to include her in some way. The wan expression on her face told him it was too late. "Might I take those inside for you?"

Leana thrust the roses into his hands, pricking his palms. "If you choose." Grabbing her skirts, she was away at once, headed for the road.

Dumbfounded, Jamie watched her disappear from sight, then turned to discover Rose near tears. *Och!* There was no accounting for women and their moods. "Rose, what is it? What have I done?"

"I'm sorry, Jamie." She tugged a dainty handkerchief from her sleeve and patted her nose, then took a deep breath. "I can think of no other way to tell you except to say it: You have chosen the wrong woman."

"I've *what?*" He threw the flowers to the ground and grabbed both her hands in his. "From the very first moment I saw you, Rose, I knew. *Knew* you were the woman the Almighty intends for me to marry."

Her eyes were like windows with the curtains drawn. "*How* did you know?"

"I knew because . . ." How *did* he know? "Because of your beauty."

She shook her head, clearly disappointed, and released his hands. "Beauty fades. Flowers are proof of it."

"But your . . ." He searched for the right word. "Your *joy.* Your joy captured my heart. And your sheep . . ."

Her eyes widened. "You fell in love with my *sheep?*"

"Nae! Not your sheep. They were impressive. Aye, they were that. But it was watching you with your sheep, your tender way with them—that's what struck me."

She nodded, as though distracted for a moment, then lifted her chin to meet his gaze again. "What if I told you that I had . . . other plans?"

"Other plans?" His patience snapped in two. "Since when, lass? You've said no such thing, not in all these days we've had together."

"That's true, but . . . but every time you've hinted at *your* plans, I've tried my best to discourage you."

"Oo aye!" He rolled his eyes. "That was a most discouraging kiss the Wednesday last."

"But you kissed *me.*"

"And you kissed me back, lass." He clasped her about the shoulders, pliant beneath his firm grip. "Or don't you know what it means to press your lips against a man's mouth?" He bent closer. "To warm beneath his touch?"

"Nae." She swayed as he pulled her closer still. "I don't know."

He kissed her hard, his teeth striking hers, his mouth making sure, making very sure she kissed him back.

When he lifted his face from hers, tears filled her eyes. Her lips, wet from his mouth, were trembling. "Jamie, I . . ."

"Rose, oh, Rose." He pulled her against him in a loose embrace, not wanting to frighten her further. "Forgive my boldness, lass. A man needs to know how a woman feels about him. Words are . . . not our way of knowing."

"I see." She took a deep breath, then released it with a mournful sigh like wind through a pipe. "Jamie, you must listen to me." She pushed him away, then stepped back, putting more distance between them. "My eyes and lips may tell you one thing, but my heart and head have decided quite another."

"But—"

"Please, Jamie. Think." Her expression was kind but resolute. "Have I said or done a single thing to mislead you?"

He glanced away from her, determined to think of something. Instead, images of Rose's avoiding his gaze and shrinking from his touch rushed to mind. When he turned to look at her once more, he was forced to admit the truth. "Nae. You have not misled me. I have deceived myself."

"I am sorry, Jamie." She touched his arm, only for a moment, then dropped her hand. "I am too young. Marriage . . . frightens me. But there *is* one who cares for you." She paused, as if he might guess before she spoke the words. "My sister."

"Leana?" *Of course.* Other images came swiftly to mind. Meeting Leana's gaze when they first greeted each other. Strolling through the village with her to kirk. Smiling at Leana across the dinner table. Finding her in the orchard. Encounters that meant nothing to him but obviously spoke volumes to her.

"But Leana is my . . . cousin. Nothing more." His shoulders sagged with the burden of his disappointment. "I care for her as I might my own sister, if I had a sister. She does not . . . well, she . . ."

"How do you *know?*" Rose persisted. "You've been so busy looking at me, you've not considered Leana properly. You've not kissed her, as you have me, nor laced your fingers through hers, nor felt the beat of her heart against yours. Jamie, she deserves a fine husband, and she cares for *you.* Cares very much, if you must know."

"She does?"

"Aye, you can be sure of it. Her words to me were, 'Jamie is everything Fergus McDougal is not.'"

He snorted. "Och, that's an encouraging thought. 'Not like Fergus'—now there's a hearty recommendation."

"Don't you see? Now that Mr. McDougal is no longer her suitor, Leana is free to marry someone else. The sooner she does so, the better. And she very much hoped to marry you."

"Marry . . . ?" He groaned, watching his plans start to crumble like a handful of stale bannocks. "Am I to understand that you feel nothing for me?"

"Oh, Jamie." She pinched her lips shut for a moment, as if holding something back. "I feel a great deal for you. But I love my sister more. Leana has been both mother and sister to me since the day I was born." Her voice broke. "I long to see her happily wed, Jamie. Loved and appreciated for who she is. Don't you see? Your love would be a dream come true for Leana."

"My dream was different, Rose." He closed his eyes. It hurt too much to look at her. "My dream was you."

Thirty-Two

The rose and thorn, joy and sorrow,
all mingle into one.
SAADI, SHAIKH MUSLIH AL DIN

Daydreaming, are we?"

Rose stepped inside the cool, dark corner of the second floor where Leana's spinning wheel held court and planted herself on a wooden stool, trying to sense her sister's mood. After the unfortunate incident in the garden, the sisters had snipped at each other all evening, then shared their box bed in silence. "I couldn't find you after breakfast."

Leana lifted her head but did not look at her. "This seemed a good place to hide."

"Och! And whom would you be hiding from?"

"You ken very well." Leana began spinning again, her rhythm sure, her long, supple fingers well suited to spinning the wool and forming a smooth twist.

Rose glanced down at her own clumsy hands, good for carding the wool and little else. "I suppose I should do my carding this morning."

"Aye, you should." Leana paused in her spinning to unfold a freshly dried fleece for Rose. "Until dinner, if you don't mind. This afternoon I'm off to Troston Hill to help Jessie stitch a new gown for wee Annie."

Rose was relieved to hear it. At least at Troston Hill Jamie wouldn't see her sister wearing those ugly spectacles. "Do hand me that wool, Leana, for it won't card itself."

She spread the coarse, tangled wool across one prickly paddle, putting the shorn ends across the top. Then she pressed the second paddle on top of it and dragged the two in opposite directions, repeating the same step over and over. With each pull of the cards, the fibers expanded and straightened until finally the wool rolled off in her hands in a neat whorl.

"Your turn." She handed the soft bundle to Leana to spin, then began the process again with a fresh handful of wool. Carding and spinning, carding and spinning, the two sisters worked side by side. The rhythm of their labors was as familiar as an old tune from their school days in Newabbey. Rose sang the first line, and Leana halfheartedly joined in.

> We were sisters, we were seven,
> We were the fairest under heaven,
> And it was all our seven-years' wark
> To sew our faither's seven sarks.

The lyrics always made Leana laugh. But not this time, although she smiled a bit. "Seven shirts in seven years?" Leana murmured. "I once sewed seven in a *week* when Father was bound for Edinburgh."

"Aye," Rose teased her gently. "Those nimble fingers of yours are the envy of the parish. Doesn't Jamie wear the shirt you made him every chance he gets?"

They sang on and on, verse after verse, while Rose carded wool and Leana sat at the great wheel, drawing out the wool fibers with practiced hands, then guiding them into a slender twist of yarn, winding it endlessly around the bobbin.

> First blew the sweet, the simmer-wind
> Then autumn wi' her breath sae kind,
> Before that e'er the guid knight came
> The tokens of his luve to claim.

"It's autumn," Leana said wistfully, "and the good knight came."

Jamie. "Soon, Leana, that good knight from Glentrool will claim you and give you a token of his love."

"'Tis a dream you speak of, Rose."

"Nae, I'm sure of it. If you'd only seen how surprised he was, and pleasantly so, to learn of your growing attachment to him."

"My . . . my *attachment?*" Leana nearly choked on the word. "Whatever did you tell him?"

"I said that you cared for him. Very much."

"Rose!"

She shrugged, her cheeks warming. "It had to be said, Leana. When it comes to understanding a woman's heart, Jamie is as daft as a three-sided guinea and thick as a post."

"That may well be. But what must he think, hearing such things from you when he obviously cares not one bittie for me."

"Not true." Rose yanked the two cards apart with a ladylike grunt. "When I told him you regarded him favorably, he raised those bonny eyebrows of his and said, 'She does?'"

"He . . . said that?"

"Aye." The look of fond desire on her sister's face gave Rose pause. Had she gone too far? Promised too much? *Nae.* Jamie would do as she'd asked. *And he'd best hurry.* Rose patted her sister's knee with the flat side of her paddle. "If our cousin doesn't move quickly, another braw lad will come to court you, and then what would Jamie do?"

Leana sighed. "Have a wee dram in celebration?"

"Och!" Rose banged her cards together with a noisy clap. "Enough of this peevishness, or you'll scare the poor lad away."

Leana's spinning wheel slowed to a stop. "The only thing that might frighten Jamie is the thought of losing you."

"Hoot!" Rose fumed. The bittersweet truth of it made her words sour. "He cannot lose what he does not have."

Leana threw her hands in the air, her spinning forgotten. "And I cannot have what is not mine to choose. Rose, don't you see? It's *you* Jamie wants."

"I'll make myself invisible then. Hide in the laundry until you've stolen his heart away."

"Stolen?" Leana's sharp tone had an edge of disapproval. "I'd rather win a man's heart than steal it."

"Stolen or won, what difference does it make as long as he's yours?"

"All the difference in the world, Rose." The wheel began to spin again. "All the difference in the world."

"Only to you," Rose grumbled.

They worked in a fractured silence, without music or laughter to weave them back together. Had they ever argued before Jamie appeared at their doorstep? Rose couldn't remember a single time. It promised to be a very trying month before he departed from Auchengray, taking his new bride with him. Rose prayed it would be Leana. Leana insisted it would be Rose. Their sisterly affection for each other had already been sorely tested, and the Lord alone knew what was to come.

Rose immersed herself in her work, keeping up a grueling pace until her wrists could bear no more. She put the empty paddles aside, then gathered the rolls of carded wool and quietly placed them in an old heather basket by Leana's foot. "I'm away to the kitchen," she murmured, standing and turning to leave. "Perhaps I can help with dinner."

"Wait." The great wheel stopped. "I'll come with you." Leana spun on the three-legged stool, and Rose saw faint tear stains on her sister's cheeks. "I'm sorry to be so kittlie."

With a sigh of relief, Rose leaned over and hugged her tight. "You *are* a bit sensitive," she whispered in her sister's ear. "And I wouldn't change you, Leana, not for all the world. You simply want to marry a good man as soon as possible. And I only want a wealthy man, and not until I'm ready."

"Dearie, you know what they say: 'Never marry for money; ye'll borrow it cheaper.'"

"Aye." Rose tossed her braid with a spirited shake. "But I've no one to borrow money from except Lachlan McBride, who won't part with a ha'penny unless it will earn him two. If I'm to be a wealthy woman, I must marry a wealthy man. Not soon, of course. Not for a very long time. But someday."

"Marry a gentleman for his money then, if your heart's set on it." Leana followed her down the hallway toward the stair. "As for me, I prefer to do as the Buik says: 'Owe no man any thing, but to love one another.' Had I the choice, I would marry for love, Rose. Only for love."

Rose murmured over her shoulder, "Then it's a good thing you're not marrying Fergus McDougal."

"Aye." Leana paused at the top of the stair. "What an awful row in the orchard. I've promised Father I won't disappoint him again."

Rose spun on her heel. "*Disappoint* him? Father

cares nothing for your future happiness. Nor for mine. He only cares about being in control of all that happens in this household. Pernickitie man!"

"Wheesht!" Leana held a finger to her lips. "The walls have ears."

"I know," Rose said, tossing her braid behind her as she started down the stair. "They have names, too. Eliza told me every word Father said in the spence yestreen."

"Shame on you," Leana whispered, though Rose heard no censure in her sister's voice. "Mind your tongue at dinner."

An hour later, when Neda brought in a cold platter of boiled beef tongue, Rose suddenly excused herself from the table, running off to the kitchen to bury her face in a towel and shriek with laughter. *Tongue!* Had Leana known?

Neda returned for more dishes and found her draped over a table, wiping away tears. "Whatever is the matter with you, child?"

"Oh, Neda." Rose could barely breathe, her stomach hurt so. "Truly, I have not laughed like this in ages. Auchengray has become far too serious since Jamie McKie arrived."

The housekeeper regarded her for a moment, brushing back the stray wisps of hair that always gathered round Rose's brow. "I canna say you're wrong, lass. A bit more joy would do the place some good." Neda nodded at the door. "You'd best join the family, or they'll think you've taken ill."

Rose composed herself and walked into the dining room with head high and her gaze firmly fixed on Leana and *not* on the dish of beef. Her sister's bemused expression told her all she needed to know. *Canny girl.* Leana had indeed known and pulled a wee joke on her. Not to be cruel, but to be kind. To prove that they were still sisters. And that she still loved her little Rose.

When Leana departed for Troston Hill after dinner, Rose resigned herself to a quiet Friday afternoon of reading while Jamie worked in the pastures with Duncan. She curled up in the window seat of Leana's sewing room, her feet tucked under her, a light plaid wrapped around her shoulders. Though the sky was bright, the wind was brisk as well, seeping through all the cracks in the window. She opened her book with anticipation, having borrowed it from Susanne, who borrowed it from a friend in Dumfries, who'd had it sent to her by a friend from Carlisle. Books were not easily acquired, especially not this one—*The History of Miss Betsy Thoughtless*—written by a woman who was an *actress* of all things. If her father found it, he would insist it be returned to its owner immediately. Rose would make very sure he didn't find it.

She liked Eliza Haywood's story from the first page: *Betsy Thoughtless was the only daughter of a gentleman of good family and fortune.* Rose sighed with immense satisfaction, settling into the cushioned window seat, ignoring the wool that needed carding, the shirts that required mending, and the sight of Annabel picking apples in the orchard. Rose was too busy pretending that instead of being the younger daughter of a bonnet laird with a tight fist, she was Betsy Thoughtless and the world was her oyster.

Hours flew by unaccounted for as the pages turned and Rose surrendered to the story. The sun, warm on her window, grew cool, then disappeared. She tucked a plaid about her and kept reading. Voices came and went in the hall, but no one came looking for her, which suited her perfectly. She was so taken by one line describing Miss Betsy that she read it aloud to enjoy it more fully: "She had yet never seen the man capable of inspiring her with the least emotions of tenderness."

"Had she not?" a male voice responded. "Poor lass."

Startled, Rose looked up from her book to find Jamie standing in the doorway. No longer the ragged shepherd, he was scrubbed and dressed for supper. "Cousin, you might have knocked," she scolded.

"I did. Twice. When you began talking to yourself, I knew it was time to rescue you before Dr. Gilchrist came knocking instead."

Rose shuddered at the thought. "The Dumfries Infirmary may have a room reserved for lunatics, but none of the beds bears my name."

"Not yet." His eyes twinkled. "May I . . . join you?"

She put aside her book with some reluctance and motioned him forward. "Leave the door ajar though, or the servants will blether about improprieties."

"What a shame." The doorway and his grin both

grew wider. "Something improper was quite what I had in mind."

"Jamie!" The man was a shameless flirt. "What *braisant* behavior from a man who once studied for the kirk."

"Right you are, Rose. And I'm about the Lord's work this afternoon." He claimed the small stool where she usually sat to do her carding and pulled it close to her window seat. Too close. He claimed her hand without asking and held it in his, lightly tracing her palm with his forefinger. His expression grew more serious. "I've been praying for you and your sister. I know I've made things . . . difficult. For both of you."

"Thank you," Rose said, not certain what might be expected. She noticed the dark circles under his gray-green eyes, the wan color of his skin. "Poor Jamie. Did you not sleep?" She slipped her hand free to brush some stray hair back from his brow. It felt like spun wool—soft yet thick, the rich brown of polished leather. She tugged on the handful of hair and said in a teasing voice, "This part always fights the rest, doesn't it?"

"Since I was a lad." He lifted his head and swept back the locks of hair himself, touching her fingers in passing. "My mother was ever smoothing it back, tucking it behind my ear, trying to cut it some way that it wouldn't pull free."

Rose smiled at the picture he painted of his child-hood. No wonder women found Jamie so appealing. He was a grown man one moment, a green lad the next, displaying his heart on his sleeve, just as her sister did. He and Leana would surely make a fine match. Odd that her sister saw that but Jamie didn't. Not yet anyway.

She laughed as the strands fell across his brow again. "Your hair has a mind of its own. As do you, James Lachlan McKie."

He chuckled, nodding. "My mother would agree with that."

Rose tucked both hands underneath the plaid to keep them warm and out of harm's way. The lazy patterns he'd been drawing on her palm had made her feel slightly drowsy. Or faint. She wasn't sure which. "Tell me about my Aunt Rowena. Have you written her since coming to Auchengray?"

"Nae. I suppose a good son would do that, wouldn't he?"

She pretended to look stern. "Aye, within an hour of his arrival."

"I regret not doing so. But I did send a letter to your father from New Galloway."

Her cheeks warmed. "Did you?" She kept her tone light and averted her eyes. "If it was delivered, Father didn't mention it."

"Had you seen it, dear Rose, you'd have discovered that my handwriting is nigh to illegible."

"Truly?" She had seen it. And it was.

"My instructors at university complained without ceasing." He placed his hand on top of her hidden ones. Even through the wool, she felt the warmth of his touch. "I know that you write with a womanly script. Perhaps you might pen a letter for me this evening before supper."

Rose brightened at the notion. She enjoyed forming words on paper, creating great, swirling loops with quill and pen. "A pleasant enough diversion. You'll tell me what to write?"

"Every word." His eyes took on a brownie's twinkle. "Most of them about a subject near and dear to you."

Leana.

Rose almost clapped her hands with excitement. *Hoot!* Jamie planned to tell Aunt Rowena all about her niece and what a fine wife Leana would make. *Och!* And she would have the joy of putting those words to paper. "Find my writing desk, Jamie." Rose slipped out her hand and waved it airily toward the door. "It's in my room—well, your room for the moment." She stifled a giggle when he nearly fell over the chair in his haste to stand. "No need to hurry, dear cousin. I'm ever at your disposal."

Thirty-Three

Kind messages that pass from land to land;
Kind letters that betray the heart's deep history,
In which we feel the pressure of a hand—
One touch of fire—and all the rest is mystery!
HENRY WADSWORTH LONGFELLOW

Jamie marveled at her hand moving across the ivory paper with ease, the letters elegantly formed and easily read. "Rosie, you are a wonder."

Her hand paused in midsentence. "I beg you, Cousin. Do not call me *Rosie*."

"Ring-a-ring o' rosies, a pocket full of posies," he taunted her until her scowl chased the old rhyme back to the nursery from whence it came. "Sorry, lass. I didn't know the name displeased you."

She gave him a sidelong glance, her nose still aimed at her writing desk. "The red-headed shepherd you met by Lochend, the one named Rab Murray. Do you remember him?"

He grimaced. "It wasn't exactly a formal meeting, you ken. They found my clothes before they found me."

"Is that so?" Her laugh was sweeter than a well-tuned fiddle. "I'm grateful I didn't come strolling by any sooner than I did, then."

"Not half so grateful as I was." He stroked his jaw. Once again Hugh's razor had done him proud. After spending the afternoon in the sheepfolds, Jamie wasn't about to appear at Rose's side looking like a hairy-chinned goat. "I do think the lad told me his name, now that you say it. Rab Murray, aye?" He peered at her, suddenly suspicious, his smooth chin forgotten. "Don't tell me this Rab fellow has intentions of darkening Auchengray's door, hoping to court you?"

"Not at all," she assured him. "Rab is simply fond of calling me *Rosie* because he knows I don't care for it."

"So you say." He stretched his legs out, cramped from perching on a chair meant for a wee lass, not an overgrown lad. "Sounds to me as if young Rab is in love."

"Och!" She wagged the feather of her quill at him. "He's the same with every lass in the parish, making up some daft name and calling her his bonny dearie."

He hid a smile. "What does he call Leana?"

"Leana?" She looked at him, perplexed.

"You just told me Rab knows every lass in Newabbey, which must include your sister."

"Ah . . . well . . ."

"And does he have names for Eliza and Annabel, your two scullery maids?"

"Nae," she said with a groan, "he does not."

"I'm right then." He stood and yanked on his waistcoat, pretending to be indignant. "Rab Murray has his eye on you. I must see it's plucked out at once."

She slapped her quill down, spattering ink on the tiny desk balanced on her lap. "James McKie! If I didn't know better, I'd think you were jealous of a poor shepherd."

"You'll ken when I'm jealous, lass." He took a step closer, then bent over to blot the stray ink with a bit of rag she kept nearby. He felt her go still and heard the catch in her breath. The same heathery scent that filled his borrowed room now wafted up from her plaid, tickling his nostrils with a heady perfume. "So, lass, are you going to tell me about this *unchancie* turn of events with the Hogmanay Ball, or will the servants' version suffice?"

She tipped her head back to look at him, her expression as smooth as the paper in her writing desk. "My father won't allow Lord Maxwell to host my debut. All else is gossip."

"Very well." He eased back onto the chair. "You are free then for me to court you."

Rose held up a slender forefinger. "Ah, but Leana

is also free. Better suited for you, in my opinion. Older, more settled, and with a much greater talent for managing a household."

"I don't want a housekeeper, lass. I want a wife. To have and to hold."

He'd hoped his honesty would disarm her. Instead, she seemed to draw away from him, fiddling with her pen and ink. "What does my father say to your suit?"

"He's not opposed to it, though he's asked me, in his words, to 'proceed slowly with my daughter.'" He lightly touched her chin and turned it toward him. "Am I going slowly enough to suit you?"

In the candlelight he nearly missed the spark that ignited in her dark eyes until he heard the fiery note in her voice. "You are going the wrong direction entirely, Jamie." She pushed him away, then folded her hands across her lap desk and straightened her back. If she was trying to appear authoritative, the effect was lost on a cushioned window seat, but he wouldn't risk mentioning it.

Instead he swallowed the smile that threatened to take over his face. "The wrong direction, meaning I should be pursuing Leana?"

"Aye, you should. And with great haste before the woman finds another suitor more worthy of her."

"Rose, Rose." He cupped her folded hands with one of his, aware of how rough and callous they felt against her soft skin, more like the hands of a farmer than of a gentleman. "You are too young to be so certain of what others want."

"What I want at the moment is to write a letter to your poor mother and see it posted in the morn's morn. It will take a week to find its way to that lonesome glen of yours. Longer, if the weather does not hold." Freeing her hands from his grasp, she held the paper steady as she dipped her quill in ink and blotted the excess. Her hand hovered over the paper, awaiting his dictation. "I'm ready, Cousin."

He could hold back his smile no longer. Rose resembled her headstrong Aunt Rowena more with every passing minute. "We'll begin in earnest then, as we've little time before the supper bell rings and we must appear at your father's table. Write as follows, if you please."

To Mistress McKie of Glentrool
Friday, 17 October 1788

Dearest Mother,

I regret not having written sooner to let you know of my safe arrival at Auchengray. The journey was difficult and costly. Walloch, unfortunately, is no longer in my possession, nor is the purse containing the silver you generously provided.

Rose lifted her pen off the paper. "Aren't you going to mention your boots?"

"I am not." The other confessions were humbling enough, though he'd neatly avoided using the word *stolen.* His mother would think him timid or care-less, which would not do at all. "I'll compose the let-ter, Rose. Your task is to make it legible."

Her lower lip eased out in a childish pout. "Go on then."

Your brother is well, as are his two daugh-ters. Leana McBride is a woman of twenty years, fair of hair and face, and skilled in the domestic arts. Her sister, Rose, celebrated her fifteenth year on . . .

He paused. "Your birthday, Cousin. When is it?"

"Aren't you the canny fellow, leaving me no choice? I'll include it if I must."

Jamie watched her hand sweep across the page, pleased with himself for gently wresting a bit of per-sonal information from her. *The first of August.* "Shall we continue, Rose?"

Your younger niece is the very picture of you, Mother. Dark hair, skin as smooth as fresh cream, a sweet mouth, and eyes that shine like onyx.

"Good heavens!" Her cheeks now resembled strawberries rather than cream. "You would write such things to your mother?"

"We understand each other, my mother and I. Make no mistake, she'll want every detail." He should have thought of writing the letter days ago.

Rose had agreed not only to listen to every word he said but to put it to paper. The perfect way to woo her. Aye, and woo her well.

Of the two sisters, Rose is the one who has captured my eye and my heart. She is not as quietly compliant as her sister, Leana, but . . .

"Jamie, that is quite enough!" Rose poked him in the chest with the feathery end of her quill. "I'll not have you telling my aunt that I'm . . . difficult."

He arched his left brow, knowing the look gave him a satisfactory air of disdain, and frowned with more disapproval than he felt. "You agreed to be my scribe, Miss McBride, which means you must write whatever I say. Did I use the word *difficult?*"

"It was bound to follow shortly."

"If it does, I trust you'll write it. Now, if you please."

. . . but her good qualities far outweigh her disagreeable traits. She is a gracious host at table, at all times entertaining . . .

"Entertaining? Jamie!"

"You know you are, Rose. Now write."

. . . and a fine conversationalist. Hers is the pen that put these words to paper, so as you can see, she writes with an excellent hand. She reads aloud tolerably well and has a good library of books at her disposal.

Her pen stilled. "Leana is the bluestocking of the family, not I. She's read ten books to my one." Her eyes implored him even more than her words. "Jamie, please say something more about my sister. Your letter speaks too favorably of me and too little of her."

Jamie rubbed his chin, hiding his irritation. Her obstinate ways could grow tiresome if the lass weren't so charming. "I'll mention Leana if you insist."

Leana and Rose are kind toward each other and respect their father, as well they should. Your brother has their future prospects well in hand and assures me he will make the best possible match for each daughter.

"That is all I intend to say of Leana," he said firmly. He cared for his cousin and thought her a wise woman of many talents, but Leana did not make his pulse quicken. The serious Leana literally paled in comparison to her lively younger sister. He would keep telling Rose that until she believed him or married him, whichever came first. "Now, lass, let me finish my letter."

I hope to send news of the banns being read and of wedding preparations made no later than Martinmas. I tarry only to please my future father-in-law, who insists I give his daughter sufficient time to be thoroughly wooed and won.

"I've yet to see any evidence of your wooing either one of us," she said with a petulant sniff.

"Och! Are you deaf as well as blind, Rose? Do you not hear me saying that you are bonny and clever, well schooled and well mannered? That you've captured . . ." He stood and jabbed his finger at the writing paper. "'Captured my eye and my heart.' There it is, in pen and ink. If it's written, it must be true, aye?"

"Aye!" Her sudden smile caught him by surprise. Had her defenses begun to crumble?

Before he could press his case further, the muted sound of the supper bell carried up the stair. "We'll speak more of this in the morning, Rose. Kindly close my letter with these words:"

I trust Evan has accepted the irrevocable decision concerning my inheritance and that Father is in good health and will remain so for many seasons.

Grateful for your prayers and your provision,
    Your son,
    James Lachlan McBride

He adjusted his cravat, absently watching her write the final words, which seemed to take longer than necessary.

"Go on, go on." She waved one hand toward the door and with the other fluttered the paper through the air. "I'll be certain the ink is dry before I seal it for you. Willie or one of the other servants will see it delivered as far as Carlinwark and sent on to the parish kirk at Monnigaff. Your mother will be sure to find it waiting there by Sabbath next."

"Now who's the canny one, to ken where to send it?"

"Oh, I'm as clever as they come, Cousin." She eyed the letter, clearly proud of her work. "Off to supper with you. Tell Father I'll be along in a moment."

"Thank you for writing the letter, Rose." He barely touched her cheek, then strode out the door, closing it softly behind him. With his concerns about the Maxwell offer of a debut put to rest, nothing prevented him from courting her properly, awkward as it was while living under the same roof.

He grinned. *Not awkward, Jamie. Convenient.* The anticipation of the chase and her parting smile warmed him all the way down the stair.

Thirty-Four

That's the nature of women . . .
not to love when we love them,
and to love when we love them not.
MIGUEL DE CERVANTES

Leana stared at the linen shirt in her hands, adjusting her spectacles, then holding the fabric up to the window for a closer inspection. The gray November light revealed neat rows of tiny stitches along the seams, precisely as she'd hoped.

Jamie had promised to wear the new shirt to Dumfries next week for Martinmas, a busy holiday of *feeing* fairs and horse sales, a day when none of the servants worked and the kintra folk flocked to the nearest market town. "You're a dear lass to make another shirt for me, Leana," he'd said on the Tuesday last. "Won't I look the gentleman again?"

She'd blushed beneath his attentive gaze. "Four-and-twenty tailors cannot make a man, Jamie. Nor does a true gentleman need a new sark to prove his worth."

"You're too generous with your praise, Cousin." He'd touched her sleeve, so lightly she'd barely felt the warmth of him through the fabric. But felt it she had. "I'm honored that you would fashion me a second one. Mary, the laundress, absconded with the first one you made me, demanding it be washed. Said it smelled like sheep." When he'd winked at her playfully, Leana wondered if he spoke to Rose with the same ease. "Now I'll look my best for Martinmas. Who knows? Your father may decide to keep me, Leana, rather then let me be fee'd by another farmer in Dumfries."

Shocked, she'd wrinkled her brow and protested, "Father would never allow his nephew to work anywhere but Auchengray!" then realized too late that Jamie had spoken in jest. Naturally he wouldn't be hired away like some of the other farm workers. They collected their pay twice yearly, at Whitsun and Martinmas. Some chose to stay, while others sold their services for the next term at the feeing fair. With a handshake and a dram to seal the bargain, the lads and lasses would pack their few belongings in a *kist* and have the chest delivered to their new home.

No, that would not be Jamie's fate. His days at Auchengray were numbered, but for a very different reason. He'd promised to work for his uncle until Martinmas. Only a week remained before he'd choose his bride and name the wedding day, with an eye to returning to Glentrool with due haste. And with his new wife. Though Rose continued to steer Jamie across Leana's path, he didn't remain there long. Lachlan often spoke of the day Jamie would make his choice, but it seemed he'd already done so.

The faint hope that he might choose her instead hung on a slender thread, thinner than any she might spin on her wheel. But she clung to it nonetheless, knowing that Rose did not love their cousin nor long for marriage.

Leana threaded her needle, then pierced the linen to begin a new seam, sewing by touch more than by sight. Grateful as she was to have Fergus McDougal gone from their doorstep, no other suitors had come to take his place. Nor would they, she feared. More than one neighbor had eyed her askance at kirk the last few Sabbaths. No one openly questioned her virtue, but she dreaded to think what cruel words might be whispered behind cottage doors. Her father had promised to see her wed, but to whom? The man would need to hail from a distant parish, far from the close confines of Newabbey. And he would need to claim her quickly, before time and gossip ruined her altogether.

Jamie fit that description like a hand inside a goatskin glove.

No one in his parish of Monnigaff had ever heard of Leana McBride or how her suitor put her aside to ease his injured pride. Since Jamie's parents wished him to marry one of his cousins, he remained her only hope. No one else could save her.

The truth, Leana. She loved Jamie McKie.

No, *love* was a strong word; *admire* might better suit. To look upon Jamie—covered with a shepherd's muck one moment, then freshly shaven and dressed for Sabbath the next—and know that he was respected in both worlds pleased her greatly. To find him alone and reading by candlelight, as she often did, or to spy him playing Neiveie-Nick-Nack by the hearth with Neda's visiting grandchildren warmed her heart as thoroughly as his fleeting touch warmed her hand.

Even her father had joined in the rhyme as the children gathered around Jamie, trying to guess which of his closed fists held the prized button while he teased them:

Neiveie, Neiveie, nick, nack,
What one will ye take?
The right or the wrong;
Guess or it be long,
Plot away and plan,
I'll cheat ye if I can.

The children adored him, as Jamie did them, mussing their hair and tweaking their noses with gentle affection.

If it was not love she felt for Jamie McKie, it was very close.

To win him, she must woo him. To woo him, she would put to use all the skills the Almighty had bestowed upon her. They were naught but the skills of hearth and home but potent in the hands of a determined woman with no time to waste.

"Leana, do you see the time?" She turned to find her father pointing at the clock on the mantel, his own face dark as midnight. "Enough of your needle and thread. Duncan expected your help with his ledgers at three o'clock. That hour is long past."

She thrust Jamie's half-finished shirt into her sewing basket and placed it a safe distance from the glowing hearth, then slipped her spectacles into the hanging pocket beneath her skirt. "Forgive me, Father. I'll fly up the stair to his quarters at once."

"Stay a moment, Daughter." His features were as somber as his tone. "Though it cost me more silver than I could afford, the matter with Mr. McDougal is resolved. The taint of it, unfortunately, remains. We must arrange for another suitor before . . . ah, before another season passes. Is your heart still set on your cousin Jamie?"

She blanched. Had her methods been so *kenspeckle?* "Wh-why do you ask, when you know it is Rose he favors?"

"What a lad says and what he knows to be true are oft at odds." He lifted his gaze to the broad oak beam above his head. "Your sister is a rosebud, tightly wrapped. But you are a fragrant bloom, ready to be snipped from the stem." His gaze dropped to meet hers. "Jamie must start a family. And you, lass, are ready to be a mother."

The frankness of his speech stunned her. "I . . . am?"

"Aye, and Jamie knows it well. Rose may catch his eye, but you, Leana, will catch the man."

She shook her head, bewildered by his confidence. "How can you be certain?"

Her father, who seldom smiled, now wore a sly grin. "Fathers ken more than their daughters credit them. And on the subject of credits and debits, you've kept poor Duncan waiting long enough." He stepped aside and nodded toward the doorway. "Martinmas approaches, with rents to be collected and bills to be paid. See that his ledgers are in order. Your eyes may be weak, but they recognize a tidy row of numbers well enough."

Leana started for the hall, then could not stop herself. "What of Jamie?"

"I'll do what I can to persuade him, lass." The grin disappeared. "But you must do your part to draw his attention away from your sister. You are older and wiser, Leana. Do what you will, and do it quickly."

She hastened up the stair, wondering what else she might do to please her cousin. Of late she had taken more time than usual brushing and braiding her hair. She cleaned her teeth with apple skins to sweeten her breath and kept a lemon in her room to scrub her hands free of vegetable stains. Still Jamie's eyes lingered on the fairer Rose.

Leana had helped Neda bake his favorite potato scones and saw that he was served a jugged hare for dinner Thursday last. Though he praised her cooking, he did not speak of her pleasing manner. Yet Rose beguiled him daily.

One rainy afternoon Duncan had filled Leana's head with the particulars of shepherding so she might impress Jamie with her knowledge of his favorite subject. Rose's easy handling of the ewes impressed their cousin more.

If she thought her sister loved Jamie—loved him as she loved him—Leana would end her efforts at once. "I am too young for love," Rose had reminded her Friday last. "And much too young to marry. Jamie is yours, dear sister." If only that were true!

Reaching the third story where the house servants slept beneath the eaves, Leana hurried down the long, narrow hall that led to Duncan's quarters. He and Neda shared two private rooms—one for working, one for sleeping—each with its own door. She knocked on the one for his study and listened for his greeting.

"Enter," he groaned, then flung open the door. His eyes were bleary and bloodshot, his face haggard. "Ye've come none too soon, lass. I canna make a bit o' sense of yer faither's scribbling."

"Let me see what I can do," she said, patting his arm. "Have Willie or one of the others bring us a pot of tea and a plate of gingerbread. Empty stomachs and full ledgers are poor companions." He disappeared down the hall to find a willing pair of hands, while she dragged the overseer's small desk closer to the window. Twilight had already fallen. The hills would be shrouded in black within the hour. She lit two more candles, brightening the room considerably, though she knew Duncan would fuss at her spendrif ways.

The minute he returned he extinguished one with a pinch of his fingers. "The other will do, lass. Now to the business at hand." They bent their heads over the ledger, which bulged with receipts. His blunt, ruddy finger followed her tapered, pale one up and down the columns of numbers. Soon they were both shaking their heads at the illegible entries Mr. McBride had insisted on making himself.

"That's a four," she murmured, taking a sip of tea so hot it nearly singed her mouth. "Mmm. And that's a three, but it could be an eight."

Duncan dropped his head in his hands. "Aye, or a two or a nine."

"Nae, I'm sure it's a three."

"What a curious conversation I've stumbled upon." Jamie stood in the open doorway, his sullied shirt torn and his breeches reeking of sheep. "My uncle said I would find you here."

Leana wet her lips, still stinging from the tea. "Find whom?"

His eyes bored into hers. "You."

The slender thread of hope around her heart drew tighter. He'd come looking for her—*her,* not her sister.

Duncan's shaggy head shook like one of his collies. "Ye canna have her, lad. She's mine, at least until Martinmas."

"What is it the shepherds say? 'Nine free nichts 'til Martinmas, and soon they'll wear awa.'"

"Yer addition is faulty, lad. 'Tis not nine days left,

but eight. Seven, when ye lift yer head off the pillow on the morn's morn." Duncan regarded him with a curious eye. "*Whatsomever* do ye need with Miss Leana?"

Jamie held up a letter. "I was hoping she might explain this. In private, if you'll allow us a few minutes, Duncan."

"Aye, take yer time. I've meikle to do sorting through this sorry collection of receipts." The overseer gathered a stack of papers and retreated to his bedroom. Leana watched him disappear, taking the cordial atmosphere in the room with him.

She turned to her cousin, who regarded her with something like suspicion. "How . . . how can I explain something I've not seen before, Jamie?"

"See it now then." He handed her the letter, a single page on heavy paper. It was from his mother, her words sweeping across the page in dramatic swirls of ink, not unlike Rose's handwriting. The usual maternal comments and cautions were included, but the last paragraph gave her pause.

> Jamie, I understand your difficulty in choosing which one of your cousins to marry. I am certain they are both good and worthy young women, but perhaps the older one is the better choice, as you say. Trust my brother Lachlan's wisdom and direction in this matter.

Leana handed back the letter without a word. Dare she hope? Was it possible Jamie truly thought her the better choice? "Jamie, I . . . don't understand."

"Nor do I." His tone was not unkind, but it was firm. "I dictated a letter, which Rose dutifully wrote for me and sent on its way a fortnight ago. I must confess, though I mentioned both of you and described your many fine qualities, Leana, I made my preference . . . ah, that is to say . . ."

The thread of hope broke in two. "You told her that you favored Rose."

"Aye." His sigh was tinged with regret. "I did, lass. However, it appears my mother received rather a different message than the one I wrote. A message I thought you might explain."

"Were you thinking I sent her a separate letter of my own?"

"Leana, I don't know what to think." He brushed back an unruly lock of hair from his brow. "I thought I'd stated my words quite clearly to Rose."

"I'm sure you did, Cousin." It was obvious her sister had written whatever she pleased, certain Jamie would trust her. *Naughty Rose.* Though she couldn't bear to tattle on her sibling, Leana gently guided Jamie toward the truth. "Did you read the letter before it was sealed?"

"Ah . . . no." His brow drew into a knot. "I didn't think it necessary." He turned toward the door, shaking his head. "What possessed the girl to do such a thing?"

"She's young, Cousin. Impulsive. But then you know that and think it charming, I'm sure."

"Charming," he repeated, not meeting her gaze. "I've offended you, Leana, and pray you'll forgive me." He bowed and was gone.

Not offended, Cousin. Crushed. She heard his footsteps fade down the stair, her stubborn heart in close pursuit. Aunt Rowena seemed willing to claim her, and Lachlan McBride was more than willing to give her away. Only Jamie remained to be convinced.

Eight days to Martinmas. Eight days to change Jamie's mind.

Thirty-Five

Oh, father's gone to market-town,
he was up before the day,
And Jamie's after robins,
and the man is making hay.
<small>RICHARD WATSON GILDER</small>

Jamie, do you mind?" Rose tugged on her skirts. Her cousin had managed to trap the fabric beneath him as they sat side by side on the two-wheeled chaise. "A bit more room, if you please."

"A wee bit." He moved just far enough to free her dress, secretly glad to have his beloved Rose so near. "We've miles to go, lass, and none of them smooth riding." He shook the reins, urging the plodding horse to lift its feet. "Have you no more smeddum than that?" Jamie demanded. The creature ignored him and continued at the same sluggish pace, his gray coat blending with the slate gray sky. The morning was dry, and that was blessing enough. Dumfries was ten miles by way of Newabbey but only nine if they'd gone west past Maxwell Park. Rose would not hear of taking the shorter, broader route. "Heaven forbid I should see Lord or Lady Maxwell after my father's rude refusal of their generosity." Jamie said nothing. Though he would never confess it to Rose, he was grateful that his uncle had intervened.

Most of the Auchengray household had headed north for Dumfries that morning. Duncan and Uncle Lachlan had departed for the royal burgh well before dawn, riding on horseback. The servants followed on foot, their spirits high despite the cold November air seeping through their garments. Before leaving, Lachlan had opened his thrifite to pay them their proper wages for the six-month term past: four guineas for the plowman, two for the dairymaid, three each for the housemaids, four for the male servants. Every shilling that passed through his fingers made Lachlan McBride groan as though the coins were minted from his own hide. Leana's careful preparation of his ledgers had made her father's task an easier one, though Jamie noticed she'd not been thanked, at least not in his presence.

"I hope Leana is feeling better," Rose murmured. Her sister had planned to join them, riding sidesaddle atop old Bess, but took ill soon after rising.

"Go on without me," Leana had insisted, her face paler than ever, her lips dry and cracked. "Willie can ride behind you as an escort. It's best I stay, with so many gone to the feeing fair." Work was not customary on Martinmas—no spinning or weaving, no miller grinding corn. Out of necessity the cows were milked and the horses fed by hands in a hurry to leave their labors behind for the day. Ill or not, Leana would no doubt be pressed into service.

Jamie reined in the horse to allow a cartful of kintra folk bound for Dumfries to pass, then turned their chaise onto the main road north. "Neda will see after your sister," he said, wanting to put Rose's mind at ease. The housekeeper was one of the few servants who remained behind to prepare the feast of the day—boiled haggis with blood pudding—so Lachlan and the others would return home to a hot supper. "How does Neda season her haggis?" he asked, knowing each household prepared the dish to its own liking. At Glentrool, Aubert favored parsley and lemon sprinkled over the chopped sheep's pluck—heart, liver, lungs, and windpipe—mixed with beef suet, onions, and oatmeal.

"Cayenne pepper." Rose wrinkled her nose. "Too much of it, if you ask me. But her black pudding is the best in the parish." She sighed, then folded her arms across her waist. "Please let us speak of something else, or my stomach will groan with anticipation."

They chatted about the late autumn air, which was too cold to be pleasant, the sky, which was too bleak to be interesting, and the farmlands, which were markedly different on either side of the dirt road. A flat *carse* stretched to the east, hinting at the marshy shores of the River Nith beyond it. To the west, the land sloped upward to hills once covered with trees. Cut down for shipbuilding in centuries past and never replenished, Rose explained.

"The Keswicks' country house sits on the crest of that hill." Rose stared wistfully up the winding drive. "A beauty, it is. Three stories tall with three handsome bay windows."

"You've visited the place?"

"A McBride call on a Keswick?" She rolled her eyes. "You've much to learn of east Galloway society, Jamie. I've not been formally invited, though I must confess I strolled along the edges of the park once and admired the view."

Jamie kept his eye on the road. "You might enjoy the view from Glentrool as well." He'd already made the mistake of sounding too eager with Rose and had no intentions of doing so now.

"But isn't your estate at the bottom of a hill?"

"The Fell of Eschoncan is no mere hill, Rose. It rises eight hundred feet behind the property." He touched the whip to the horse's back to hide his irritation. "And though we're situated in a glen, the view is still bonny. The loch, the hills—"

"We have Lochend and Criffell," she countered, slapping him with her braid as she turned her head smartly to the right. "Loch and hill enough for my eyes."

Jamie ignored her childish rebuff, reminding himself that she was fifteen. She would grow to love

Glentrool, even as he hoped she might grow to love him. Eventually. Her reticence confused him, angered him at times. "Too young," she said. "Too soon," she insisted. "Not ready," she complained.

He had not told her—might never tell her—that for him, marrying a McBride sister was not a choice but an expectation. His only choice was which sister. And that decision was made weeks ago. Time had run out for them both. Today would be the day. If Rose refused him, Lachlan would force her to marry him. A grim way to begin a life together. But it was Rose whom he loved. And Rose he would marry.

They rode in silence for another mile or so, until the sharp *tik tik* of two robins caught their attention. Staking out their territories, the male and female birds scolded one another, their red breasts puffed out like angry shields as they flew about, the male claiming the female's land, then flying away to guard his own. "By midwinter those two will pair off," Jamie explained. "They'll share the same home come spring."

Rose snorted. "You made up every word of that, Jamie McKie!"

"Not at all, lass. That sort of fighting and wooing is peculiar to robins."

"Aye, and cousins." She swatted him with her braid, this time on purpose. "Jamie, tell me truly: Why won't you marry my sister?"

"Because I don't love her, Rose." The chaise jostled over a rocky patch of road, then the springs settled into a steady rhythm again.

"Why, Jamie?"

He looked down at her with an even gaze. "You know why."

"Because you love me. At least you say that you do." Rose bit her lip, as though chewing on his words "How can you be so certain?"

"I was drawn to you from the first day we met. Surely you noticed."

She shrugged. "I pretended not to."

"Aye, you did. Even so, that attraction soon became affection." In the distance a kirk bell rang the hour. "That affection has grown to love, now that I know you better."

"And what do you know, Cousin, after a month at Auchengray?"

Patiently he tallied her best qualities. "You are lively and imaginative, enthusiastic and spontaneous—"

"What man cares about *those* sort of things?" she teased him.

"This man." Rose seemed to require an accounting of her virtues on a weekly basis, as though she doubted their existence, perhaps because her father seldom spoke a kind word about her in her presence. Her need for praise touched him. If it earned her love, Jamie would tell her what she needed to hear a thousand times. He finished naming her admirable qualities, intentionally saving her beauty for last. "So. Will that keep a smile about your face for an hour or two, lass?"

She smiled and closed her eyes, as though she'd taken the last bite of a fine meal. "'Twill last an entire day, Jamie."

"Are you believing it then?"

One dark eye slowly opened. "Aye, I'm beginning to."

They rode on, their silence less strained, more companionable. Because they sat so close in the narrow chaise, a rough section of road often threw them against each other, sending them scurrying to right themselves amid much apologizing and smoothing of feathers. It was more embarrassing than enjoyable, Jamie decided, as he gazed down the lane toward the outskirts of Dumfries. Already the foot traffic on the main road had increased. Families and their servants walked side by side, near equals for the day as debts were paid and a new term of service began.

The road turned sharply north to run parallel with the River Nith. "This is Troquire," Rose informed him, perched on the edge of her seat, her hands gripping the leather upholstery. "It's the last parish before we cross over the bridge to Dumfries. Is Willie still behind us?"

Jamie glanced over his shoulder. "Aye." He waved at the servant, urging him to draw closer. Willie's duty for the day was to mind the chaise and horse by the wayside while they continued on foot into the town proper. The Troquire kirk and nearby manse, with its wide, grassy glebe, seemed the most convenient spot. Jamie chose a patch of uncultivated ground, handed the reins to Willie as he stepped down, then turned to help Rose, who grasped her skirts and hopped to the ground without his assistance.

"Here at last!" Her eyes shone with a contagious excitement. "Well done, Willie. Neda tucked some hard cheese and bannocks and a slice of mutton behind the seat of the chaise for you." She touched the servant's arm. "You'll not mind being here by yourself?"

"Hardly by meself, lass." He nodded at the glebe, where other wheeled carts were starting to gather. "I'll have plenty o' company. Go on with ye now, and find yer faither. He promised to be watchin' for ye round the Midsteeple." Willie fixed a stern gaze on Jamie. "Sir, I'll thank ye to keep Miss McBride close by yer side, 'specially in the village of Brigend. 'Tis a lawless place, full o' *gaberlunzies* lookin' to steal yer purse." His eyes shifted toward Rose. "Or worse."

Jamie cupped his hand around Rose's elbow. "I'll see that she's properly looked after, Willie. We'll return by three, well before the gloaming." They headed north on the kirk street, following the flow of human traffic. Well-built homes on substantial lands soon gave way to smaller farmhouses, then mean cottages crowded closer to the street, until the rough sounds and pungent smells of Brigend enveloped them.

Jamie's grip on Rose's elbow tightened when they were nearly knocked off their feet by peasant children scurrying past with sticks in hand, swatting at a ball. Merchants spilled into the street with their wares—bakers and tailors, coopers and smiths, clog makers and rope makers—while less industrious men lurked in doorways, eying the crowd for easy marks. Jamie did not intend to be one of them. Lachlan had provided a dirk for his boot and a paltry amount of coin, well hidden beneath his waistcoat. Rose had no reticule to tempt the riffraff, only her bonny self, which was temptation enough. Jamie lifted his chin and squared his shoulders, challenging any passerby who stared too intently at Rose, threatening them with a piercing gaze of his own.

She patted his arm and pointed to a flesher arranging slabs of meat. "Duncan will stop there on the way home and collect our *mart.*"

Jamie nodded; his mother would be purchasing the same today in Monnigaff. An ox, butchered and salted on Martinmas, kept a family fed all through the harsh winter. The mob swelled as the street beneath them converged with the main road into Dumfries, carrying them past the old Brig House Inn and across the red freestone span with its graceful arches. "Devorgilla's Bridge," Rose said, raising her voice above the din.

"The same woman buried at Sweetheart Abbey?"

She glanced up at him with a look of surprise. "Listen to you, Jamie McKie! Already knowing our local history."

He smiled, glad he'd pleased her, then surveyed the royal burgh situated at the other end of the bridge. To their right stretched the Whitesands of Dumfries, where hundreds of black cattle and horses were to be sold.

Rose waved a hand in the same direction. "The ground is dry today, but when the river is in spate, the water floods the Whitesands and travels up past the Coach and Horses Inn halfway to the High Street. I can't imagine how the townsfolk can bear having water up to their windows."

Jamie glanced up the narrow alley, then turned for a final look at the many horses already assembled for market day. A promising collection of bays, chestnuts, and piebalds whinnied and stamped the ground, steaming the frigid air around them. All at once the guilt of losing Walloch to a band of brigands on the Edinburgh road rose in his throat like bile. He would not likely ride so fine a horse again. Nonetheless, perhaps another would do for the time being. A gentleman needed his own mount. It was a matter of pride and of practicality. Jamie touched his waistcoat, feeling the lump of coins beneath it. Not nearly enough for a horse. Nor could he bring himself to borrow such a sum from Lachlan.

He groaned and muttered a sad reminder. "A man without silver goes fast through the market."

"And did your mind ride off without you?"

He turned and discovered Rose standing in front of him, hands on hips, eyes narrowed. "Beg pardon, lass. I was distracted by—"

"The horses, as anyone with eyes can see." She patted his cheek—affectionately, he thought—then turned to slide her hand in the crook of his elbow as they resumed walking. "Is it poor Walloch you're thinking of?"

He stopped again and gazed down at her, grateful she understood. "Aye, it is. His coat was black. Dark and gleaming as your hair—"

"Like that one?" She pointed toward a riderless horse some distance ahead.

Jamie followed her gaze, then nodded. "Aye, very much like . . . in truth, quite exactly . . ." He measured the mount with his eyes, noted the long mane and tail, the peculiar gait. "Forgive me, lass, but I . . . I need to be sure." He pulled her along, his heart beating like a drum. The nearer they came, the more Jamie was convinced the horse was Walloch. Hadn't he mounted the beast every day for half a dozen years?

When he caught a brief glimpse of the man leading the horse, his blood froze.

A broad back. And bright red hair. *Evan.*

Thirty-Six

There is no mistake; there has been no mistake;
and there shall be no mistake.
ARTHUR WELLESLEY, DUKE OF WELLINGTON

Surely it isn't Walloch!" Rose struggled to keep up
with Jamie as he lengthened his stride in pursuit of
his horse. His *stolen* horse. *The very idea!* Her
pulse quickened along with her pace. "Might you be
mistaken?"

"No mistake, Rose," he shouted over his shoulder. "It's Walloch." Jamie plunged them both into the
teeming horde on High Street. He dodged barefoot
servants and gentlemen in silk hats, ox-drawn carts
full of whisky barrels, and Gypsies with heather

creels strapped on their backs, ignoring them all in his singular pursuit of the gelding not far ahead. "Faster, lass!"

She clung to his hand as they veered south on the High Street, narrowing the distance between them and the animal in question. A perfectly ordinary black horse, from her viewpoint, with a too long tail. He was an impressive size though. Broad enough to conceal the man holding the reins. She caught a glimpse of bright red hair before a throng of high-spirited peasants blocked her view. The Midsteeple of Dumfries, though, was easily seen looming before them. A tall, square building that served as the burgh's courthouse, it was topped with a pointed cupola and wrapped in a wrought-iron rail.

Rose quickly scanned the crowd at the base of the Midsteeple, looking for her father, knowing he would be watching for her. Intent on her search, she hardly noticed the man careening toward her with an armful of kindling until he barreled into her, knocking her forward. "Oh!" She stumbled across the flagstones, grasping wildly for Jamie's coat to keep from falling and being trampled. "Jamie, wait!"

He turned to catch her and pulled her to her feet, his strong hands gripping her arms.

Less than a stone's throw away, the black horse came to a halt. "Come, lass," Jamie muttered. "I think I know this blackguard who stole my gelding."

The stranger holding Walloch's reins turned toward them, his face a dark scowl. Rose noticed only that he had broad shoulders, thick arms, and bright red hair. But Jamie's face blanched for a moment before his color returned and he managed to speak.

"That horse, sir, is stolen property."

The man's jaw hardened. "It was not stolen by me. I bought it with good silver. An hour ago from a man down on the Whitesands."

"So you say." Jamie's eyes narrowed. Somewhere in those green depths he was weighing whether or not to believe the man.

Rose didn't know what to believe. She only knew that Jamie frightened her almost as much as the stranger did.

Jamie slowly released his grip on her hand. "Go find your father, Rose. And Duncan."

"Will you be—"

"Right here," he assured her. "Go."

She staggered through the crowd, blinking back tears, gasping each time she saw a man with a dark gray coat like her father's or a woolen bonnet like the one Duncan wore. A glance back at the two men gave her no comfort. Though they hadn't resorted to blows yet, their necks were thrust out, and the black horse strained at his halter. She aimed her sights toward the Midsteeple area and at last spied the men lingering by the outer steps to the second floor. "Father! Duncan!"

They turned, taking awhile to find her with their eyes and even longer to make their way across the sea of people.

"Hurry!" She waved impatiently at them. "Come, Jamie needs you!"

The moment she could snag the men's sleeves, she tugged hard, pulling them back the way she'd come, breathlessly trying to explain what she could. "Jamie's found his horse."

"The stolen one?"

"Aye, Father. A gelding named Walloch."

"*Walloch?*" Duncan chuckled. "Ye mean to tell me the horse dances?"

"*Och!* Duncan, we've no time for foolishness. Pick up your feet."

The three of them fought their way across the High Street, keeping the horse in view even when the brothers couldn't be seen among the masses. "Jamie!" she called, certain he could hear her, relieved when he poked his head above the crowd and signaled to them.

Moments later the Auchengray party reached Jamie's side. His face still had the look of a dark storm cloud, but his voice was surprisingly even.

"Uncle, come see what we've found in the streets of Dumfries."

"Was this the horse stolen from you on the Edinburgh road?" Lachlan angled his head to look over the gelding. "A worthy animal." Lachlan gathered the reins in his hands, then pressed them into Jamie's palm. "How thoughtful of this gentleman to return your mount to you."

"*Return* him?" The veins in the man's neck turned an ugly purple. "I *bought* the horse, sir, at Whitesands. With my own coin."

Lachlan appraised him, much as he had the horse. "Did you really, good fellow? And if I asked the horse seller at Whitesands, he would tell me the same?"

"He would, sir." The man glared at Jamie. "Though this man charged me with thievery before he looked me in the eye."

Jamie's face grew red. "I thought you were . . . someone else."

"But still a thief," the man growled.

Jamie dipped his chin. "If I wronged you, sir, I do apologize."

"There you have it," Lachlan said loudly, as if to bring things to a close. "How much did you pay for the gelding?" The red-haired man begrudgingly told him. "Then it seems I'm going to purchase a butchered ox for Martinmas and a saddle horse as well." Lachlan smiled and held out his hand, palm up. "Duncan, my purse." Without ceremony her father dropped the stated amount into the man's waiting hand, down to the last shilling.

Rose had never seen her father spend money so effortlessly, with nary a wrinkle on his brow. He'd bought Jamie his own horse, of all things. Whatever had gotten into him?

Lachlan held out his arms. "Come, family. We've servants to hire and others to bid farewell. Good day to you, sir."

Jamie shook his head, the color in his face starting to fade. "Uncle Lachlan, I hardly know what to say."

"My nephew speechless?" Lachlan placed a hand on each of their elbows. "No more likely than my Rose to be caught without a word on her lips."

"But Walloch—"

"Was a bargain, Jamie. Auchengray can always use another horse." Lachlan glanced at the animal, his gaze no longer meeting Jamie's. "Feel free to ride him home if you like. Though the animal belongs to me now, of course."

Rose saw Jamie stiffen ever so slightly before he answered. "Of course."

Lachlan squeezed their elbows, then released them. "Duncan, we'll leave you to your duties. See that you fee only those willing to work for their wages." The overseer tipped his cap, then disappeared into the crowd while Lachlan rubbed his hands together. "What do you say, children? Shall we find some dinner?"

He craned up and down the High Street, its *closes* and vennels harboring half a dozen public establishments, their doors propped open to invite paying customers. "This way," he finally said and aimed them toward the Globe. "Mistress Hyslop will have just the thing, I'll wager. A bite to hold us until Neda's haggis."

Rose held her skirts above the filthy street, hurrying to keep in step, bewildered by her father's jovial demeanor. Something about it made her uneasy. And the silver he'd spent so easily. *Och!* That was not the Lachlan McBride she had known since the first day she opened her eyes. Whatever devious sort of stew he was brewing, she prayed she would not be forced to dine upon it.

When they reached their destination, Jamie entrusted Walloch to the stable lad on the premises, then returned to her side. "I paid him most of the coin in my purse for Walloch's safekeeping." He smiled down at her. "I don't want our time together to be disrupted."

Before she could ask Jamie what he meant, or why it mattered, Lachlan guided them through the Globe's open door. A steep, narrow stair rose before them. Two sizable rooms to the left were spilling over with patrons and ale. To the right she noticed a cozy alcove with two tables and a noisy gathering room beyond it with a roaring hearth.

Lachlan addressed the proprietor with some familiarity since the man hailed from Newabbey parish. "Mr. Hyslop, we have need of your snuggery." He pointed to the two vacant tables in the alcove. "Feed and water us if you will, sir, for we've had a de'il of a morning." They were promptly seated and served steaming bowls of Scotch broth, a McBride favorite. "Not horn spoons, ye ken, but silver." Her father winked, proud of finding them a proper meal on a busy day in Dumfries. Rose couldn't remember when she'd seen the man so amenable. She could hardly taste the broth in her bowl for worrying what his behavior might mean.

The men ate and drank their fill, then Lachlan called on a waiter to clear the table. "Kindly provide as much privacy as these walls will allow, man." In short order they were closed in with both doors to the adjoining rooms shut tight.

Rose touched her linen napkin to her lips, then exchanged glances with Jamie. Had he noticed the change in her father? Lachlan was ebullient, almost giddy. It made her nervous to watch him, fussing with his cravat, yanking on his cuffs, fiddling with his waistcoat buttons. "Father, have you news for us? You seem—"

"Grateful," he interjected. "Grateful is what I am. I have a nephew who understands the meaning of hard work and displays a keen eye for breeding ewes." Lachlan folded his hands in his lap, regarding them both with a smile of satisfaction. "You've done a great service to Auchengray this past month, Jamie."

Jamie acknowledged him with a nod, though his eyes looked wary. "A month exactly, come the morn's morn."

"Been counting the days, have you, until you're free of your obligation to me?"

"Nae, Uncle." Jamie dropped his hands into his lap as well, though Rose noticed him folding and unfolding them. "I have wondered, though, what my efforts might be worth to you."

"Aye, well, no point to hard labor without earning an honest wage. How is it you'd like to be paid, Jamie?" Lachlan's eyes twinkled. *Twinkled!* Rose had never seen the likes of it.

Jamie cleared his throat, and his hands stilled. "If you recall, the past month was meant to give me time to . . . ah, woo a certain daughter of yours." Beneath the table his knee lightly pressed against hers, startling her.

Lachlan's smile was too broad to be believed. "Which daughter might that be?"

"This daughter, sir." Jamie looked down at her,

even though she would not meet his gaze. "I have wooed your fair Rose, with her raven hair and ivory skin, though it's a mite pink at the moment."

She wet her lips, bone dry with fear, but no words would come.

"Tell me, Daughter, what you think of this braw nephew of mine?" Both men looked at her with anticipation in their eyes. Her father's gray ones masked something else she couldn't decipher. Jamie's green ones shone with a boundless love she might never match, no matter how she tried.

"Come now," her father prompted. "You've kept the man waiting long enough."

"What do I think of him, you say?" She gulped, hoping her face would not give her away. "He is everything good and fine and strong and kind."

Jamie bent his head over hers. "Then say you'll marry me, lass."

Marry? Not me, Jamie. Leana!

He cupped her cheek, gazing at her with sheer adoration. "I've worked a long month for this moment. But I've waited a lifetime for you."

"Nae, Jamie." *Not for me.* Overwhelmed, she pushed away his hand and dropped her chin, unable to speak another word without choking on it. It was Leana who loved him. Why hadn't he listened? *Why hadn't he listened?*

"Rose? What are you saying, lass?" Jamie leaned closer, his voice low and strained. "Please, Rose. Please look at me."

She lifted her head and looked at her father

instead. His face was a mask. Even before she asked, she knew the answer. "Do I have a choice?"

Jamie's eyes widened with pain. "A . . . choice? Would you choose another, Rose?"

"Nae, she would not." Lachlan answered for her. "She has chosen you."

The word came out on a sob. *"Father!"*

"Aye, it is well that you remember I'm your father, which means that I choose whom you will marry." He did not raise his voice, but he did raise one hand, as though to stop any protest that might rise to her lips. "What you do not know, lass—a fact which Jamie has been loath to tell you—is that he *must* marry you. Or he must marry Leana. Those are his only two choices, by his parents' design. And he has chosen you. Be grateful."

"Grateful?" She could not look at the hurt in Jamie's eyes. *Not hurt. Devastation.* "Aye, Father, I am grateful to be loved by a good man. But I'm too young. I'm not . . . ready."

"Och!" Lachlan growled like a collie cornering a sheep. "No woman is ready. Nor is any man. You simply make your vows and you keep them. Jamie loves you and has chosen you, so the matter is decided. What say you, Rose? You will have him?"

"Aye, Father," she whispered, looking down at her hands clasped tightly in her lap. "I will have Jamie, if Jamie will have me." It was the most she could say and remain honest before God. The rest would have to follow.

"And you will learn to love him?"

"Aye," she said faintly. *Forgive me, Leana.* "I will try."

"Will that do, Jamie? Is her promise enough?"

"Nae." His voice was sharp as broken glass. "But it is a beginning."

"Guid." Her father nodded rather abruptly. "To business then. What do you offer for your young bride, James Lachlan McKie?"

Jamie was nonplussed. "Ah . . . offer?"

"You've lands and sheep coming to you, lad. Someday. But for the moment, have you silver to seal the betrothal?"

"Uncle, you know the only silver I have in my pockets is yours."

"Hmmm." Lachlan tapped his finger beside his brow. "And the horse you'll ride home is mine as well. Still, better you than some other man, eh? I've a decent *tocher* set aside for my daughter, a suitable sum for one so young, and the provision of a lady's maid. Now what can you give me in return for my blessing on your marriage?"

Rose stole a glance at him, wondering what he might offer. Perhaps Jamie had nothing to give. Perhaps it would all end here and now, and she would be free.

Jamie's gaze darted about as though looking for a solution on the paneled walls. Finally his gaze settled on her. "I might . . . well, I could *work* for your younger daughter, sir."

Work. At Auchengray. At least she would still be home; she would still have Leana by her side. She clutched her skirt in her hands. *Say yes, Father.*

"I'd be willing to work hard, sir, and do anything Duncan asks of me. Until . . . until Hogmanay? Would that suit?"

Lachlan bobbed his head slowly, counting on his fingers. "Seven weeks then. In truth, seven months would be better." Her father's laugh, seldom heard at Auchengray, echoed about the snuggery walls. "Seven years would be better still."

"Until Hogmanay," Jamie said firmly. "Might I marry Rose then?"

"You might."

Thirty-Seven

But I love you, sir;
And when a woman says she loves a man,
The man must hear her, though he love her not.
ELIZABETH BARRETT BROWNING

Leana lifted three slender brown bottles of syrup from her wooden medicine box in search of something that might bring her relief. *Rose hips.* Aye, that could ease the congestion in her chest. *Elderflower.* Her sore throat might be grateful for its soothing touch. *Heartsease.* Rest would come more easily if her cough abated. She held the bottles closer to the flickering taper on her bedside table, musing over her choices, until she finally uncorked each one in turn and measured out generous teaspoons of the honey-drenched syrups, swallowing all three with a prayer.

She hadn't been truly sick for several seasons, and it frightened her. Common colds had an unpleasant habit of developing into pneumonia, which had claimed her childhood friend, Janet Crosbie, last November. Leana had tended to Janet, as had old Mistress Bell and the parish minister, desperately turning the pages of *Primitive Physic, or an Easy and Natural Method of Curing Most Diseases,* all for naught. Janet's body was carried to the kirkyard soon after Martinmas. It made Newabbey folks nervous to watch a healthy lass of eighteen succumb so quickly. The neighborhood had kept a constant vigil for pneumonia's deadly symptoms ever since.

As a precaution Neda had spent the day filling Leana with hot tea, all the while giving orders to Annabel, who'd stayed behind to help with the Martinmas feast. Leana had remained abed with the family Bible by her side to comfort her all through the long and lonely day. Now that the gloaming had nearly faded to black, the household would soon return from Dumfries, and Jamie with them.

Dear Jamie.

Leana pressed the cork stoppers back in place, then returned the three bottles to her medicine box, wishing another syrup among them might relieve the pain that ailed her most. "No herb will cure love," she reminded herself with a weary sigh that set her to coughing once more. The deep, painful coughs bent her in two. It was several minutes before her chest settled and her breathing became more even. Still holding the box in her lap, she dropped back onto her pillows, exhausted. No autumn in memory had ever worn her down like this one.

The parish gossips, scattering lies like falling leaves, had busied themselves spreading the news of Fergus McDougal's refusal to marry her. Remnants of their stories were whispered in her ear each Sabbath by well-meaning friends. None of the far-fetched tales resembled the truth. Some said she'd slipped a sprig of blackthorn in Mr. McDougal's pocket, hoping he'd prick his finger on its wicked spines. Another insisted Leana had refused to bear him children, since he already had an unruly brood of his own. The most common fabrication was that something untoward had happened in the orchard with her cousin and she was no longer worthy of the bonnet laird or anyone who called himself a gentleman.

Though such blether did not hurt her feelings, it had mortally wounded her marriage prospects. Since All Souls Day, her father had discreetly inquired of several more eligible gentlemen in the parish and had been soundly turned down. Jamie was her only chance and her heart's desire. He'd promised to remain at Auchengray until Martinmas, and that dreaded day was here. Had he made his final choice of a wife? Would her hopes, which had waxed and waned since the moment he'd arrived, come to naught?

Spurred on by mounting desperation, she'd spent the last week doubling her efforts to catch

Jamie's eye. Elaborate meals, flattering dresses, meaningful glances, ballads sung round the hearth—none of them seemed to draw his attention away from Rose for longer than a minute. "How kind of you, Leana," he would murmur, then go on as before. Was he daft not to see what she was trying to say? Was she more so, wearing her heart boldly on her sleeve?

From outside the window came the merry clatter of horse and carriage. *Jamie!*

Leana lifted her head from the pillow, feeling her spirits lift as well. Her handsome cousin had arrived, and her father and sister with him. They would be looking in on her any moment. She must appear well, or she'd scare them senseless. Her medicine box, which Duncan had fashioned from hazel branches, needed to be hidden, lest they fear the worst. She gripped the hazel handle, then nearly let it slip from her hands when an old wives' tale came to mind: hazel wood was unlucky. When a woman wished to put aside her beloved, a twig of hazel made her heartless wishes known without a word.

Fear not, Jamie. She could never be so cruel.

Leana threw back the covers, then padded across the room and slid the box behind the stack of books she'd borrowed from a neighbor's library for her winter reading. Nothing warmed a cold, dark afternoon like a well-told story. The eight volumes of Samuel Richardson's *Clarissa* beckoned, but she turned her back on them, thinking only of Jamie and the others who would soon come knocking on her door, inquiring after her health. By the time the knock came, she was freshly combed and well under the covers, seated straight up, with her hands washed and neatly folded on the bedcovers. The bittersweet taste of elderflower lingered on her tongue. Though her voice was husky and her chest sounded full of brose, she forced herself to sound cheery. "Come in!"

Her father entered first, followed by Jamie, then Rose, with Eliza and another of the house servants trailing behind them, eyes wide with concern. Jamie looked the picture of health, his color high, his thick hair tousled by the long ride. Rose, standing rather close by his side, was bright eyed and pink cheeked. Leana, conscious of her own wan face and red-rimmed eyes, knew she was a poor match for her younger sister's beauty.

"Welcome . . . home . . ." Overcome by the smell of horseflesh and heath hanging about their clothes, Leana sneezed violently. It was not at all the way she'd hoped to greet them.

"What remedies have you taken thus far?" Lachlan demanded. He listened to her litany of herbs and seemed satisfied. "You'll heal soon enough, Daughter." With a wave of his hand, her father summarily dismissed the servants and asked Rose and Jamie to wait downstairs. "I've need of my older daughter's ear for a while. Come back shortly. And mind you, knock first."

Leana's stomach tightened at their hasty departure. Something was wrong. Her father's uneasy manner confirmed it. Lachlan paced the room, hands folded behind his back, eyes to the ceiling.

The last footfall died on the stair before his gaze finally met hers and he spoke.

"You missed a bit of excitement in Dumfries, lass."

"Nothing bad, I hope." She sneezed again as he pulled a chair to her bedside and sat.

"Jamie found his stolen horse."

She stared at him over her handkerchief. "His *horse?*"

"Aye, most unexpectedly." He pressed on with his story as Leana dabbed at her nose, trying to read her father's face in the candlelight.

"And what of Jamie? Will this be his last day with us?"

"He'll be staying a bit longer." Lachlan's gaze remained fixed on hers. "Until Hogmanay, at the very least."

"I don't understand." Though she'd had no fever all day, her entire body flooded with heat, making her shiver in the chilly room. "Why is Jamie staying?"

"For a time and for a purpose." Her father did not blink, nor did his face reveal his thoughts.

She sat up, pushing back the covers so she could breathe, so tight was her chest. "A purpose?" *Aye, to marry!* Perhaps he'd asked for her hand after all! "What purpose, Father?"

Lachlan pinched his mouth shut, causing the stubble of his beard to stand out, then frowned and released a heavy sigh. "They say God shapes the back for the burden, Leana. I trust the Almighty has strengthened yours to bear what I'm about to tell you."

And then she knew.

"Tell me," she whispered. Her shoulders sagged, preparing to receive the awful weight of truth.

His words cut like sharpened steel. "Jamie McKie has asked for Rose's hand in marriage."

Tears welled in her eyes. "Did you not tell him of my . . . my feelings for him, Father?"

"Och, lass." He groaned, sounding a mite frustrated with her. "The proper time and place for such revelations never presented themselves."

She fumbled for the handkerchief tucked in her nightgown sleeve, then attended to her nose, her hands still shaking, though now from grief instead of joy. "Only a week ago you said that Rose might catch his eye but I would catch the man. But I . . . I did not, Father." She broke down, her tears flowing in earnest. "I did not capture his eye. Nor his heart. I tried, truly I did, but . . ." Her moan was a keening, from deep inside her. "Jamie . . . Jamie would not . . . even . . . look . . . at me." The words were lost among her sobs.

Jamie. Oh, my sweet Jamie.

When her father spoke at last, his voice was low. "It does not give me pleasure to see you suffer, child."

She nodded glumly, blowing her nose yet again. He sounded as though he meant what he said, but she could not be certain.

"Leana, I had no choice but to agree to a wedding. His father ordained it. His fortune requires it. I am bound by blood to honor Jamie's desire for marriage."

"What of my desire?" she whispered, ashamed the moment she said it.

"Your desire is for Jamie alone? No other man?"

"No other man will have me, Father, and you ken it well."

Her father leaned back, letting one hand drop to his side while with the other he stroked his chin. "Then we've a problem, Leana, and not one easily solved." After a long silence, he made an enigmatic statement, which she was too weary to examine. "Alec McKie's purse may be deeper and his boundaries wider, but I am still laird of Auchengray, am I not?"

"You are, Father." She tried to smile, though the corners of her mouth barely lifted.

"Well then." He stood, smacking his thighs as he did. "I hear your sister and cousin on the stair. They will want to tell you more of this, I jalouse. Do what you can to look happy for them, Rose in particular. The less she knows of your true feelings for Jamie, the better. You ken my meaning, Daughter?"

Leana nodded. "Send her in alone, if you please. Then Jamie by himself, if you might allow that. Only for a moment, I promise."

"Aye," he agreed, though his brows knitted in warning. "When you speak to your cousin, see that the door is wide open and your bedcovers pulled up to your neck."

He swung open the door and called in her sister, who slipped into the room and softly closed the door behind her. Leana caught a fleeting glimpse of Jamie's handsome face before it disappeared with a click of the latch. Rose took the seat her father had just vacated, her sprightly form perched on the chair, her young face brimming with compassion.

"Father has told you everything then?"

Leana pressed her lips together, not trusting herself to speak.

Rose's eyes filled with tears. "Oh, dear. I see that he has." She pressed her hand against Leana's, which rested in her lap, balled around her damp handkerchief. Her voice was a hoarse whisper. "I'm so sorry, Leana."

"Why would you be sorry when Jamie has chosen you?" Leana looked away, unable to bear the pity on her sister's face.

"Don't turn away." Rose touched her cheek with a trembling finger. "Please, Leana. Jamie cares deeply for you . . . as . . . as his cousin. He simply had his mind made up from the start. Nothing I said or did seemed to alter his opinion. A stubborn and prideful man, our Jamie."

"Not 'our' Jamie. Yours." Leana's heart gaped like an open wound. Her sister's words felt more like stinging nettle than soothing comfrey. "I'm pleased for you, Rose. A wealthy bridegroom, the very thing you wanted."

"But not *now,* Leana. And not Jamie." The strain in Rose's voice was palpable. "Leana, will you not look at me?"

She turned slowly back toward her sister. Rose, the motherless child whom she'd loved and cherished from birth. *My wee Rose.*

Rose's face was white as bleached linen. Her

dark eyes streamed with tears. "Please, Leana. Father gave me no choice. Please forgive me. I cannot bear to see you hurt."

Leana lifted a weak hand to her sister's cheek. "I know. I know, Rose. Don't cry, dearie. Be happy, and know that God will see to my happiness. So will Father. There's no need for tears." She wiped them away with her thumb. "Send Jamie in so we might make our peace."

Rose bobbed her head, then ducked out the door, barely looking in Jamie's direction as she shared Leana's request. He entered the room with hesitant steps, pushing the door wider as Leana pulled the bedding around her neck.

"Rose said you wanted to see me . . . alone?"

"With my father's blessing," Leana explained, nodding to the chair. "This will not take long, Jamie. I simply want to ask you something."

He sat as she requested, his eyes canvassing the room as though seeking an avenue of escape. "How . . . how are you feeling?"

"If you mean this common cold that has afflicted me, I will recover."

His boldly chiseled jaw, in dire need of Hugh's razor, turned a ruddy color. "I . . . I meant about the . . . wedding. About Rose and me."

"I am . . ." What could she say? *Disappointed? Heartbroken? Undone?* "I am . . . happy for you," she said at last. "But you must know . . ." The words caught in her throat. "You must know, Jamie . . . that I loved you."

"And I'm grateful for it, lass." His gaze was kind,

nothing more. "No cousin in Scotland could be made more welcome than I was."

"Nae . . . nae!" She shook her head. He must understand; he *must.* "Not merely as my cousin. I loved you as a woman loves a man. I love you still."

He stood abruptly, touching a finger to her lips. "Say no more, Leana." The scarlet tint was gone from his face. His expression was grim. "We will always be family. And I will always care for you, as good cousins should. But it is Rose I love and Rose I will marry, come the last day of December. Promise me you will not speak of this . . . of your . . . feelings for me again."

Leana fell back on her pillows, limp. "As you wish."

Thirty-Eight

Each time we love,
We turn a nearer and a broader mark
To that keen archer, Sorrow, and he strikes.
ALEXANDER SMITH

Leana wished the floor of the kirk might split open and swallow her whole: her gray serge dress, her ugly bonnet, and her broken heart.

Her father, seated next to her in the pew, turned and threatened her with naught but a raised eyebrow. He would brook no sentimental display of tears, no sense of injustice on her face. Lachlan had dutifully paid the *cryin siller,* the coins required for the marriage banns to be cried out three Sundays in a row. All of the Auchengray household knew; soon the entire parish would know.

A certain tension hung in the room at the crying of the marriage banns. More than one parish member had stood in the kirk and protested a match. Only a year ago a woman in another parish asked to have her banns stopped, on the grounds that she'd changed her mind and loved another. *Och!* The uproar in Mauchline that day.

Leana's gaze took in the soberly dressed assembly, bathed in the harsh gray light that streamed through the windows. None would speak against Jamie and Rose. Nor was the couple present to defend themselves if someone did. Jamie had taken Rose by chaise to Kirkbean parish that morning, nearly five miles south of Newabbey along the River Nith, because it was unlucky to hear their own banns read. Leana would listen on their behalf and keep her opinions to herself.

As the session clerk stepped forward, Jessie Newall, seated in the pew in front of her, turned her head slightly. Their gazes met, and Jessie nodded in silent support. Hadn't Jessie seen her with Jamie by the hearth his first Saturday at Auchengray? Jessie turned forward again but held Annie up to her shoulder, kindly making sure the child's sweet face was pointed toward Leana.

Her pink cheeks wet with drool, Annie's eyes grew round with wonder at seeing familiar Leana. She started to squeal and was quickly hushed by her mother. Leana swallowed her sorrow and smiled at Annie, seeking comfort in the innocent joy before her, praying for the child to have the happiest of lives. If Annie was a lucky girl, she would grow up to love a man who loved her in return.

The session clerk lifted his hand, signaling silence for the crying of the marriage banns. All murmuring ceased. "I hereby proclaim the names of those seeking to be married in Newabbey parish. From Auchengray, James McKie wishes to wed Rose McBride on 31 December. Are there any present who claim some impediment to this marriage?"

Leana gripped her handkerchief. *Aye.* There were two impediments: Rose did not love Jamie enough, and she loved Jamie too much.

No voice raised an objection.

"And from neighboring Kirkbean parish, Fergus McDougal of Nethercarse wishes to wed Sarah Clacharty from Drum Mains in Newabbey parish on 4 December."

Leana gasped. So did others. Whispers ran up and down the pews like mice. Heads turned. Faces stared at her, dark with accusation. Fergus had located another willing bride. No longer would the muddy waters of their ill-spent courtship splatter on his boots. Leana's skirts alone would be covered in shame.

She looked down at her hem, expecting to see the evidence. Her crime? Refusing to marry a man she could never respect, let alone love. Fergus had made it known that he'd withdrawn his proposal of marriage. Leana knew the truth: that she'd never heard his offer nor accepted it. But a woman's view of things was seldom published abroad. Sarah

Clacharty was a young lass from a poor farm family who must have jumped at Fergus McDougal's suit. Poor Sarah would jump for the rest of her days to do the man's bidding. Leana did not envy the girl's bleak future; she only envied her wedding ring.

The congregation settled down, though sharply tipped arrows still found their way to Leana's pew. She fixed her gaze on Annie's face and pretended not to notice the others. She would endure the hours ahead and pray to God for mercy. When Jamie and Rose joined them after the first service, to share the family meal in the pew and stay for the afternoon sermon, she would pray for strength.

Leana bowed her head. The banns had already been read. The worst was over.

It was nearly one o'clock when Reverend Gordon spoke his benediction: "The grace of our Lord Jesus Christ, the love of God, and the communion of the Holy Ghost be with us all. So be it." *The love of God. So be it.* Leana let the words sink in for a moment before slipping out the door to watch for Rose. The couple came riding up at a fast trot. Jamie held the reins high; Rose clasped her hat on with one hand and waved wildly at Leana with the other.

The wheels of the chaise had barely stopped turning when Rose leaped down, her face alight with news. "*Och,* Leana! Strange doings in Kirkbean. The banns—"

"For Fergus McDougal. Aye, they were read here as well."

Rose rolled her eyes. "Sarah Clacharty is in for a

sorry time of it. How like that old haggis to find himself another bride."

Jamie reappeared, having parked the chaise for the afternoon. He nodded curtly at Leana, then grinned at Rose. "Did I understand you to say we're having haggis for supper, my bride?"

She made an adorable face at him. "You know very well we've a cold supper waiting at home and a cold dinner waiting in our pew." Rose steered Leana toward the door. "We'd best go inside and eat first, Leana, before Neda's smoked herring vanishes inside Jamie's pockets."

Walking to their pew took the couple longer than they expected. Leana watched as one young person after another came alongside and rubbed shoulders with them—the lads against Jamie, the lasses against Rose—so they might catch a bit of luck in finding their own true love. "Your turn, Leana." Rose pulled her against her, eying her closely. "Will you rub shoulders with me, sister?"

Leana wriggled free of Rose's grasp, feeling foolish and a more than a bit hurt. "Perhaps my ill luck will rub off on *you,* Rose." When her sister's countenance fell, Leana was sorry she'd spoken unkindly. "That is to say, I wish you only good luck, dearie. Though you need no such wishes from me."

"Aye, I do." Rose took her hands and pulled her down onto the pew, ignoring the crowd of well-wishers around them. "It is your blessing that matters most, Leana." She glanced up at Jamie, who was engrossed in discussions with their neighbors, then turned back to give Leana her full attention. "I know . . ." Rose groaned and started again. "I know that you've been dreadfully misled and ill used. By Father. By Fergus McDougal. By Jamie, unintentionally."

"It's true. I have been." It pleased Leana to confess it in the kirk, even if only to her sister. "Yet I fear I must bear some responsibility—"

"Nae." Rose's tone was adamant, her dark eyes sparking. "You did what your heart told you was right. You said yes to loving Jamie and no to marrying Fergus. Doesn't the Buik say, 'Let your yea be yea; and your nay, nay'? You ken that it does. And that is what you did. God Almighty sees your honest heart."

Leana managed a faint smile, but inside she shivered. Her heart was anything but honest. Her love for Jamie still burned there, bright as ever, and her unending hope that he might change his mind before Hogmanay was alive and well too. Neda knew. Jessie guessed. Jamie would never know, not unless he came to her and confessed the same.

Leana squeezed her sister's hands, grateful for the covering of noise around them. Even so, she lowered her voice. "You've asked for my blessing, Rose, and you shall have it. But only if you can tell me that you love Jamie with every bone in your body."

Her sister glanced up at her betrothed, and the corners of her mouth twitched. "I care for the lad, that much I know. But *love* is a word that scares me, Leana. The only kind of love I've ever known is yours: a sister's love, almost a mother's love." Her gaze drifted toward Lachlan seated at the other end of the pew, busily chewing on his mutton. "But you'll never convince me that Father loves either of us. Not as Mr. Elliot loves his daughter Susanne." Rose hung her head. "I'm confused, Leana. Does Jamie love me as you do? Or does Jamie love me the way Father does?"

Leana's heart sank at the thought of her young sister having to grapple with such weighty matters. "I will pray that Jamie loves you as I do, and more. And I will pray that you love him completely, as you should."

Her sister nodded, though she made no promises, then gazed up at Jamie when his hand accidentally brushed against her shoulder. "I enjoy his company. He makes me laugh. And he *is* the handsomest of men." A winsome smile decorated her sweet face, as pink and shining as Annie's. "The wedding will be fun, won't it? And all the presents? And the dancing at the bridal? But the best part . . ." She ducked her head beneath the brim of Leana's hat and giggled like a schoolgirl. "The best part will be not having to answer to Father ever again!"

Thirty-Nine

O happy is that man an' blest!
Nae wonder that it pride him!
Whase ain dear lass, that he likes best,
Comes clinkin' down beside him!
ROBERT BURNS

Seven weeks of hard labor.

Jamie smiled at the thought of it, filling his shovel and hoisting it toward the dunghill, now covered with frost. Three of those weeks had already passed, yet they seemed more like three days to him, all for the love of Rose. *Sweet Rose.*

Unless he was mistaken, she had warmed to him a bit. That morning she'd greeted him at breakfast with a hesitant smile and a gift waiting by his plate. "'Tis December, Jamie."

He unwrapped the ribbon and cloth, knowing what waited inside, yet pretending surprise. "A *waddin* sark! And well stitched it is, Rose." He held up the fine cambric shirt so the household could admire Rose's needlework, then winked at his betrothed. "Did you do this on your own, lass, or did a certain skilled seamstress under this very roof offer some assistance?"

A bonny blush tinted her cheeks. "You know very well Leana helped me." She gazed at her older sister with a respect bordering on reverence. "Without her needle, our bed linens and tablecloths would be a sorry sight indeed." The bottom drawer of Rose's dresser, empty only weeks earlier, could barely be pushed shut for all the linens and sheets, tablecloths and curtains Leana and other women in the parish had carefully stitched and placed in the sacred drawer, which every bride hoped to fill before her wedding day.

Jamie had nodded his thanks in Leana's direction, not quite meeting her steady gaze. The awkwardness between them had eased but not disappeared. Whenever he was in her presence, the words she'd spoken on Martinmas stretched between them like an unseen silken thread: *I love you still.* Had he misled her somehow? With all his heart, he hoped he had not. As long as Rose was in his life, Leana would be on hand as well, hovering in the wings, providing support and guidance. He needed her on his side and on Rose's as well. It was a thorny arrangement, like three points of a triangle—stable but sharp edged nonetheless.

Jamie pushed his worries aside and plunged his shovel into the refuse, making quick work of it. The days grew shorter, yet Duncan's list of duties for him grew longer. Mucking out the byre was the worst of them, so he'd tackled it first, even though it meant his clothes reeked for the balance of the day. By four o'clock, when the sun ran its course, he'd be free to scrub himself clean and dress for supper. *For Rose.*

Thinking of her made his labors lighter. Over Neda's haggis on Martinmas night, they'd made their formal pledge of betrothal with the entire household serving as witnesses. Moistening their right thumbs, Jamie and Rose pressed them together, hands and hearts joined as one. Then he spoke the traditional vow, and Rose repeated it after him, her voice high and thin:

Receive it, then, with a kiss and a smile
There's my thumb, it will ne'er beguile.

The wedding banns had been cried aloud by the session clerk in Newabbey kirk on the last three Sabbaths in November, with nary a complaint from the congregants, despite Rose's youth and Jamie's recent arrival in the parish. It was clear that Lachlan McBride's consent had sufficiently convinced the townsfolk of his merits as a son-in-law. Though much remained to be done in preparation, Jamie knew Neda and Leana would see to the details. His primary responsibility was to appear at kirk and claim his bride on the last day of the year. December could not pass swiftly enough to suit him.

The day was well chosen. Among Scots, Hogmanay was the luckiest day of the year to marry. Jamie prayed it might be very fortunate indeed. After spending their bridal week in Dumfries, he would take Rose home to Glentrool and pray she carried his heir in her womb.

"Well, lad, I see you've pit the brain asteep for a moment." Duncan ducked his head to enter the stables, where Jamie had paused to warm himself on Walloch's obliging horseflesh.

"Aye, I'm meditating on a certain dark-haired lass," Jamie confessed. "Give me another minute to thaw my fingers, then I'll be back to my labors."

"Och! I've no fear of that, Jamie. Ye're the hardest worker Auchengray has seen in mony a day." Duncan joined him at his task, smoothing a brush over the gelding's back, their tandem strokes falling into the same rhythm. "I venture even now Lachlan McBride is thinkin' of how he might convince ye to stay on a bit longer. On through the spring lambin' and the summer shearin'."

Jamie brushed harder, hiding his irritation. "'Twill not be the way of things, Duncan. When Rose is mine, so is my freedom."

"Aye." The overseer's checked bonnet bobbed up and down. "Ye've more than earned the right to both. Though I believe ye were the one to name the price, were ye not? Seven weeks o' labor without a

ha'penny earned, when a bag o' silver from Glentrool would've spared ye even one day of it."

Jamie frowned at the reminder. "McKie silver was
provided once and stolen. I was not about to ask for
more."

Duncan stopped brushing and looked him in the
eye, his demeanor more serious than usual. "It's yer
pride that's put ye here, doin' the work o' a peasant.
Naught but pride. And ye ken what the Buik says:
'When pride cometh, then cometh shame.' Ye've let
Lachlan McBride get the better o' ye, and mark me
words, lad, he's not finished with ye. The laird kens
a bonny bargain when he comes upon it."

"But I've made a bargain as well. A bride like
Rose is worth seven years of work."

"So ye say, lad." Duncan resumed his brushing.
"Me faither would say it's dear-cost honey that's
licked off a thorn. Enjoy the sweet taste of it while
ye may, Jamie. Mind that yer tongue isn't pricked
when ye're not payin' attention."

Jamie merely nodded, vaguely disturbed by the
overseer's comments. Were they the idle musings
of a man more familiar with a farm steading than a
laird's house? Or were Duncan's words a warning?
"I do appreciate your concern," Jamie murmured,
patting Walloch's withers, then moving toward the
midden walk that circled round the dunghill. "For
now, I've more stalls to muck and a doocot that
needs attending."

"Aye. See ye don't get so wrapped up in yer work
that ye miss Leana's potato scones." Duncan followed him out into the frosty forenoon air. "Made

them specially for ye, I ken. Neda will have them at the kitchen door aboot one o'clock or whenever yer stomach starts to growlin'." Duncan stamped off across the hardened ground, leaving Jamie to press on with his work and stave off his hunger.

He was unwelcome at the family hearth covered in filth, and rightly so. Instead, he stopped by the kitchen door at the dinner hour and let Neda feed him something plain and nourishing to hold him until supper. Potato scones with a bit of hard cheese and the hottest mug of tea she could brew would be a cheery sight on a December day.

He tipped his head back to discover the sky above him had no color at all. Neither blue nor gray nor white, it was naught but a backdrop for the black branches of the orchard trees, stark and bare. The wind was blessedly still and the air cold but not bitterly so. Around him shuffled stable lads lugging saddles that needed cleaning and young shepherds bound for the hills. They greeted him as an equal, and for that he was grateful. To be blethered about behind his back and ignored to his face would be a miserable lot.

Jamie stamped his feet as he worked to keep the blood going and his mind off the waddin sark safely hanging in the oak clothes press. *Four weeks and two days.* It was agony to have her sonsie self so near—beneath the same roof, sleeping in the next room, breathing the same air—and know that he must wait to claim her, wait to touch her, wait to kiss her the way he wished. Not the chaste kiss he'd stolen from a shepherdess two months past, but the kiss of a husband ravishing his wife and her relishing it. Aye, that was the image seared across his mind when he lay in bed at night, counting the hours. *Four weeks and two days.*

Rose had honored him with the traditional bridegroom's sark. Now it was his turn to provide for his bride, and he'd not disappoint her. His mother—no doubt without saying a word to Alec—had sent a package by post from Monnigaff, a charge which Lachlan had begrudgingly paid when he learned its contents. "Gifts for the bride," was all Jamie told him, but it was enough to keep the man from insisting he empty the box while the curious household gathered to look, Rose among them.

The first token of his affection would be placed by her plate at supper that eve: Rowena's silver brooch, bought by Alec's father decades ago at the *luckenbooths,* a cluster of locked stalls selling jewelry and silver on the High Street in Edinburgh. The tiny pin, no bigger than his thumbnail, boasted two silver hearts intertwined and his mother's initials engraved on the back. *R. M.* for Rowena McKie. Rose might think they were her own initials and be charmed by his cleverness.

The box also held ribbons and lace for the ladies and silver buttons for the bridegroom's sark. Rowena generously included a pouch with sufficient silver to buy a wedding gown—a tailor in Newabbey village had already taken the measurements—and a week's lodging in Dumfries. The inn was his mother's idea and a fine one. He would enjoy Rose's company in blissful privacy before they bade farewell to Auchengray and braved the January storms en route to Glentrool.

Not all in the package was fortuitous. Evan was still breathing threats, his mother's letter explained. "Do your best to bring your bride home with a babe in her womb," she cautioned. "Your foolish brother wouldn't dare threaten the lives of all three of you." Rowena went on to say that his father was too infirm to travel east for the wedding and unwilling to send her without him, meaning no McKie would witness his marriage. It grieved Jamie to think of standing in the kirk without his family seated behind him beaming their approval. But it could not be helped; he would not fret over things that couldn't be changed. He and Rose would see them soon enough.

Jamie glanced at the watery sun as he walked toward the back door, guessing the time, then brushed enough soil from his clothes to keep Neda from holding her nose as she fed him his scones and cheese. "Your Uncle Lachlan has a present for Rose too," the keeper of the house whispered, her eyes bright with the news. "He's promised to let her open it before supper. I've a clean shirt and breeches waiting in your room, lad." She waved him away, wrinkling her nose after all. "See that you're presentable."

By seven that evening any remnant of Jamie's lowly labors had vanished. His face, hands, and hair were gleaming, his chin freshly scraped with a razor, his clothes carefully pressed by one of the maids who'd taken a fancy to him. Lachlan was ringing the tableside bell as Jamie hastened down the stair, the brooch tucked in a velvet pouch in his palm.

Jamie nodded to the usual assembly round the table, then placed his gift by Rose's plate, brushing her arm as he did so. She giggled and pulled away, batting her braid at him playfully. Much as he loved her, it made him uncomfortable to see her behave so. More like a schoolgirl than a young woman about to be wed. Leana, seated next to her, neither blushed nor simpered but sat gracefully in her chair, the mistress of Auchengray. Perhaps she might teach Rose how to wear the mantle of marriage in a more becoming manner.

His uncle stood, quieting the room at once. "I've two announcements of interest to our future bride. Rose, I've arranged for you to spend the week before your wedding with your Aunt Margaret in Twyneholm. 'Tis the custom, you know."

"Aye." Rose sighed with a hint of drama, her eyes seeking Jamie for sympathy. "I know."

She'd warned him this might happen. Aunt Margaret Halliday—Meg to her two nieces—was her mother's older sister, a maiden who'd seen sixty summers and still lived in the two-room cottage where she and Agness were born. To hear Rose's description, the woman was an eccentric character—keeping bees, distilling spirits, and hiding smuggled salt brought to her door by the free traders of the neighborhood.

"An unco woman," Lachlan confessed. "But with a stubborn will and a good heart to match it. 'Twill be a most interesting week, of that you can be certain.

Now, lass, you've noticed two packages by your plate, aye? Open the one from Jamie first if you like, then the larger one, before we ask the Almighty to bless our meal."

Rose pulled open the velvet pouch and shook out the brooch with a satisfactory gasp of delight. "Jamie, how bonny!" She held it up for all to see, then pinned it to her gown with trembling fingers. "Jenny Copland has been showing off her lucken-booth brooch for months. Won't *she* be the quiet one next Sabbath morning!"

"Now, Rose." Her father held up a pointed finger. "Mind your manners."

She ducked her head, even as she pulled the second package toward her and carefully untied the plain linen wrapper. Both sisters stared at the folds of lace waiting inside, their eyes wide, their mouths hanging agape. "A *kell!*" Rose lifted up the fine white cambric with its pulled thread work done in an intricate design. "To wear with my gown. Oh, Father, it's a treasure. Wherever did you—"

"Dresden." Lachlan sat down, clearly pleased with himself. "It just arrived today, courtesy of . . . ah, Mr. Fergusson." All at the table knew of Fletcher Fergusson, one of Galloway's more renowned smugglers, who'd no doubt charged Lachlan dearly for the headdress, meant to be worn only by young, unmarried women. *Like Rose.*

She stood, stepping well back from the table, and tried to drape the delicate fabric over her head without success. "Leana, help me. Something's gone wrong in the back." The ever-efficient Leana quickly arranged the lace over Rose's hair and along her shoulders, spreading it out so that it showed off the delicate needlework to best advantage.

"Roses," Leana sighed at last, shaking her head. "It's covered with roses. How utterly perfect."

Jamie gazed at the beautiful lass beneath the lacy kell, and his concerns evaporated. "Aye," he whispered. "Perfect indeed."

Forty

The sun that brief December day
Rose cheerless over hills of gray,
And, darkly circled, gave at noon
A sadder light than waning moon.
JOHN GREENLEAF WHITTIER

Fit a bride's gown on a Friday?" Joseph Armstrong, the tailor from Newabbey village, shook his scissors like a scolding finger. "Whose daft idea was this, I'd like to know?"

Leana touched Rose's arm to keep her from confessing the truth. "It was mine," Leana said coolly. "Had I looked at a calendar before I chose the twelfth of December, Mr. Armstrong, I'd have known better than to have my sister fitted on such an unlucky day."

"Aye, well," he grumbled. "'Tis too late now, lass. The gown and I have made the hour's journey to Auchengray, so dress the bride we will." With a noisy huff, the tailor knelt to the floor once more, poked half a dozen straight pins between his teeth, and returned to his hemming. Between mouthfuls, he directed his apprentice to pin the sleeves as well. "Set up the smoothing board first, lad, and be quick about it. See that ye don't drop the goose on Miss McBride's toes, or she'll be limping at her sister's wedding."

The small lad, so thin he appeared not to have eaten for a month, placed the heavy smoothing iron by the fire, its gooselike neck silhouetted in the glowing peat. His own neck was almost as narrow. The collarbones sticking out of his shirt begged for meat. Leana would see that he left with a bannock and some pickled mutton in his pocket. As to the tailor, he, too, bore the look of poverty. The marked hump on his back and cruel bend to his posture meant he'd had a difficult way of it from his first breath. She vowed to pay the man twice his wage and face her father's disapproval.

Leana lit another candle, knowing frugal Lachlan would object to that as well. Still, the room was too dark for the tailor to see clearly. The forenoon sun was out but hardly shining, its meager rays lighting the room's two casement windows. Leana moved the candles closer, then gave the men room to work as she circled the nervous bride, who stood on a stout wooden box in the center of the sisters' bedroom. Praying as she walked, Leana begged the Almighty for patience with Rose and a generous spirit. She had known this day would be difficult and had prepared herself for it, or so she'd thought. Now that it was here, her words felt wooden and her heart like a stone.

Jamie, oh, Jamie. How his eyes would light at the sight of Rose in so becoming a gown. If Leana thought it might win Jamie's affections, she would gladly pay the tailor to make a second one to match it. A foolish notion, of course. No dress, however flattering, could make such a dramatic change in Jamie's heart. He would simply say, "Don't you look fine, Leana." But his eyes would never show what she longed to see reflected there, nor his lips say the words she ached to hear: *It's you whom I love, Leana. You alone.*

Leana shook her head, dislodging the traitorous thoughts, and forced a smile to her face. She must be happy for her sister. *Must.* If Rose were marrying another—any man but Jamie McKie—Leana would be overjoyed. *Think of that then.* What she could not dwell on were her own feelings for Jamie, which had strengthened rather than diminished. The reason was simple: The worst had already been endured. Jamie would never be hers, so she had naught to fear, and little to lose, in loving him.

True, her love was one-sided, but it was love in its purest form. Chaste. A love born of admiration and respect, not youthful lust. Whether he knew it or not, Jamie *needed* her love, needed a constant and steady source of support, something she feared childish Rose could never manage. Leana kept the secret of her continuing regard for Jamie well hidden. Once the wedding was past and all hope lost forever, she would bury her feelings for Jamie in the frozen soil of her garden beside the sharply pruned Maiden's Blush. For now, her love grew in silence, like the mistletoe in the crevices of her apple trees, unseen yet potent.

Comforted by her thoughts, Leana watched her sister hold her arms akimbo, struggling to accommodate the tailor's wishes and not lose her balance. Rose's voice trembled as she asked, "How does it look, Leana?"

She could only speak the truth. "Wonderful, dearie. The color especially." It was far and away the most fashionable gown Rose McBride had ever worn. The damask was a pale dusky rose, the robe styled high above her waist, the seam covered with a sash of a darker hue. The petticoat beneath it matched the kell from Dresden, as creamy white as Rose's flawless skin. A shoemaker in Newabbey had managed to make damask slippers to match the dress. Neda recommended the shoes be carried to the kirk for the ceremony and not worn until the last minute, and Leana had agreed. Come Hogmanay, east Galloway weather could be frightful.

Leana nodded at the tailor and his apprentice. "Thank heaven you two had a dry day for your walk from the village, or my sister's gown might have been ruined before the neighborhood ever saw her wearing it."

Rose pressed a hand against her chest. "What a horrid thought!"

"So it is, lass." The tailor stood to his feet, his crooked back even more pronounced. "Once I've pressed it smooth, ye're not to wear the dress again until your wedding day, nor can it be altered on the morning of your marriage, not by one stitch." He turned to Leana. "Ye'll see to it, Miss McBride? Bad enough that our fitting took place on a Friday without yer sister handing ill luck an invitation to the wedding."

"Och!" Rose's hands flew to her cheeks, which now matched the rosy gown. "The invitations! I completely forgot." She waved her arms up and down, pins flying. "Jamie and I planned to deliver our invitations this afternoon. Surely we've finished here." She nearly jumped from her perch before the tailor placed his hands firmly on her waist.

"Steady, lass. I've more of the hem to mark, and the sleeves still need fixing." He consulted his watch, shaking his head all the while. "We've another hour of work that can't be managed without ye."

Rose wrung her hands, imploring Leana with her eyes. "Is there nothing to be done? We were to deliver the invitations round the parish on Tuesday, but the rain was so fierce we feared we'd be soaked to the skin. You'll remember on Wednesday, Neda had every woman in Auchengray making treacle candy. Then on Thursday a north wind blew down from Queensbury . . . *Och!* We must leave at once. Leana, *think* of something!"

Leana looked at the apprentice, nigh to cowering by the chimneypiece, and the tailor, whose face resembled that same north wind, cold and foreboding. "Gentlemen, if I may make a suggestion. Might I . . . that is, would it be acceptable to you if I took my sister's place? Just for the balance of the fitting?"

The tailor threw up his hands with a lengthy groan. "Ye've no regard for tradition, Miss McBride. The wedding gown is not to be worn before the bride herself has been married in it."

"Ill luck again, is it?"

"Ill?" The tailor shook his head, rolling his eyes as he did. "Disastrous, if ye want to know the truth."

The sisters gazed at each other across his wagging head. Would it really be such a risk for a mere fitting?

Rose made the decision for them. "Mr. Armstrong, we're grateful for your concern. If it were anyone other than my sister, I would never risk such a foolish thing. But since it *is* my dearest Leana, and since I *must* deliver my invitations today . . . well, we've been wearing each other's dresses for several seasons. I don't suppose it will matter just once more."

"Whatever ye say, lass. It's yer wedding."

The men left the room while Leana and Rose switched gowns amid much laughter and sticking of pins. Rose stood back to admire the dress. "The color suits you as well, Leana." She knit her brows in mock annoyance. "See that you don't grow too accustomed to the feel of this dress on your bonny shoulders. The gown is mine, don't forget. And so is the bridegroom who goes with it."

Leana stilled, swallowing a sour taste in her mouth. "How could I forget such a thing?"

"Leana." The color drained from her sister's face. "I'm . . . I'm sorry. I meant it only in jest. I never . . ." She shrugged, dropping her chin to her chest. In a small voice she added, "Forgive me."

"There's naught to forgive, dearie. You were only teasing." Leana reached out and pulled her sister into a loose embrace, not wanting to prick her with a pin or tear a fragile seam. "Go on, see to your invitations. Your friends are no doubt wondering if they'll be invited at all and will be most glad to see you appear at their gate. Mr. Armstrong and I will make certain your gown is perfect."

Rose hugged her back and whispered a teary thank-you in Leana's ear. "My dress is the one thing that doesn't concern me. All the rest of it scares me witless." She slipped out the door, her cheeks still pale, and sent in the tailor and his apprentice, who wasted no time getting to work.

Leana patiently stood while they pinned and measured, relieved when Mr. Armstrong assured her, "Ye and yer sister are nigh to twins, so close are yer measurements. 'Twas good of ye to do this for her, Miss McBride, ill luck or no. Yer sister seemed eager to take her leave."

"Aye." She stared out the nearest window, the gray hills in the distance as bleak as her future. Any moment the chaise would be summoned and Rose sent safely on her way with a maid to keep her company. Astride Walloch, Jamie would deliver his own invitations—precious few since he'd been in the parish less than three months—while she, the older sister, stood proxy for the missing bride.

"Come, miss." The tailor reached for the kell. "Nothing remains but to see this hung round your head." He shook out the long headdress with surprising grace, then stood on tiptoe to drape it over her hair. It landed softly, as pure as early December snow falling on Lowtis Hill. He tugged the folds around her face, covering her hair. "A pretty piece of needlework, to be sure. From Dresden, ye say?" He stood back, nodding his approval, then walked around her, muttering to himself. "A pity you can't see for yerself, Miss McBride. From the back, ye'd never know it wasn't yer sister." He continued around until he stood before her once again, then gave her a sly wink. "Even the bridegroom himself might be *swicked,* aye?"

Forty-One

When I was at home, I was in a better place;
but travellers must be content.
WILLIAM SHAKESPEARE

Rose peered out the bedroom window into the wintry darkness, touching the silver brooch pinned close to her heart. Dawn was an hour away, yet already she heard Willie working outside the stables below, harnessing old Bess to the chaise. "Promise you'll take good care of my bridegroom while I'm gone, Leana?"

"Aye." Her sister's voice was nigh as chilly as the room. "Jamie will be well looked after."

Rose turned to touch Leana's cheek in tacit thanks, wishing her sister's smile didn't look so strained. Since the afternoon nearly two weeks past when Jamie and she had delivered the wedding invitations, Rose had sensed Leana pulling away from both of them, quietly folding inside herself like a handkerchief about to disappear in a pocket.

And now *she* was the one preparing to vanish from sight. Custom required the bride to flit for the week before her wedding, so flit she must. "'Tis improper to have you and Jamie living under the same roof before you wed," her father had cautioned. "Your Aunt Margaret will keep your mind off things and well out of harm's way." Rose had offered to stay closer to home—visit Susanne Elliot's family in Newabbey perhaps—but her father had been firm. "Twyneholm," he'd said. Twyneholm it was.

She would return on the morning of her wedding day with her Aunt Meg in tow. The women of Auchengray would await her arrival, gown and kell at the ready, while down the hall Jamie would be in Hugh's capable hands.

A week! Hardly enough time to know her own heart, let alone alter it.

Her father was right: Twyneholm was the ideal diversion.

Leana folded a pair of long woolen stockings and tucked them inside Rose's traveling trunk. "I can't imagine how Jamie will survive without you for seven days," Leana said, her tone more amiable. "Duncan and I will see that he's occupied. And what will you find to keep you busy in Twyneholm, do you suppose?"

"If I know Aunt Meg, she'll put me to work scrubbing the floor or polishing her silver."

"Her silver?" Leana's slight laugh warmed Rose's heart. "Have you forgotten? Our dear aunt has one silver plate she uses to impress her neighbors. Your polishing chores will last all of an hour. And the flagstone floor will not require more than a wet rag on a dry morning to set it to rights. Do it first thing so you won't come home with chapped hands for your wedding day."

"Heaven forbid!" Rose glanced down at her hands, already more pink and rough than she liked. "Mother's gloves will do for the ceremony, but I dread thinking of Jamie touching these pitiful hands on our wedding night."

"Come, let me see them. I've a remedy for everything, you know."

When Leana lightly brushed her outstretched hands, Rose felt a lump creep into her throat. Leana's touch was as gentle as their mother's must have been. *Oh, Leana.* What would she ever do without her sister when the time came to leave for Glentrool?

Leana turned her hands over, inspecting the palms. "Beeswax and pine resin make a fine healing balm. Aunt Meg will have plenty of wax stored from her hives. I'll see that Willie slips some fresh pine boughs in the chaise before you leave. Won't that add a lovely fragrance to your journey?"

"Mmm." Rose closed her eyes at the thought of it. "Like Christmas."

"Wheesht!" Leana held a finger to her lips.

"Father might hear you." She laughed in spite of her warning. "Or worse, Reverend Gordon."

The kirk had long ago banned any celebration of Christmas or the Daft Days that culminated on Twelfth Night—too pagan, too papist, and entirely too frivolous. Each winter Neda reminisced about one December in her youth when a certain minister had visited his parishioners unannounced on the 25th, checking to see that all were busy about their labors and that nothing festive was cooking on the hearth. Neda, it seems, had hidden the roasted goose beneath the bedcovers in the spence and banished the puddings to the cellar, biting her tongue to keep from wishing the dour man a blessed Christmas as he left.

Hogmanay, however, remained on every Scottish calendar, a practice which the kirk reluctantly condoned. More than any other year in recent memory, the McBride family would have reason to rejoice when the kirk bell rang in the New Year. Until then, Rose was off to another parish to count the days, with only her aunt for company. Not that she minded. Aunt Meg was, to put it mildly, an original, though she had no use for the womanly arts. Rose handed her sister a few last items to include in her trunk, groaning as she did. "Pack my sewing kit and darning needle as well. I fear I'll have need of them both."

The corners of Leana's mouth lifted into a genuine smile, her first of the morning. "And soap to scrub your feet?"

"Oo aye! I'd almost forgotten." Rose stared down

at her stockings, dreading to see how the skin beneath them might look by the light of day. "Yestreen was a bit of nonsense, wasn't it?"

Neda stuck her head in the doorway. "Necessary nonsense, lass. 'Tis your wedding, and all must be done according to custom, including the foot washing."

Last evening Jamie had gathered with the men of the neighborhood in the front room, with Duncan serving as the proper overseer. In the kitchen, Susanne Elliot supervised the lasses. "Stockings off, Rose, and plunk your feet in the tub of water Neda's drawn for you. Nice and warm, eh?" Amid much giggling and splashing, Rose's wet feet were rubbed with candle grease and soot until they were black as could be. "Doesn't our Rose make a lovely bride?" Susanne teased. No sooner had Rose's friends washed her feet clean with soap than another blackening ensued, even as the men blackened Jamie in the next room. The night's revelry dissolved into laughter and song, not ending until Rose and Jamie sent their guests home long past midnight.

The couple had met on the stair—stockings in hand, feet streaked with black, her skirts soaking wet, his breeches the same. Their smiles were weary but their hearts full. She'd tugged on his shirttail, hanging out in shameless disarray. "You look a fright, Mr. McKie."

"As do you, Miss McBride." His gaze had traveled the length of her, making her shiver on the moonlit stair.

"One more week, guid sir."

"Seven verra lang days, my bonny wee bride."

Tears stung her eyes. "Jamie, am I too young for you?"

"Never, lass." He smoothed her hair back from her brow, his gaze lighting her face like a candle at midnight. "Am I too old?"

She'd shaken her head, then kissed his palm and hurried up the stair, afraid to say more, wary of exploring the unfamiliar sensations that sang inside her.

Aye, Twyneholm was the very thing to get her mind off her handsome bridegroom and the moss green eyes that saw more than she dared imagine. Whether she loved him, she could not say. But he was bonny; aye, he was that.

In the murky light of approaching dawn, Willie waited for her by the chaise. The orraman was as patient as their old mare Bess, whose breath filled the morning air when she whinnied, her tail swishing, her huge eyes half closed. Leana appeared while Willie was loading the trunk. In her arms were freshly cut pine boughs, and on her face was naught but a sister's love. *Dear Leana.*

Leana handed Willie the evergreens to store, then wrapped her arms around Rose in a last embrace. "Godspeed, Rose," she whispered beneath the hood of her wool cloak. "See that Willie keeps a firm hand on the reins and a careful eye on the roads."

"Aye." Rose blinked away the tears pooling in her eyes. "Tell . . . tell Jamie good-bye for me." She glanced up at the window to her bedroom, where Jamie should have been fast asleep. Instead, she caught a glimpse of him at the window before he stepped back, away from view. According to custom, Jamie was not to see her for a full week, not until he walked into the kirk and found her waiting for him. *Soon, Jamie. Soon.*

By the time she'd climbed into the chaise, Neda and Duncan had come out to wish her a safe journey, joined at last by her father. He kissed her cheek, his unshaven chin scraping against her skin. "See that you're home by noon on Hogmanay, lass." His features were drawn in a scowl, yet his eyes shone. "If you're late, Jamie may grow weary and marry another."

Rose laughed merrily, grateful for her father's jest. It eased her leaving, which was becoming more difficult by the minute. In two weeks she would be leaving for Glentrool forever. *Och!* It didn't bear thinking. "Farewell, dear family." She patted Willie's arm to signal she was ready. "My prayers are with you all."

"And with you, dearie." Leana waved as Bess jerked forward, pulling the chaise down the drive. "Hurry home, Rose!"

The harness bells jingled in the frosty air, drowning out the last of their farewells. Rose settled back in the chaise, grateful for the heated brick beneath her feet and the warmth of her fur muff and heavy green cape, for the winter morning was bitterly cold. They turned onto the road that took them west along Lochend, its surface glassy and still. She gazed at Maxwell Park as they trotted past, admiring the enormous front door festooned with garlands and the windows bright with candles. Lady Maxwell had no doubt been awake for hours, putting the final touches on her plans for Hogmanay, so different from her own.

What if, on the day Lord Maxwell's letter had arrived, Lachlan had approved her debut after all? How different the past weeks would have been! Better or worse, Rose could not say. She only knew that Jamie loved her.

Forty-Two

Every winter,
When the great sun has turned his face away,
The earth goes down into a vale of grief,
And fasts, and weeps, and shrouds herself
in sables,
Leaving her wedding garlands to decay.
CHARLES KINGSLEY

How long, Willie?"

Her gray-haired companion grunted beneath his checked bonnet. He'd often teased her about being a troublesome traveler, complaining about the weather, asking how much farther they had to go, much like an impatient child. "Five miles to Milltown, where we take the military road south for another ten miles to the Brig o' Dee and on to Twyneholm."

"Hours, Willie," she said, nudging him playfully with her muff. "Not miles."

"Five hours, Miss McBride. We'll arrive at dusk, if the road is good and the toll takers are quick about their business. And if we're verra lucky."

"Och! I'm weary of hearing about lucky this and unlucky that." She poked her lower lip out, then thought better of it. An almost-married woman should behave like an adult, much as it pained her to think of leaving her pouting days behind. "If you'll not object, Willie, I'll doze a bit. 'Twas a short night."

With nothing to draw her attention but gray skies, gray fields, and a meandering gray road, she nodded off, rocked to sleep by the swing of the chaise and the steady clop of Bess's hooves on the hard ground. By the time Rose was jolted awake along a rough patch of road, they'd traveled nearly halfway and were gaining speed on the long downhill slope at Haugh of Urr. They stopped at a stable near the parish kirk, where the mare enjoyed her oats while Rose and Willie dined on cold mutton and crumbly bannocks. Willie let the horse drink her fill from a swift-moving burn and rest her legs for a short time before they pressed on for Twyneholm.

They passed a few gentlemen on horseback, some peasants on foot, and a carriage or two, but the road was otherwise a barren track across the rolling Galloway landscape with the freezing wind as bitter company. The winter sun never showed its face, hiding from dawn until dusk behind heavy clouds that boded snow. They crossed the Brig o' Dee with a noisy clatter, then climbed round Kelton-hill. Willie pointed his face southwest, directly into the wind. "An hour and we're knocking on yer aun-tie's door, lass." Bess must have understood his words, for her hooves fairly flew across the ground, the bouncing chaise forgotten.

"Twyneholm!" Willie cried, pulling back on the reins as the parish kirk came into view. Situated at a high crossroads in the center of the parish, sur-rounded by a cluster of cottages and houses, Twyneholm was not large enough to call itself a proper village but offered a pleasant prospect nonetheless. The main road led downhill, where a burn ran through the center of things. Bess trotted toward it, even as Rose sat up straighter, her spirits lifted by the sight of the thatch-roofed cottage nes-tled by the water's edge. *Aunt Meg.*

She was watching from the window and bounded out to greet them before Willie managed to rein Bess to a full stop. An older version of Leana, her fair hair now faded to silver, Aunt Meg had skin like fine parchment, pale gray eyes, and a full set of teeth, displayed in her welcoming smile. "Rose!" she sang out, ignoring convention and helping her from the chaise without waiting for Willie to do so. "My bonny niece, come to see me before her waddin!" Her aunt hugged her mightily, fur muff and all, and then nodded at Willie. "Attend to your horse, man, then hurry in for a dram to warm you and a hot meal to hold you 'til the morn's morn."

Rose was ushered over the threshold without

ceremony, her eyes quickly adjusting to the dim light inside the cozy house. Her aunt's stone cottage was as neat as a pin, every surface gleaming beneath the rushlights. Rose wondered if there would be any work for her after all, since the flags were well scrubbed and the curtains carefully mended. Aunt Meg's one silver plate, prominently placed above the hearth, had been polished to a fine sheen. "The place looks grand, Aunt Meg. How ever will we pass the time?"

Her aunt rolled her eyes dramatically. "Talking, of course! Getting you ready for your new life as James McKie's wife."

Rose put aside her muff and unwrapped her cape, noticing at once how toasty warm the two rooms were. "But, Auntie dear, you . . . you've never been married."

"*Och!* Do you think I don't ken the way of things? Lachlan sent you here so I might explain certain matters no father should discuss with his daughter. Especially not a girl sae *green* as you, Rose."

She had been in the woman's house only a minute, and already the conversation had waded into shocking waters. How like Aunt Meg!

Rose found an empty peg to hold her cloak, then moved to the fireside, rubbing her frozen fingers to warm them. "Coal, Auntie? Not peat?"

"The mosses in the southern half of the parish have plain given out." Her aunt joined her at the hearth, poking at the coals on the grate with her cane. "Have to order coal from Whitehaven now. A guinea a ton, if you can imagine."

"Poor Auntie! At least you have fresh water at your doorstep and every drop free."

"Glad I am that you reminded me." Her aunt disappeared out the door, a wooden pitcher in her hand, and returned moments later, her hair windblown but her wide smile triumphant. "Drink," her aunt demanded, filling a wooden cup of water for her. "Fresh and cold from the kirk burn."

"I thought hot tea might—"

"Aye, tea soon enough. But first, drink."

Rose complied, not wanting to upset her. She felt the icy water all the way down, shivering in spite of the coal fire.

Her aunt grinned with satisfaction. "I hope it's twins you're wanting, lass."

"Twins?"

"Aye. We've had five women in Twyneholm give birth to healthy twins. Five pairs of twins in two years! Who ever heard of sic a thing in a wee parish like this one? It's the water, you ken. The verra water you just drank."

"Twins." Rose shook her head, bewildered by it all. "Jamie is a twin."

"Hoot!" Her aunt crowed like a rooster. "Drink up, Rose! We'll have you primed for two bairns by next harvest, or my name's not Margaret Halliday."

On the hour, it seemed, Rose dutifully drank water drawn from the kirk burn—in tea, in brose, in soup, in punch, and by the chilly cupful. She didn't believe for a moment that the water contained any special powers, but if it pleased her aunt, drink she would. The balm made of beeswax and pine resin brought more reliable results, smoothing her hands until they looked like Lady Maxwell's, silky and white as the Damask rose in Leana's garden.

When she returned to Auchengray, Jamie would hold her balm-softened hands in his. She would touch his skin, and he, hers. They would become in all ways husband and wife. If Aunt Meg was right, 'twould be a fine and honorable thing they would do in the darkness of their bedroom. Although it frightened her more than a little, Rose was eager as well. Could she tell Jamie she loved him? Give herself to him completely?

Her girlish fears whispered, *No, no!* But her woman's heart said, *Yes.*

Each hour they were apart she found herself longing for him, like a great ache inside her. Surely it was love and not mere cousinly affection. Each day that passed in Aunt Meg's cozy cottage Rose remembered Jamie's kind words and thoughtful deeds. The tea and biscuits he had Eliza serve her in the sewing room. The endearing notes slipped inside the pages of *The History of Miss Betsy Thoughtless* for her to find.

Whenever they came near one another, he brushed a tender finger against her hand or cheek. He had not stolen a single kiss, but he had borrowed a few. Sweet, they were. *Oh, Jamie.* She missed him. She needed him. Aye, she could deny it no longer: She loved him. Her heart was young and untried, but at last it was truly ready.

Saturday, while she and Aunt Meg made stew for their Sabbath meal, Rose sang Jamie's praises as her aunt listened, smiling a crone's smile. "Faraway fowl have fair feathers. That's what I told your father, and wasn't your auld Aunt Meg right about that? When you're a good distance away from a lad and have time to miss him, then you learn what your true feelings are. He's a braw lad, is he not?"

"Oo aye!" Rose giggled.

Her aunt raised a stern eyebrow, like her father's, only so much kinder. "And he loves you true, does he?"

Rose nodded, very certain of her answer. "He does, Aunt Meg."

"And have you told this Jamie of yours that you love him?"

"Sully girl that I am, I have not." Rose threw a handful of cut potatoes in the stewpot. "But I will, Aunt. The very moment I lay eyes on him next Wednesday I will tell Jamie and anyone else who will listen." *Even you, Leana. Forgive me, dear sister.*

On the Sabbath her aunt's parish minister, Reverend John Scott, prayed mightily over her while the congregation, as sober and devout as any in Galloway, bowed their heads and asked for God's blessing on her impending wedding. Monday and Tuesday passed quickly, the hours filled with visitors stopping by to tuck small gifts into her hands and plant kisses for luck on her cheek. By the time she woke in the wee hours of Hogmanay morning, Rose felt certain any ill fortune had been chased away by the good folk of Twyneholm. Willie had returned safely on yestreen and was outside at that very moment, preparing the chaise for their departure at six o'clock, hours before the sun would show its wan face.

The wind outside sounded fierce, but Rose was too excited to fret about the weather. She dressed in her warmest clothes, thinking of the rose-colored gown waiting for her at Auchengray. In a few hours she would be wearing it. A few hours more and she would be married! Joy and apprehension sang a merry duet in her heart, making her hands tremble as she pulled on her gloves. *Soon, soon.*

Waiting for Aunt Meg to finish her ablutions, Rose listened more carefully to the wind blowing hard against the cottage's tiny panes and realized it was more than mere wind. It was an icy snow. The joyful song in her heart grew silent, while the fearful tune played on. *Not today. Not now.*

When Willie blew in the door, his expression grim, she knew the awful truth. "I'm sorry, Miss McBride," he said, wiping his face with the back of his gloved hand. "We've a weatherful day, I'm afraid. A snowstorm. Blown down from the Rhinns of Kells, I reckon. It's sae thick ye canna walk without fallin'."

"It's *what?*" Rose grasped the wooden box bed, feeling faint. "But we're not w-walking, Willie. We'll be dry enough in the chaise. It will be cozy with the three of us—"

"Listen tae what I'm sayin', if ye will." He wrapped a hand around each arm to steady her. "A body canna ride, nor walk, nor crawl in sic terrible weather, and neither can Bess. She's shakin' sae badly from the cold, I canna hardly harness her. We'll have to wait, lass. Wait until the storm lets up. By daybreak perhaps. Could be noon—"

"Nae!" She tore herself away from him and threw open the cottage door to see for herself. A gust of wind tore through the room, thick with icy pellets. She fought to close the door, then fell against it, tears spilling from her eyes. "Willie, Willie, what am I to do?"

He slipped his icy bonnet off his head and gripped it between his fingers. "Wait, lass. 'Tis all ye can do."

"*Wait?* But it's my wedding day!" She threw her arms in the air as she spun in a dizzying circle, nigh blinded by her tears. "Don't you see, Willie? We must try. We *must!* The kirk will be filled with neighbors, the house with food enough for all of Galloway—"

"Aye, and the road will be filled with carriages with broken wheels, ours among them, if we try sae daft a thing." He patted her arm, but she jerked it away.

"You don't understand! Jamie is waiting. He's . . . he's waiting . . ." She put her face in her hands, unable to bear the thought of it. "I can't . . . keep him waiting."

"Now, now," Willie said in the same soothing voice he used with the horses. "Ye've naught to worry about, lass. Jamie will wait, however lang it takes." He patted her shoulder while her aunt put water on the hearth for tea. "After all, Miss Rose, they canna have a waddin without a bride, now can they?"

She lowered her hands and groaned in resignation. "Nae, Willie. Of course they can't have the wedding without me." Rose sank onto a stool by the hearth and stared at the glowing coals, wiping away her tears with her sleeve. "They'll be terrible fash though, wondering what's happened to us."

Aunt Meg stepped behind her, smoothing her hair. "I've no doubt the same dreadful weather we're having here has covered Newabbey with snow as well. They'll ken what's happened, Rose, and put a stopper on their plans until they see your bonny face."

Her aunt crouched down beside her, her face aglow with confidence. "A day or two at most, sweet niece, and you'll be walking through the doors of Auchengray, ready to tell a certain lad you love him at last. Jamie will be waiting for you. You'll see."

Forty-Three

Every delay is too long to one who is in a hurry.
SENECA

Jamie paced the stone floors of Auchengray, his black boots buffed to a high sheen, the polished buttons on his coat reflecting the blazing hearth. "I'll not leave for the kirk 'til I know my bride is safe. Is that understood?"

Lachlan held up his hand, saying nothing. All through the house servants tiptoed about their work, speaking in hushed tones. The mantel clock clearly stated what no one could bear to mention. It was well past noon, nearly one, and nary a word from Rose.

Jamie paused to stare out the window at the

frozen sky, willing her to come careening up the drive. He could almost see her jumping down from the chaise—breathless from the journey, cheeks pink from the cold, eyes sparkling with anticipation. "I'm home, Jamie!" she would say, running through the door and throwing herself into his embrace. His vision of her was so real that he folded his arms across his chest and was dismayed not to find his bride wrapped inside them. *My bonny Rose, what's keeping you?*

He swallowed his disappointment, grown to a sizable lump in his throat, and sought his heart for answers. Had she changed her mind? Was she afraid of marriage? Afraid of him? Or was it something else entirely? Had she suddenly taken ill? Encountered an accident on the road? *Och!* The uncertainty was the worst of it. Perhaps she *was* too young and he in too much of a hurry to claim her. Or she might have run off to Maxwell Park, determined to have her debut at the Maxwell's Hogmanay Ball after all.

Every idea was more ludicrous than the last.

Jamie glanced at the timepiece once more. *One o'clock.* Maybe Rose was simply delayed. Aye, she might be minutes away. He would hope for the best and refuse to consider the worst. He turned toward Lachlan, who was comfortably seated at the head of the dining table, sipping a wee dram. "How long is the journey, Uncle?" Jamie was vaguely aware of having posed the same question earlier, but the answer evaded him.

"I told you at breakfast. It takes five hours from

Twyneholm by chaise." Lachlan stood and joined him by the window, a second dram in his hand. "Drink up, lad, and calm your nerves. You're more fash than a tup in October." Jamie, who seldom drank whisky, tossed down the dram in a searing gulp. Lachlan took the small glass from him and quietly filled it again. "Much of the journey home is uphill, so it could take a bit longer. Never more than six hours though."

Jamie felt the whisky's heat move through his limbs. "Might we send one of the servants along the same route? See if there's been"—Jamie hated to say the word—"an accident with the chaise or some trouble with Bess?"

"Aye, that might be prudent." Lachlan rang his handbell, and Neda stuck her head in the room. "Kindly have Duncan dispatch one of the servants on the road to Twyneholm. They'll have gone west to Milltown, then down the military road. Have him bring back news or the bride herself if he finds her by the roadside in a broken chaise. See to it, Neda."

Lachlan turned back to the window, and together they peered at the featureless expanse of thick clouds and the hard, dry ground beneath it. "Thank heaven we've had neither snow nor ice dampen our plans. I suspect the weather is much the same in Twyneholm."

"Are you certain, sir?"

Lachlan shrugged. "One can never be certain about the weather, Jamie, especially closer to the Solway coast. What is it the wise wags say? 'In winter be well-capped, well-shod, and well on porridge fed.' 'Tis good advice, that."

"Rose was properly dressed for the cold, wasn't she? Surely her aunt filled her with porridge before they set off. And isn't Willie an able driver and Bess the most dependable horse in your stables?"

"All of those things are true, Nephew." Lachlan licked a stray drop of whisky from his lips, then cleared his throat. "Have you given any thought to another possibility?"

"Namely?"

"That Rose changed her mind."

Heat flooded the skin beneath Jamie's waddin sark. "That's not possible!" *Liar.* It was more than possible. But how could Lachlan be privy to such information? "Perhaps Rose made a confession to you before she left for Twyneholm . . . is that it?"

"Perhaps." Lachlan shrugged, averting his eyes. "Or perhaps I'm a father who wants to see his daughter happily wed."

"So you say." Jamie resumed his pacing, frustrated by his uncle's cryptic comments when more pressing concerns demanded their attention. Wedding guests arriving. A full kirk. And no bride. Jamie threw his hands in the air and banged them down on the mantel. "What's to be done, Uncle?"

Lachlan's gaze drifted to the clock, then back to Jamie. "We proceed with the wedding."

Jamie's jaw dropped. "We *what?* Without a *bride?*"

Lachlan held up a cautionary finger. "I did not say that, Jamie. I said we proceed. Carry on to the kirk.

Go through the ceremony. Return home for the bridal—"

"How can we have a bridal supper *without a bride?*" Jamie nearly shouted the words, incredulous. "What sort of swickerie are you suggesting, Uncle?"

Lachlan shrugged, his demeanor maddeningly calm. "I'm not trying to deceive you, lad. On the contrary, I'm as eager for this wedding as you are. After all, it's my thrifite that's been emptied on your behalf, is it not?"

Jamie grimaced. "So you've mentioned. Many times." With his uncle, all roads led to money. His own courtship of Rose had quietly lined Lachlan's pockets with silver saved on farm labor, yet every penny spent on the wedding had been duly announced. "You've yet to tell me how we can have a wedding without a bride, Uncle."

"Simple." The sweep of his hand took in the whole of Auchengray, as if he'd scrubbed and polished it himself. "Our mounts are groomed, the piper and fiddler arranged, the feast prepared and paid in full. Up the stair your cousin is holding a wedding gown that lacks only a wearer. Let Leana serve as Rose's proxy, and this day is half-done."

"Her . . . her proxy?" Jamie's mouth dried to dust. "Can such a thing be done?"

"Oh, aye." Lachlan looked pleased with himself. "Leana would merely be standing in Rose's place for the ceremony itself. The proper names would be spoken, the binding vows said. If at any moment

Rose should appear, Leana would exchange places with her at once."

Jamie shook his head in disbelief. "Even if it made sense to do so, Leana would never agree to it."

Lachlan's gaze was even. "She will, if you're the one who asks her, Jamie."

"But I cannot ask *Rose,* and it's her opinion that matters. Does the lass not deserve to attend her own wedding?"

"Jamie, Jamie." Lachlan slowly shook his head, as though dealing with a stubborn schoolboy. "Rose will be along any minute. We're just moving things forward. Getting ready for her to join us."

Jamie rubbed the heel of his hand across his brow, wishing the tension would ease. "If I could know that Rose would want this—"

"What Rose wants is to be married," Lachlan interrupted, his tone persuasive. "Just as you do, Jamie. If she arrives later tonight, she'll simply join the bridal supper, and then you two can . . . ah, begin your . . . your own *private* ceremony without further delay." Lachlan's voice dropped to a warm drone. "It's the marriage that matters, Jamie. Not the wedding."

Jamie stared at the man, troubled by his smooth words and easy answers. So like Rowena. *So like you, Jamie.* The realization stunned him. Weren't his own words to Alec McKie smooth as old whisky, gliding down easy, yet with a fearsome bite at the last swallow? The memory of that painful night swirled in Jamie's head, stirring up troubling questions with no simple answers. Was Lachlan

McBride merely being practical? Was money the only concern, or were there other reasons his uncle didn't bother to mention?

No matter. He could not risk disappointing Rose. "I say we postpone the wedding. Wait until Rose is safely here."

Lachlan arched his brows. "And what if that is tomorrow, or the next day? How could we inform our guests on such short notice? It would be days, even weeks, before all the preparations could be made again. Not to mention Neda's efforts in the kitchen gone to ruin. And my good money thrown on the dunghill, let us not forget."

"No danger of forgetting that," Jamie muttered. Lachlan was a canny one, anticipating every argument and answering it as well. It was true; they could hardly keep everyone waiting indefinitely. What the man suggested had some merit. Be done with the ceremony. Formalities held little appeal. It was all over in an hour, no matter who might be standing in the kirk.

"Give it some thought, lad." Lachlan placed another dram before him. "And while you do, drink to your health in the new year."

Jamie sipped the whisky absently, his mind traveling the road to Twyneholm, looking for a lost bride. A peal of laughter at the front door startled him from his reverie, as a chorus of boisterous voices burst into song.

> God be here, God be there,
> We wish you all a cantie year.

God without, God within,
Lat the auld year out an' the new year in.

Lachlan swept his arm toward the door. "Your wedding guests. The first of many. If the ceremony is to start on schedule, we must begin our procession to the kirk at two o'clock, accompanied by our neighbors. What shall we tell them, Nephew?"

Jamie tossed down the last of his dram and stood, weaving ever so slightly. "Tell them we'll wait." He swallowed, difficult as it was. "Wait all day and all night if we must."

"Wait?" Lachlan's cordial tone lost its warmth. "Wait for what?"

"Wait for Rose."

Lachlan turned his back to the door and his face toward Jamie. His features grew hard as flint and his eyes sharp as tinder. "We will not wait, Jamie. This wedding will take place today, or this wedding will not take place at all."

"Not take place?" Jamie stared at the man, stunned. "You cannot mean what you're saying."

"I mean every word. I've tried to make this easy for you, James, but since you insist on being stubborn, then I must be firm." His uncle stepped closer. Instinctively Jamie drew back. "If you do not proceed with your wedding as planned, you will have no choice but to work for me seven months to return all the money I've invested in this *ill-paid* day. And then we shall see whether or not you'll be marrying my daughter."

"Seven months?" Jamie fell another step back,

reeling. The man was mad. "Uncle, I'll not work for you *seven more hours!* When Rose arrives—and she will soon, or I'll go find her myself—we'll make haste to Gretna Green and marry there."

"Gretna Green, with a lass of fifteen? *Och!* You do not know the documents of your own faith. According to the First Book of Discipline, 'No persons should be married without consent of the parents.' *My* consent, Jamie."

Jamie throttled him with his words. "They do not require such things at Gretna Green."

"Aye, but some things *are* required, Jamie. Gretna Green is forty miles hence. Unless you intend to walk, you would be riding on a mount stolen from my stables, with the sheriff on your heels, and no silver in your pocket." Lachlan folded his arms across his chest, a victor's stance. "Would you spend your wedding night alone, under a jailer's lock and key? Or would you prefer to be sleeping soundly in your bed, waiting for your bride to join you? The choice is yours, Jamie."

Forty-Four

Near the kirk, but far from grace.
SCOTTISH PROVERB

I have no choice." The admission cost Jamie everything.

Lachlan lifted one eyebrow in acknowledgment.
"Then I suggest you tap on Leana's bedroom door
and find out if the lass is willing to serve as her sister's proxy. See that she wears her sister's gown as
well, or the cost of it will be wasted."

Leana. His last hope. Jamie tugged his waistcoat
in place and smoothed his cravat. "Your older
daughter may put an end to your scheme and
refuse. And when she does, I will ride off to find
Rose."

"Nae, you will not, for my stables are not yours to command. As to Leana, you've naught to fear on that score, lad." His uncle lifted his empty glass, his eyes merry as Auld Nick's. "I know my daughter better than you do at the moment. Here's to your success in wooing Leana to our plan."

"*Your* plan." Jamie ground out the words, heading for the door.

"Yours now," Lachlan called after him.

No, yours. Jamie strode toward the stair, led by his chin. It was his mother all over again, forcing him to lie to get what he wanted. He'd wanted Glentrool; when he'd done as Rowena said and fooled his father, Glentrool was his. He wanted Rose; if he did what Lachlan said and persuaded Leana, Rose would be his.

Since he wanted an heir, and quickly, would that also require a bit of swickerie?

Gritting his teeth, he took the steps two at a time, anxious to have his discussion with Leana behind him. He did not know her as well as her father did, but he knew her well enough. She would be angry or hurt or appalled, all for good reason.

Lilting voices floated down the stair to greet him. When he reached the door, he took a deep breath to steady his nerves and wished he'd had another whisky. Better still, none at all. He knocked sharply and heard the room grow silent.

The door opened. A flock of females in colorful gowns stood before him, eyes wide, mouths agape. He placed one foot in the room, and the women shrank back, except for Leana. She stepped out from among them like a flower being lifted from a bouquet.

"Y-you're not meant to come in, Jamie." She moved closer, blocking his view. "Rose's gown is here, remember?"

"Aye, but Rose is not." He took her firmly by the hand and pulled her into the empty upstairs hall. Promising the others he would return her in due course, Jamie shut the door soundly behind them and led her toward a quiet corner. "We must speak, Leana."

"What news of Rose? We've been wound as tight as spools, listening for her voice on the stair."

"No news." He could not mask his concern. "Lachlan sent a servant to look for her, though it may take hours before we hear word."

"Poor Jamie." Her eyes filled with sympathy. "How hard this must be for you."

He nodded, drawing the first deep breath he'd taken all morning. "More difficult than I can say." How like Leana to think first of him and not of herself.

She was dressed in a new gown, he noticed. Dark as claret and covered with embroidery. The rich color warmed her skin, adding roses to her cheeks where there were none, the contrast making her eyes more like a May sky than a December landscape. A white silk chemise above the neckline covered what the gown did not, exposing her long, pale throat. Her hair was down, as befitted a maiden, flowing like a golden wave across her shoulders, with a spray of white satin flowers and pearls crowning her hair. He hadn't paid attention to the others. Were they all dressed so bonny?

His tongue seemed to stick in his mouth for a moment while she waited patiently for him to explain himself. Perhaps it was the whisky. Fractious stuff, that. "Leana, we don't know how long Rose may be delayed. Could be another hour or another day. Even two." When she only nodded, he plunged in without giving his words much thought. "Your father suggests we go on with the wedding."

"Go on?" Leana stared at him as though he'd sprouted horns. "Without Rose?"

Jamie nodded. "My response exactly." He saw in her eyes the same disbelief he'd felt moments earlier. But he had no choice. Neither did she. Leana must be convinced.

He hurried to share the rest of it while he still could recall Lachlan's endless list of reasons. "As your father sees it, the plans are made, the guests are here, the horses are groomed, the bills are paid, the minister awaits at the kirk, the piper and fiddler are engaged, the tables groan under the weight of the bridal supper, and news of the wedding has been spread about the parish. All will be for naught if we postpone the wedding."

"Jamie, I don't understand." Leana studied his face, seeking answers he hoped she wouldn't find. "All those things are true, but without Rose, there can be no wedding. She's the bride, Jamie. It is her day, don't you see?" She smiled, though only with her mouth. "You can hardly stand before Reverend Gordon and speak the vows to yourself."

"Nae," he agreed, meeting her gaze, "but I could speak them to you."

Leana's hand fluttered to her throat. "Wh-what do you mean, you could speak the vows to me?"

Och! He'd already made a mess of things. "I . . . that is, your father and I . . . thought you should serve as Rose's . . . proxy."

"Proxy?"

"Aye. You would stand in for her. At the kirk."

She slowly shook her head. "Jamie, I know what a proxy is, but why? Begging your pardon, the idea makes no sense at all. Don't you want to wait for Rose?"

"Aye, I do, more than I can possibly say. But we can't wait. I mean, we shouldn't." He touched her sleeve, imploring her. "Don't you see, Leana? The wedding gown, the bridal supper, the musicians— all will be for naught if we tarry much longer. Your father put it best: 'Tis the marriage that matters, not the wedding."

"How like my father to say that." Her blue-gray eyes regarded him so keenly Jamie feared she might see the truth. And she did. "Jamie, I have a feeling this notion of a proxy bride is not your idea."

What had Rose told him once? That it was impossible to lie to Leana? *Aye, lass. You were right.* He cleared his throat as though doing so might clear his muddled mind. "Whose idea it was, I cannot say. I only know that if there is ever to be a wedding, it must be today."

"Ah." Her gaze reflected what was not said. "And if Rose arrives, she would take my place?"

He nodded gamely. Leana had all but agreed. "That's the happy ending all three of us would hope for, isn't it?"

"Is it?" She turned her head to stare out the window at the darkening sky. "Jamie, how will you feel saying those vows to me?"

"Grateful." He gently turned her face back toward his. "Grateful to have a cousin who cares for me enough to help me out of a thorny predicament."

"You forget, Jamie. My feelings go deeper than that."

Oh, Leana. How could he make her understand? "I've not forgotten, lass." His voice lowered yet another note. "Your . . . your devotion touches me."

"Touches you where? Here?" She brushed her fingers across his brow. "Or here?" She pressed her hand against his heart. "I am not a child, Jamie. You need not hide the truth from me, afraid I might run off crying."

"I'm not afraid of your tears, Leana." He captured her hand and kissed it lightly, then lowered it to her side. "Heaven knows, your sister weeps enough for five women. And I have nothing to hide." When a faint smile appeared at the corners of her mouth, he realized the folly of his words and shrugged, making light of it. "Nothing hidden that matters anyway. Nothing worth seeing or hearing."

The smile faded without blooming. "Jamie, I know why you came to Auchengray."

He froze. "What is it you know?"

"Your parents insisted you marry one of your cousins, and your only choice was *which* cousin.

You chose Rose almost from the very first. That is what I know."

She did not know the worst of it then. But she knew enough to be wounded.

"Forgive me, Leana. I realize what I am asking of you today."

"Nae," she said, her lower lip beginning to tremble, "you do not."

"If there were some other way . . ." Jamie dropped his chin, unable to look at her. He'd told her he wasn't afraid of her tears, but he was. Another lie.

"Wait for Rose," she said softly. "*That* is the other way."

He forced himself to face her, even if it meant sharing her sorrow. "Your father insists we've waited long enough, Leana. He's made his wishes very clear."

"As he always does."

"Rose knows your father's pernickitie ways. She'll not blame either one of us for doing his bidding, least of all you, her dear sister." His voice faltered as the truth came out unbidden. "I believe Rose loves you more than she does me."

An odd light came into Leana's eyes. "You may be right, Cousin."

He swallowed the last of his apprehension. "Then you'll agree? You will do this thing, be a proxy bride for Rose? For me?"

"Aye, Jamie," she whispered. "I will. For you."

Forty-Five

Nothing is more easy than to deceive one's self,
as our affections are subtle persuaders.
DEMOSTHENES

I *will not cry. I will not.*

Leana pressed her hands against her skirt and bowed her head. "I'm ready, Neda."

The airy kell wafted over her head, falling in graceful folds around her shoulders. She eyed the pulled thread work, marveling at its intricate rose pattern, a subtle reminder of whose bridal veil she was wearing. *Forgive me, Rose.*

For the last half-hour, she'd moved as though in a dream, checking every moment to see if she might wake and find it all gone. Yet it was not a dream at all. It was real. Before the sun disappeared from the sky, she would stand beside her beloved Jamie in her own parish kirk and hear him vow to love and cherish her. Not by name, no, but she would hear the words. His hand would touch her hand when he slipped on the ring, his eyes would look into hers when they turned to speak the vows, his lips would say the words she longed to hear: *Even so, I take her before God and in the presence of his congregation.*

Take me, Jamie! By the law and all that was holy, she knew he could not.

Leana touched the kell, letting the solid feel of it bring her thoughts in line. "Thank you, Neda." She gazed into the long mirror, a borrowed treasure from Susanne, brought to Auchengray on Mr. Elliot's ox-drawn cart. Leana blinked as she stared in the glass. She touched the delicate petticoat beneath her gown, then held out her foot for the matching shoes.

Neda stood back, her face knitted with concern. "Are ye sure about this, lass? Seems a bit hasty to go on with the waddin. What if yer sister comes ridin' up with Willie?"

"Nothing would please me more, Neda." She nodded at Rose's gown, stretched across their box bed. "See that her gown and shoes are carried to the kirk. We can dress her in the manse, if need be."

Neda's brows arched. "I thocht Jamie said *ye* were supposed to wear it."

"I'll not ruin my sister's lovely gown. I agreed to

wear the kell to appease my father, but the gown will wait for its rightful mistress."

"Now who's the heidie daughter?" Neda teased, though her eyes shone with approval.

Leana turned back to the mirror, smoothing her hands across the elegant cambric veil, secretly pleased at the chance to wear it once more. Might Jamie be swayed by the sight of her in such fine array? Men never seemed to care about a woman's clothing. Still, unless she was mistaken, her new claret gown had caught Jamie's eye earlier.

Though it wasn't his eye she longed to catch. It was his heart.

Her conscience wisely reminded her of her role that day: *A proxy bride. No more than that.*

"Come, Neda," she said, keeping her tone light. "Finish pinning the kell in place. They're shouting for a bride on the lawn." Susanne and the others had already swept down the stair to join the wedding guests gathered for the procession to the kirk. Jamie had agreed to explain the unusual turn of events. Leana could only imagine what their neighbors would think of it all. When Fergus McDougal had put her aside last month, gossip had flown thick and fast through the parish hills. A proxy wedding would keep them blethering until Candlemas.

Neda pressed a pair of gloves into her hands. "Best put these on, and say a prayer for your sister in her travels. If your mother were here, that's what she'd be tellin' ye."

Leana slipped her fingers inside the white silk,

smoothing the fabric in place, then dropped her hands to her side with a pensive sigh. "What would Mother think of all this, Neda?" Leana turned aside to circle the room, afraid of what she might see in Neda's eyes. "Would Agness McBride be in this room, helping me dress to take my sister's place? Or would she be busy in the spence, sending notice to our neighbors that the wedding must wait for Rose's return, never mind the trouble and expense?"

"I . . . canna say, lass."

"Then you *have* said." Leana turned to find Neda's coppery head bowed with regret. "You think what I'm doing is wrong."

"Nae, I do not." Neda lifted her chin to meet her gaze. "I think what your faither is doin' is wrong, putting his thrifite before honor. And I think what Jamie is doin' is wrong, marryin' a child who does not love him instead of marryin' a woman who loves him with all her heart."

"Neda, please!" Leana glanced at the door to the hall in dismay, dropping her voice to a terse whisper. "Do not say such things."

The housekeeper folded her hands before her and straightened her back. "I will say this, and then I will say no mair: This day was not of yer choosin', but it's a day the Lord has made, and so we're to rejoice and be glad in it. Take it as a gift. Hug it close to ye. Make merry with yer friends. And show James McKie what a fine wife he might have had."

Leana wrinkled her brow in confusion. "Am I to . . . punish Jamie then?"

"*Och,* not at all! Ye're to please him, lass. He deserves a fine waddin as well." Neda fussed with the kell for a moment, as though considering what she might say next. "I think young Jamie will not mind havin' ye for his proxy bride. I've watched him look at ye when he thinks ye dinna see him."

"You have?" Leana's hands grew cool inside her mother's gloves.

"Aye. Niver with disrespect, mind ye."

"But he loves Rose," she protested.

Neda shrugged. "So he *aften* says. But he looks at you. Like a man who wishes for somethin' he canna have."

Leana pushed down the hope rising inside her like yeast dough on a warm hearth. "He has no need to wish for me when he has Rose."

"Aye, but *does* he have yer sister?" Neda regarded her evenly. "If so, whaur is the lass? Have ye not considered that she might be stayin' away on purpose? She was *sair* afraid of marriage, Leana. And not in love with Jamie McKie, best I could tell."

"Neda, don't . . ." She pressed her hand to her mouth, the faint scent of lavender from her mother's gloves calming her, giving her strength. "Don't . . . tempt me with this."

"'Tis not a temptation if he loves ye back."

"Jamie doesn't love me, Neda, and I cannot pretend that he does."

Neda chuckled softly. "Nae, but I can, if only for the day, watchin' ye take yer vows." Brushing a last bit of lint from Leana's gown, the housekeeper nodded with satisfaction. "It's time ye made yer appearance, or yer faither will be stormin' up here lookin' for ye." Neda touched a hand to her cheek, then hurried out the door, leaving Leana with naught to do but follow.

Out on the lawn the Lowland bagpiper was filling his bag, preparing to pipe the bridal party to the kirk in Newabbey. With squeaks and grunts, the cylindrical chanter came to life as the notes of a lively reel accompanied Leana down the stair. By now Jamie had likely been spirited away to the barn with some of the young men of the parish, prepared to follow discreetly behind the bridal party, well out of sight. Judging by the noise beyond the front door, the rest of the household had moved to the lawn. Some waited on foot, others on horseback. All bore bridal favors and libations to share with travelers they might meet along the way.

Her father waited for her at the bottom of the stair, dressed in his best coat and waistcoat, his ebony hair gathered into a severe knot. His dark eyes appraised her as she drew near, though she saw no affection in his gaze and heard even less in his voice. "Where is Rose's gown?"

"I could not bring myself to wear it, Father." Seeing his brow darken, she hastened to explain. "If Rose arrives in time, she'll have need of it. And if she does not appear until the morn, I want her to find her gown clean and pressed, waiting for her."

"Never mind your sister just now." He glanced about, as though looking for attentive ears, then lowered his voice. "Your gown is bonny enough to catch Jamie's eye."

A chill ran down her back. *It isn't his eye I long to catch.* Her own thoughts only moments ago! What else might her father know? She looked away, lest he read her face like a book. "It is too late to catch Jamie's eye."

"You're about to be a bride, Leana. The kell, the kirk, and the vows. I believe I've made the best of the situation, don't you agree?"

"Father!" Her head snapped back as panic beat a path to her heart. "Don't tell me that's what this proxy business is all about!"

"This 'proxy business,' as you call it, is meant to bind your cousin to this property in marriage. Though it matters not which daughter he claims, you are the better choice."

His cold logic frightened her. "But I cannot simply *steal* Jamie, as though he were a wedding gift left unattended."

"But that's exactly what the lad is: unattended." Lachlan looked about him. "I see no sign of Rose. For all we know, the lass has no intentions of going through with this wedding. But I do. I've paid for it, and I'll see it done. With you as the bride."

"*Why,* Father? Why like this?" Distraught, she asked more boldly than she should, "If I was, as you say, the better choice, why did you not insist Jamie marry me from the beginning?"

He wagged his head, as though only fools asked such questions. "I cannot tell my nephew whom he will marry. I can only tell him which of my daughters he may *not* marry." His lips curled, but he did not smile. "A father's rights only extend so far, Leana.

I'd hoped your appearance in kirk today might give Jamie a reason to change his mind."

"Your hopes are in vain, Father." Determined not to be swayed by his twisted sense of reason, she led him toward the door, her chin held high. "I am merely Rose's proxy, as you requested."

"Your sister is too young to grasp the meaning of love, and we both ken it well." He stepped close behind her, placing his hands on her shoulders and bending over to growl in her ear. "Let me say this more plainly: Jamie stole your heart months ago. See that he lays claim to the rest of you before the morn's morn."

"Father!" Stunned, she spun around to face him. "I will not behave like a—"

"Wheesht!" He grabbed her roughly by the arms and pulled her away from the door. "Need I remind you that no man will have you?"

The truth at last: Her father wanted rid of her.

She turned her head, feeling ill. His face was too close, his contempt as thick as the whisky on his breath.

Lachlan shook her, as though she'd not heard every terrible word. "I promised to get you a husband, Leana, and I have done my duty by you. See that you do yours before this day ends."

"My . . . duty?"

He released her as abruptly as he'd seized her. "You ken very well what I mean."

Leana swallowed the bile that soured the back of her throat. "And if I do not do this . . . duty?"

He threw words at her like stones. "Then you will

never marry. Never. It is Jamie McKie, or it is no one. The wedding vows you speak today will not be spoken by you again in your lifetime. Do I make myself clear?"

Forty-Six

Oh, why should vows so fondly made,
Be broken ere the morrow,
To one who loves as never maid
Loved in this world of sorrow?
JAMES HOGG

*Even so, I take him before God and in the presence
of his congregation.*
Leana held back her tears, whispering the vows
in her heart, practicing for when she would say
those words aloud to Jamie. *Even so I take him.*
Aye, she would gladly take him as her true husband.
But not with tricks and threats, her father's stock in
trade. Not by seduction or deception. Not simply
because Rose was not there to stop her. *Nae.*

Leana would bravely show Jamie her heart, in as many honest ways as she could, and let him choose her or not, once and for all. She could bear a lifetime alone; she could not bear a lifetime of wondering if one last appeal might have changed his mind.

The assembly prepared to leave for the kirk, most of them on horseback. A volley of pistol shots rang through the wintry air, followed by girlish screams and male laughter. The horses whinnied and shook their heads but kept their feet on the ground, while a startled wren took to the sky. The piper abruptly changed his tune, and the gathering ambled forward with Duncan leading the way, pulling her horse's reins as she clung to the pommel.

The day was colder than any Hogmanay in memory. Though the air was dry at the moment, the low gray clouds seemed thick with possibilities. Jamie rode well behind her, since tradition required the bride to arrive at the kirk first. A groom waiting for his bride was considered most unlucky, though in truth Jamie was doing just that: waiting for Rose.

"Say a prayer for your sister in her travels," Neda had said. *Aye, but what to pray?* That her sister would arrive shortly and claim Jamie forever? Or that her sister be delayed in Twyneholm another day or two? Leana was ashamed to admit which prayer she favored, and so she simply prayed for Rose's safety and trusted God for the outcome.

Around her, neighbors linked arms and serenaded her with the usual wedding fare: "There Cam a Young Man," and "I Hae a Wife o' My Ain." When they begged her to sing "I Gotten the Laddie That I

Like Sair," she politely refused. "He is not my laddie, and you ken it well." Nor would wishing make it so.

"Leana!" Jessie Newall rushed up to join her, her eyes bright with Hogmanay cheer. "Aren't you the bonny bride?"

"Proxy bride," Leana reminded her, but Jessie only laughed and drew closer, chasing off the shepherds who served as her escorts.

"I've seen Jamie," her friend announced, her hoarse whisper none too soft. "Is he not a fine sight to behold?"

"Aye, he is that." Leana could hardly argue with so obvious a fact, having seen him earlier. His velvet coat and waistcoat were the same color as her gown, only darker, the perfect contrast to the brilliant white of his waddin sark and the cool green of his eyes. "'Twill be a shame if my sister does not see her own bridegroom looking so braw."

"Och! That's not what I'm thinking." Jessie tugged on the kell, pulling Leana's head down a little. Her friend winked like a free trader with a saddlebag full of smuggled goods in search of a buyer. "I'm thinking Jamie McKie looks very pleased for a man whose bride is miles away in Twyneholm."

"Jessie!" Leana rolled her eyes and straightened. "You must not say such things."

"And why not, when they're true? He cares for you, Leana. He will make this day special for you."

Leana stared down at her, aghast. "Do you mean . . . ? Did he say . . . ?" She could not put words to her thoughts, they were so scandalous.

Jessie only laughed. "I'm a married woman, and I know longing on a woman's face when I see it."

Leana started to argue, but her friend prevailed. "Make the most of this day, for as long as it lasts. Above all, listen with your heart when Jamie speaks his vows to you."

"To *Rose,* you mean."

"Aye." Jessie flapped her hand as though she were brushing away midges. "But you'll be the one hearing those vows. And the one saying them."

Even so I take him before God.

By the time the bridal party straggled through Newabbey village and up to the kirk door, after handing out bridal favors to every passerby, the gray sky had faded to black. No stars pierced through the night's thick canopy. Nor was the waning moon anywhere to be found. Those who'd brought lanterns held them aloft, guiding everyone through the narrow doors and into the hallowed sanctuary. Even the most boisterous lowered their voices, intimidated by the pews that spoke of the Sabbath and all things holy.

Reverend Gordon, none too pleased with the late hour, greeted them with naught but a solemn nod. "It's not even five o'clock," Duncan grumbled under his breath. "Must be eager for his supper and a warm bed."

Either that or the minister disapproved of the proxy marriage. They would learn his opinion shortly. Handing her cape and gloves to Neda for safekeeping, Leana followed Duncan to the bride stool, the pew set aside especially for weddings. She took her place before it, praying her knees would hold her. The sanctuary was icy cold and dark as a tomb, despite the roaring wood fire and the smattering of lanterns around the room.

"I'll be back with the bridegroom," Duncan promised, then left her shivering by the minister's side while the guests jostled for the best seats.

"Most irregular," Reverend Gordon murmured, looking over her shoulder. "I haven't performed a proxy wedding in twenty years, Miss McBride."

She nodded, not knowing what response might be appropriate. As their guests continued to whisper among themselves, Leana turned to find one man still standing in the back of the kirk. *Jamie.* Her breath caught. Though she'd seen him earlier by the bright light of day, in the glow of the flickering candlelight he was a braw sight indeed.

Jamie walked toward her, his eyes wide, almost as if he were surprised to find her waiting for him. "Leana," he said softly, taking her hands in his, "thank you for doing this."

"It is my pleasure." She dipped her knee in a gentle curtsy. "My pleasure to be of service, that is." When she straightened, he continued to gaze at her, squeezing her hands more tightly. "What is it, Jamie? Have you . . . changed your mind?"

"Nae, I . . . I'm quite convinced we're doing the right thing." His gaze swept down to her slippers and up to the cambric kell covering her hair. "I never expected . . . that is . . ."

"Oh." She wet her lips, wondering if they could be trusted to form words, let alone vows.

Jamie's gaze rested on hers. "The kell looks lovely."

Only the kell.

He stepped back and held her arms out to get a better look. "I'm only sorry Rose isn't here to see you wearing it." He bit his lip, as though regretting his words. "I know this day has been awkward for you, Leana. For me as well. Shall we make the best of it? For Rose's sake and yours?"

She smiled and spoke the truth: "I want nothing more than to make you happy, Jamie."

His eyes shone like jade in the firelight. "You are a finer woman than any man deserves, Leana McBride. I hope you will stand in this kirk again soon with a worthy bridegroom by your side."

She swallowed her pride, leaving only the taste of hope on her lips. "Might I pretend that worthy man is you?"

His brow creased with concern. "Leana, I . . ."

"Just for this hour, I mean?" Her eyes were beggars. *Please, Jamie.*

"So be it, lass." His smile turned winter into spring. "For this hour, on this night, you will be my bride and I your bridegroom. Like a stage play, with us as the actors, playing our assigned roles." He touched his forehead against hers, wiggling his eyebrows playfully. The whisky on his breath was stronger than before. "By the time the curtain falls, our audience will be thoroughly persuaded we're well wed. Are we agreed, Leana?"

"We are." *Oh, Jamie!* She would agree to anything, anything at all, if it kept him by her side. "Shall
we begin then?"

"We shall." With a gallant movement, he released
one of her hands, then placed the other against his
arm, now tucked across his chest in formal fashion.
"Reverend Gordon, we are yours to command."

Quieting the congregation with a sternly arched
brow, the minister drew himself up, his chin pushed
out as though daring anyone to question his authority. "We are gathered here on this most solemn
occasion to join James Lachlan McKie of Glentrool
and Rose McBride of Auchengray in holy matrimony. The bride's sister, Leana McBride, will serve
as proxy and speak on Rose's behalf. Stand for a
reading from the Book of Common Order."

The gathering stood as one and dutifully listened
to the words penned by John Knox two centuries
earlier. Leana leaned on Jamie's arm, glad to have
his strength so near at hand. When the minister
wasn't paying attention, Jamie glanced over at her,
offering a wink of assurance or a slight smile. She
barely noticed the chilly room, so thoroughly did
she bask in the warmth of his attention.

"Now then." The minister closed his book, holding
it shut before him, one hand pressed on either side.
"Is there any impediment to this marriage? Any reason why the two of you should not be joined
together as husband and wife?"

None whatsoever. Leana's lips remained sealed
in a gentle smile, even as her heart cried out to be

heard. *Please, Jamie!* Behind her, she detected furtive whispers and sensed curious stares pressing against her back.

"None," Jamie stated, loudly enough that all might hear and be silenced.

Reverend Gordon stepped aside to address the congregation and posed the same question. "Is there any reason why these two should not be joined in holy matrimony?"

"None," came the immediate reply. Lachlan McBride had answered for all of them.

"We will proceed then." The minister nodded at Jamie, who produced a simple silver ring. He slid the narrow band onto her left hand, only to the knuckle, holding it there while her hand trembled at his touch, awaiting the minister's next words.

"Do you, James Lachlan McKie, take this woman, Rose McBride, to be your lawfully wedded wife?"

Jamie glanced at Leana, if only for a moment, before his voice rang out with sincerity. "Even so, I take her before God and in the presence of his congregation."

The minister turned to Leana, his brow stern. "And do you, Rose McBride, take this man, James Lachlan McKie, to be your lawfully wedded husband?"

Never had Leana spoken with more conviction. "Even so, I take him before God and in the presence of his congregation."

The minister intoned, "Give diligent ear then to

the Gospel that ye may understand how our Lord would have this holy contract kept and observed and how sure and fast a knot it is, which in no wise should be loosed."

She held her breath as he read, not pressing the ring in place until he finished. How easily the marriage knot was tied! And how difficult it would be to unravel her heart from its knotted threads.

"For this cause shall a man leave father and mother, and shall cleave to his wife: and they twain shall be one flesh."

One flesh. Her dream could not extend so far. This moment, this holy hour, would be enough. *Must* be enough, unless Jamie deemed otherwise.

"What therefore God hath joined together, let not man put asunder."

"Hear, hear," a besotted voice added from the congregation, followed by subdued laughter.

Ignoring the outburst, Reverend Gordon held his hand over the couple and pronounced his blessing: "The Lord sanctify and bless you; the Lord pour the riches of his grace upon you, that ye may please him and live together in holy love to your lives' end. So be it."

So be it.

Leana closed her eyes. Praying, wishing, hoping, begging she knew not what. There remained the possibility, slender though it was, that Rose had chosen to stay away. And that Jamie would choose the older instead of the younger. Willingly. Joyfully.

The congregation sang loudly, without regard for key or pitch, the traditional wedding psalm:

Thy wife shall be a fruitful vine
By thy house sides be found
Thy children like to olive plants
About thy table round.

Jamie bent down to press his mouth against the curve of her ear. "Cousin, you look more like a fragrant flower than a fruitful vine," he whispered, pretending not to see Reverend Gordon's pointed stare. "I do wish you many children, lass. May your house be filled with them someday. And lucky is the man who will sire them."

She hid her warm cheeks behind the lacy kell, barely listening as the minister offered a closing prayer. The play was nearly ended; the curtain soon would fall. Nothing had changed, and yet everything had changed. They'd spoken vows to each other, vows they were bound by a holy God to keep. Did the spoken name matter when her intentions were pure?

Not pure, Leana. Nae, not entirely so. She'd let her thoughts wander far beyond convention's gate. *Forgive me, Lord.*

"Amen," Reverend Gordon said, and it was finished.

Awash in emotions, she held tight to Jamie's hand and followed him down the aisle, past the smiling faces and teary smiles, out the kirk door, and into the freezing night. Reverend Gordon led the way, then turned to her, his face as dour as ever. "Well done, Miss McBride. Or should I say, Mistress McKie?"

"You should . . . kiss me, Reverend Gordon," she stammered.

"Aye, right you are. That's the custom." The minister leaned forward, pressed his dry lips against hers for only an instant, then stepped back. "The best of luck to you, Mr. McKie." He turned to Duncan with an expectant air and was duly paid for his services from the overseer's leather pouch.

Leana remembered her hostess duties and inquired, "Will we be seeing you at Auchengray for the bridal feast?"

"Nae, I'm afraid Mistress Gordon has already cooked up our supper, a steak and kidney pie for Hogmanay. Forgive me for missing the festivities." His brow darkened. "See that things don't become, shall we say, *unseemly,* as wedding celebrations are inclined to do."

"Not this one, Reverend." Jamie slipped his hand behind Leana's waist, barely touching her gown. "Not when good Leana, the kindest and best among us, is the reigning bride." He looked over her head toward Duncan. "Come, let us shower the village children with coins, then hasten home before moonrise. 'Tis ill weather for a jolly occasion."

The minister looked askance. "Aren't you going to kiss your bride? Proxy or not, it's most unlucky for her next kiss not to be yours."

"Unlucky?" Jamie gazed down at her. "Is it really?"

"Aye, very unlucky." She made certain her voice did not give away her anticipation, but her thoughts brought a flush to her cheeks.

When Jamie turned and drew her near, the warmth of him traveled from her kell to her toes. He cupped her face in his hands and brushed his thumbs across her cheeks. "May I kiss you, Leana?"

She let him see her heart in her eyes and whispered the truth. "I wish you would."

"Then I will." His mouth moved toward hers.

Forty-Seven

Drink, my jolly lads, drink with discerning;
Wedlock's a lane where there is no turning.
DINAH MARIA MULOCK CRAIK

She tasted like butterscotch. Warm, sugary, fresh from the pot.

Leana was truly kissing him. Not an actress playing a part. A bride kissing her bridegroom. Responding instinctively, Jamie leaned closer, tilting her head back, molding his lips to fit hers, tasting her again. *Sweet.*

"Enough, lad, or you'll be drunk." Rab Murray, the young shepherd, tugged on Jamie's shoulder, easing the two of them apart as their wedding guests spilled out of the kirk and gathered round to watch.

Jamie released his hold on Leana, already ashamed of himself. Whatever was he thinking? "Forgive me," he whispered, low enough that only she would hear it. He stepped back slowly, making certain Leana would not faint, for she looked very much as if she might. She swayed a bit, her face still turned upward, then her eyes opened—reluctantly, Jamie thought—and gazed steadily at him. If she heard the ribald laughter, she did not acknowledge it or look away, not for a moment.

What he saw in her eyes made his chest grow tight: *love.* Pure, selfless, unbounded love. The very thing he'd longed to see in Rose's eyes shone in her sister's, clear as moonlight.

"Jamie." She said his name softly, reverently. Like a prayer.

"Leana, I—"

"Enough o' that." Rab appeared again, her wool cape in his hands, a determined look in his eyes. "Come along, ye two, or ye'll set the gossips' tongues waggin' for mony a Hogmanay to come." Rab dropped the cape over Leana's shoulders and steered her down the street shouting, "Make way for the bride! The bride goes first!"

Jamie found himself caught up in the flood of parishioners, pulled forward by hands eager to see him take his rightful place behind the bride. The two maidens who served as his escorts, Eliza and Annabel, hooked their arms through his and delivered him to the front of the procession, one step behind Leana, who turned and watched him approach, her face luminous.

"I thought I'd lost you, Jamie."

He shook his head, still a bit unsteady from the whisky, the kiss, and the look in her eyes. "I'm not so easily lost as that."

"Good." She regarded him for a moment, as though waiting to see what else he might say, then smiled and turned back to mount her horse for the procession to Auchengray. Rab Murray stood on one side of her and another young shepherd, Davie Tait, on the other, both grinning like naughty schoolboys. Jamie remembered that Rose had chosen the young shepherds to serve as her protectors en route to the kirk, a practice from the days when warring clans would kidnap a bride and ride off with her.

Leana laughed at their attentive stances. "Gentlemen, you've nothing to fear. Nary a soul will be dragging me away to another parish."

Rab Murray gave her an appraising glance. "From where I'm standin', ye'd be a bonny prize for any man to steal. Hold, lass, while the guns are fired. Can't have yer mount tossin' ye on the dirt in yer pretty dress."

Jamie had to agree, it was a pretty dress. And she had a regal seat on the horse—her back straight, yet her shoulders relaxed, and her head pointed forward. Had they ever ridden together? *Foolish question, Jamie.* Naturally they hadn't. He'd gone riding with Rose.

The piper dispensed with his opening fanfare and proceeded to the wedding jig, "Wooed an' Married an' All," which the assembled party sang whether they knew the words or not. Endless verses followed, with a chorus between them. Only the last verse caught his attention and only because Leana was singing the words with joyful abandon:

Out spoke the bride's sister
As she came in from the byre;
O, if I were but married
It's all that I desire.

"Sing another round, Mistress McKie!" the crowd shouted, stumbling and staggering as they made their way along the dark road to Auchengray with few lamps to guide them and naught but whisky to keep them warm.

Leana answered primly, "Call me Miss McBride, if you please, and I'll gladly sing it again." Which she did, in a voice like laughter itself. Jamie joined in the chorus, thinking she might sing one more verse, but the piper launched into a reel, which none could sing for all the exuberant dancing. Someone had slipped a flask of whisky into his pocket, and he took advantage of it now, letting the heat of it seep into his limbs.

They neared the last hill when a murmur ran through the crowd. "The water! The water!" Tradition required that the bridal party cross moving water twice on the route home from the kirk. In front of him, Duncan guided Leana down to the burn that ran close by the road and forded the icy stream once, then back again, before her mount had time to protest. Jamie and the others came splashing behind her, whether on horseback or on foot, making a wet mess of things.

Through it all, Leana was a brightly lit taper, casting her glow on the neighbors and friends she'd known all her twenty years. She was meant to have this day. After her ill-fated suit with Fergus McDougal, Leana might never have a true wedding day of her own. A tragedy, when she was a good woman in every sense of the word. No wonder Rose loved her.

Rose. His heart thudded to a stop. Rose would never have a wedding day of her own either. *This* was her day, nearly spent. Had they made a terrible mistake going on without her? Would she ever forgive them? *No, Jamie. Will she ever forgive* you?

Leana, who knew Rose better than anyone, might have some idea of how such a delicate thing should be handled. As they turned the corner onto Auchengray's drive, Jamie drew up next to her and leaned over. "We must talk, Leana. About your sister. About . . . what to tell her . . . when she arrives."

Her brows lifted in mock amazement. "You mean you've not thought that through?"

"Not . . . exactly."

"This was your idea, Jamie."

"And your father's," he reminded her.

"Aye, my father had a hand in it as well. As for me, I was the willing accomplice but not the mastermind." She smiled demurely. "That task falls on your broad shoulders, dear cousin."

Without thinking, he pressed her for an answer. "How willing? How willing were you, Leana?"

Any trace of artifice disappeared from her expression. "Very willing, Jamie."

God, help me. "Then were you—"

"Mr. McKie!" One of Auchengray's servants suddenly appeared at his side, wild eyed and out of breath. "Mr. McKie, I've news from Twyneholm."

The wedding party came to a ragged halt, some stumbling ahead, others dropping behind to hear the report. The young lad crumpled his bonnet between his fingers, bobbing his head. "Me name's Ranald, sir."

"Ranald." Jamie offered a curt nod. "Tell me what you've learned."

"I rode hard, sir, and fast, as far south as I could go. Made it halfway to Twyneholm before I was turned back by a frichtsome snowstorm."

Jamie's nerves snapped to attention. "A *snowstorm?*"

"Aye. Carts and wagons stranded all over the road, axles broken, lame horses. *Och!* Ye've never seen sic a *fankle.* Not the sort of thing we aften have in Galloway."

"But no sign of Rose . . . ah, of Mistress McKie?"

"Nae sir. Yer lady and her aunt and Willie—none of them was anywhere to be seen."

Jamie exhaled, grateful for some good news. They'd not been caught traveling in the storm then. "Anything else you can tell me?"

"Well, accordin' to the folk I met on the road, the storm started in the black o' night, lang before the morn. Willie—he's a smart man, ye ken. He'd never do anythin' daft. Willie no *dout* plans to keep the ladies there in Twyneholm 'til the roads are passable."

"And when might that be?"

Another male voice answered. "I'd expect your bride tomorrow, Nephew." Jamie turned to find Lachlan strolling up with a lady neighbor on each arm. "Probably about noon, I'd say. In time for dinner."

Jamie rubbed his chin, hiding a smile. "The lass is headstrong enough, she might insist Willie bring her late this evening, storm or not." He leaned down and added for Lachlan's benefit alone, "The door to my room will be unlatched, should my bride sneak into the house at a wee, dark hour."

Lachlan chuckled at his braisant suggestion, though Jamie noticed his uncle's eyes fell on Leana as the man responded, "In that case 'twould be well after midnight, I venture." Lachlan raised his voice then and lifted his hand to catch the crowd's attention. "Dear guests, we've food that needs eating and a fiddler whose bow is itching to scratch. The feast awaits and then Hogmanay."

There was a mighty rush to the barn, where the great meal was laid out on rough tables draped in fresh linens. Candles gleamed amid evergreen boughs, giving the place a festive air. The servants had outdone themselves, scrubbing and setting the place to rights. Such a throng would never fit in the house, nor did it bode well for the new couple to invite them all under their roof. For country weddings, the barn was best. With Leana properly seated at the head of the table, Jamie assumed his rightful task of waiting on her and her guests, and the courses commenced: barley broth, then beef, mutton, and goose, bread and oatcakes, and finally puddings swimming in cream. And cups of ale, from first to last, with drams of whisky for good measure.

"Had I more daughters, I'd host a penny wedding every month," Lachlan boasted, as each guest provided a shilling for his meal, more for his drink. Jamie saw him count the coins when no one else was paying attention and then spirit them safely away in Duncan's pockets. Lachlan's thrifite would be overflowing long before the New Year bells had rung. Many more folk came to the bridal feast than attended the wedding, eager to partake of the bonnet laird's bounty and the fiddler's jolly tunes. Even Gypsies and other travelers were welcome to avail themselves of the feast, if they could scrape up a shilling.

By the time the moon rose low in the winter sky, the tables had been pushed aside to make room for dancing. "Bride's reel first," the piper called. Leana stepped forward to do her duty and held out a hand for Jamie to join her, her eyes twinkling, but not from the ale. Unlike him, she hadn't drunk a sip. Her gaze glowed with something else he was only beginning to understand. It frightened him, this love of hers, yet fascinated him as well.

Jamie walked to the center of the barn, aware of the silent anticipation that hovered around them. It'd been easier to play their roles at the kirk. Here, in Auchengray's barn, pretense was put aside. Bonnet lairds and beggars sat at the same table. Gentlemen and peasants ate from the same dish. For one night all souls were equal in this place. He was not the great McKie of Glentrool, but only Jamie, warmed by whisky, about to dance with his proxy bride.

She'd carefully stored the white kell in the house earlier, leaving her hair unbound, gleaming like spun gold in the candlelight. Her eyes were gray-blue pools, and her mouth curved into a smile. Leana was not as bonny as her sister, but she was as bonny as he'd ever seen her. He slipped one hand behind her waist and loosely clasped her hand with the other. Leana felt natural in his arms and vibrantly alive. "Will you dance with me, lass?"

"Aye, Jamie." She lifted her free hand and placed it lightly on his shoulder. "I will." She called out a tune, and the fiddler complied, striking his bow as the piper pressed his bellows. On the first note they swept to the right, moving clockwise, not *widdershins,* holding ill luck at bay once more.

Within seconds Jamie realized he was the lucky one. Leana was the perfect dance partner, sailing gracefully across the dirt floor as though it were polished oak in a Brussels salon. Round they went, joined in the second reel by Eliza with Rab and Annabel with Davie, all four blushing as they swirled past them. By the third tune, the barn floor was crowded with couples, forming long lines as they prepared to greet their partners and join in the reel. As the bride, Leana had the right to dance with anyone she pleased, yet Jamie was the only partner she chose, dance after dance, strathspey to jig.

The hour was late when someone hollered, "It's nearly Hogmanay!" and another year knocked on their door. The youngest among the revelers called out, "We are but bairns come to play! Rise up and gie us our Hogmanay!" Neda appeared as though by magic, bearing trays of black bun. The yeasty Hogmanay favorite was flavored with cinnamon, nutmeg, cloves, and caraway, mixed with currants, orange peel, and almonds soaked in French brandy. Handfuls were gathered up and passed about the dance floor, tucked into hungry mouths, and washed down with ale.

Breathless from dancing, Jamie and Leana found a bench where they might rest their sore feet, repeatedly trampled upon. He nicked a bit of black bun off Neda's tray as it passed by and waved it under Leana's nose. "A taste for you, my proxy bride?" She nodded and popped open her mouth expectantly, catching Jamie by surprise. He hadn't meant to feed her. His hands were less than steady from too many cups of ale as he broke off a piece and pressed it between her lips.

After quickly swallowing, she pinched a taste for him as well and placed it in his mouth. He swallowed with some difficulty, so tight was his throat. She fed him a second bite, whispering as she did, "I must go, Jamie. When the kirk bell rings at midnight, I need to be inside the house."

Jamie nodded, understanding. It was unlucky for her to remain outside. Once Hogmanay began, their guests would depart Auchengray to roam the neighborhood and celebrate "first-footing," calling at

any house where a light still burned. In their pockets waited pieces of coal to wish the hosts a warm
house through the year and black bun to fill their
stomachs. In their hands would be *het* pints of ale
mixed with spirits, eggs, cream, sugar, and nutmeg.
A cup of cheer would be shared, then it was off to
the next house and on until dawn.

"The first foot across each threshold should be a
man," Leana reminded him, standing to leave. "A
dark-haired man, like you."

He stood as well, taking her hands in his, willing
her to stay a moment longer. "But a bachelor is
best. As you well know, I'm no longer single."

"Yet I am still a maiden and a fair-haired one at
that, which makes me unlucky indeed." She shook
her hair like a filly with a newly brushed mane. "No
one would care to have me knock on their door
tonight."

I would. Fearing she might hear his traitorous
thought and bolt away, he gripped her hands.
"Leana . . . Leana, thank you. For everything." What
else could he say? A dozen things, all of them without honor. "I will see you in the morning then."

"You will."

When he finally let go of her hands, she touched
his cheek, then slipped off the silver wedding band
and pressed it into his hand. "Good night." Her eyes
wet with tears, she turned and disappeared into the
throng, quickly lost from sight.

Leana.

"Son?" Lachlan came up behind him and clapped
a firm hand on his shoulder. "You look like a man

who might benefit from a dram of Hogmanay cheer." His uncle—his father-in-law now—pressed him back onto the bench and dropped down beside him. "I have just the thing for a lonely bridegroom."

"I am that, sir." Jamie sighed heavily, fingering the warm ring.

"Aye, and rightly so." Lachlan slapped a pewter cup on the wood between them and produced a flask, pitching the cork aside as soon as it pulled free. "You've a long night ahead and a longer day after. A man needs his strength, and I've just the thing for it." He poured a dram of whisky and tossed it down, then immediately poured another and handed it to Jamie. "Drink up, laddie. Drink up before I change my mind and keep it for myself."

Jamie slipped the ring in his waistcoat pocket, drank the whisky in a single swallow, then held out the empty pewter cup. "I've need of another, Uncle. To keep the winter cold from my door."

"Oo aye!" Lachlan chuckled. "A young man's bed should ne'er be cold."

Forty-Eight

A winter's night, a woman's mind,
and a laird's purpose aften change.
SCOTTISH PROVERB

Leana sat at the top of the stair and listened to the empty house breathe. The night wind moaned outside, making the shutters rattle and the floorboards creak, while the stone walls remained solid and immovable.

Be like the stone, Leana. And not like the supple wood, bending at the strong wind's command. She felt like neither stone nor wood but rather like the rose petals she'd strewn that morning across the bed in Rose's room. *Jamie's room.* The petals were no longer fresh but brittle, easily broken, meant to release a last sigh of fragrance when crushed beneath the weight of a husband and wife becoming one flesh.

Jamie, Jamie! He had broken her heart a thousand times, only to mend it with a gentle touch, a warm glance. Did he know that he held such sway over her? That whatever he asked she would do and more? She pressed her palms against her eyes, holding back the tears that would not stop. She had never known what it meant to love a man, and now that she knew, she wished—oh, how much she wished!—that she did not.

Before Jamie walked through Auchengray's door, the only love she'd known had been pure, righteous, and honorable. Love for her mother long ago. Love for her dear sister now. Love without compromise. Love that required sacrifice. The love of a child for its mother, a sister for a sister. Love that grew like a garden, always lovely, fresh every season.

But this . . . this obsession with Jamie was a garden full of weeds, choking out the beauty in her life, twisting and binding itself to all living things until they withered and died. Her sweet sister would return tomorrow, if not this very night, yet all Leana could think of was Jamie. How he looked at her, how he touched her hand, how he kissed her mouth. *Forgive me, Rose!* She could beg for forgiveness, but still she could not stop wanting him.

Jamie had looked at her—at her, not at Rose—before he pledged his troth. And for one splendid moment outside the kirk, he'd shown his true feelings for her. At least they seemed genuine, for his kiss was not that of a cousin but of a husband, a lover. She'd nearly swooned when he finished with her.

Somewhere outside in the darkness of the new-born year, the fiddler struck up a final tune. It faded as he played on, walking down the drive toward home. The musicians were always the last to leave, the others having gone off to celebrate Hogmanay while the servants were kept busy cleaning the barn. Jamie and her father were nowhere to be found. And Rose was yet to be seen on her wedding day.

Leana hummed the familiar fiddle tune, then realized with a sinking heart that she knew the words as well:

O! how can I be blithe and gay,
When this is my sister's wedding day?
For I should first have been away.
O! she has beat me clean.

"Aye, dear Rose, you have," she said aloud, her voice echoing down the stair. "I was to marry first, remember? I don't mind that you've taken my place, dearie. Only that you've taken my love."

All at once the front door banged open, and familiar voices chimed through the empty hall. *Father. And Jamie.* She scooted closer to the wall, knowing they could not see her, yet fearing they might find her there, drenched in tears and sorrow on this happiest of nights.

"Wait, Uncle. Wait." Jamie's voice was rougher

than usual. She recognized the sound. *Whisky.* He seldom drank spirits and would sorely regret it come the morn's morn. In the quiet house she could hear every word Jamie said. "I'm supposed to carry my wife across the threshold. This threshold right here."

"Aye, and break the bride cake over her head as well," Lachlan said, equally besotted.

Leana hung her head, ashamed to recall she'd managed those wedding customs by herself less than an hour ago, leaping over the threshold for good luck, then crumbling a bit of black bun over her head as well. A pathetic gesture, but she'd done it nonetheless.

"Never mind all that, lad," Lachlan was saying. Their footsteps moved closer to the stair. "To bed with you now. The hour is long past midnight, and you've need of a good night's sleep."

"And a good wife to sleep with!" Jamie chuckled at his own jest.

When the men's boots touched the bottom step, Leana bolted to her feet and backed toward her bedroom door, wondering how she might open it without giving herself away. By the time her hand touched the latch, it was too late. They'd rounded the landing and were staring straight up at her. "Happy New Year," she said lamely.

"And to you, lass," her father said, continuing to climb toward her, his arm around Jamie's sagging shoulders. When they reached the top of the stair, Jamie stopped directly in front of her, with Lachlan behind him providing support.

"Leana." Ever the gentleman, Jamie made certain his bleary gaze traveled no lower then her face, even though her wool wrapper covered her from neck to toe.

"Leana," he said again, "how can I ever thank you for all you've done?"

Oh, Jamie. She didn't want to be thanked. She wanted to be loved. Could he not see that? Was it not written across her face in a bold hand?

Lachlan peered over Jamie's shoulder, his eyes sharper than she'd expected. "Leana, your cousin has asked you a question: How might he show his thanks?"

Leana could barely breathe, let alone think, with Jamie's eyes boring into hers. She saw desire there. Aye, and a bit of fear. How well she understood them both.

"Father, I . . . I believe Cousin Jamie has already . . . expressed his gratitude. In many ways."

Lachlan would not be dissuaded. "Have you something to show for it, lass? A gift perhaps? Something solid, such as coin for your tocher or coal for your grate?"

Jamie glanced over his shoulder. Something in his expression made her father lean away from him ever so slightly, though Jamie said nothing. When he turned back to her, his gaze was filled with regret. "I have nothing to give you, Leana. Even the clothes on my back were bought with your father's money."

"Jamie . . ." She touched his arm. "There is nothing I need. Nothing except the one thing you cannot give me."

The muscles in his neck tightened. "I would if I could."

"I know," she whispered, feeling a fresh spate of tears springing to her eyes. "Good night, Jamie." She released the latch behind her and disappeared into her room, closing the door behind her, then falling against it in a crumpled heap.

The men's footsteps faded down the hall and their voices as well. Pressed against the door like a common eavesdropper, she heard the door to Rose's room open and close with a soft bang. Silence filled the second floor of the house. Her father had gone in to speak to him, it seemed. *To bed, Leana.* Sleep could not cure a broken heart, but it was a beginning.

She slipped beneath the woolen covers, leaving one taper burning high on the dresser where it would not disturb her slumber. Clouds had moved in and blotted out the moon, for the window was dark, and her whole room, except for the tiny flame, remained pitch black. "As dark as a Yule midnight," Neda would say. Darkness was nothing to fear. Far greater fears gnawed on Leana's soul. A life without love, without a husband, without children. For her it was no life at all. But what if that was the life the Almighty had chosen for her? If it pleased him, could she bear it?

The knock at her bedroom door was so soft she almost didn't hear it until it came again, three light taps in a row. *Jamie?* She threw back the covers and reached for the candle, laying her other hand across her neckline in a moment of modesty. Foolish. He'd already seen her heart; the rest of her held no secrets. She took a slight breath to give herself strength, then lifted the latch, holding the taper in front of her as she opened the door.

She blinked in surprise. "Father?"

Lachlan lifted one finger to his lips to silence her, then pushed open the door, inviting himself in. His gaze darted toward the latch, and she quickly closed it, shivering from the cold and his icy, sober stare.

"What is it, Father?"

"You know verra well what brings me here. To convince you to take what is rightfully yours."

"Rightfully mine?" She balked, distancing herself from him. "*What* is rightfully—"

"Not *what!*" he hissed, his face reddening. "*Who!* Jamie McKie, the cousin you married in the kirk today, with the whole parish as witnesses. That's who is rightfully yours, by God's law and man's law as well."

"Father!" He could not have shocked her more. "I was merely a proxy, standing in for my sister. It is Rose who has the right to claim Jamie. It is Rose who married him today."

His eyes were slits. "Did you not hear me say earlier that this would be your only wedding? Your only hope for a husband?"

She stood her ground, though the candle in her hand trembled. "I would rather be alone forever than steal my sister's husband."

"Och! What a stubborn child you are." His voice was low but frighteningly even. "Did you think by speaking your sister's name in the kirk the deed was done?"

"Aye . . . I did think so." She nodded, swallowing great lumps of fear that kept rising to choke her. "I . . . I *do* think so, Father. You can be certain Reverend Gordon thinks so."

"I am laird of this property, and it is only what I think that matters." He deliberately stepped closer, holding up one finger as though to shake it at her. "And I say it's not the wedding that matters, it's the marriage. The kirk can be paid to believe it was you who were meant to be the bride all along. Marriages are not made in kirk; they are made in bed."

She looked away from him, ashamed. "What if Jamie does not want me in his bed?"

Lachlan thrust his finger in the direction of Jamie's room. "You cannot tell me that my nephew is not thinking of you—*you,* Leana—this very minute. Imagining you in his arms and meikle more, I'll warrant."

"Father, I . . . I have no reason to believe that's so." Inside her, another voice begged to differ. *His eyes said so. His kiss said so. It could be so.*

"I've watched Jamie all day, lass. Gazing at you like a besotted schoolboy. Dancing with you and feeding you sweets from his own hand. And kissing you." He rolled his eyes. "*Losh!* I've never seen such a vulgar display by the kirk doors in all my long life."

She'd not heard him use the Lord's name so freely. *Forgive him, Father. And forgive me as well.* For what? For loving a man who very well might love her after all?

Her father pressed his case, leaning so close he nearly burned his waistcoat on her candle. "He wants you, lass. No matter what your cousin may say with words, his heart, his eyes, and his body cannot deny the truth. What did his body tell you, Leana? When he held you, when he kissed you, what message did he send?"

Need.

"Aye, I can see it reflected in your own eyes, even in the dark of night. And what do his eyes tell you, lass? What story do you find there?"

Desire.

"So be it. And when you look into his heart—and don't tell me you can't, Leana, for I've known you these twenty years, and no one has a better grasp of such things than you—in that heart of his, what do you find?"

Longing.

She turned away from him, weary of being forced to reveal what she'd kept hidden, tired of being probed so deeply by one who knew her better than any man on earth. "Father, what would you have me do?"

"Jamie asked you, as clearly as any man could, what he might do to thank you. Did you hear him say those words?"

Leana nodded. It was fruitless to argue.

"And his last words to you: *I would if I could.* Well, Daughter, he *can* and he *will!*" His voice, still tinged with whisky, sharpened to a low hiss. "It is Jamie McKie, or it is no one, remember." Lachlan stepped back, like a barrister releasing the jury. "I leave you to your thoughts, Leana. Do what you must." He blew out her candle and unlatched the door, leaving as quietly as he came.

Leana stood there, the candle wax cooling even as her limbs began to tremble from the cold. Or from fear. Or from desire. It was impossible to separate them now. Her father could not be trusted, that much she knew. But could she trust her own eyes and ears to tell her the truth when her heart wanted Jamie so desperately?

Not only her heart. Her body wanted him as well. She was not a girl, like Rose. She was a woman, and she could not pretend otherwise.

Forgive me.

She put the candle aside, shivering as she tightened her wrapper. Her father's demands alone could not make her climb into Jamie's bed. Even her own longings would not be enough to open his door. But if Jamie desired her . . . if Rose did not love him . . . if their spoken vows might be valid after all . . . if his kiss was true and his warm gaze genuine . . . if he meant what he said . . . *I would if I could.*

Could he? Could Jamie decide for them both?

Her mouth fell open in astonishment at the simplicity of the answer: *Aye!* She could not trust her father, but she could trust Jamie. He would welcome her openly, or he would refuse her soundly. Jamie would decide. Not Lachlan, not her.

Leana spun about the room, bumping into things, caring not for the bruises. *Jamie!* She would go to him tonight, now. Her fear was gone, and in its place anticipation thrummed through her limbs. She ran her fingers through her long hair, imagining him doing the very same with his hands. *Jamie.*

Even in the dark room, the white kell caught her eye. Without thinking, she pulled off her wrapper and chemise and draped the cambric veil over her head. Earlier in the day it had only brushed against her face, but now it touched her back and covered her breasts. She tiptoed toward the long mirror, her heart beating so loudly she was certain Jamie could hear it in the next room. The reflection was faint but enough to show her what she'd hoped to see: She was bonny enough. Not so beautiful as Rose, but in the darkened room she could go to him without apology.

If he rejected her, she would survive. Had he not already refused her love before? He and Rose would leave for Glentrool and take her shame with them, leaving her to pick up what was left of her heart and build a new life without Jamie.

But if he did want her . . . if he did *love* her . . . then she must go to him, for his marriage to Rose would be a sham. And her own life without him would be a travesty.

Leana clasped her hands for a moment, seeking the courage she needed, then unlatched her door and stepped into the darkened hall. The servants were all outside. Not a sound could be heard any- where in the house. Jamie's door, only three steps away, was slightly ajar. It would swing open with the slightest touch.

She would not knock. She would not speak. But she would go to him and seek his blessing. Leana gathered her love about her like a veil and moved toward his bedroom door.

Forty-Nine

I love the night because she brings
My love to me in dreams which scarcely lie.
PHILIP JAMES BAILEY

Jamie did not remember when or how he'd removed his cravat, but he must have done so. His
neck was bare. So were his legs, which meant he'd
done away with his breeches before falling into bed.
Well and good. Only his shirt remained, as was
proper. His valet would approve. The few times in
his life when Jamie had consumed that much
whisky, he'd collapsed in a chair fully dressed, hat
to boots, and slept till noon.

It was not noon now; it was night. Well past midnight, though no moonlight filtered through the win-

dow to tell him so. How long had he slept? Less than an hour, for his body still ached for a great deal more sleep. The taper on the tall dresser, left burning lest he need to move about in the night, had lost little of its height. Aye, not long then. He rolled over on his back, folding his hands behind his head, making himself comfortable beneath the new linen sheets, enjoying the clean feel of them against his legs.

The whole box bed smelled like roses. How had the women of the house managed that? He drank in the scent until he was nigh to dizzy with it. *Rose.* It had been her idea, he was sure of it. To make him think of her. To make him long for her until the moment she walked through the door to his bedroom—well, *her* bedroom. Now it was *their* room. At least it would be when she arrived at Auchengray, which couldn't happen soon enough to please him.

Lachlan had said . . . What *had* the man told him? That she might appear after midnight? Or had he suggested that himself earlier? His memory was playing tricks on him, confusing him. Jamie groaned, then sat up, determined to sort out what he did and did not remember from the day before. The last day of the year.

When Rose hadn't walked through the door at noon, the time she was expected, he and Lachlan had agreed that Leana would serve as her proxy. Or had that been Lachlan's idea? It mattered not. The fact was, Leana did stand in for her sister, and a very good proxy bride she was.

She was bonny.

He remembered that quite clearly. Leana had made a bonny bride, dressed in a wine-colored sort of gown. Or was it dark blue? He rubbed his forehead, hoping to ease the pain that throbbed inside his head. She wore a white kell, of that he was certain. A soft, filmy thing all around her sweet face. Aye, her face was *douce,* but her kiss was more so. He rubbed his brow harder, thinking it prudent to erase that memory altogether. A sudden urge for a dish of butterscotch overwhelmed him.

He shook his head, then wished he hadn't. The room spun a bit. They'd kissed, he and Leana, outside the kirk. In the cold. With the lanterns. For a moment he'd forgotten—or pretended to forget, which was it?—that they weren't alone. They had kissed for a long time, as though it mattered, as though it meant something. *Och!* And her eyes. Jamie smiled in the dark, remembering her eyes, which were filled with pure light and immeasurable love. So much love that it scared him senseless.

Had he ever seen a woman's eyes so filled with regard for him? Even his mother, who'd plainly adored him from infancy, never looked at him that way, nor had Rose. Only Leana. Dear, misguided Leana. Whatever did she see in him to warrant such devotion? He knew what he was: a liar and a thief. He'd lied to his father and stolen from his brother. If Saint Leana knew that, she would pack her bags and move as far from Auchengray as her feet might take her.

Which might be very far, because her feet carried her across the barn floor more gracefully than any woman he'd ever seen. He remembered *that;* aye, he did. They'd danced for hours, the two of them. No wonder he was so thirsty yestreen. No wonder he drank more ale in a night than he had in a year.

He fell back on the heather mattress, and the scent of roses wafted up to greet him. *Rose.* He needed to be thinking of her, of his bride, his love. Not of her sister, her proxy, his cousin. *Leana.*

Leana had told him more than once that she loved him. *I love you still.* She had said the words, realizing he did not love her in return, knowing that he intended to marry her sister. She was a brave lass, that Leana. A woman, not a child. Was Rose a child? She would be sixteen next August. *And you will be twenty-five next September.* It made him feel old to think of having so young a bride. His father was much older than Rowena. *Aye, and look how the woman regards him.* Without nearly as much respect as Alec McKie deserved, nor with as much affection.

Jamie sat up again, suddenly ill at ease. Would Rose look at him the same way in years to come? As a man who could be tricked and deceived, whose will could be bent to suit hers? Was he as blinded by his beautiful Rose as Alec was by his sonsie Rowena?

Nae. He wouldn't entertain such foolish thoughts, because they weren't true. Rose had an innocence about her that Rowena might never have possessed. Rose was beautiful, yes, but she was also sweet tempered, kindhearted, and utterly good. *Or was that Leana?*

He slapped the mattress. *Enough about Leana!* He was not in love with his wife's sister, not in the least. Rose had stolen his heart completely and left for Twyneholm with it tucked inside her reticule. When she returned—please God, might it be soon—she would come home bearing his heart in her hands. Lovely Rose, with her black hair swirling all around her ivory skin. Bonny Rose, with her dark eyes snapping at him. Clever Rose, behaving like a child one moment, like a grown woman the next. Charming Rose, with her sweet laugh and her sweeter lips and her small waist and her . . .

Well.

He could think of her no more, or he would ride Walloch all the way to Twyneholm to claim his bride that very night. *Let her come to me.* He stretched his long limbs, satisfied to hear his joints crack and pop, then wrapped himself in the rose-scented sheets, closing his eyes and dreaming of his new bride, of Rose.

Let her come to me. Tonight. Soon.

Yes, that was the last thing Lachlan had said to him before they'd said good night. That his daughter would slip into her bridegroom's bed in the wee, dark hours of the night. That Jamie should leave the door unlatched. He'd said he would, and he did. Lachlan told him to be certain that all was in readiness for her arrival and that Jamie should not be alarmed to wake and find a woman in his bed.

He would not be alarmed. He would be delighted.

Jamie's eyes drifted shut, and his body relaxed into slumber. Far down the stair, above the hearth, the mantel clock ticked so loudly he could almost count the seconds. *Tick. Tock.* He fell deeper into the twilight world of sleep. *Tick. Tock.* Beyond the dark edges of the room, a door creaked open. Jamie was so thoroughly exhausted he paid no attention to a door closing, or a candle snuffing itself out, or a curtain being drawn closed. Instead, he rolled over and slept the sleep of the dead.

The dream—for it had to be a dream, it was too vivid to be real—began with the brush of a woman's hand across his cheek. Aye, definitely a woman. Her fingers were supple and slender, her touch as light as an angel's wing. Like the angels that climbed up and down the ladder to heaven. Jacob's ladder. Not the leafy plant. The vision, the dream, his dream. At last he'd remembered it! His dream, all of it, spread before him, clear as day in a room black as pitch. Angels and stairsteps and a voice from above.

"Don't leave me," he whispered, afraid to open his eyes.

"I will never leave you." A woman's voice, soft as air.

He believed her completely.

"Jamie, it's me."

Not merely a dream. A dream come true. Sweet Rose.

She had come to him, just as Lachlan had said she would. Traveling through the night, through the wind and the snow, just to be with her bridegroom. He opened his arms to her, and she slid into them as though they'd already spent a thousand nights together. "Welcome, beloved," he said. Her sigh was a song.

The box bed curtains were drawn tight. Not a sliver of light entered their world. It was only the two of them, and no other existed. He could not see, but he could feel, and what he felt was more than enough. Time and the night would stand still until he had his fill of her. *My love.*

But would she say it now? Would she tell him that she loved him?

"Say you love me," he whispered.

"I love you," she whispered back. "I've always loved you, Jamie."

"And I you, dearest. Always. From the first. But then, you knew that."

"Aye." In the darkness she smiled. He could tell, could feel her lips on his neck, curling up at the corners.

She was wearing something long, a single cloth, nothing more. "Is this . . . your kell?"

"It is. My bride's veil. Will you lift it away now?"

"I will." He tossed it aside and his shirt as well. "And will you let me love you?"

"I will." She kissed him. Not as she'd kissed him when they met, with sheep bleating all about them on a grassy hill, nor as she'd kissed him in the garden, a frightened girl. This was a bride's kiss. A lover's kiss. His young Rose was blooming that very moment into a woman.

Fifty

Our lips, without words, find the way to the heart.
GEORGE ALEXANDER STEVENS

Leana was stunned to silence.

It was almost as though Jamie expected her. As though he *knew* she would come to him. As though the moonless night and the dark hour and the curtained bed had prepared themselves for her quiet entrance.

All that was required was to slip into his waiting arms. Which she did. Oh, so willingly. *Jamie.* His bed was warm, and he was warmer still. Welcoming her with an eager embrace. *Jamie.*

He'd said he loved her, as simply as that.

"I love you, I love you," she'd whispered back,

kissing him again. And again. He tasted like whisky, but she told herself she didn't mind. That tomorrow night he would taste like Jamie again. His words were slurred, but not terribly so. What few words he said were everything she needed to hear. *I love you.* His sighs were poetry and his soundless touches a symphony.

He seemed hungry to taste her skin. "Like honey," he said, and so she let him do as he wished, too overwhelmed to speak. There was nothing to say. She wanted to whisper his name again, but—selfishly perhaps—she needed to hear her own name first. *Leana.* He would say it soon enough. She would wait. And while she waited, she would love him and hold nothing back.

Jamie.

He had chosen her for his bride after all.

Forgive us, Rose.

Surely her father was right about Rose's name in the ceremony being nothing more than words. Jamie had made his vow to her, to Leana. And to God, in the presence of his congregation. That vow would be consummated soon, very soon. Now, this night.

Mine, Jamie. You are mine.

The rose petals that she'd scattered across the bed released an intoxicating perfume. In a moment she would be drunk with flowers. She giggled at the thought, until he kissed her into silence once more. When he stretched himself against her, their toes touched. His feet were heated from the warming pan; hers were cold from the hall floor. "Warm me," she whispered, and he did, until there was no part of her that was not heated to a flame.

Everything was different, all was new, and the old Leana was lost forever.

They drifted in and out of sleep, finding each other in the darkness, twining themselves together. Time was locked outside the room, barred from their bed. There was no hour of day or night, only love, and for that they had all the hours in the world.

When Jamie finally drifted off to sleep for good, Leana found herself more awake, more alive, than she could ever remember. *Oh, my dear husband!* To be so loved and shown such love was beyond her most cherished dreams. She wanted to laugh, she wanted to sing, she wanted to run into the hall and shout of her love for James Lachlan McKie so the whole household might know what a transforming thing true love could be.

Did every bride feel the same way? *Surely not!* She buried her face in the covers to hide her laughter. No bride could possibly feel as she felt, for no bride had come so close to losing everything. Jamie was the husband she'd almost let go. Jamie was the man God had put across her path, and she'd nearly walked away from him out of fear. Fear that he did not love her and never could.

But he did love her and had thoroughly proven so. She would never doubt again.

In the murky interior of the box bed, she found the white kell, more by touch than by sight. She could feel the intricate patterns carefully wrought across the fabric, stitched by a loving hand in another country. Did that woman know how greatly she would bless a Scottish lass this Hogmanay? Leana could never place it over her head again, for a kell could only be worn by a maiden. The thought both saddened and thrilled her. A maiden no more. A woman, a wife.

She smoothed her hand across the veil, an unspoken farewell. The thin cambric was covered in roses, and so was her marriage bed. She must now think of how to tell Rose, her dear, precious sister, that Jamie had chosen her instead. Might the lass be crushed, or would she be relieved? After all, Rose was young and had often confessed she was afraid to marry. With many years left to find a husband, a society debut could still be in her future. Besides, hadn't Rose pushed Leana in Jamie's direction since the moment he arrived? *You were right after all, Rose!* That's what she would tell her sister. That her instincts had been right and her efforts had not been in vain. *Dear Rose.*

A hint of daylight crept between the bed curtains. From down the stair came familiar sounds, a household stirring from a winter night's slumber. Jamie slept on, his breathing even, his smooth face that of a younger man, free of any cares that might wrinkle his brow. She curled up against him, pressing her cheek against his shoulder and draping one arm across his broad chest.

Perhaps she would sleep, just for an hour. It was bound to be a hectic day, and she had so much good news to share when she awakened.

Fifty-One

Awake thee, my Lady-Love!
Wake thee, and rise!
The sun through the bower peeps
Into thine eyes.
GEORGE DARLEY

Jamie's eyes opened only a crack, then he squeezed them tight, shutting out the invading light of day, which had thrust its bright saber between his bed curtains, the unsheathed point aimed directly at his throbbing forehead.

The year 1789 was off to a very bad start.

Pain droned between his eyes, like a bagpipe playing one long, bleating, endless note. The chanter's tune that danced around it was a taunting one. *Nae mair whisky for you. Nae mair whisky for you.* Jamie vowed that come next Hogmanay he would remember that dreary song and be more prudent with his drinking. One cup of ale. Nae mair.

He forced himself to swallow, disgusted by the bitter taste in his mouth. A fresh pitcher of water and Hugh's razor would be a welcome sight. But he'd have to part the bed curtains to get there, and it was entirely too bright in the room to suit him. Perhaps if he pushed the fabric aside a bit at a time, the light would not be so painful.

Stretching out his hand, he tugged at the curtains, and a pool of daylight fell across his arm. In the far corner of the room, the narrow window was flooded with sunshine. It seemed that while he slept, the gray skies of yestreen had transformed themselves into a canvas of pale, shimmering blue stretched across the heavens. In January? Unheard of.

He longed to know the time. Was it late morning? Noon? Later still? He rubbed his eyes, then his brow, moaning as he did. *Happy New Year, laddie.* Though his head remained foggy, his eyes slowly adjusted to the dim light around him as he pulled the bed curtains open further. It was noon at the earliest. Strange that no one had come knocking on his door. Lachlan would be ringing the bell for dinner before long. And whatever was his shirt doing on the floor? Had the fire burned so brightly he'd torn off the sark in his sleep?

Jamie lifted himself with great difficulty into a sitting position. He threw back the covers, absently turning to look over his shoulder as he did.

Leana!

Jamie snatched his hand back, as though bitten by an adder, and stared at the sleeping woman. It *was* Leana; there could be no doubt. She was curled up with her back to him, her hands tucked beneath her cheek, her slender legs drawn up against her chest. Her flowing, blond hair covered some of her pale skin but not enough of it. Not nearly enough. She was naked. In his bed. Fast asleep.

His heart pounded in his chest, the pain in his head already forgotten. One thing was certain: He was sober now. Wretchedly so. What had happened? Where was Rose? He tried to swallow but could not manage it. Water, he needed water or he might choke on his own spit. Slipping one leg over his side of the box bed, he eased one foot to the floor, then the other, as gingerly as possible, not wanting to wake her, not until he sorted things out. What had happened? Where was Rose? And why, in heaven's name, was her sister asleep beside him?

Jamie stood, then yanked the bed curtains shut, trying to block out the sight of her, desperate for a moment to think, to remember. What had he done? What grievous sin had he committed in the dark hours of the night? It was obvious, wasn't it? Her scent was all over him. He bolted to the washstand and splashed the pitcher of water over his hands,

his face, his mouth, his chest, like a man possessed.

The vivid images that appeared unbidden were
not as easy to scrub away. His falling asleep,
dreaming of Rose. A woman slipping into his room,
slipping into his arms. *Jamie, it's me.* Rose. He'd
been certain it was Rose. *I've always loved you,
Jamie.* She'd said his name, said that she loved
him.

I love you still.

Leana.

His blood rising, he grabbed a towel and dragged
it across his face and arms, drying them with a
vengeance as the truth sank in: She had come into
his room, pretending to be Rose, and ruined his
wedding night. And not just his wedding night, his
marriage. No bride would ever stand for such wan-
ton behavior from her bridegroom. To be unfaithful
to her, on their wedding night, *with her sister!*
Unthinkable, unspeakable. Rage seethed inside
him, drenching him with heat, despite the empty
hearth and the freezing cold room.

He'd not been cold in the wee hours of the night.
Oh no, he'd been very warm indeed. Awakened
memories suddenly washed over him, burning him
from the inside out. The intimate things they'd done,
the countless ways he'd bared his soul to her. The
endearments he'd whispered in the dark, in the
sanctity of their marriage bed. To Rose, he'd
thought. To his wife. *Not to her sister!*

Jamie drew the ends of the linen towel taut
between his hands, stretching it, twisting it, nigh

pulling it to shreds. *How dare she! How dare Leana do this to her sister and to me?* But she *had* dared. It was done.

He stared at the curtained box bed, wishing he could turn back the clock. Twelve hours would be enough to save him. *God help me.* Such things were impossible. But one thing he could do was rid himself of every trace of her. Aye, he could do that. He plunged the towel into the bowl of water, then scrubbed his skin clean from head to foot, disgusted with himself for having been part of such swickerie, however unwittingly.

It was Leana's fault, from start to finish. Not his. Not Rose's. Leana's alone.

What had she called herself? A "willing accomplice"?

Very willing, Jamie. Aye, she'd certainly been that.

His conscience assaulted him. *You were willing as well. Very willing.* The towel tightened in his hands, threatening to stop the blood from flowing to his fingers. Of course he was willing. He thought she was Rose. Leana knew what she was doing. And he did not.

He pressed the towel between his teeth, biting down hard on it, forcing himself to think of every careless word he'd ever spoken to Leana that might have led her to believe, to foolishly convince herself that . . .

The vows.

True, he'd spoken them with feeling and conviction but only because in his mind he was saying them to Rose. Leana heard him pledge his troth, but those vows were never meant for her.

The kiss.

He lowered the towel, remembering how it had been when he kissed her. Aye, after the ceremony. Outside the kirk. That must have been it. Somehow he'd given her the wrong sense of how it was between them. They were cousins, they were friends, they were in-laws, but they were not lovers. Not then. Not now. It was only one kiss. And hadn't she been the one who said, "I wish you would"?

The dance.

He'd held Leana in his arms but no more than any other partner whirling about the floor. Had his touch been too familiar? Had his gaze told her something he'd never meant to say?

Good night.

There, in the hall, at the top of the stair. What had he said to her? "I would if I could." But he could not, of course. Could not even consider it. He was married to Rose. Leana knew that and had chosen to ignore it.

I love you, I love you. How many times had she told him that last night? Why hadn't he listened to her voice instead of her body? How could he have been so deceived?

Nae. She was the one who was deceived. Her sort of love wasn't genuine at all but a delusion, a hope based on air. Not a blessing, as love should be, but a curse. A curse . . .

Aye, that's it!

Gripping the towel in one hand, he snapped it

through the dry air, pleased with the crack it made, like a whip against a post. What had his father said when he'd blessed him? "Cursed be anyone who curses you." *Let Leana be cursed then!* She deserved that and more.

Flushed with a sense of justice, he threw the towel to the floor and marched over to the clothing press, yanking out the first shirt he found. He dressed with a haste born of anger and tied the laces on his breeches with a brutish hand. Suitably dressed for the grim day ahead, Jamie yanked the bed curtains aside without ceremony, no longer caring how much racket he made or how rudely she was roused.

"Get up, Leana."

She sat up with a start, shaking her head, her pale eyes wide but not quite focused. Her hair fell around her shoulders as she lifted her face to him and smiled. "Jamie."

Fifty-Two

When lovely woman stoops to folly,
And finds too late that men betray,
What charm can soothe her melancholy?
What art can wash her guilt away?
OLIVER GOLDSMITH

Don't speak my name."

Leana gasped. "Jamie, I—"

"Don't." He pressed his hand against her mouth, stifling her. She felt his palm, cold as granite in winter, flat against her lips, his fingers digging into her cheek, the hem of his coat brushing her knee. He told her again, every word distinctly formed so she would not miss the import of his message. "Do . . . not . . . speak . . . my . . . name."

His message was clear but not the meaning. *Why, Jamie? What has happened?*

Desperate to say something, she formed her lips into the shape of a kiss beneath his hardened palm. When he pulled away his hand, the release of her tender smack was surprisingly loud in the silent room. But it did not please him. It infuriated him.

"How dare you kiss me!"

"But . . . I only kissed your hand."

"Yestreen you kissed my mouth more times than I can count." His eyes were colder than his hands. Moss green had turned to a frozen loch, with unseen depths too dangerous to fathom.

Tears began gathering in her eyes. "I admit I kissed you, J—"

"Don't—"

"But I *did* kiss you, and you kissed me. Willingly, I thought." Though how could she know? She'd never kissed a man before, had never before done any of the things they'd done. She'd misunderstood him completely, it seemed, and disappointed him thoroughly. "I did not know I—"

"*Och!* You knew, Leana. You knew exactly what you were doing. Did you hope I simply wouldn't notice?"

"N-notice what?" The first tear spilled out, landing on her bare skin. Suddenly desperate to hide her nakedness, she pulled the bed linens around her, furtively tucking them underneath her, covering everything she could.

He repeated himself, as though for a child. "Did

you hope I wouldn't notice the difference between you and Rose?"

"Of course you would notice the difference." She shook her head, trying to make sense of words that made no sense at all. "We are . . . very different, Rose and I. Nothing alike."

"Enough alike it seems. In the dark." He leaned over her, his hands clenched by his side, his lip curled in disgust. "In the pitch black of a moonless night very much alike. As you well know."

"I know . . . *nothing!*" Except that she loved him, loved Jamie. After all he'd done to please her, in this room, in this bed, why was he being so cruel? "I don't know what you're saying. I don't know—"

"You knew I was drunk. You knew I was hoping to see my wife—"

"But *I* am your wife. At least, I will be—"

"You knew and took advantage of it. That's what you knew."

"Jamie—"

"Don't!"

"Nae!" She held the bedsheet against her and scrambled to her feet, forcing him to take a step backward. "I will not! I will not stop saying the name of the man I love. Jamie, Jamie. Please, dear Jamie." She stretched one hand toward him, but he jerked away from her touch. "Tell me what I've done that's upset you."

"*Upset* me? You've ruined me." He spun on his boot heel and paced the room, back and forth on the hardwood floor, crossing the yellow square of light pouring through the window.

Jamie spoke again, his voice low, taut as the strings on a fiddle. "Today my young bride will return to this house—her own home—not even knowing there's been a wedding, let alone imagining there's been a wedding night. Without her."

"Ah. I see." Leana sighed with a small measure of relief, beginning to understand. He, too, was worried about how her sister might receive the news. "You're afraid Rose may be disappointed."

"*Disappointed?* Have you not heard one word I've said?"

She tossed her hand into the air. "None of your words have made sense, Jamie."

"Then I will make myself quite clear. But first, you will get dressed. Since it appears you brought no clothes of your own to this room, you can wear this for the time being." Jamie snatched his discarded waddin sark from the floor and threw it at her.

Her hands shook as she let the sheet fall to the floor and slipped the shirt over her head, struggling to weave one hand through a long, voluminous sleeve, then another. A shirt she had stitched. For her sister. For her husband. Leana tugged it over her head, pulling her hair free, grateful to be covered at least to her knees. She shivered inside the sark. It wasn't the cold that troubled her; it was Jamie. His heartless gaze made her feel soiled. Discarded.

"Please, Jamie. I'm dressed, after a fashion, and I'm listening. Tell me what this is all about."

"It's about deception, Leana." He walked closer, yet still kept his distance. "It's about pretending you were Rose and stealing what was rightfully hers."

Her mouth fell open. *Surely not.* He couldn't possibly think she would do such a dreadful, sinful thing. "N-no, Jamie. I stood in the kirk before God and man and vowed to take you as my husband."

"That was not the way of it, Leana. You were speaking for Rose."

"Aye, the minister said her name, but, Jamie, you must have known in my heart—"

"I did *not* know!"

"But you kissed me as though you cared for me. As though you loved me—"

A spark flared in his eyes. "I never said the word *love.*"

"But we danced. You held me. You . . . you fed me, you touched my lips."

"Aye, fool that I was and drunk as I was, I did." He exhaled, his anger abating. "I wanted my bride there, but you were there instead. Perhaps my actions were not completely honorable. For that—for that *one thing,* Leana—I do apologize."

She closed her eyes for a moment, shutting out the painful light and the hard look on his face, only to be tormented by the scent of him on his shirt, in her hair, on her skin. "You did much more than that, Jamie McKie." She opened her eyes to be sure he was listening. "You told me you loved me. And I believed you."

His ill temper returned, first on his face, then in his voice, which pierced her heart like a sword. "I never said I loved you!"

"Aye . . . you . . . did." She choked on the words. "Yestreen you did."

He spoke through clenched teeth. "I thought I was speaking to your sister."

A chill ran along her spine. *He truly thought I was Rose.* If he meant that, if he was being honest with her . . . *Please, God. Don't let that be the truth of it.*

"Jamie." She spoke slowly, trying to grasp how it could have happened. "I came to you as myself, as Leana. The moment I climbed into your bed I told you who I was."

"Nae." He shook his head and kept shaking it, as though doing so would make it so. "You did not tell me who you were."

"Aye," she persisted, "I did." That much she knew to be true. "I said, 'Jamie, it's me.' I was certain you'd know my voice."

"But you whispered."

"I did not want to startle you."

"The woman was worried about *startling* me?!" He gripped his hair for a moment, as though to yank it out of his head. "When morning came, I was more than startled. I was undone." His voice rose to a fever pitch. "Do you understand, Leana? I'm a man with two wives. Or *no* wife. Heaven knows what the kirk will do with all of this."

Her legs began to tremble. "Jamie, I thought I was doing the right thing. I thought *I* was the one you wanted. After everything that happened between us at the kirk . . . and then in the barn . . . and then on the stair . . . I thought . . ."

"Nae, you did *not* think, Leana. You felt. But you did not think."

Leana sank into a chair and bent forward, letting her hair touch the floor and cover her bare legs, though nothing could cover her shame. "I knew only that I loved you. And I thought that you loved me. When I came to your bed and I said your name . . ."

"Och! You should have said *your* name. Before it all began." He was standing over her, his voice bearing down on her like thunder. "Why didn't you, Leana? Why didn't you say your name, just once?"

"I was waiting . . . I was waiting . . ." Her heart, broken and mended many times before, shattered into pieces. Tears streamed across her knees and down her legs. She could not say anything for a long time, and when she finally spoke, her confession sounded as foolhardy and selfish as it was. "I was waiting for *you* to say my name, Jamie. Just once."

Fifty-Three

Thou hast stept in between me and my hopes,
And ravish'd from me all my soul held dear.
Thou hast betray'd me.
<small>NICHOLAS ROWE</small>

Leana!" A woman's voice, followed by a series of light taps on the door next to his. "Sleeping late are we, dearie?"

Jamie's head snapped in the direction of the hall. The world had come looking for them; they could hide no longer. He bent over Leana and spoke in a terse whisper. "Do you hear? It's Neda. She expects to find you in your room."

Leana, folded over like a lifeless doll, merely shook her head but did not speak. Jamie groaned in frustration. Apparently the lass cared nothing about preserving her reputation, not even under her own roof. He'd have to handle things and without delay.

He straightened, then slicked a hand across his damp, unbound hair. "I'll send Neda down the stair on an errand. Haste to your room and find something to wear. Something that's yours." He strode across the room and flung the door open, flashing his most disarming smile. "Neda Hastings!" He closed the door firmly behind him. "The very woman I need this morning."

"Is that so, Mr. McKie?" The older woman regarded him evenly, her wise eyes measuring him and, he sensed, finding him lacking. "Yestreen at the bridal feast, sir, the only woman ye needed was Leana. Yer sister-in-law. No wonder the puir lass is sleepin' later than usual. Ye wore her out dancin'."

"Aye," he agreed. The knot in his stomach loosened. "I'm afraid we enjoyed one strathspey too many." Neda didn't know, it seemed. Or she knew very well and was pretending otherwise. "Is there news from Twyneholm?"

Neda bit her lip. "Nae, nary a word yet. But since the weather is sae mild here for the first of January, we're praying 'twill be fair there as well. By dinner, please God, ye'll be seein' yer young bride."

"Please God," he echoed, eager to see her, dreading it as well. *Oh, sweet Rose.*

"The pair of you missed my fine wedding breakfast," she scolded him, stepping away from Leana's door and lowering her voice. "And without the usual wedding night excuses."

"Forgive me, Neda." He'd forgotten it completely. "I must confess, I did indulge myself more than necessary at the feast yestreen."

"Aye, well, so did Mr. McBride, though he found his way to the breakfast table by nine."

Jamie glanced at the slanted rays streaming through the hall window. "What time is it?"

"Nearly one. Dinner is a bit later today. New Year's Day and all. Your uncle is in the spence, should ye have need of him. Ye can be certain he will ring the bell at two o'clock and expect ye promptly at his table." Neda turned to Leana's door and raised her knuckles, prepared to knock again.

"Wait." He captured her hand, lowering it to her side. "Let her sleep, Neda. I promise I'll knock again for you in a bit."

She arched a brow at him. "All well and good, sir, but ye'll not help her dress."

"Nae." The skin beneath his cravat grew warm. "I'll leave that to your able hands. Might you give the lass another half-hour though? 'Twas a long day."

"So it was." She gathered her drugget skirt in her hands and started down the stair, calling over her shoulder, "Comb yer hair, lad. Ye look like ye've not slept a wink yerself."

Jamie stepped back into the room, grateful when the latch closed behind him. Leana was standing by Rose's dressing table, her back to him, still wearing his wrinkled waddin sark loose about her shoulders. She'd pinned her hair up and was bathing herself with a wet cloth, the mirror reflecting her pale skin, painted gold by the sun. He closed his eyes and pleaded for strength. Was there one moment in the darkened box bed when he'd known it was Leana? And hadn't minded?

"Leana." He kept his voice low but heard the tremor in it. He moved toward her, averting his eyes. "You must dress for dinner. To be served at two o'clock, Neda says."

"What . . . what else did she say?"

"We've had no word from Rose, but they're looking for your sister to arrive any moment."

She turned toward him, love and sorrow pooled in her eyes. "Jamie, I can never say I'm sorry enough."

"Nae, lass. You cannot." He looked away, unable to bear the burden of her grief as well as his own.

"What . . . what will you do now, Jamie?"

"Speak to your father. Explain the situation."

"Good." She nodded briskly, clearly relieved. "Father will help you understand."

"Understand what?" The knot in his stomach returned.

"Why I served as your proxy bride to begin with." Her gaze was guileless, her expression sincere. "Why I danced with only you and came to your room to claim you as my husband. My father will explain everything." She took a step closer, her hands clutching the towel. "Perhaps then you will find it in your heart to forgive me. I realize now that you do not love me. But I cannot bear for you to hate me."

Jamie scarcely heard her last words, so stunned was he by her bold statement: *My father will explain everything.* Was the deception not Leana's alone then? His jaw hardened. "What has my uncle to do with this?"

Her gaze shifted to the floor. "He told me . . . that is, he assured me I would be doing the right . . . well, that it was . . . necessary."

"Necessary?!"

"Please, Jamie. Go." Her eyes pleaded with him even more than her words. "Now, before Rose arrives. Ask Father all the questions you like. He can explain . . . everything."

"Och! Whatever lies he told you, you can be certain they benefited Lachlan McBride. He will indeed explain himself this very hour."

Jamie turned to leave and glanced at the box bed in passing. Its covers were thrown back, the bed linens exposed to the unflinching light of day. *God, help me.* The cloth was faintly stained with blood. *Leana.* A maiden no more. The thought sickened him. If Lachlan had done such a heinous thing, sacrificing his daughter's innocence for his own gain, the man deserved to be shot.

"Be ready by two o'clock." He said it as calmly as he could, not wanting to wound Leana further. Not now. Not when the whole sordid picture was coming into focus.

Jamie did not recall storming out the door of his bedroom, or pounding down the stair, or striding through the house, or flinging wide the door to the spence. He only remembered the look of satisfaction on his uncle's face when Lachlan looked up and saw him.

"Good morning, Nephew." Lachlan put aside the book he was reading, taking his time about it. "Or should I say good afternoon?"

Jamie balled his fists to keep from hitting him and unleashed his fury in words. *"What have you done to me?"*

"Done? A great favor, from my point of view." Lachlan waved toward the empty chair across from him. "I've provided for your every need for a week, then for a month, then for another seven weeks. Most men would call me generous."

Ignoring the offered chair, Jamie stepped closer, his neck thick with rage, his voice meant to convey what his fists could not. "I would call you something else."

"Aye, you should." Lachlan nodded calmly, reaching for his dram of whisky. "You should call me your father-in-law, for that is what I am."

"Wheesht!" Jamie knocked the pewter cup from the man's hand, sending a spray of dark liquid across the cover of Lachlan's bed, staining the embroidered fabric.

"Pity." Lachlan merely shook his head, ignoring the outburst. "Leana worked long and hard on that bit of needlework."

"We will speak of Leana in a moment." Jamie forced himself to breathe, to keep his mind clear and his temper in check, at least until he had some answers. "But first, we will speak of Rose. And those seven weeks you mentioned. I worked hard, Uncle, mucking out your filthy stables and feeding your starving sheep, every day except the Sabbath. I worked for Rose, for her bride price."

"For Rose? I thought you worked for me."

Jamie chewed on his words, then spat them out. "We had an arrangement, Lachlan. At the Globe in Dumfries, you told me—"

"Aye, I remember every word of our short conversation, Jamie. You agreed to work until Hogmanay. You asked, 'Might I marry Rose then?'"

"Exactly!" Jamie roared, no longer caring if his temper claimed the upper hand. "To which you agreed."

"Wait." Lachlan shook his finger at him. "I did not say 'aye' or 'we are agreed' or 'it will be so.' I simply said, 'You might.' There is no promise in the word *might,* now is there?"

Jamie sank into the chair in utter dismay. *"Why?* Why have you deceived me? All these months thinking Rose would be mine. From the very day I arrived. From the first hour I saw her."

"She's a wee bonny lass, I'll grant you." Lachlan retrieved his pewter cup and poured another dram as though nothing had happened. "Too young for marriage though. We both know that's true. Even Rose knew, but you wouldn't listen to her."

Jamie dropped his head into his hands, feeling it throb against his fingers, while Lachlan went on explaining himself, spinning a web Jamie feared he might never untangle.

"In east Galloway it is not our custom to give a younger daughter in marriage before her older sister is wed. Is it not the same in Monnigaff?"

Jamie could only nod at the terrible truth.

"Well then. You have married a fine woman. Leana loves you, Jamie—"

"Nae!" Jamie lifted his head, his jaw clenched. "She may love me, but *I* do not love Leana. What did you tell your older daughter to convince her that I did? Did you use the word *might,* Uncle? Did you tell her that she *might* be welcome in my bed, that I *might* have room for her in my heart and in my life?"

"Nae, I did not." Lachlan pressed his lips in a tight line and shook his head firmly. "I only told Leana that the choice was hers to make."

"I don't believe you, Uncle. Not for one minute. You filled Leana's head with hopes and dreams and promised her what you could not deliver."

"But you delivered it for me, didn't you, Jamie?" Lachlan smiled broadly, revealing a crooked line of teeth that seldom saw the light of day. "Leana needed a husband. Rather desperately after Mr. McDougal put her aside. She wanted you, Nephew. And you complied." He leaned back in his chair, pressing against the upholstery as though to make himself more comfortable.

Jamie ground out the words. "I thought she was Rose."

When Lachlan laughed, Jamie shot to his feet, his fists clenched against his chest. "How dare you mock me!"

"You are the one who has made a mockery of your marriage bed, Jamie. When Leana appeared by your side in the wee dark of night—of her own free will, mind you—did you honestly think she was Rose? Did she look like Rose? Did she sound like Rose? Did she bear Rose's heathery scent or have her sister's soft, lithe hands? Why couldn't you tell the difference between my two daughters, Jamie?"

"Because I was expecting Rose, not Leana!"

"Oh?" Lachlan's brows arched. "The way your father was expecting Evan, not you?"

Jamie's knees gave way beneath him, dropping him onto the chair, nearly tipping it over. "Don't tell me . . ."

"Aye, but I will tell you. You're a fine one to be blaming me for deceiving you! No one else in this house knows the twisted path that brought you to our door. The lies, the trickery. Wearing your brother's plaid, stealing his inheritance. Your innocent Rose does not know, nor does your wife, Leana. Only I know." Lachlan leaned forward, thrusting his face into Jamie's. "Do you not see the hand of justice at work, James Lachlan McKie?"

Jamie only saw red swimming before his eyes. Evan's red hair. A ruddy bowl of broth. Goat's blood in Glentrool's kitchen. A maiden's scarlet blood streaked across his bed linens.

Lachlan's voice droned on, cutting Jamie's skin with his words, slicing open his heart with the deadliest of dirks. "Did you think that you could lie and steal from your family and God Almighty would simply look away? Turn the other cheek? Do you not know what the Buik says? 'Behold, ye have sinned against the LORD: and be sure your sin will find you out.' Did you not learn that verse at your father's knee?"

Jamie nodded as best he could. There were no words left.

"You are angry with me, lad, when you've only yourself to blame. As you have deceived others, so have you been deceived. You fooled yourself into thinking Leana was Rose, just as Alec McKie convinced himself you were Evan."

"Leana," he moaned.

"Aye, another of your victims. She's ruined forever, lad. That blood can only be spilled once."

Jamie lifted his head, the weight of it nearly crushing him. "What am I to do?"

"Leana is your wife now, Jamie. You made your choice. So did she. You cannot go back."

"Aye, but I cannot go forward either." He glanced away, ashamed of his emotions. "Rose is the one I love. *Rose,* not Leana."

"Do you think the lass will have you now, after the unseemly things you have done?"

Jamie gathered what hope he had left. "She might."

"Aye, that word again. *Might.* If she does still want you, Jamie, whatever would you do to deserve her?"

He didn't deserve Rose, not after what he'd done. But he could *earn* the right to ask for her hand, could he not? "I would work." He squared his shoulders, wiping at his damp eyes with the heel of his hand. "The lambing season is not far off, then the shearing. I'll work hard—"

"For me?"

"Aye, for you, Uncle. But for Rose's hand. Let there be no misunderstanding this time."

His uncle chuckled. "Jamie, you canna keep two wives."

Heat filled his cheeks, a shame he deserved to have displayed. "Leana will not want me for a husband. Not after . . . not after what I said to her this morning."

"Don't count on that, lad. She loves you sorely, Leana does. Did she not make that clear to you?"

"Aye, she did." *Abundantly.*

Lachlan stared in his empty cup for a moment, twisting it back and forth in his hand, then he tipped it over his mouth for the last drop and banged it on his desk like a judge about to pronounce a sentence. "You've arranged for a week in Dumfries at the King's Arms Inn, paid for with Rowena's silver. Take Leana there for her bridal week. Be a husband to her in every sense of the word. 'Tis only fair when she's ruined for another."

"But Rose—"

"Young as she is, the lass can easily wait for another seven months, if she's willing. When she turns sixteen on the first of August, seven months from today, you may put Leana aside and marry Rose."

Jamie shook his head, incredulous. "You mean divorce Leana?"

"I do, with my blessing, come August. But first you are required to give Leana seven days of your undivided attention in Dumfries. *Undivided.* Do I make myself clear?"

Jamie nodded. It was only fair. "Aye, seven days with Leana."

"Then seven months of hard work to earn Rose's hand."

Jamie exhaled, blotting out the memory of cold mornings in the byre and clothes smeared with dung. "Aye, you shall have it. Seven months of work for Rose."

"There is only one thorn in our plan, Jamie." Lachlan leaned forward, lowering his voice as though curious ears were pressed against the spence door. "If Leana conceives a child—your child—in those seven months, then you are bound to remain her husband. I'll not have a grandson without a father."

"You shall not, Uncle." The corners of Jamie's mouth twitched, tasting his first victory of the new year. Leana could not conceive without him. After her bridal week, she would not have the chance.

Fifty-Four

Let none but Him who rules the thunder
Put this man and woman asunder.
JONATHAN SWIFT

Leana missed Neda's skillful fingers dressing her hair, buttoning all the tiny buttons of her gown. But she could not call down the stair for Neda to help her. Could not bear to see the look on the kind woman's face if she overheard Jamie and her father—arguing, no doubt, in the spence—and came to an obvious conclusion. Could not bear to think of the names Neda might mutter under her breath. *Hizzie. Tairt.*

Nae. Neda loved her. Neda would not condemn her. Scold her, aye. Lecture her on proper Christian behavior, aye, for hours on end, and deservedly so. But Neda would see the way of things, that Leana had only meant to claim the man she loved and whom she thought, at last, had come to love her.

I never said I loved you.

His words rang like a deid bell through her weary head.

And what of Rose? Would her sister's love for her die as well? *Please God, may it not be so!* Not dear Rose, the wee lass whom she'd raised with the tender care of a mother all her young life. Rose would understand. Wouldn't she?

Not if she loves Jamie as I do.

Leana's busy hands paused, stunned at the possibility. Though she knew her sister considered their cousin braw and likable enough, Leana had never heard Rose confess to actually *loving* Jamie. Yet what if her feelings had changed? What if Rose genuinely loved him now? *Oh, please, Rose. Not my Jamie!* Fresh tears poured down her cheeks, already irritated from an hour of weeping. Jamie was her only hope. She not only loved him; she had given herself to him.

If Jamie would not claim her, she would be alone and unloved the rest of her life.

It is Jamie McKie, or it is no one.

"Then it must be Jamie McKie," Leana whispered to the mirror, wiping away the last of her tears with her handkerchief, then tucking it inside her skirt. The day was young, and Rose had not come home yet. There was still time to make things right with her father and with Jamie. And then with Rose.

Her resolve strengthened, Leana brushed her hair with firm strokes and pinned up the long locks as best she could. What had her father said a few months ago? Something about having no saicrets in their household? Let him be the first, then, to speak the truth this new year.

Leana tucked the last of her curls in place, pressed her hand to her chest to calm her quickening heart, and hastened down the stair. The servants greeted her with subdued voices, not looking up as she passed. "The day has eyes, the night has ears," Neda would say. It seemed the whole household knew. She went straight to the spence and lifted her hand to knock on the door until she realized all was quiet inside the closed room. Had the men left the house, gone for a walk before dinner? She leaned one ear against the door panel to see if she could hear voices, then jumped slightly when her father's voice rumbled across the room.

"You've arranged for a week in Dumfries at the King's Arms Inn, paid for with Rowena's silver. Take Leana there for her bridal week."

Jamie all to herself for a week! Leana grew light-headed at the thought, resting one hand against the wall to hold her steady, nearly missing what her father said next.

"When she turns sixteen on the first of August . . ."

Her heart sank. *Rose.*

". . . seven months from today, you may put Leana aside and marry Rose."

Put me aside? He cannot mean . . .

". . . divorce Leana?" Even Jamie sounded shocked. Her knees sagged under the weight of it, lowering her closer to the floor.

She heard a note of caution in Lachlan's voice. "You are required to give Leana seven days of your undivided attention in Dumfries."

Seven days. That was all. However glorious that bridal week might be, it would end all too soon, and Jamie would come home to Rose. For good.

"There is only one thorn in our plan, Jamie."

A thorn? She tried to breathe, to stand, but could not.

"If Leana conceives a child—your child—in those seven months, then you are bound to remain her husband."

She straightened, as though filled with air. *A child! And Jamie as well!*

Lachlan's voice brooked no argument. "I'll not have a grandson without a father."

Nor I a son without one. Leana clasped her hands and pleaded with God, *Please let Jamie agree. Please!*

Jamie's words rang out like a benediction. "You shall not, Uncle."

Leana threw her hands in the air, spinning in a circle, nearly bumping into the door. Not seven days—*seven months!* She and Jamie would live as husband and wife after all. There, at Auchengray. Surely she could conceive a child in seven months. There would be no need for a divorce. *Please God, may it be so.* To think that she might be a wife and mother after all! Leana patted her cheeks, willing them to cool, then tapped on the door. The sooner she faced both men, the sooner she and Jamie might put the past hours behind them and move forward.

"Who is it?" her father barked.

"'Tis Leana." Opening the door, she ducked her head around it, hoping her gaze would not give away what she knew. "May I come in?"

Her father waved her inside. "Your timing is excellent, Daughter. Your husband and I were just discussing you."

Jamie gave him a withering look, but Leana would not be dissuaded. *Seven months, Jamie. And then, please God, forever.* "Thank you, Father." She swept into the room with all the grace she could muster and folded her hands demurely before her. Jamie, his cravat askew, his dark beard showing, looked exhausted, beaten down. Lachlan, pressed and neat as the day before, looked delighted with himself.

"What news have you for me, gentlemen?" She lifted her brows in anticipation, infusing her expression with all the love and hope that were hidden in her heart, while her father patiently explained the unusual terms of their agreement. The same terms he'd just spoken in private, she noticed. For once perhaps her father could be trusted.

"Will you agree to abide by my wishes, Leana?"

She spoke her vow as clearly as she had in the kirk. "I will."

"And you, Jamie? Will you agree, with Leana as your witness, to assume the role of her loving husband for seven days in Dumfries and to work seven months at Auchengray for Rose's hand in marriage?"

Before Jamie could speak, Leana quickly added, "Unless I am found with child. Then Jamie . . ." She turned to him, praying he would not change his mind. "Then Jamie must remain my husband and be a loving father to our firstborn." *First of many. Please God.*

Jamie's jaw hardened, though he nodded in assent. "I will."

Lachlan clapped his hands together, rubbing them with obvious glee. "It is settled then. Shall we pour a dram to seal our bargain?"

Jamie's voice was sharp. "We shall not."

Lachlan shrugged. "Aye, well. No doubt you had whisky enough last night to quench your thirst for a day or two."

Jamie's gaze darkened. "Longer than that, Uncle."

"Seven months, I'll wager." Lachlan unlatched the door and gave them both a parting nod. "You have much to discuss and a sister whose appearance you should prepare for momentarily. I expect the two of you to break the news to her. 'Tis only fair." He left them standing there, staring after him, the silence in the spence thick with unspoken misery and spent passion.

Leana closed her eyes and waited. *Let Jamie speak first.*

When he didn't do so after a moment, she looked about for somewhere to sit and noticed her neatly stitched bedcover had been badly stained. "Goodness," she murmured, touching the fabric. "Something's been spilled here."

"Whisky," Jamie said with no emotion in his voice. "Knocked from Lachlan's hand."

"I see." The dark, ugly stains would not come out. "It doesn't matter." She chose the less comfortable of the two chairs pulled close to the feeble hearth and eased into it, not able to look at him yet. "I'll embroider another."

Jamie took the upholstered chair—her father's favorite—and sat down heavily. "What of our marriage bed, Leana?" His tone reeked of sarcasm. "I suppose you'll embroider bedcovers for that as well?"

She looked up and met his gaze. "You forget. I already have. Some of the linens that fill Rose's bottom drawer were the fruit of my labors, remember?"

He leaned forward in his chair, his hands pressed against his knees, arms akimbo. "And what of the fruit of your womb, Leana? Yestreen at the kirk we sang about your 'fruitful vine.' Is that your expectation? That you will have my child and thereby claim me as your husband?"

She lowered her gaze, hurt by the edge of anger in his voice, the look of a trapped animal in his eyes. "It is not for me to decide, Jamie. The Buik tells us that children are an heritage of the Lord and that the fruit of the womb is his reward."

"*Och!* And you deserve a *reward* for last night's performance, is that it?"

"Jamie, please." Leana touched the back of his hand. "It was not a performance. You thought I was Rose. And I thought you loved me. We were both—"

"Deceived. By your father." He threw his shoulders against the chair, frustration flowing off him in waves. "The man's motives and methods are canny beyond imagining. He saw a clever way to marry off an older daughter who has no prospects and to keep his lovesick nephew bound to him for seven more months, nigh to a year from when I arrived. Without wages, without any guarantee of getting what I want in the end."

She swallowed the sickening taste in her mouth. "You mean Rose."

"Aye. Rose. The woman I love, who will be here shortly." He stood, straightening his clothes with brief, sharp movements, as coolly efficient as his words. "See that you are packed for our journey to Dumfries with due haste. My bags have been waiting by the door since Wednesday morning."

Leana stood, feeling as though she might be ill. "When . . . when will we leave?"

He smoothed his cravat, then folded his arms over his chest. The same chest she had used for a pillow. How was it possible? Where was the Jamie who'd loved her yestreen?

"We won't leave until Rose returns."

"Of course." Leana held her breath and prayed for strength, her empty stomach tied in a knot. When was the last time she ate? *The Hogmanay black bun.* Fed to her from his fingers. Touching her lips.

Leana gripped the corner of Lachlan's box bed. "Which one of us will . . . will tell Rose?"

His gaze remained even. "You will."

Fifty-Five

Sorrow and ill weather come unsent for.
SCOTTISH PROVERB

Rose poked Willie in the ribs. "Cannot we ride a bit faster?"

"Auld Bess has seen more than her share of winters, Miss McBride, and they've taken their toll on her legs." To appease her, the orraman shook the reins and called out a sharp word of encouragement to the mare. Rose groaned when the horse merely tossed her mane back at him and kept plodding forward, no faster than before.

She had to know. "How much—"

"Twa miles," Willie snapped. "Twenty minutes at

most. And that's the last time I'll tell ye, lass, so busy yerself with yer knittin'."

Poor Willie. It had been a difficult two days for him, stuck in the tiny cottage with her eccentric Aunt Meg and her two collie dogs. He'd refused to set out before daybreak, concerned at what they might find. What they found was sunshine, great shining pails full of it, poured over the Galloway landscape. On the first of January of all things!

Hogmanay—her wedding day—her Aunt Meg had fallen on the polished flagstone and twisted her ankle, poor woman. Then, when they'd packed to leave that morning, her aunt had refused to come to Auchengray after all. "I'll just be a burden, hopping about on this bad foot. Best stay home and tend to it. I'll send you off with your present, lass, and regards to your sister, Leana. Write and tell me all about the wedding."

Write she would, the moment Rose knew when the ceremony would be performed. What a dreadful nuisance it must have been for her father, canceling the wedding on the very day it was planned! Leana probably handled every detail. *Dear Leana.* Rose had missed her terribly, almost as much as she'd missed Jamie.

She closed her eyes to picture him, as she had many times a day, all eight days she'd spent in Twyneholm. Jamie, with his dark brown hair in a sleek knot, and his green eyes gazing at her, and his full mouth curved into a sly smile, and his carved chin with a hint of a beard, and his long legs, so handsome in his new boots, and his strong, broad shoulders. *Oo aye!* Picturing James Lachlan McKie had become her favorite pastime. Who could have guessed that spending a week apart from a man would make her feelings grow so much deeper and multiply like wildflowers in May?

Twenty minutes.

I love you, Jamie.

She would tell him the very second she laid eyes on him, no matter who was listening, no matter how it might embarrass him.

To keep her mind off her bonny bridegroom, Rose dutifully pulled out her knitting bag, untouched since the day before, and found the heel of the stocking she'd been working on. She eased it out of the bag so it wouldn't unravel. The needles were poked into the wool, right where they belonged. She'd no sooner sorted out the skein of yarn when Willie glanced over and brought Bess to a sudden halt.

Willie's eyes were tea saucers. "When did ye start knitting that stocking, lass?"

"Monday." She held it up, proud of how much she'd finished. Knitting was her least favorite pastime. "They're for Jamie. Aren't they a lovely shade of blue?"

"Did ye . . ." He gulped, a sheen of sweat on his forehead. "Did ye . . . leave the knitting needles in the stocking like that . . . all night?"

She gaped at him. "Willie, whatever is the matter with you? Aye, naturally I left the needles there." She glanced outside the chaise for some explanation. "Why have we stopped?"

He sighed heavily, shaking his head like one of Aunt Meg's collies. "There's no cure for it now, lass. D'ye no ken how unchancie a thing it is to keep knitting a stocking from the old year to the new?"

She stared at the wool in her hands. "It is? Unlucky, I mean?"

He jerked the reins to start Bess on her way, though his gaze was still fixed on Rose's hands. "Wise is the woman who finishes knittin' her stocking before midnight on Hogmanay and puts the needles safely awa."

"Hoot!" Rose laughed gaily, trying to conceal her uneasiness. "You are the most superstitious old Scotsman I've met in many a day, Willie."

"Aye, lass, but I've lived long enough to ken what I'm telling ye to be true. They say on the last day of the old year, a great gust of wind blows across the face of the earth, and all the earth is changed. 'Tis our job to keep the old ways so that change will be for the better."

Willie sank down into his overcoat, two sizes too big for him, still shaking his head. "Seems to me a lass about to marry would need all the guid luck she can gather around her."

"I don't need guid luck," she told him, tossing her black hair the way Bess tossed her tangled mane. "I have Jamie."

They rode on in silence, past Maxwell Park, then Lochend, then Glensone, each farm and cottage bringing her closer to home. She discarded her knitting, lest the needles themselves bear some unco curse, and clasped her hands in her lap, breathing in the crisp, cold air and basking in the brilliant sunshine, all too aware that such fine weather never lasted.

When they turned into the drive at Auchengray, her heart was in her throat. Would Jamie be waiting at the window, watching for her? Or come running out the door, breathing out steamy puffs of air as he hastened to help her down from the chaise? She closed her eyes for the briefest of wishes—*Let him hurry out to meet me!*—then opened them wider than ever in joyful anticipation. *Jamie! Jamie, I'm home!*

There was no sign of him at the door or at the window. Willie relaxed the reins, knowing Bess would find the shortest path to the stables, and stopped in front of the house long enough to help Rose climb out. "Go on, lass. Dinna keep yer man waitin'."

She planted a kiss on Willie's leathery cheek, then fairly skipped to the front entrance. After pushing open the heavy door, she sang out her greeting, not waiting for someone to come as she pulled off her hat, scarf, and coat, laughing at how Aunt Meg had bundled her up from head to toe. She discarded her things in a careless heap by the door and went straight to the dining room, certain the family must be finishing dinner and hadn't heard her arrival.

Finding them in their usual places, their untouched food sitting before them, she swept into the room, flashing them a brownie's grin. "Is there no one in this house eager to welcome a weary traveler?"

"Rose!" Jamie stood so quickly his chair tipped back for a moment. He held out his arms, a sheen of tears in his eyes, and she threw herself into his embrace.

"Jamie, Jamie!" She stood on tiptoe to whisper in his ear the news she'd waited all week to tell him. "I love you, Jamie. I do, I love you."

"And I love you, beloved." Jamie's arms tightened around her, even as servants quietly slipped out and the room grew strangely silent.

Her father's stern voice cut through the air. "That will be quite enough, Rose."

She eased back, hating to lose the warmth of him, though Jamie's gaze embraced her still. "Forgive me, Father. I was . . . that is, I've missed Jamie."

"You've made that abundantly clear, lass. Find your seat at the table so we may begin our dinner."

It was only then she turned to look at Leana more closely. Her pale skin was smudged with shadows, and her eyes rimmed with pink, as though she'd been crying for hours on end. "Leana?" By the look of her face, her sister had aged a year during the last week. She hurried to Leana's side, taking the empty seat next to hers. "Dear sister, what is it? What's wrong?"

Her father answered before Leana could take a breath. "Your sister is . . . tired. It's good to have you home, Rose. Would that ill weather had not prevented you from arriving at this hour yestreen."

"Aye, Father. No one is more sorry than I am." She patted Leana's hand, resolving to keep an eye on her, and sniffed the pungent air, famished for some of Neda's steak and kidney pie. "Forgive me for throwing your plans in such an uproar. Did you not have the same ill weather here in Newabbey?"

Leana spoke, her voice timid, almost apologetic. "We . . . did not."

"Och!" Rose squeezed her sister's hand, noticing how limply it rested in her lap. "No wonder you're exhausted. All our guests must have arrived, not knowing what had happened. Dear me, what a bother, moving all our arrangements to another day." She looked expectantly around the table. "What day have you chosen?"

The three of them exchanged glances, then her father spoke. "No day as yet." He exhaled with obvious impatience. "We have already blessed the meal, child. Let us bless your safe return and enjoy our food while it is hot. In silence, if you do not mind, as we have no guests to entertain, and it has been a . . . difficult two days."

Rose bowed her head slowly, watching the others, a knot of fear tightening in her chest—a knot made of wool yarn, with knitting needles sticking out of its center. Why were they all so solemn, as though they weren't pleased to have her home? It was common for them to eat without speaking during the meal, but why today of all days?

Her father prayed, filling the room with long, dour phrases that sounded very holy indeed, though the pie grew cold beneath her nose. At last he finished, and they lifted their silver, cutting and chewing with nary a word spoken for the longest dinner hour

Rose could ever remember. She and Jamie exchanged glances when the others had their heads down. His love for her shone in his eyes, but there was sadness there as well. *Poor Jamie.* Her delay must have put a terrible strain on the household; their grim faces were proof of it.

Another long prayer closed the meal, and then she could bear it no more. "To your feet, Leana. Willie should have deposited my things in our room by now." Rose stood, tugging her sister's sleeve. "We shall see what sort of wedding present Aunt Meg has sent along for Jamie and me." She rolled her eyes, giggling all the while. "Smuggled salt, judging by the feel of it." She glanced at Jamie, whose sorrowful gaze—there was no other word for it, the man appeared positively grief-stricken—followed her to the door. He looked as if he hadn't slept in two days.

She pranced into the hall, letting her fingers brush the walls, she was that glad to be home. Everything looked different, as it often did after a time away. Shabbier, a bit plain compared to Aunt Meg's cheerful cottage, but still Auchengray, still home. However would she bear leaving it behind for Glentrool?

Leana turned to her at the bottom of the stair, her expression as gloomy as Jamie's. "This way, my sister. I've a rather . . . delicate matter we need to discuss."

Fifty-Six

Oh! how many torments lie
in the small circle of a wedding ring.
COLLEY CIBBER

Come now, it can't be as bad as all that." Rose pushed Leana ahead of her up the steps, cajoling her as they went. "I can see that Auchengray needs my speeritie ways, loud as they may be. While I've been gone, joy has positively vanished from this house."

"Aye," Leana agreed, nodding as she slowly climbed the stair, two steps ahead of her, "that it has."

The knotted bow in Rose's chest tightened further. What *was* this all about? She followed her sister into their shared bedroom and found her trunk and packages neatly stacked in the center of the room. How she'd missed home! Her gaze took in the familiar box bed, Leana's reading chair by the window, the stacks of books, and two gowns hung out to air—Leana's new embroidered one and her rosy wedding dress, still waiting for her.

"We'll be wearing these soon enough." Rose sighed with delight as she hurried over to inspect the two dresses. Her gaze was drawn to the hem of Leana's claret gown, and her eyes narrowed. "Heavens! How ever did this get soiled?"

"Rose." Leana was standing beside her now, her hand gently touching her elbow. "I have much to tell you." Rose turned, dismayed to find tears streaming down her sister's face.

"Leana! Dearest, whatever has happened, it cannot warrant such tears."

"Oh, but it does. I only wish my tears were enough for both of us." Leana inclined her head toward their box bed. "Please, sit with me. Here, where I can look you in the eye and hold your sweet hands."

Rose sensed her own well of tears beginning to fill as she sat, her sister's clammy hands gripping hers. Was Leana ill, desperately ill? Was that it? *Please God, no!* She could not imagine life without her sister. "Tell me. Just begin. I cannot bear it another moment."

Leana swallowed, then moistened her lips. "I must start by asking for your forgiveness. What I have done . . . what we . . . Nae, what *I* have done is . . ." She choked on her words, releasing Rose's hands to smooth away the flood of tears, though it did not stop them. "Rose . . . oh, Rose, when you did not appear on your wedding day, Father thought it best . . . in truth, he demanded that we . . . continue with the . . . ah, ceremony. With me as your proxy."

"Proxy?" Rose felt the knot in her chest rise into her throat. "What . . . what does that mean, Leana? A proxy?"

Leana squeezed her hands over and over, struggling to get out a single word. "It means that . . . I stood in the kirk and . . . said your vows for you."

"What?" Rose shot to her feet, throwing her sister's hands aside. "Why? Why would you do such a thing, Leana? It was *my* wedding!"

"I know, dearie, but—"

"What possible benefit was there to go on without me?"

"Father said . . ." Leana looked up, her gaze filled with despair. "He said we could not postpone the wedding because of our many guests and because of the expense—"

"Money!" Rose threw her arms over her head, now furious with her father as well. "I should have known! With Lachlan McBride, it always comes down to what a thing costs." Storming about the room, she noticed her kell discarded in a wrinkled heap on her dressing table and gasped, snatching it up. "And *this!* I suppose you wore *this* when you said my vows."

"Aye." Leana's head hung so low Rose could not

see her face, only the coil of yellow braids on top of her head. "I did wear your kell. Father insisted." Her voice thinned to a vapor. "He wanted me to wear your gown as well, but I refused."

"Och! And I'm to thank you for that, no doubt."

"You are to thank me for none of it, Rose," Leana said softly. "We kept hoping you'd come. We didn't learn about the snowstorm until we arrived home for the bridal supper, and even then we prayed you might come riding up."

"If you expected me, why didn't you *wait* for me?" Rose swatted at her dress, her face crinkled with tears. "Why didn't you *wait?*"

"We should have waited. I know that now only too well." Leana stood and began pacing back and forth across the room, wringing her hands as she tried to explain. "We had both gowns with us at the kirk so that you could dress at the manse and slip into the kirk in an instant. We never imagined the whole day would unfold without you, dearie."

Rose hated when her sister sounded so sincere. "*We,* meaning you and Father, I suppose."

"*We,* meaning all of us. Jamie, Neda and Duncan, Susanne—everyone in the neighborhood kept thinking you might appear, riding up in the chaise with Willie."

Rose pouted, not caring if it made her look twelve years old. "You were feasting on *my* bridal supper while I sat with old Aunt Meg, eating porridge."

"I'm so sorry, Rose. I would do anything, *anything* to have refused to stand in for you. How I wish I had." Leana whispered those words again under her breath, turning away from her for a moment, looking as though she might be ill. "Father did not allow us much choice."

"And I had no choice at all. *Och!*" Rose groaned, dropping into the chair by the window. She had missed her own wedding. *Her own wedding!* "It's all Father's fault. He can send a person spinning like a top with his endless reasons why a thing must be done."

"Aye, he can. But Rose . . ." Leana sank to her knees by the chair, laying her hands on Rose's lap. "That is not the worst of it. Wearing your kell, saying your vows, looking into Jamie's eyes . . ."

Poor Leana! Rose nodded, understanding at last what she was trying to say. "It was terrible for you, wasn't it? To stand next to Jamie, saying those vows yet knowing that he loves me." She squeezed Leana's hands, suddenly feeling generous. "You cared for him a great deal once. Shame on Father for expecting you to do such a difficult task."

"But, Rose, it wasn't difficult. It was . . ." Leana sank back, folding up on herself as though she could not bear to be seen. "God forgive me, it was . . . wonderful. We kissed outside the kirk . . ."

A cold wave of shock ran through Rose's body. "You kissed . . . Jamie?"

Leana only nodded as tears splattered her dress, staining it. "Reverend Gordon insisted it was . . . unlucky not to do so."

Rose fell back against the chair, her mouth agape, her emotions reeling. "Unlucky?" Knitting needles clicked in her addled mind. A dress fitted on a Friday. A wedding gown worn by another. "It seems I'm the unlucky one, to have missed seeing my beloved Jamie hold someone else in his arms. My sister. *My sister!*" She shrieked the last words, unable to restrain herself. "How could you? *How could you,* Leana?"

Leana held out her palms, unable to speak, struggling to breathe.

Rose rocked back and forth, feeling sick, feeling faint, trying to swallow, trying desperately to grasp what Leana was saying. The image of her sister in Jamie's arms, their lips, their bodies pressed together in a kiss. "Do you no longer love me, that you would treat me so ill?"

"Of course I love you, Rose!"

"You can't, you can't!" she wailed, her own tears flowing now, forgiveness abandoned. "*My* sister, kissing *my* husband, pretending to be me! *Pretending to be his bride!* Heaven help me, this day cannot get any worse."

"Aye, it can, Rose." Her sister clenched her tear-drenched hands and pressed them against her mouth. "Much worse."

Fifty-Seven

Grasp me not, I have a thorn,
But bend and take my being in.
HARRIET PRESCOTT SPOFFORD

Worse?" Rose cried. "How can it possibly get worse?"

Leana sank her teeth into her knuckles, pleading for mercy, knowing it was useless. God was nowhere to be found. "Please, dearie."

"Don't call me that." Rose stood, her skirts brushing Leana aside as she abandoned her chair to pace. "I cannot be *dear* to you, or you would not have kissed my Jamie."

"You are more than dear to me." Leana hastened to her feet, needing to be near her, to look her in the face when she told her the worst news of her young life. "You are precious to me, Rose. You are my only sister, my closest friend, a daughter—"

"Nae!" Rose whirled about, her braid slapping Leana's cheek. "I am *not* your daughter!" Pain and anger sparked in her dark eyes, though her chin trembled like a child's. "And *you* are not my mother. My mother is dead."

Leana could barely speak for the tightness in her throat. What lies had she whispered to herself in the wee dark of yestreen that had brought her to this? *Jamie would decide.* Aye, he had done that. Unless she bore him a child, that decision would stand. She swallowed, trying to make room for the painful words that must come. "If Mother had been here, perhaps none of this would have happened."

"None of *what?*" Rose tossed her hands in the air. "You being my proxy? You speaking my vows? You kissing Jamie?"

"Aye. And none of the . . . rest." She feared she might be sick so tightly clenched was her stomach. *God, help me.* A fool's prayer, that. What had she told Jamie their night together was? *Necessary.* Rose would not consider it necessary. Rose would think her sister was the worst kind of woman that ever took breath. And she would be right.

"The rest of *what?* Leana, you are not making sense." Rose groaned, walking back and forth in front of her, her boots, still muddy from the morning's journey, making marks on the wooden floor. "Kissing my betrothed is quite enough. My own *sister!* It's appalling."

"Aye, it is," Leana agreed, heaping guilt upon herself like kindling on a fire. "What is more appalling still is that I thought . . . that is, I convinced myself . . . that Jamie . . . enjoyed it."

"He did not!" Rose stamped her foot, as though her words were not loud enough to make her point. "I *know* he didn't."

Her own words hurt more. "You are right. He did not."

Rose eyed her askance. "Then why did you *think* he enjoyed it?"

"Because that was what I chose to believe." Leana's fingers found a loose thread on her dress to worry with as her mind struggled to find words to say what should never be said. "When Jamie looked at me, I saw affection where there was only . . . where there was . . . nothing. Nothing at all." The thread, pulled taut, turned her fingertip pink, brighter than the sweetbriar in the hedgerow. She stared at it, willing it to hurt more so she wouldn't notice the pain growing inside and threatening to engulf her.

Rose shrugged. "Jamie once told me he cared for you as a sister." Her tone soured. "Though a sister's love is not always what it appears." Dry for the moment, her eyes narrowed. "You *did* say my name when you spoke the vows?"

"Aye." *But my heart whispered my own.*

"So, our cousin is my husband now, by the law of the kirk?"

Leana released the thread. She could not bring herself to respond.

Rose did not seem to notice, for she'd spun around to walk the floor again. "Jamie is . . . well, he *must* be my husband now. My silver ring is safe in his pocket, is it not? Waiting for me to claim it."

Leana could answer that one. "Aye, it is." She'd seen him studying it moments before Rose appeared in the dining room.

"So then." Her sister paused by the hearth, disbelief giving way to wonder. "I must be . . . his *wife?* No longer Rose McBride but Rose *McKie!*" Her eyes widened, and a flicker of apprehension came and went from their dark depths. "A wife who might be expected to . . . share her husband's bed this night."

Leana closed her eyes. *Nae, Rose.* She must say those words. Now. *Nae, Rose.*

She could delay no longer, hoping to be struck dead by a vengeful God or spared by an impatient Jamie bursting into the room. She must tell her sister the wicked thing she'd done and cast all the blame upon herself. Not on Jamie, not even on her hatesome father. She alone had yielded to temptation. She had wanted Jamie for herself. Wanted him so blindly that she saw love where it did not exist and desire that was not hers to satisfy.

She could not hope for forgiveness. She dare not even ask. Leana opened her eyes and looked directly into her sister's bonny wee face. "Nae, Rose. You will not share Jamie's bed this night."

Rose jerked her chin. "And why not, if he's my husband?"

"Because he will be sharing his bed with me."

The room grew so still she could hear the clink of dishes in the dining room below. Rose stared at her, like a doll with black buttons for eyes. Her mouth hung open as though she would speak but had forgotten how.

"Rose, I cannot begin . . . It was . . . a mistake."

Coward. It was a sin.

Her sister's mouth closed, then opened again as she breathed out the word. *"Mistake?"*

Leana swallowed. She would do better this time. She would tell her the truth. She would not hold back. "Yestreen, I persuaded myself that Jamie loved me as I loved him. I did not know yet that I was . . . mistaken. When I went to him in his darkened room, he . . . well, he . . ."

Rose spoke so softly her voice barely dinted the air. "He . . . what?"

Leana turned away, unable to bear the agony on her sister's face. "He thought I was you."

Color slowly seeped into Rose's cheeks. Not a maiden's blush. The heat of anger. Her eyes came to life, and her words seared like flames. "Then you are no longer my sister. You are a *howre.*"

Fifty-Eight

In the election of a wife, as in
A project of war, to err but once is
To be undone forever.
THOMAS MIDDLETON

I will *never* forgive you!"

"Rose, please, please . . ."

"*Never!* I trusted you. I *trusted you,* Leana!"

Jamie cringed at the harsh words pouring from beneath the door to the sisters' bedroom. He'd not intended to eavesdrop yet could not drag himself away. He edged closer to the door, ready to bolt at the slightest footfall on the stair.

Leana had not handled things as well as he'd hoped. Rose was hysterical, and no wonder. "You have stolen my Jamie!" she cried. "You have stolen my *love!*"

Jamie's heart swelled to hear Rose's confession again. She *did* love him. Why had he ever doubted it?

Leana's voice was strained to the breaking point. "Rose, don't you see? *I* love Jamie, even more than you do."

"How *dare* you judge my feelings? I *do* love him. I realized it in Twyneholm."

Of course. Apart from him Rose had come to her senses. Jamie leaned against the doorpost, his head aching, as Leana's words echoed his thoughts.

"Oh, Rose. If only I'd known your true feelings. I never meant to hurt you."

"*Hurt* me? You've *ruined* me!"

Leana's voice was low, emotionless. "Nae, sister. I am the one who is ruined. I meant only to let Jamie choose."

"But he *did* choose, and he did not choose *you,* Leana. He chose me! He loves *me!*"

For a moment the room was silent. Jamie felt his heart pounding against his chest, grateful they couldn't hear it.

At last Leana spoke. "Feelings sometimes . . . change, Rose."

Nae. Jamie reached for the latch, pausing only long enough to take a full breath. He would not, not for one minute, let Rose think he no longer loved her. Pushing open the door, he walked into the room unannounced, then latched the door behind him. The two sisters were standing an arm's length apart, both their faces ravaged with tears, looking more aghast the closer he came.

"Rose. Leana. Forgive my intrusion." Tension came off them in waves. "Since I was an unwitting party to all this . . . this . . . well, I thought . . . perhaps . . ." There was naught to be done but say what he'd come to say. "You must know, Rose. You *must* know that I love you. Have loved you from the moment we met."

"Then why, Jamie?" Her eyes implored him. *"Why?"* Her broken voice tore him asunder. "If it was my kisses you missed, could you not have waited one . . . more . . . day?"

"Rose, dear Rose." Swallowing hard, he drew closer, taking her limp hands in his. "I would have waited a lifetime for you. Had I known, had I realized . . ." He lifted her hands to his lips and lightly kissed the tender center of each palm, first one, then the other, gazing steadily at her all the while.

She would no longer look him in the eye nor acknowledge his touch. "I trusted you, Jamie," she whispered. "Just as I trusted Leana. You have both deceived me all these weeks."

"Nae!" Jamie and Leana spoke in unison, their gazes meeting for an instant.

"Nae," he said firmly, turning back to Rose. "I never thought of Leana . . .in that way. Only of you, Rose. What happened is most un-fortunate."

"Unfortunate?!" Rose yanked her hands free and wiped away fresh tears. "Is that what the kirk is calling *hochmagandy* in the new year?"

"Rose!" Leana's shocked expression mirrored his own. "Such words are not proper for a young woman to—"

"Och!" Rose shook her skirts at Leana, as though flicking dirt from her hem. "How *dare* you speak of what's proper after what you've done? *You* have forced me to use such words, Leana. You, who taught me all that I knew and everything I believed. Now I don't know *what* to believe! You have stolen my husband and my future, *all in one night!*"

"Dearest . . ." Leana reached out to her, only to have Rose shrink back from her touch. "I will keep saying I'm sorry until you believe me, until you understand that I never meant to harm you, that I did what I did because . . ."

"Because you loved him." Rose's dark eyes narrowed to pinpoints, the corners of her pretty mouth turned down into an ugly frown. "What a pity, Leana, that he does not love you in return."

Jamie took a step back, giving the sisters a wider berth. He had foolishly waded into very deep water and found himself at a loss how to make his way back to dry ground. He looked at Leana, a host of emotions churning inside him. He did not envy her this day. She had brought it upon herself, upon all of them, but a spark of sympathy warmed his heart toward her. However misguided her love for him, it was genuine. And her love for Rose was beyond question.

"Leana," he said softly, barely touching her elbow, "have you told your sister about your father's . . . terms?"

"The seven days? The seven months?" Leana turned toward him, her eyes washed clear as quartz by her tears. "Those arrangements were made for your benefit and for our father's. Not for mine. And certainly not for Rose's. Suppose you explain them to her, Jamie, while I pack." Turning away from them both, Leana pulled a dress from the clothes press and a handful of necessities, then disappeared into the hall, calling softly for Neda.

Fool! To have walked into their room as though he had a perfect right, when these women had known each other all their lives and known him all of three months. Aye, he was a fool, and now he would pay for the stupidity that had brought him there.

"Rose," he began, praying she would understand, "I asked your father if there was any way I might still earn your hand in marriage . . . that is, if you want me . . ."

"*Want* you?" She stared at him, incredulity on her features. "Jamie, I *love* you. It will take time to sort through my feelings, but this much I do know: You have been badly used, as I have. I hold my sister accountable for all of it."

"Wait." He held up his hand, shocked at how quickly he came to Leana's defense. "Your father played a part in this, Rose. Do not blame your sister, not completely. All three of us were deceived, I most of all." *Deservedly so.* A thread of guilt wound itself around his windpipe, making it harder to breathe.

She clutched a handkerchief in her hands, wrapping it absently around her fingers. "What sort of arrangements did Father offer you?"

Jamie carefully explained the terms, watching as her face registered each scandalous detail.

When he finished, she sank onto her dressing table stool in a near faint. "Jamie, I can't bear the thought of it. Of you . . . of my sister."

"Don't think of it, Rose." He knelt beside her, but she pulled back from him. "Don't think of any of it. Spend the week with Susanne, if you like. Or perhaps Aunt Meg might come to Auchengray."

Her eyes, swollen and red from crying, took on a spiteful glare. "Fine plans you're making for me, Jamie. A visit with a friend who attended my own wedding when I did not. An aunt who would fuss and cluck over me as she does her chickens. While you and Leana . . . while you . . ." Her voice broke on a sob, and she turned away, soaking the chair with her tears. When he reached for her, she swatted his arm. "Don't . . . touch . . . me!"

Och! The situation was impossible. He spun about the room, giving her time to cry unabated, thinking of what he might say. *The future.* Aye, that was what they must discuss. Not the week ahead and certainly not yestreen. "Rose," he murmured, kneeling beside her again, "this time next Thursday all will be as before: Jamie and Rose, anticipating our wedding day. The first of August." He rested no more than his fingertips on her sleeve. "Summer is a fine time for a wedding, don't you think?"

She fell back against the chair to face him, her face blotched with red, drained of emotion. "Jamie, we've already *had* our wedding at Newabbey. Reverend Gordon will not put up with such . . . irregularities."

"Your father has already agreed to meet with the kirk session. The parish records will show that on 31 December I married Leana McBride. Since the marriage has been"—even saying the word brought a flush to his neck—"has been consummated, Reverend Gordon will have little choice in the matter."

"And the gossips?"

He waved his hand dismissively. "Let them talk. It is not *you* they will find fault with, Rose. It is Leana. And perhaps me. Never you. Once she is . . . put aside, we'll be free to marry. In Monnigaff if you prefer. The kirk is older but a fine building."

She eyed him, a newfound cynicism in her raised brow. "Would you divorce a wife so easily as that?"

"Not easily, Rose. I am grieved for your sister. Her future is bleak, as you well know. No man will have her as his wife. She will spend the balance of her life in quiet disgrace, caring for your father into his old age. Should the kirk session choose, they may assign her several Sabbath days on the repentance stool."

Rose sat up straighter. "Jamie, they wouldn't dare!"

"They might, lass. 'Tis rare to see the stool of repentance used in the kirk of late, but Monnigaff keeps theirs polished, and I suspect Newabbey does as well." He dearly hoped Leana would not be subjected to such public humiliation. To mount the wooden stool in front of the pulpit, dressed in a coarse white linen gown, her head and feet bared, her grievous sin announced to the whole congregation, her penance addressed in the sermon—Jamie would not wish that on anyone, not even a woman who'd stolen into a man's bed under false pretenses.

Rose knew what the repentance stool entailed as well; its terrors were written all over her face. "Is there . . . no hope for her?"

"Aye, but that hope is at your expense, Rose. If Leana conceives a child during those seven months, then I am bound to remain her husband."

Rose's countenance fell. "Leana is healthy and very much wants a child."

He lowered his voice. "That would require my . . . ah, my cooperation. And I have no intention of being cooperative once this appalling week is over. Do we understand each other, Rose?"

She nodded, her features softening for the first time since he'd entered the room. "Yes, Jamie."

"The first of August then." He leaned forward and kissed her forehead, then each cheek, and finally, when he knew she would allow it, her mouth, wet from her tears. Soft, sweet, innocent lips. Untouched and untried. "I will buy you a new kell, my fair Rose," he murmured. "More lovely than this one. We will start anew, the two of us. If you will wait for me another seven months, I will prove that my love for you has never faltered."

"I will wait, Jamie McKie. But I cannot promise those months will be easy for any of us." She sighed, frown lines erasing any remnant of childish innocence from her face. "For the moment, Leana awaits you. Your . . . wife."

"For the moment," he reminded her, standing to leave. "We will return to Auchengray the Thursday next. Until then, know that you are the woman I love, Rose." He bent to brush his lips against her hair. "You alone."

Fifty-Nine

When the heart's past hope,
the face is past shame.
SCOTTISH PROVERB

You canna fool me, Leana." Neda wagged a work-worn finger at her. "Lining your basket with pine cones, tying on sprigs of mistletoe. I ken what ye're aboot, lass."

Leana offered the housekeeper a slight nod, grateful to have one friend left at Auchengray. Most of the household simply avoided her, though some raked her with their eyes or whispered as she hurried past them gathering what she needed for her bridal week in Dumfries with Jamie. He was still upstairs with Rose, though Leana expected him to appear shortly, impatient to be off, even more eager to return home. They would be traveling by dark, and though the day had been unusually bright, the long winter's night promised to be bitterly cold. Jamie, colder still. *Please God, let it not be so.*

Determined to make the most of her time with Jamie, Leana had filled her traveling basket with the necessary ingredients for a fruitful week, gathered from her neatly stored collection of seeds and nuts, roots and plants from the stillroom. Neda peeked over her shoulder, making noises of approval. "Hmmm. Cucumber, mustard, and poppy seeds. Guid. A bag of currants and hazelnuts for ye to nibble on. Aye, that's right. And wild carrots from the cellar for Jamie. Well done, Leana. If yer heart's desire is to fill yer womb with a wee babe, ye've certainly packed yer basket well. Anythin' else in there?"

"Hope." Leana tucked the last of the seeds into a safe corner. "Hope that Jamie will not treat me unkindly. Hope that I can please him as a wife. Hope that I will come home next Thursday bearing the seed of a son inside me."

"Or a daughter," the older woman teased, regarding her with a kind smile. "Hope is the wisest medicine of all. Me mither always told me if it weren't for hope, the heart would break."

"My heart is already broken, Neda." She sighed heavily, swinging the basket over her arm. "Jamie will never love me. Rose will never forgive me. Our neighbors will never invite me through their doors again."

"That's a lot of nivers for a young woman to worry over." Neda gently took her basket from her and placed it on the cutting table, then grasped both her hands, squeezing them as only Neda could, with a firm yet gentle grip. Her voice was low, soothing, a mother comforting a hurting child. "Ye made a mistake, lass."

Ashamed, Leana lowered her head, biting back tears. "Aye."

"Ye're not the first woman whose heart took her places she never meant tae go." Neda ducked her head to catch Leana's eye. "Who knows? Ye may already be carryin' Jamie's babe. Have ye thocht o' that?"

Leana's head lifted slightly and her spirits with it. "Nae, I'd not even considered it."

"Ye see?" Neda's ruddy face smiled from brow to chin. "Swallow yer herbs and seeds if ye like, but remember who has the power to fill yer womb, and I dinna mean yer husband."

Leana nodded and offered a faint smile in return. "I ken your meaning: 'Children are an heritage of the Lord.' But, Neda, I can barely bring myself to ask God for his forgiveness. How dare I ask him for a blessing?"

"D'ye think the Almighty blesses only those who deserve it?" Neda laughed softly. "None of us is worthy, lass. Not one. He blesses whom he chooses, and we thank him when he does. That's the way of it."

Leana sniffed, squeezing Neda's hands. "You make the most difficult things sound simple."

"They are simple, dearie."

Leana looked up to find the light of mercy and grace shining in the older woman's eyes. "Oh, Neda." Overcome, she fell forward and pressed her teary cheek against Neda's weathered one. "Whatever would I do without you? You have truly been a mother to me."

Neda's whispered words warmed her ear. "Ye honor me, child. Agness McBride was goodness itself."

Too good to have borne such a daughter. Leana leaned back, struck afresh with guilt. "What would Mother have said?"

Neda studied her for some time before she answered. "She would've cautioned ye to spend mair time thinkin' of God and less time thinkin' of yer braw cousin."

"Is it . . . too late to do that now?"

"'Tis niver too late to think of God." At the sound of Jamie's footsteps on the stair, Neda slipped the basket of herbs back on Leana's arm and kissed her cheek in farewell. "Pray. Listen. Show Jamie yer true heart. Let him see the goodness inside ye, Leana, for there is meikle of it."

"But his temper—"

"Och!" Neda waved away her concerns. "Anger's short lived in a guid man."

Leana gripped the basket. "What of our dear Rose?"

The smile on Neda's face dwindled. "Let me tend to your sister while ye're gone, for she needs a mither as well." When Leana tensed, the older woman shook her head briskly. "Nae. Do not burden yerself further, lass. Rose is not yer concern this week. Think on the Lord Almighty and yer new husband, in that order. And see to it that ye worship at Saint Michael's on the Sabbath. Are we agreed?"

"We are." Thanking her with her eyes, Leana hurried through the kitchen and out the back door, circling around to the front of the house, where the chaise was waiting. Jamie stood beside it, the planes of his face hard in the fading light of day as Willie stored her trunk behind the seat.

Neda had included her favorite scented soap, her best nightgown, and one good dress. Not the claret gown though. Leana feared Jamie might be reminded of the first moment he saw her wearing it when he'd come to her room, asking her to serve as proxy, putting their misfortune in motion through no fault of his own.

"Thank you for waiting while I filled my basket." She took his hand as he guided her into the chaise.

"There's no room for that behind you," he said curtly, climbing in beside her.

"I'll gladly hold it on my lap."

He glanced at the odd assortment of goods, then at her. "What's all that *rubbage?*"

"Hope," she said simply, settling into her seat as he shook the reins and their journey began. "'Tis a basket full of hope."

He snorted, the look on his face nearing disgust. "If by 'hope' you mean some foolish notion of winning my affections, then leave the basket behind,

Leana. My heart is spoken for. You may have the rest of me for seven days but no longer."

The basket nearly spilled from her lap. "But Father said I would have seven *months!* That it would be August before you and Rose might marry."

He looked at her, the knowing gleam in his eye not at all like the Jamie she loved. "*You* have seven months to produce proof of an heir in your womb. But I promised your father that I'd give you my undivided attention—weren't those the words he used?"

She nodded, her eyes widening with fear.

"Aye, my undivided attention for just seven *days.* So there you have it. One week, lass. No more." He urged their horse forward with a light crack of his whip, smiling grimly into the deepening twilight. "Your father is not the only one who can twist words to suit his needs."

"One *week?*" she whispered, feeling sick. "Jamie, a week is hardly enough—"

"Nae, it's more than enough. Ask any woman who has conceived on her wedding night."

She sat up straighter, remembering Neda's words. "And what if I've done just that?"

His expression darkened. "I sincerely hope you have not. Is it . . . . possible?"

Heat flew to her cheeks. She'd discussed the intimate details of a woman's monthly courses with her sister and Neda but never with a man, and especially not Jamie. Still, he was her husband, and he deserved an answer. "It's possible, though not likely," was all she said, then counted the calendar days in her head. *But possible.* Leana pressed her lips together and patted her basket. "I shall make the most of my week and be satisfied with that."

"That's settled then. When we return to Auchengray, it will be as though it never happened. There will no mention of this . . . this *bridal* week. Especially not to Rose."

"I would never hurt my sister like that." She touched his arm to be sure he heard her. "Despite what you may think, I love Rose even more than I love you, Jamie."

He glared at her, his entire countenance frowning. "Do not say those words again, Leana. It will not change my opinion or my feelings concerning you. I do not love you and never have."

Must he repeat it again and again? Did he not realize that once would last her a lifetime? *I never said I loved you.* She forced herself to speak the unspeakable. "But you will *love* me, as a husband. Do what you can to . . . give me a child."

He turned away. "Have you no shame?"

"I'm covered in shame, Jamie." When her chin began to tremble, she willed it to remain steady. "The only thing that will take away my shame is to bear your heir and claim you as my rightful husband. You must know it is my only hope and my deepest desire. I will not pretend otherwise. Nor will I grovel and beg for your affection each night."

"See that you don't. It's most unbecoming in a woman. I will do as I've promised. Let us speak no more of it."

She had her answer. The pleasures of yestreen were lost to her, like a thick mist evaporating with the light of day, leaving no trace. All that was left was duty.

Her heart broken yet again, Leana gripped the sides of her basket as though drawing strength from the woven heather itself. "I only have one favor I might ask during our week."

"Favor?" He already looked unwilling to grant it.

"May we attend Saint Michael's on Sunday for our *kirkin?*" She hesitated to mention the wedding custom, for theirs would include no friends nor the traditional feast that followed.

He exhaled evenly. "Aye, the kirkin, for our first Sunday at kirk together."

And our last. He did not need to say it for Leana to hear it.

Jamie fished in his waistcoat pocket and produced the silver wedding ring. He tossed it into her basket as though it were a worthless trinket. "Wear this, lest our innkeeper heave us out on the cobblestones."

She found the slender ring among her bundles of seeds and slipped it onto her finger, the cold silver warming quickly. *Let Jamie warm to me as well.*

The last of the light was gone. Darkness wrapped them in a black, woolen blanket of cold. She was grateful the air was calm, that no night wind pierced her hooded cape or Jamie's sturdy coat, yet she moved a bit closer to him for warmth. He did not move away, nor did he acknowledge her. They ran out of words to say and rode in silence, passing through the crowded streets of Brigend, winding their way to Devorgilla's Bridge and across the span into Dumfries. Sandstone and red brick houses loomed over neatly paved streets, the interiors brightly lit with candles and glowing hearths. Turning down the High Street, Leana imagined young and old gathered behind the many doors, celebrating the start of another year.

As their chaise drew up to the King's Arms Inn, its noble patrons coming and going with much ceremony, Leana prayed—how hard she prayed!—that 1789 might end on a more promising note than it had begun. And that her first week with Jamie would not be her last.

They were greeted at the door by a convivial bellman, their chaise and bags promptly attended to and a key placed in their hands. "Will you be joining us for supper?"

"Aye," Jamie answered.

"Nae," she said just as quickly.

The portly man grinned. "We can arrange for dinner later if you're hungry, sir. That is, if Mistress McKie will permit you to leave her side."

"She will," Jamie said shortly and stood back for her to start up the elegant stair, thanking the man as she went. They found the room spacious and well furnished, with a sitting desk by the window and a good store of candles for the handsome wall sconces. A manservant appeared at the door with their few belongings and plunked them onto the floor, his palm eager for Jamie's coin.

"Will ye be needing anything else?" the gaunt lad asked.

Leana shook her head, then turned to Jamie when the door latched. "May I unpack for you?"

"If you like." He sat on the edge of the bed—not a box bed with curtains like the one at Auchengray but a standing bed with four corner posts and no tester stretched above it. The openness of it made her feel uneasy. Exposed.

Her hands shook as she lifted out his linen shirts and wool stockings, stacking them in a chest of drawers the same as she might for her father, uncertain how Jamie preferred such things to be stored. He did not comment, so she did what seemed best, placing her things in a separate drawer, lest the fabrics touch.

She finished—too quickly, she feared—with no plans for what might come next.

He stood abruptly. "Are you sure you won't join me for supper?"

"Jamie, I'm more tired than I am hungry. Perhaps a nap would be in order. Do you mind?" He assured her that he did not and disappeared into the hall, while she hung her discarded cape on a hook by the door, then undressed for bed. It was better this way. He would find her resting, perhaps wake her for a short time, then leave her to her sleep. Much needed after yestreen.

She hung her gown, hid her shift and stockings in the chest, and slipped into her best nightgown made of fine cambric, embroidered around the neck, sleeves, and hem with Scottish bluebells. It was her design, meant to match her eyes, though Jamie would not notice. Raiding her basket, she nibbled on seeds, nuts, and currants, praying as she did for a blessing she knew she did not deserve. A tepid glass of water from the pitcher and her appetite was sated.

Leana slid between the chilly sheets and rested her cheek against the wedding ring that felt so strange on her hand. A wife, yet not. Only one week to make it so. Never would a man be wooed more thoroughly than Jamie McKie. After much tossing and turning she drifted to sleep, lost in a dreamless world.

"Leana?" Jamie woke her with a low-pitched whisper.

Half-asleep, she smiled at the sound of it, so close to her ear. "How was your supper?"

"The meat was tough, the ale watered down, and the potatoes harvested some other season entirely." He yawned, then blew out his candle, extinguishing the shadows in the darkened room, the curtains drawn tight against the cold. "Perhaps their specialty is breakfast."

"Perhaps." Leana rolled toward him in the feather bed, suddenly wide awake. *Oh, Jamie.* He lay very near, the tails of his long shirt brushing against her nightgown. "Jamie, I pray this night will—"

"Shh." He touched a finger to her lips. "Let us speak no more of it, remember?" Not another word was said, though his hands and his mouth were not silent, and in the darkness she heard him speak her name. Just once.

Sixty

Let us embrace, and from this very moment
Vow an eternal misery together.
THOMAS OTWAY

The bluebells on her gown. That was the first thing
he noticed. Though the morning light was faint, he
could still make out the delicate embroidered flowers circling her neck as she slept on her back. He
stroked one flower along her collarbone, feeling the
small loops of thread beneath his fingertip, and
imagined her huddled close to a window, spectacles perched on her nose, squinting at her needle
and hoop, stitching a nightgown no man was meant
to see.

'Tis your fault, Leana. He kept reminding himself

of that, holding guilt at arm's length, determined not to be sullied by it. But his conscience was ever vigilant, prodding him with the truth: The first night, his whisky-soaked mind had thought she was Rose. Yestreen, sober, he'd known she was Leana, and still he'd responded to her touch.

With a certain resignation, Jamie propped his head on one elbow to study her features. She was not a beauty. Her face was too long, her eyebrows thickly drawn, her nose and mouth a bit full for a gentlewoman, her coloring wan. In her spectacles she looked like a stayed lass of thirty years. But in the dark of the night, when she'd smoothed her hands across his chest and whispered his name, all those unappealing details had flown out of his head. *Leana.* He'd spoken her name aloud once, not meaning to. She'd wept without making a sound, even as he cursed himself for being careless, for giving her false hope. Heaven knew she'd brought enough of that in her cone-lined basket.

Nothing could come of this week but misery. Not love, not marriage, not a future. And not, he prayed, a child. He was bound to honor the terms made by his scheming uncle and bound to do his duty by Leana, but he would do as little as possible. Rose was waiting for him, his dark-haired, dark-eyed, darling Rose. He would not dishonor the girl's newfound love for him by allowing himself even a moment of genuine pleasure with her sister.

Her sister. It was beyond comprehension how such a thing could have happened. He only knew his uncle was somehow behind it. Lachlan had threatened to withhold Rose's hand in marriage to force the proxy wedding. Might the pernickitie man have vowed to ruin Leana's life as well? Jamie would not ask her, fearing the answer. Such knowledge would not make the week ahead easier. Only more difficult.

She stirred, turning toward him, her eyes still closed, her generous mouth open. Jamie rolled to his feet in one swift movement, shivering from the cold room and the fear that rose inside him. He could not love two women. Half measures were not his way of doing things. If he loved Rose, then he must spurn Leana. Discourage her at every opportunity. Give her no room to build a nest inside his heart.

Turning his back on her, he used the chamber pot and dressed quickly. The dark sky matched the inn's fine pewter plate: thick, gray, with a dull sheen. He was almost out the door when Leana awoke, catching him with his hand on the latch.

"Jamie. Are you off to breakfast then?"

He did not look at her. "Aye."

"Please let me join you." She slipped from the bed, a silhouette in the murky light. "Will you wait while I dress?"

"I'll wait downstairs." His words were curt, his movement abrupt. He practically threw himself down the stair, then warmed his hands around a cup of steaming tea while he put his emotions in order for the hours and days ahead. He would be polite, but distant. Honest, yet risk nothing. Kind, without being warm. A gentleman, not a husband.

When Leana appeared, her hair neatly braided, her dark blue gown complementing her pale skin, he merely nodded in greeting. She took her seat, her expression serene. "Shall we see if their porridge has more to recommend it than the potatoes they dug up for your dinner?"

Jamie looked at her, suppressing a smile with some effort. "Our host has been instructed to deliver two bowls when you came to the table. Tea and bannocks as well and a rasher of bacon. Will that suffice?"

"More than enough," she murmured, folding her hands in her lap. "My appetite is easily sated."

He ignored the teasing comment that sprang to mind—a lover's response, not at all appropriate. Breakfast was served and consumed with little discussion, their napkins put aside within the hour. A long day stretched before them. And, since it was the second of January, an even longer night. He looked at her across the table, hiding his feelings behind a mask of indifference. "What are your plans for the day?"

She did not flinch at the sharpness of his tone. "Whatever you please, Mr. McKie. If it suits you, I would very much like to see what secrets Dumfries might be keeping from us."

Secrets? Aye, he had enough for the whole burgh. "And if it does not suit me to accompany you on this cold morning?"

Her smile was sufficient to warm the room. "Then I will gladly pull a chair to the inn's hearth and lose myself in a novel."

He could not keep the surprise out of his voice. "You brought a book for your bridal week?"

"Aye." She blushed a bit. "*Evelina,* in three volumes. I was not certain how the . . . weather might be in Dumfries. As well, I cannot remember when I last enjoyed seven days without working." She stretched, beaming at the handful of patrons scattered about the inn's dining room. "'Twill be a luxury to read without some task being thrust into my hands."

Jamie stared at her, taken aback by her calm, almost confident demeanor. Where was the shy Leana he'd met months ago? She was not cheerful, like Rose, but she seemed most sure of herself for a woman who had no future to speak of. Her manner so intrigued him that, before he could stop himself, he offered to take her on a stroll up and down the streets of Dumfries.

She smiled, amused by something. "I suppose *Evelina* and her adventures might wait until later." When Leana stood, he did as well. "If you'll kindly retrieve my cloak from our room, Mr. McKie, we can begin at once."

McKie again. He pinched back a frown. "What happened to 'Jamie'?"

"I've been asking myself that all morning," she said evenly, her blue gaze fixed on his. "Your formal tone and cold reception suggested I might best treat you as a stranger. For you see, I have one ambition this week, and that is to please you so completely that you cannot imagine life without me."

Stunned, he fell back into his seat. "Then our goals are quite at odds."

"I am not surprised." She sighed, as though clearing her thoughts, then turned toward the door. "Shall we walk out then?"

A courting term. Indeed, that's how it felt, as though they were courting. But that was impossible. He was married to the woman . . . or *not* married, if things could not be smoothed over with the kirk session. He was bedding her, yet she called him *Mr. McKie.* A most unsettling situation. Shaking his head, he hastened up the stair for her cloak and returned to find her waiting for him by the door, which was propped open to welcome the gentry to the King's Arms.

They fell in step, climbing up the High Street. Though it was cold, no bitter wind tore at their scarves. Instead, they kept a leisurely pace and poked their heads into every establishment with a yawning door. Leana, more at ease than he could ever remember, carried on intelligent conversations with glove makers and apothecaries, greeted fishermen avoiding their boats—for all men of the sea agreed that Fridays bore naught but ill luck—and chatted with opinionated writers at the next table when they stopped at the George Inn for a dinner of roast lamb.

Leana did not flirt with men, as Rose did without

meaning to. Instead, she engaged merchants and tradesmen in thoughtful dialogue, asking perceptive questions. Leana had Lachlan's mind for business but none of his devious ways. No wonder Duncan sought her counsel with the ledgers at Martinmas.

By day's end she was no more bonny than at the start of it, but Jamie found himself smiling when he should look grim and praising her when he meant to be silent. Supper was a pleasant plate of broth and bread before they retired and found themselves huddled beneath the bed blankets earlier than he'd intended. When he reached for her in the darkness, her response was immediate, her love for him undeniable, though he took care not to speak her name nor whisper any endearments. It was true; he appreciated her attentions. But he did not love her, not in the least.

Saturday he slipped out before she awoke, leaving behind a note advising her to spend the day with *Evelina* while he attended to business. It was a ridiculous ploy; he had no business in Dumfries. He simply could not bear another day of misery, torn between his will and his desire, between what he knew to be proper and what he knew to be honest. He returned to the King's Arms very late to find Leana fast asleep, her book still clasped in her hands, her candle guttering. Relieved, he undressed quickly, only to have her open one eye and smile at him. "Come to bed," she whispered, and he did.

The Sabbath morning dawned cold and damp, a

steady rain overnight saturating the air. Seagulls soared above the High Street, their long, mournful cries a sad, two-note melody, then a series of short calls, as though the birds had changed their minds and started laughing.

Jamie glanced at Leana as they walked down the sloping street toward Saint Michael's kirk, wondering if she'd noticed the gulls as well and heard the irony in their call. She tipped her head back to watch them swooping back and forth. "Are they sad or happy, do you think?"

Leana missed very little. "I suspect they are both," he said. *Like us.*

The kirk bells began ringing on both ends of the High Street—one for the New Church, as the townsfolk called it, the other for Saint Michael's. Jamie had planned to hear Dr. Burnside at the New Church, but Leana had assured Neda they would worship at Saint Michael's, so he obliged. A small compromise. It was not the kirk in Newabbey, so it hardly mattered. They would see no familiar faces, and their visit would be quickly forgotten.

They stepped aside to make way for a carriage when the heel of her boot caught on a crack in the paved street, and Leana pitched forward. Without hesitating, Jamie slipped his arms around her waist and pulled her against him to keep her from falling onto the muddy street. He held her only for a moment until she righted herself but long enough to flood his mind with vivid images. His resolution to make her bridal week a miserable one was crumbling like Neda's shortbread.

Four more nights and it would end, forever.

It was best that way; it was right. Rose was still his first love, his only love. He would remind himself of that until he held the young lass in his arms.

Sixty-One

I've done my duty, and I've done no more.
HENRY FIELDING

They climbed the steps to Saint Michael's, its kirkyard littered with immense gravestones in chaotic
array all the way to the front door. As befitted the
custom of kirkin, Jamie had walked Leana directly
there without taking any side streets and arrived
after the service had well begun. With some reluctance, he offered her his arm before they entered,
bewildered by her eagerness to observe the tradition when it was for naught.

She tucked her hand in place, close to his heart,
and they stepped through the doors. Every head
turned, though only for a brief second. The two

were strangers, a perfectly ordinary husband and wife come shamefully late to service. One couple did not turn back though. They smiled and waved the two of them forward.

Leana's eyes widened. "Neda!" she whispered. "Duncan!"

Jamie's jaw tightened at the sight of the overseer's lanky frame. *Duncan Hastings.* The one man from Auchengray who could break down his defenses with a single kind word.

Leana dragged him forward to the pew where the couple sat waiting. It was the custom for the bridegroom's good friend to come to the kirkin, and the bride's favorite as well, though they'd hardly expected them so far from home.

"We had to come," Neda explained in hushed tones, seating the couple between them, then squeezing Leana's hand in greeting. "Quiet now, and give the Almighty his due."

Jamie merely nodded at Duncan, not quite meeting the man's piercing blue gaze.

"O Eternal God and most merciful Father," the minister intoned, "we confess and acknowledge here before thy Divine Majesty that we are miserable sinners."

Jamie bowed his head and felt Leana do the same, their shoulders and knees brushing against each other in the crowded pew. *A sinner.* Aye, Leana was that. The worst kind of sinner: pretending she was innocent. Convincing herself on his wedding night that he loved her, wanted her, welcomed her as his bride.

Yet the more he tried to tally Leana's flagrant transgressions, the more his own assaulted him. He'd sinned when he'd asked Leana to serve as a proxy bride, too impatient to wait for Rose and not caring that the lass might miss her own wedding. He'd sinned when he'd kissed Leana too thoroughly, danced with her too gaily, drunk too freely, and enjoyed her body so completely. The last was her sin as well, but try as he might, he could not put all the blame on her shoulders.

He'd sinned again by agreeing to Lachlan's despicable plans for his daughters so he might claim Rose for his bride, not caring what it might cost the two women. Selfish. Thoughtless. *Sinner.*

Not Leana. *You, Jamie.*

And those were far from his first sins. He'd sinned when he'd bartered a birthright. He'd sinned when he'd stolen a brother's blessing. He'd sinned when he'd deceived a beloved father.

Forgive me. He'd said the words by rote hundreds of times. *Forgive me.* Yet this time the tightness in his chest was real, and his plea came from not only his lips but his heart as well. *Forgive me.* Bent with the weight of his shame, his forehead nearly touched the pew before him.

He felt more than heard the answer: *Behold, I am with you.*

Nae. Jamie pressed his lips into a hard line, fighting against the very mercy he'd pleaded for. How could Almighty God remain by his side when he couldn't live with himself?

The minister droned on, yet his words were alive.

"Nothing is able to remove thy heavenly grace and favor from us. To thee, therefore, O Father, with the Son and the Holy Ghost, be all honor and glory, world without end. So be it."

"So be it," the congregation responded.

Can it be? Jamie lifted his head, troubled by a promise of favor that required nothing of him. He'd stolen a blessing from his father. Was it right to steal one from God as well?

The precentor led the parishioners in a hymn, familiar yet not. The tune was the same, but the words had been altered in the new edition of the *Paraphrases,* forcing him to listen carefully. On his left Leana sang with a steady voice, seemingly unaffected by the words. For him they struck too close a chord.

> The wretched prodigal behold
> In misery lying low,
> Whom vice had sunk from high estate,
> And plunged in want and woe.

Aye, far too close. He'd run away from home and found himself up to his ankles in sheep dung. His pockets were empty of silver and his heart full of misery, some of it by his doing. If God was with him, then why had his troubles increased tenfold? His stomach churning, Jamie was grateful when the many verses were finished and even more relieved to have the sermon and prayers over and find himself standing beneath a gray January sky again, his temporary anguish left behind in the pew.

"May we treat ye both to a kirkin feast?" Duncan asked when they reached the High Street. "Our coin won't stretch far enough to cover the fare at the King's Arms, but we might be able to feed ye proper at the Hole i' the Wa'. Will that suit?"

"Aye," Jamie agreed, resigned to play the part of the doting husband, if only for the afternoon. The foursome enjoyed a simple meal at the old inn, then a long winter's walk. It was three o'clock before Duncan and Neda rode off for Auchengray, Neda's skirts modestly kilted about her. Jamie waved them off with Leana by his side, then steered her through the inn door toward a warm hearth, for the air had grown frosty.

"I'm glad they came," she admitted, climbing the steps by his side. "I fear that when we return to Auchengray, nothing will be the same."

He paused on the stair, firmly grasping her elbow. "It cannot be the same, Leana. I am doing my duty here, nothing more. See that you don't pretend otherwise, or you will be sorely disappointed."

She lowered her gaze and her voice as well. "You could never disappoint me, Jamie. My expectations are such that anything you do delights me."

Such a woman did not make spurning her easy. Pleasant by day and passionate by night, she was the answer to every man's prayers except his, constantly putting his resolve to the test. One minute he was grateful for her companionship; the next he was furious for allowing himself even the smallest measure of enjoyment. Wednesday night arrived too soon, yet Thursday could not come quickly enough to end his misery.

True to her promise, Leana had never groveled or begged for his attention. She'd simply showered him with love. Warm glances, gentle touches, sweet words, and an honesty that took his breath away. Leana's love knew no bounds and required no bindings, yet he felt inexplicably tied to the woman. 'Twas a cord that would need to be sharply cut come the morn's morn.

On their last night in Dumfries, the weather took a turn for the worse. "The hour grows late," he murmured, extinguishing the last candle. A biting wind from the north rattled the inn's windowpanes, the cold air whistling through the cracks and seeping beneath their bedcovers where they huddled in mutual despair.

"This will be the last then." Leana spoke without giving away her true feelings.

"It must be," he said, not needing to explain why. "I hope that I have . . ."

"You have." She kissed him, and he tasted the tears on her lips. "Jamie, my sweet husband," she whispered, wrapping her arms around his neck. "I love you still."

Long after the Midsteeple bells rang at ten o'clock, they drifted into a fitful slumber, waking each other throughout the night without meaning to, tossing to and fro, trying to keep warm, trying to stay apart. At dawn they dressed quickly, avoiding each other's eyes, hastening down the stair to break their fast and be on their way to Auchengray. The bitter night had frozen the muddy ground solid, making it easier for the two-wheeled chaise to manage the road from Dumfries. When they paid their toll four miles south of the burgh, Jamie noticed how few coins were left of his mother's gift, though the week had cost him more dearly than silver.

At least it had not cost him Rose. Her beauty, her laughter, her lively ways would be a welcome change after her plain, quiet sister. Yet Leana had stolen a part of him that he feared he could not retrieve. She'd touched his soul deeply, and Jamie resented her for it. For reaching a part of him he'd kept to himself, for exposing his weaknesses. As they rode in silence, a seed of bitterness grew inside him, turning into a smoldering anger the closer they came to Auchengray's gate.

They made the final turn east at Lochend about noon. Two short miles remained. He snapped his whip, eager to get home to innocent Rose and away from her older but wiser sister. Whatever had taken place between them in Dumfries was over and best forgotten.

"I don't want any unnecessary scenes," he cautioned her. "From the moment we arrive, we are not to be alone in a room together nor to touch in any manner."

"As you wish, Jamie." Leana's cool voice infuriated him. He'd meant to hurt her, to push her away with his heartless request, and she refused to be vexed.

"If there should be some . . . unhappy news

resulting from our time together, I trust you will let your father and me know as soon as you are certain."

She regarded him evenly. "Would a son be unhappy news to you, Jamie?"

A son. There could be no better news in the world. But not like this. He shrugged to hide his feelings. "I am thinking of Rose and how her hopes for the future would be crushed, along with mine."

"But if *my* hopes are crushed, that is without consequence to you?"

"I cannot please two women, nor will I try to." *There.* He'd ruffled her feathers. Let them stay so and keep them farther apart. Leana knew him too well, and that made her dangerous.

Rose was waiting for him at the window when they brought the chaise to a halt near the front door. "Jamie, Jamie!" She ran out the door without coat or hat, her cheeks pink from the cold, her long braid flying behind her. *Like a child.* His spirits lifted at the sight of her. *My sweet Rose!* She practically pulled him out of the chaise, ignoring her sister. If Leana climbed out on her own, he did not notice.

Duncan, Willie, and several of the others who labored in the farm steading strolled up, hiding something in their midst. "Dinna be walkin' awa from us, lad." Duncan produced a wicker creel weighed down, not with fish, but with stones. "In case ye dinna know, today marks yer first day back to work. Or have ye been workin' hard all week?" Duncan winked at the others, whose good-natured laughter made Jamie's neck grow warm. "Ye must face yer *creelin,* Jamie McKie. Come, let me strap this basket on yer back. If ye've been a worthy husband and assumed yer manly role, yer wife can cut ye free of it."

Jamie asked Rose to wait for him, then walked toward the group, hiding his irritation. Such customs were for common working folk, not for well-bred gentlemen. *And which are you, Jamie?* With a grimace he offered his back to Duncan, who took his time strapping the creel on his shoulders while the others taunted Jamie about his manhood. "A more ridiculous wedding custom could not be found in all of Scotland," Jamie fumed, which only made them laugh harder. When the weight of the heavy basket was fully on his back, he fought to keep his balance, refusing to bend more than necessary.

"Do yer part, Mistress McKie," Duncan chided, motioning the silent Leana to join them and handing her a sharpened dirk. "If Jamie's done right by ye, cut him free."

Leana took the dirk in one hand and the cord tightly wrapped around his shoulder in the other, keeping her pale gaze fixed on his.

Please, Leana. His eyes pleaded with her. *Cut me free.*

Sixty-Two

A maid whom there were none to praise
And very few to love.
WILLIAM WORDSWORTH

Daughter, a word, if you please."

Lachlan was waiting for Leana inside the front door. Without preamble he steered her through the house and into the spence, latching the door behind them. "I have met with the kirk session and explained the situation to them."

Her cheeks, flushed from Jamie's creelin, suddenly cooled. "The . . . situation?"

"Aye." He regarded her evenly. "I told them you convinced Jamie to marry you instead of your sister, knowing there would not be sufficient time to change the kirk records before the vows were read."

"But, Father, I—"

"I also told them God had revealed his will on the matter, demonstrated by the ill weather and Rose's providential delay."

"Do you really think—"

"Finally I assured them the marriage was swiftly consummated and legally binding."

"Then, I'm . . ." Her mouth dropped open in astonishment. Her father had managed the impossible. "I truly *am* married to Jamie?" Dazed, she pulled off her cape, longing to run up the stair and hang it on a hook in Jamie's room, claiming a small corner of his world. "You are sure, Father, that Jamie and I are bound by God's law and man's as well?"

"Sit down, lass, for you look about to faint." He gestured toward a chair, then folded his arms across his chest. "Almighty God sees that you are married for the moment, Leana; that much is true. As to man's opinion, Jamie requested before he left for Dumfries that you be moved as far away from his bedroom as possible. He is my nephew, my guest, and my son-in-law. I could hardly refuse him. It seems he has a healthy fear of you, Leana. Is it any wonder?"

"But in Dumfries—"

"Och! You know as well as I do that those seven days were his punishment for not recognizing you in his bed. One week of forced husbandry, no better than a tup put to the ewes." Her father eyed her, curiosity in his gaze. "Was it a . . . fruitful week?"

She lifted her chin, unwilling to give him any hint. "I won't know for a little while."

"See that you don't keep the news to yourself. Whatever the outcome, others' lives will be greatly affected."

"I know, Father." She took a deep breath, fearing what his next answer might be. "Will I be permitted to attend kirk on the Sabbath?"

"Permitted?" He snorted. "Your presence will be *required* at both morning and afternoon services and a weekday sermon as well."

The shadow of the repentance stool fell across her heart. "And will I be publicly—"

"Nae. Nothing so harsh as that. The kirk session was willing to overlook the irregularities, but not without some . . . ah, consequences. I assured the session that I would see that you and Jamie are disciplined here at home, as is my rightful duty."

"Disciplined?" Her breath caught for a brief chilling moment. Discipline could mean anything, from hours spent reciting the Shorter Catechism to scrubbing out the scullery. She prayed her father would be merciful, even as she asked, "For how long?"

He shrugged. "For as long as it takes for you both to be sorry."

"Sorry?" Leana clasped her hands, anxiety creeping along her limbs. "I could not be sorrier than I already am." She could not speak for Jamie, but she was certain of her own remorse.

He poked his forefinger at the cover of the Buik. "God Almighty is the only one who knows the heart, wicked as it is. He alone will say when you two are sorry enough."

Without thinking, she cried out, "Are you not sorry too, Father? For sending me to Jamie's room on his wedding night?"

His brow knit together in a dark line, like storm clouds moving in from the west. Thunder rumbled through his voice. "I did not send you, Leana. You walked into that room of your own accord."

Beneath her skirts, her knees began to shake. She'd accused him, however foolishly, and he would demand that she prove herself or beg his forgiveness. "Father, you clearly said, 'Do what you must.' You *sent* me. You said, 'It is Jamie, or it is no one,' remember?" She bit her tongue to keep from adding an old proverb of Neda's: *Liars should have guid memories.*

"Aye, I said those words. But you alone decided what 'must' be done."

She pressed her hands to her knees, willing them to be still. "Father, you gave me little choice. You wanted me in Jamie's bed, I know not why."

He regarded her for a moment, as though weighing his words. When he spoke, his voice was cold and his words more so. "I will not lie to you, Daughter. I wanted you to marry Jamie. Don't pretend you did not want that as well." She hung her head, stung by the truth, and he continued. "I wanted you off my hands and firmly placed in his so there would be no question of which woman he'd married, come morning. And I wanted some means of tying your cousin to Auchengray for another term of labor, for the lad is verra skilled, and his willingness to work without being paid in silver is . . . ah, difficult to resist."

With Lachlan McBride, it always came down to what a thing cost.

Oh, Rose. You were right.

"But what of Jamie?" Leana's voice grew as thin as the wool on her great wheel, pulled taut by pain. "Have you not considered what he might want?"

Lachlan's shoulders did not shrug, but his words did. "What Jamie McKie wants is to marry your sister. Perhaps he might still get his wish. Unless you carry his child, which means Auchengray will be his someday." He spread his hands out, as though the matter were finished. "The lad has no cause to complain."

No cause to complain. Leana felt suddenly ill. "Where am I to sleep, then, if not with Jamie?" After Dumfries, might he be willing to change his mind? She would know soon enough. "Shall I sleep in my own bed with Rose?"

Lachlan scratched the back of his neck, avoiding her gaze. "Nae, Rose has declared you unfit company. Anger's a thirsty passion, they say. I fear you'll be a long time regaining your sister's trust." He gestured toward the door. "Willie's in the hall, waiting. He will show you to your new quarters."

Quarters?

Eyes full of apology, Willie walked her up one staircase, then another, to a storage room under one of the third-floor eaves. The narrow space had been fitted with a low dresser and a *hurlie* bed, which trundled about on wheels, more suitable for a child than a grown woman. Willie explained, with much blushing and stammering, that her own bedroom—hers since she'd moved from the nursery fifteen years ago—now belonged to Rose.

"I'm sorry, lass." Willie spread out his hands, the picture of helplessness. "When I moved yer things up here, yer sister's words to me were . . . well, I canna bear to repeat what she called you."

She swallowed, tasting the cruel word in her mouth. "I think I know."

Numb with shock, Leana sent Willie on his way, then unpacked her bag from Dumfries, moving with wooden gestures like a puppet on a string. She washed her face and hands in a plain porcelain bowl that sat in the dormer, glancing out the small window, its cracked panes stuffed with rags. With some difficulty she brushed her hair and pinned it up without a mirror to guide her, certain she looked exactly as she felt: ugly and unkempt, no longer wanted by the people she knew and loved. And trusted.

Help me, Neda.

Neda would not put her aside, declaring her—how had Rose put it?—*unfit company.* Neda understood what it meant to forgive someone. But when Leana hastened down the stair to find the housekeeper, the dinner bell was already ringing, and Neda had her hands full in the kitchen. The housekeeper only had time for a compassionate gaze in her direction before turning to attend to the meal. With a weary sigh, Leana let the kitchen door swing shut. She would seek out the older woman later for comfort and wise counsel.

Leana turned toward the dining room, her spirits lifted by the aroma of haddock in brown sauce, only to discover her place at the table had been moved. Jamie and Rose sat side by side, while she sat alone, some distance from them. Conversation would be difficult, by intent.

She took her place without a word, waiting for someone to notice her, beseeching each of them with a lengthy gaze, praying someone might simply look at her. Welcome her. Acknowledge her.

Please. Please see me.

None of them turned a head in her direction.

After Lachlan's solemn prayer, Leana poked at the haddock with her fork, unable to find the appetite for a single bite. Even the apples picked by her own hand and sliced into one of Neda's tasty pies did not tempt her at meal's end. The others ate quietly as well. Perhaps they stole glances at her, just as she did when their heads were bowed over their plates. The wedding was not mentioned, nor was Dumfries, nor the kirk session. It was as though none of it had ever taken place.

No longer content to keep secrets, Auchengray was now steeped in lies.

A rhyme from her childhood rang through her head like a clanging gong.

Liar, liar lickspit,
In behind the candlestick!
What's guid for liars?
Brimstone and fires.

The family Buik, waiting in the wooden box by the hearth, cried out for a hand of mercy to fall upon its pages. Was there one to be found at Auchengray? Leana rose from her chair, unsteady on her feet. "Please . . . excuse me, Father." She bolted for the kitchen, not waiting for his permission, not watching to see how the others might respond.

Neda.

The housekeeper waited for her inside the stillroom, as though she knew Leana would come running, just as she had as a child. "Come, lass." Neda gathered her up in her arms, sticky from cooking, fragrant with herbs, a proper homecoming. Leana sank into Neda's warm embrace and breathed a grateful prayer as the housekeeper brushed her hair back from her brow. Tears sprang to her eyes from the gentleness of Neda's touch.

"What am I to do, Neda?" Leana leaned back and sniffed, wiping her nose on her sleeve, not caring. "Rose has banished me to the third floor."

"For a wee while perhaps." Neda produced a cotton handkerchief from her hanging pocket and tucked it into Leana's hand. "Rose will weary of havin' to tramp up tae the third floor every time she's needin' yer advice."

Leana shook her head, dabbing at her tears. "My sister won't come to me for the time of day, let alone advice about Jamie or marriage or anything that matters." She paused to eye Neda more closely. "Were you able to . . . comfort her while we were in Dumfries?"

Neda's thin lips disappeared into a firm line. "Nae," she said at last with a weary sigh, "she was too hurt and too angry tae listen. Blamed herself, she did, for not tellin' Jamie how she felt afore she left for Twyneholm."

"Rose said that?" Leana gasped in dismay. "She's the innocent party in all of this."

"Och! No one is innocent, Leana. The Buik tells us that." Neda moved to the cabinet in the stillroom and began straightening bottles. The woman never sat still except in kirk. "Yer sister said mony an unkind word about ye these last seven days. Yer new bedroom was the least of her curses. She's not without her own sins tae repent of, lass."

Leana absently plucked a stem of dried lavender hanging over her head and pinched off the flowers with her thumbnail, dropping them into her waiting palm. "Did you know of all this when we dined in Dumfries on the Sabbath?"

"Aye." Neda ducked her head, trying to hide the color in her cheeks. "But Duncan and I were not aboot tae spoil yer time with Jamie, not for anythin'. Mr. McBride was waiting for us when we returned though. Standin' in the stables. Chastised us for visitin' ye, he did."

When Leana tried to apologize, Neda hushed her with a shake of her copper head. "Hoot! We were pleased to come." She patted her arm, her freckled features brimming with sympathy. "Ye must understand, yer faither does not know the word *forgiveness.* He insists ye both pay for yer sins."

"How much?" Leana sank onto a stool. "How much must we pay?"

Neda closed the cabinet door with a muted bang. "Yer father sets the price, I'm afraid."

Exhausted, Leana leaned her head against the damp stone wall behind her. "I thought God set the price long ago. You taught me that, didn't you? That the price was the spilling of innocent blood." Hot tears, held at bay through dinner, pooled in her eyes. "I've already spilled mine . . . on Jamie's bed." Leana pressed a hand to her mouth to keep from sobbing, but it was too late. Her face crumpled and her hopes with it. "I have . . . nothing . . . left. *Nothing!*"

"Now, now." Neda gathered the lavender from her palm and put it aside, then smoothed her hand over Leana's with tender strokes. "It was not our blood God wanted. It was his son's. No matter what yer faither may say, yer sins have already been paid for, Leana. All of them." Neda ran a finger along Leana's chin, collecting tears. A wry smile creased her face. "D'ye remember the task I gave ye when ye went tae Dumfries?"

Leana nodded with a noisy sniff. "You told me, 'Think on the Lord Almighty and your new husband, in that order.'"

"And did ye?"

Leana nodded but averted her eyes, giving her secret away.

"Ye thought more about yer new husband, didn't ye, dearie? Well, then, think of yer first love now, yer first Bridegroom. The Buik says we're tae go tae him in prayer. Tell God where it hurts, lass, and tell him what ye need. He loves ye more than Jamie ever could."

"So you say, Neda." Leana pressed the hem of her apron against her cheeks and stood, bound for the third floor. "So you say."

But Jamie did not love her at all, a fact that became more evident as each dreary January day unfolded. He was polite to her, even kind, but there was no spark of love in his eyes. She wore his wedding ring, and they sat together at kirk to quell the gossips. But within the walls of Auchengray, Jamie and Rose were inseparable and Jamie's love for Rose unbearable. Leana kept her eyes down as she went about her endless tasks, feeling unwatched and invisible.

Curled up in her bed, in a lonely corner of the house that creaked in the stiff breeze and groaned from the cold, Leana warmed herself with her prayers. "Almighty God, do *you* see me? Do you see my emptiness?" The wind moaned but did not speak. "Fill me with his child, Lord." She whispered into the dimly lit closet that was her refuge, her eyes on the window that looked toward the heavens. "Let a son be growing beneath my heart. Maybe then Jamie will love me."

When her courses, dependable as the full moon, did not appear that month, Leana kept the news to herself and did not breathe a word to a soul, not even to Neda. It was too soon to be sure and too deep a secret to tell. She would wait. Aye, and she would pray.

Sixty-Three

Thorny rose! that always costeth
Beatings at the heart.
JEAN INGELOW

Rose stole a furtive glance up and down the third floor hall, then ducked into the room beneath the eaves where her sister had been exiled. She'd heard from the servants that it was a cramped and gloomy space, and they'd not exaggerated one bit. Seeing the poorly lit closet—for that was all that it was—almost made her feel sorry for Leana, until she reminded herself that it was Leana's fault and not hers. *She* had not thrown herself at Jamie and thrown away her innocence.

Father was right to chastise Leana, hard as it was to watch. And it was very hard.

Now it was her turn, for Leana had wronged her as well. Leana, the sister who'd once loved her, cherished her, mothered her. A lump rose in her throat, but she pushed it down, refusing to let herself care too much.

It was the last day of January, the day Rose should have been celebrating one month of marriage to Jamie. Instead she had six long months of waiting, six more months of wondering if Jamie would manage to stay away from her sister's bed and avoid getting her with child, an unthinkable outcome that would ruin everything. Leana never looked at Jamie, but Jamie looked at Leana when he thought Rose's thoughts were occupied elsewhere. His eyes were filled with longing. Not love, but longing. It frightened Rose to see it, to know that her sister had some claim on Jamie's affections, however base it might be.

She had to do something. She *had* to.

Rose tiptoed over to Leana's hurlie bed and lifted the thin mattress. From her reticule, she pulled a handful of hawthorn leaves she'd found among Leana's herbs in the stillroom, pressed flat between the pages of a physic book. They looked harmless enough, but Rose knew better. The leaves of the thorn held a special power. Placed under Leana's mattress, they would keep any man from her bed, though only one man mattered. *Jamie.* She spread out the leaves from one end of the bed to the other, sobered by the sight of them. Some said it was dangerous to bring hawthorn into the house.

There was more in her reticule—dried myrtle leaves and willow sap in a tiny bottle—which Rose intended to put to good use as soon as she reached the kitchen. She smoothed the cover on Leana's bed, then backed out of the room, latching the door behind her with a sigh of relief. *Stay away, Jamie.*

She hastened down the stair, wondering if Neda was using her teapot at the moment. The kitchen was quieter than usual, which made things easier. *Ah.* The empty teapot was sitting on the shelf waiting for her, and a pot of water was boiling on the hearth. After pouring the hot liquid over the myrtle leaves, she added a drip of the willow sap, then dropped the lid onto the pot while it steeped. Three days in a row, that's what the old wives said. Three days in a row to keep a babe from a woman's womb. From now until Candlemas, Rose would see that her sister had tea each afternoon, served by her own hand.

Deep inside, something tugged at her conscience. "Nae, it must be done," she whispered to herself, finding a cup and saucer and cutting a square of Neda's gingerbread. What woman would want a child by a man who did not love her? After placing the tea items on a tray, she gingerly lifted it and carried it across the brick kitchen floor toward the dining room, knowing she would find Leana there, polishing silver.

Her sister glanced up as she walked in, her face

as gray as the sky. Leana appeared exhausted most of the time but today even more so. Rose ignored the twinge of guilt that twisted inside her and walked toward the table, holding her offering aloft. "You've been so tired of late, Leana. I thought you might benefit from a pot of tea."

She placed the tray in front of her sister, chagrined to see Leana's eyes fill with tears. *Please. Not tears.* She could bear many things, but watching her sister cry was not one of them. Leana needed to be punished first; she needed to pay for what she'd done. 'Twas only fair, just as their father had said.

"Th-thank you, Rose." Leana lifted the cup to her lips, her hand trembling.

Rose could not stop herself from asking, "Are you . . . all right, Leana? You don't look well."

"Just tired," she sighed, sipping the tea. Her brow wrinkled, and she lifted the saucer to her nose. "What sort of brew is this?" Leana sniffed, then quickly drew back from it. "Bog myrtle, Rose?" She put it aside with a wary eye and reached for the gingerbread instead. "Reverend Gordon says it's ideal for treating worms in children, but as I have neither a child nor worms, it seems an odd choice for tea."

Rose stared at the teapot. Something was wrong. Hadn't that old hen Mistress Millar told her to use bog myrtle? Or had she said simply *myrtle?* Perhaps the willow might still serve its purpose. She joined her sister at the table and pushed the tray closer. "Come. Drink up, Leana. I have it on good authority that tea will cure anything that ails you."

"Forgive me, dearie." She put the gingerbread aside. "Nothing tastes right lately." Leana stretched her hand across the table, her gaze an entreaty, her heart held open before her like an unseen book. "*Will* you forgive me, Rose? Truly forgive me for how I've wronged you?"

Rose dropped her chin, hoping to hide the shame that heated her face. She'd avoided Leana all month, afraid of her own anger, afraid of her feelings for her sister that would not die, much as she fought them. *I will never forgive you!* That was what she'd screamed at her the day she'd returned home from Twyneholm. And she'd meant it then. She hadn't known what a burden it would be to stay angry day after day, hating someone she'd once loved so much.

"I do not know," she finally confessed, the first honest thought she'd had in weeks. "I will try, Leana. But you've hurt me . . . deeply." Tears stung her eyes, and she blinked them away, furious with herself for being so weak. "You . . . you . . ."

"Aye, so I did. Without meaning to, I hurt you desperately." Leana leaned forward, taking Rose's hands in hers, smoothing her fingers across her skin, a mother's loving caress. "I was selfish, Rose. I was thoughtless. I was wrong, utterly wrong, to think that Jamie loved me when he doesn't. He loves you, dearie. I know that now, and I'm sorry, so very sorry . . ."

Rose could hold back her tears no longer. She let them flow, not caring whether she was strong or not, whether she held the upper hand. This was her sister, her only sister, her dearest Leana. She tried to speak, but the words would not come. How could she tell her what hurt most of all? It was not losing Jamie for a moment. It was losing Leana forever.

"Leana . . ." She swallowed her tears. "Don't you see? You are my sister and the only true mother I've ever known. Without you, I'm . . . lost."

"Oh, my sweet Rose! I could never leave you."

The sisters fell into each other's arms, their wet cheeks pressed tightly together, their halting sobs filling the empty room. They whispered in each other's ears words of comfort they'd spoken since childhood. Gentle words. Caring words. It was some time before they were able to let go of each other long enough to attend to their runny noses and dripping chins, sharing one linen handkerchief that soon was soaked.

"You look a fright," Rose announced, then giggled in spite of her tears.

"And you look no better," Leana said firmly, though a smile graced her reddened features as she touched the handkerchief to the corners of Rose's eyes. "Whatever am I to tell Father, who expects me in the spence any minute, prepared to recite passages from the Shorter Catechism?"

"Tell him nothing." Rose quickly stood, brushing the last of her tears from her cheeks, then the wrinkles from her dress. "I will speak to Father myself, tomorrow evening when we return home from services. Jamie and I both will. We have all been punished long enough, Leana. None of us can bear a house full of misery for another long winter's month."

Leana's clear gaze searched her, disbelief etched on her pale features. "How can you be so kind to me, Rose?"

"That's easily answered." Her sister leaned over and pressed her cheek against Leana's. "I had a kind mother."

Sixty-Four

Truth is the work of God;
lies are the works of man.
MADAME DE STAËL

Leana's heart crept into her throat as she watched Jamie and Rose disappear into the spence Sunday evening. She would not let herself crouch near the door, not this time. For truth to reign in their house of secrets, she needed to be honest with herself and with others. In honor of Saint Bride's Day, the portent of spring and all things new, she would put aside her eavesdropping and simply knit.

It was dark outside her window, a white winter's night with a light blanket of snow draped across the hills. Pulling her chair closer to the hearth for warmth and light, she sang a tune suited to the day. As a child, she'd thought the song had been written just for her, a lass named McBride:

> O Bride, O Bride, come with the wand
> To this wintry land;
> And breathe with the breath of the Spring so
>   bland,
> Bride, Bride, little Bride!

Leana had indeed been a bride. For a day, then a night, then a too-short week. Before the brief month of February ended, she would know whether the bride would also become a mother. Hope had made a nesting place in her heart, though she tried not to disturb it by adding feathers. God alone decided such things. She was learning by the hour to trust him with her future.

Moments later the spence door opened, and Jamie startled her by calling out. "Join us, Leana, if you would, please." Just hearing him speak her name warmed her more than the fire. She put aside her knitting, smoothed a hand across her hair, then walked toward the open door where Jamie waited for her, his gaze giving away nothing. She bobbed her head at Rose and her father in silent greeting, then tried to catch her breath in the tense, peaty air. Lachlan and Rose were seated, and Jamie took his place between them, his hands resting on the corners of their high-backed chairs. Perched on the edge of the box bed, Leana longed for someone to break the silence.

To her surprise, it was Rose. "Father, I am glad you agreed to meet with us."

"It seems I had no choice in the matter." His jaw was hard, his eyes narrow as he drummed his fingers on the Buik in his lap.

Rose wisely responded first with a smile. "All the more reason for us to be grateful."

After a brief pause, Jamie spoke, clearly choosing each word with care. "Uncle, I think we would all agree that this . . . unfortunate situation has put a great strain on everyone at Auchengray. You in particular, I imagine."

"A presumption you have no right to make." Lachlan's lips hardly moved, so rigid were his features. "Unlike my daughters, I assign feelings little value. I simply do my work and see that others do theirs. You, for example." His gaze bored into Jamie's. "Have you been keeping up with your labors? I thought the stables looked a mite slitterie when I last saw them."

Leana saw Jamie's hands flex, then curl into lethal-looking fists. Sometimes words cut mair than swords, Duncan would say. *Be careful, Jamie.*

"You are mistaken, Uncle," he said evenly, though his voice was anything but calm. "The stables are well cleaned and in good order."

Lachlan's blatant look of disregard would earn him a throttling in any public house. "Then Duncan is doing his job. As, it seems, are you."

"It is that precise obligation which is the point of this evening's meeting." Jamie stepped around her father's chair so that he addressed him directly. "It would seem that Leana has not . . . that is to say, she does not carry my child." Jamie glanced over his shoulder at her for a moment, though his gaze did not quite meet hers. "I can think of no good reason to put this household through another six months of misery. Could we not have the marriage quietly annulled so that Rose and I might marry and leave for Glentrool at once?"

Nae! Leana's hand pressed against her stomach.

Lachlan smiled, but there was no joy in it. "I can give you one verra good reason to remain at Auchengray another six months: because that was the bargain we made, Jamie. Those were the terms, that you would work for Rose's hand in marriage."

"Then it's only my work that concerns you." Jamie paced in front of him, well armed, it seemed, with arguments. "I will see that sufficient silver is provided to more than pay for a farm laborer through Lammas. Two, if need be. My presence in the steading will hardly be missed."

Leana's face grew cold, then her arms, then her hands. Jamie's days at Auchengray were at an end. His words would not penetrate her father's hard heart, but money would.

"You would prefer to buy your wife with Alec McKie's silver rather than earn her by your own efforts?"

Jamie scowled, his pacing halted. "You forget, my father's money is mine."

"And *you* forget that I know why that is so."

Leana watched a series of emotions move across Jamie's features. Anger, but only for a moment. Acceptance perhaps. Then something like resolve. Jamie spoke again, his voice neither hot nor cold. "You are speaking of deception, are you not? Then let us speak openly, with all of us here, about my wedding day. A day of whispered half-truths and unreasonable demands. Of threats made to Leana, and to me."

Leana gripped the edge of the bed, desperately wanting to leap into the air. *Jamie!* He had come to her defense. He had stood up to their father. He had spoken the truth in a room littered with lies. *Dear Jamie.*

"Threats, is it?" Lachlan quietly put the Buik aside, then smoothed his waistcoat in place as though he had no other concern but his appearance. "Half-truths? Are you calling me a liar?"

Jamie thrust out his chin. "I am."

Lachlan's voice was unnaturally calm. "A deceiver?"

"If you like."

"You should know, Jamie McKie. You, who are a master at lies and deception."

The atmosphere in the room thickened, as though fresh peat had been thrown on the grate. Jamie's skin grew ruddy. "There is no need to discuss that here."

"Oo aye! I think there is." Lachlan stood, thrusting his face in Jamie's. "It is past time that my daughters know what manner of man they've entrusted with their affections."

Leana stared at him, a sense of dread growing inside her. "Father, whatever do you mean?"

His eyes were sharp as dirks. "I mean that Jamie fled to Auchengray because his brother threatened to kill him if he remained at Glentrool."

Both sisters gasped. Jamie stood stiff as a corpse and said nothing while Lachlan continued to fill the air with accusations. Could they be true? *Oh, Jamie.*

"He stole his brother's heirship. Evan, the first-born, should have been the heir. Instead his clever younger brother, Jamie, fooled their decrepit father into thinking he was Evan and claimed the whole of Glentrool for himself."

Rose was near tears. "Is that . . . true, Jamie?"

Jamie ground out his words, rough as sand. "It was my mother's plan."

"Aye, and it was a good plan," Lachlan agreed. "Which makes Rowena the canny one and you no more than a willing party to deceit." He eyed Leana. "'Tis a weak child who cannot bear a test of his moral strength."

Nae. She turned away, sickened by his words, poisoned by their venom. No matter how she tried to swallow, the bitter taste remained. *Jamie, a deceiver. Just like my father.*

She stood, the room spinning around her. "Forgive me, but I'm . . . ill." Fleeing from the spence, leaving their startled faces behind, she headed for the front door and dashed out into the freezing night, struck with a sudden need for fresh air and a discreet bit of shrubbery where she could empty her stomach in private. She felt no better when she finished, as though she were still full of something foreign. What had she eaten for dinner at kirk that noon?

She tipped her head back, drinking in the cold air in great gulps, hoping it might calm her stomach. Tiny flakes of snow fell on her cheeks and hair, cooling her feverish brow. Nothing would calm her thoughts, which spun in sickening circles. Jamie would leave. Rose would leave. And she could do nothing to stop them.

Sixty-Five

Hear ye not the hum
Of mighty workings?
JOHN KEATS

Leana!" Rose slipped toward her on the icy lawn,
eyes wide with fear. "You look positively dreadful.
Are you sick?"

"I . . . was." Leana swallowed, resting her hand
on Rose's arm until the stars above stopped spinning. "If you might help me to my room."

Rose guided her up the stair, clucking like a hen.
They passed Rose's room, then Jamie's, before
mounting the stair to the third floor while Eliza
located a warming pan and hartshorn shavings to
clear Leana's head and keep her from fainting.

Leana drank a glass of water, then slid beneath the covers of her hurlie bed, grateful even for the thin mattress.

Her sister knelt by the bed, undoing Leana's braids, then brushing her hair back from her brow. "Leana, is it true what Father said? About Jamie deceiving his family?"

"Jamie did not deny it, so I fear it must be true." Still shivering from the snow, Leana pulled the covers tighter beneath her chin. "Let Jamie tell you the details himself, dearie. Father has a way of twisting a story to his advantage. Perhaps it is not so bad as it appears." *Or perhaps it is worse.*

Rose wiped Leana's brow with a damp cloth, gnawing her lip as she did. "Leana, I must speak with you about something else. Your illness may be . . . well, it could be my fault."

"*Your* fault?" Leana tried to sit up but thought better of it and sank back down. If she was with child—though she dared not hope for such a blessing, not yet—Rose was the one person whose fault it was *not.*

Poor Rose was busy wringing the cloth in her hands, her features distraught. "I put . . . I put *leaves* under your mattress. Here, beneath the hurlie bed. Oh, Leana! That's what must have made you sick!" Rose fell onto the mattress with a loud groan.

Leana bit back a smile. How she'd missed her sister's dramatic ways. "What kind of leaves were they, dearie?"

"Hawthorn!" Rose blurted out, starting to sniffle.

"Ah." The leaves of a thorn. Meant to keep Jamie away from her bed. "You had no need of that old superstition, Rose. Jamie has eyes for you alone."

"'Twas not his eyes I was worried about," Rose murmured, and Leana laughed, despite her queasy stomach. Rose did not laugh. "He looks at you, Leana. Did you know that?"

"Looks at me?" A cool chill danced up her arms. Neda and Jessie had both said the same.

"Aye, when you're not looking at him." Rose sighed heavily, straightening back up. "I believe he loves me, Leana, though he professes it so often I fear he's trying to convince himself."

Leana kept her voice even. "And do you love him, my sister?"

Rose nodded but said nothing for a moment. Finally she confessed, "I do love him, Leana. I do. But not, I think, the same way you do. Not with the same . . ." Her gaze darted about the room, as though the word she needed sat propped on the washstand.

"Passion?"

"Aye." Rose hung her head. "I am still young, Leana. And there are many things about . . . about men that I do not understand."

Leana smiled, reaching out to tug Rose's braid. "That will not improve with age."

"Will it improve with marriage?"

"Most definitely." Her sister would be wedded someday, she consoled herself. Even if it was not to Jamie.

A light tap sounded on the open door. "May I come in?"

Leana lifted her head only long enough to see Jamie bent inside her doorway before she collapsed back on her pillow. "Aye," she said, suddenly exhausted. "With both of us here, you may come in."

He ducked his head and made his way toward her, his expression filled with genuine concern. Or so it appeared. She did not know what to believe about him now. He knelt next to Rose, but his gaze remained locked with hers. "Your father and I were both anxious to know of your . . . your condition, Leana."

Her neck warmed. "My condition?"

"Aye. If you are still ill or feeling better. If a doctor should be called . . ."

"A doctor?" She and Rose exchanged glances. "Father would hardly pay for a doctor to come all the way from Dumfries. Not unless I was on my deathbed." *Or my childbed.* She touched Jamie's hand, which rested lightly on her bedcovers. "Do let Father know I will be fine once my stomach settles."

Rose wrinkled her pretty nose. "What do you suppose is the cause of it?"

Jamie stared at Rose for a moment, as though gauging her grasp of the possibilities. "Perhaps her dinner did not agree with her," he said at last. "Why not run and get Neda? She might have just the concoction to help Leana sleep."

Leana watched her sister's buoyant departure with a heavy heart. It was clear Rose did not understand what might be happening. But Jamie did. Leana saw the fear in his eyes. He had run from his responsibilities at Glentrool. Now he wanted to run from Auchengray, and there was only one thing that would stop him.

Jamie bent forward, his eyes searching hers. "Leana, I'm sorry you had to learn about what happened at Glentrool from your father and not from me."

She turned her head away. He was too close, and she loved him too much. "Does it matter what I think of you? Isn't Rose's adoration enough?" When he did not answer immediately, she turned toward him again, sorry for speaking so bitterly. "Forgive me, Jamie."

"Forgive you? *Och,* Leana. It is quite the other way round, and you ken it well. This eve I did my best to shirk my duty to you, to end this pretense of a marriage and spirit Rose off to Glentrool."

She kept her voice light and her apprehension hidden. "Has Father agreed to your offer of silver rather than labor?"

His groan answered for him. "He insists that our terms have not changed and that we cannot be certain that you are not with child. 'Not yet,' he said, as though he understood such private matters." Jamie leaned closer, his eyes wide, his gaze pleading. "Unless *you* know, Leana. If you were certain that it . . . that a child was no longer a possibility, your father might reconsider and send us packing."

He was too near. Her hand moved of its own volition, stroking his rough chin, cradling his handsome cheek. Though he blinked, he did not move away. "Jamie, my father is right. I do not know, not yet."

Rose's sharp voice startled them both. "Know what yet?"

Jamie stood abruptly, almost cracking his skull on the low ceiling, while Leana slipped her hand beneath the covers, still feeling the warmth of his skin on her fingers.

She answered smoothly, "Know whether or not Jamie might be free to leave for Glentrool. With you."

"Ah." Rose smiled, apparently satisfied to know they'd been discussing her happiness. "Neda says she will be up shortly with peppermint tea. Come, Jamie. Duncan has need of you down the hall. Something about his ledgers."

Leana watched him leave, glancing at her over his shoulder. His expression gave away nothing. She made sure her own was blank as well. *Soon,* she wanted to say. She would know very soon, but for now, they could only wait.

The next ten days were spent poring over a calendar, counting and recounting the days from Hogmanay, wondering if her symptoms were an illness or a babe. There had not been a birth at Auchengray in all her years there, not since Rose, and she'd hardly asked any pertinent questions then. Most servants were unmarried, coming and going from year to year. Duncan and Neda's children had arrived long before she was born, then left Auchengray to start their own families.

She could not bring herself to ask Neda what the weariness and nausea meant, the tenderness and the swelling, afraid that a hope spoken would become a false hope. She would wait and trust God to show her. He had heard her cry. He knew her heart's desire. If a son was growing inside her, he was already in God's hands.

On the twelfth of February, a perfectly ordinary Thursday, Leana woke to find snow blowing hard on her third-floor window and nary a drop of blood on her bleached linen sheets. *Please, God.* She bathed to be sure, to keep hope at arm's length until she could be certain. But the cloth was clean. For the second month, her courses did not flow.

But her tears did. With joy. *Bethankit!*

"A child!" she whispered to the snow piled against her window. "A child!" she said again, laughing into her pillow. She dressed with trembling fingers, filled with energy for the first time in a week. *A child!* Even the coldest of winter days could not steal her joy. Pausing to brush away a fresh spate of happy tears, she slipped her toes inside her leather shoes, grateful for their warmth, grateful for everything. The Almighty had blessed her womb and Jamie's seed. There were too many signs now for it not to be so.

Scrubbed and dressed, she headed for the stair with Lachlan's words ringing inside her like a bell. *If Leana conceives a child—your child—in those seven months, then you are bound to remain her husband.* Her smile broadened with each footstep. It had not taken seven months, perhaps not even seven days. It might have taken only one night, the most glorious night of her life, when she believed herself innocent and truly loved for who she was. *Leana.* Not Rose.

   She turned on the landing, the hall waiting below her and the spence beyond it. Her father had demanded that he be the first to know, even before Jamie. She could not wait to tell him the news.

Sixty-Six

Master, master! news, old news, and such news
as you never heard of!
WILLIAM SHAKESPEARE

Neda knew first.

She stopped Leana on the stair, her brows
arched, her hands planted on her hips. "I would
speak to you at once, in private," the housekeeper
said, the gleam in her eye softening her stern
expression. Leana obediently followed her through
the house and into the kitchen, where she was
escorted through the scullery and into the chilly
laundry. Neda closed the door behind them, locking
them safely apart from the rest of the house.

"Now then." Neda planted her on a stool. "I am the mither of three grown daughters and the granmither of eight. Ye may fool the rest of this household, lassie, but Neda Hastings knows a pregnant woman when she sees one. Aye?"

"Aye," Leana whispered, then leaped to her feet, clasping her hands. "Aye, it's true! I am, I am!"

"God be praised!" Neda swept her into her arms and nearly lifted her off the stone floor, dancing her about in a tuneless jig, wiping away tears, and laughing all the while. When they stopped to catch their breath, Neda held up her finger as though she'd thought of something important and dove into her box of sewing goods on the shelf over the sink.

She pulled out a needle and quickly threaded it with nimble fingers accustomed to the task. "Sit ye doon on that stool and lean back for me, will ye, Leana?"

Leana sat, looking at the needle with misgivings. "Is this something all expectant mothers must do?"

Neda chuckled softly. "Only those who care whether they're having a lad or a lass." She held the threaded needle over Leana's womb, then paused. "'Tis one of the old ways, though many set store by it. Do ye want to know? Does it matter?"

"It does not." Leana glanced down at her flat middle, still amazed to think of a child nestled inside her, growing by the minute. "But I do want to know." She looked at the needle askance. "As long as it won't hurt."

"Nae. I would niver hurt one *gouden* hair on yer sweet head. Now then." She held the two threads and lowered the needle. "If it swings in a circle, they say it's a wee lass. And if it swings back and forth, it's a wee lad." Both women watched as the string barely moved at all. But when it moved, it did so in a short, straight line. Back and forth.

"Have ye chosen any names yet, child?" Neda grinned broadly. "Perhaps Alec, for Jamie's father?"

"I haven't given it a thought," Leana confessed. "I must tell Father first. Then Rose, because I've done her a terrible injustice." She groaned, already dreading it. "God help me, Neda, it will break her heart. Then I will tell Jamie."

"And how will this news affect Mr. McKie's heart, d'ye suppose?" When Leana only shrugged, Neda pulled her to her feet and kissed her brow. "Listen to yer auld mither: I saw ye and Jamie on yer waddin day. Jamie can protest all he likes about bein' deceived, but the man who loved ye that day and loved ye that night loves ye still, though he does not ken the truth himself yet."

Leana searched the woman's face for assurance. "Is this a word from God Almighty . . . or from Neda Hastings?"

Neda smiled and patted her cheeks. "Sometimes we speak the same words, the Lord and me. Trust in his blissin and know that the news will be yers alone to tell. I will speak nary a word. Yer faither is readin' by the hearth. Take a cup of tea to him, Leana. I'll see ye're not disturbed."

A few minutes later Leana carried the tea tray with exceeding care, not trusting her trembling hands or her unsteady feet. "Father, I've brought a bit of refreshment." Neda closed the door silently behind her, which her father noticed immediately.

"You're not bringing me tea, Daughter." He regarded her with a jaded eye. "You're bringing me news. Aye?"

"Aye." Perhaps it was best if he'd already guessed. "The babe will arrive in early October."

"When Jamie arrived. A fortuitous month, it seems." He leaned back in his chair, ignoring both his book and her tea, a satisfied smile creasing his face. "I did not expect this so soon, Leana. Your . . . ah, fruitfulness surprises me." His smile faded a bit. "You understand, you and Jamie will not be running off to Glentrool. Jamie will still need to work here until August. That was our agreement."

"Aye, it was." She hoped Jamie understood that as well. It would be hard enough to tell him the news, without adding to his misery. "I am off to find Rose now and then Jamie. Might I ask you, Father, not to . . . not to tell anyone until I've spoken with both of them?"

He waved his hand dismissively. "As you wish. I don't envy you the task. You might remind Jamie it's best to be off with the old love before he puts on the new."

"That is how the saying goes," she murmured, bowing her head as she took her leave. Her father was pleased. But Rose would be devastated.

Leana hastened up the stair, praying with each step. After a bit of searching, she found Rose carding wool in their workroom on the second floor.

"Dear one," she said, sitting down at her wheel. "I should be spinning if you're carding."

Rose rolled off a freshly carded bit of wool. "Here you are then."

Leana held the soft bundle in her hands, thoughts of knitted baby bonnets floating through her head. "Rose, I am already spinning but not on the wheel." She pressed her hand to her stomach to steady her nerves. "I have something to tell you, my sister. News you will not want to hear."

"News?" Rose stared at her, a look of fear in her eyes. "It's about Jamie, isn't it?" When Leana nodded, the fear in Rose's eyes turned to anguish. "Please don't tell me his child grows in your womb?"

"Aye." Leana swallowed. "It does."

Rose gasped and turned away, holding up her carding paddles so Leana could not see her face.

"Rose, I'm sorry! Please, don't hide. Let me talk to you. Let me tell you—"

"You've told me," Rose whimpered. "Now go."

"Forgive me, dearie." Leana hated to ask, but she had to be certain. "You know . . . what the terms are? What this means?"

"I do," Rose said, her voice high and soft like a child's. "It means you will have Jamie as your husband. And I will not. Ever."

"Aye, it means that. I'm so sorry, Rose. I know that you love him and that he loves you. If it's any consolation, this will be even more burdensome news for Jamie to hear."

"Och! It's the best news in the world for you though."

Leana could hardly argue with her. She could only console her. "'Tis the best for you as well, young Rose. It means you are free to seek the richest man in Galloway for a husband. To have a debut, if you like. To go to school in Dumfries. Or spend the summer with Susanne. Or—"

"Nae!" Rose slapped her paddles down on the worktable with a mighty crack. "I'll not have you planning my future for me any longer."

"I only wanted—"

"You only wanted Jamie!" Rose stood, her chest heaving, her face flooded with tears. "That's all you've ever wanted, from the minute he arrived. I may not have loved him as soon as you did, Leana, but I love him all the same. And he loves me. He loves *me!*"

"Aye, he does, my sister," Leana admitted. "And that will be a very difficult thing for me to live with. Knowing he loves you more."

"Not *more,* Leana! *Only!*" Rose's voice rose to a fevered pitch. "He loves only me. He told me so. He told *you* so. Why can't you keep this babe of yours and let me keep Jamie?"

"Rose, Rose." Leana reached out to her, but Rose backed away, swatting at her as though she were a hoard of bothersome midges. "Be reasonable, Rose. The child must have a father, as our own father insisted, and to which Jamie agreed. You knew this might happen, dearest." She made sure their gazes were linked. "You knew, or you wouldn't have given me myrtle tea with willow sap."

Rose was shocked into silence.

"Aye," Leana said evenly. "I realized what you were up to, Rose. All those herbs in the stillroom come from my garden, remember?" She leaned forward, able to touch her sister's hand at last. "I understood why you did it. And I understand your pain now."

Rose brushed away Leana's hand, her voice petulant. "Nae, you do not."

"Perhaps not. I have wronged you in so many ways, and this is the worst of them. But children are a gift to us from God's hand, Rose. I cannot refuse that gift or the man God chose to deliver it."

"My Jamie," Rose said, sniffing.

"Aye. Your Jamie." *And mine.*

Rose stared at Leana's belly, her eyes narrowing. "Does Jamie know?"

"He does not. Not yet."

"Then *I* will tell him the terrible news." Rose leaped for the door, slamming it shut behind her, screaming his name as she ran down the hall. "Jamie! Jamie!"

"Nae!" Leana jumped up to follow her, then grabbed her wheel, dizzy from standing too fast. "Rose, wait!" When she finally regained her balance, Leana hurried after her sister, fearing it would be too late.

And it was.

Sixty-Seven

The greatest griefs are those we cause ourselves.
SOPHOCLES

Jamie was scattering grain for the hens when Rose came flying out the back door and across the frozen lawn, calling for him, her voice taut as an arrow aimed straight for his heart.

"Jamie, Jamie! The worst has happened! The very worst!" She threw herself at him, knocking his sack of grain to the ground. Her face was hot with tears, her body limp.

He pulled her against him, stroking her hair. In the nearby doocot, the doves cooed and ruffled their wings, flustered by the commotion. "Rose, please. Calm down, beloved. Tell me what's happened."

"Leana is . . . Leana is . . ."

And he knew.

"I'm sorry, Rose," he whispered, his chest so tight he could barely speak. *The best news. The worst news.* "I'm so sorry."

"You said . . ." She hiccuped, nearly drowning in her tears. "You said you would not be . . . cooperative."

"I'd agreed to the bridal week, remember? Only one week, only in Dumfries. I've not been alone with her since." His conscience nagged him. *Except on Saint Bride's night and only for a moment.*

Rose wriggled out of his embrace, wiping her tears away with the back of her hand. Her mouth curved downward in a bitter frown. "But you've looked at her."

More than you know. More than I should.

He kept his voice even. "No more than necessary, for politeness' sake. She is my wife, if only by law—"

"And now in the flesh." Rose backed away from him, holding her hands up. "Our love is finished, Jamie. I cannot bear to think of . . . of sharing you with her." She turned and ran off, her skirts rustling in the cold morning air.

He watched her disappear through the back door at the very moment her older sister appeared, walking toward him across the lawn. Like some stage play, with actors stepping onto the boards on cue and he, the director, without a script.

Leana. His wife. Soon to be the mother of his child.

She glided toward him, her head held high, her eyes dry, her chin firm. How had he ever mistaken her for Rose? Rose was a beautiful child. Leana was a woman. Plain, but graceful. There was a purity about Leana, even after all that had happened between them.

"You've heard." She'd reached his side and stood before him, her face paler than ever, but her eyes bright.

"Aye," he said, brushing the grain from his hands. "Rose told me."

She touched his fingers, so lightly he almost didn't feel the warmth of her. "I'm sorry, Jamie. I wanted to tell you myself, but my sister . . ."

He nodded, as did she. Both of them knew Rose. "When?"

Leana's cheeks colored. "The first of October."

He gritted his teeth, knowing she waited for his reaction. "I'm sorry to hear it, Leana."

Her head snapped up. "Sorry?" She choked on the word. "Jamie, I'm not sorry in the least. You know that I love you."

He couldn't stop himself. "And you know that I don't love you."

"How could I not, when you've told me so many times?" She stepped closer, the toes of her soiled shoes touching his. "I wonder if you're trying to convince me or trying to convince yourself? I believe you when you say it. Do you?"

"Aye," he said grimly. "With all my heart."

Her eyes closed, as though shutting out the sight of him. And no wonder. The woman had come to him with the happiest news of her life, only to be reminded that she alone considered it so. He said he was sorry, and he meant it. Sorry he did not love her. Sorry he could not rejoice at her news. But sorrier still that he'd crushed her sister's hopes. And his own. *Forgive me, Rose.*

When Leana opened her eyes again, they were clear as ever, without a trace of tears. "What shall we do then, Jamie? Shall we make a life together, live as husband and wife?"

"A life?" He waved his arms at the frozen barnyard with hens clucking about their feet, pecking at the spilled grain. "This is not the life I imagined for McKie of Glentrool."

"Nor will this be your life forever, Jamie. Your duties here will end. Not long after, your duties as a father will begin." She took his hand and pressed it low against her body. "God has blessed my womb and your seed, Jamie."

The land you sleep upon, to you will I give it, and to your seed.

He snatched back his hand. Her touch was too familiar, the blessing of God too clear. "I suppose what God has chosen for us, we must accept."

"As a gift, Jamie. Not a burden."

But it *was* a burden, and it was not light.

Leana bit her lip, her cheeks turning pink from the cold or from shame. "Shall I have my things moved from the third floor to . . . your room?" She glanced away, her gaze trained on the noisy doocot. "That is, if you want me. If you'll have me."

Want. Have. "Aye." He could not say no. Because

she was his wife. And because there were moments in the wee, dark hours of the night when he did want her, for all the wrong reasons. *Forgive me, Rose.*

A pair of magpies landed by their feet, interested in the grain, hopping about with their black tails raised, their pied plumage stark against the colorless ground. Leana smiled faintly at them. "Do you know the old nursery rhyme?" she asked, nodding at the birds as they flew off. "One magpie for sorrow . . ."

"Two for joy . . ."

"Aye, for joy," she whispered, pinching her lips. "Three for a wedding . . ."

He grew still. Fearing, hoping. "Four for a boy."

"Would you . . . welcome a son, Jamie?"

He shrugged as though it hardly mattered. "I have no son yet."

"But you will. I know it, Jamie, as only a woman can. 'Tis a son that I carry inside me. Surely that must please you."

"Now you're insisting I be *pleased* with this news? You ask too much of me, Leana." He swung away from her, scaring the chickens as he strode about, wanting to shout, wanting to shake something hard until it broke in his hands. "I need time to think. Time to reason things through."

She touched her fingers to her lips, as though holding back what she wanted to say. At last she spoke, her voice low. "You will have more than enough time. Nearly six more months of work. Then we must haste to Glentrool while I can still travel—"

"Glentrool?" He bit off the word, then spit it out, so bitter was the taste in his mouth. Leana had no right to speak of his home, the home where Rose was meant to live. "Do you think my brother, Evan, will welcome our arrival in the glen after all that happened between us, knowing the birth of this child will seal his fate?"

"It is sealed already, Jamie. God alone knows the time and place."

"The time and place for *this* child's birth is here, at Auchengray, where he can be safe." *And where I can be near your sister.* Rose, who made him feel young and carefree, without responsibilities, without risk, without asking him to be a father before he'd learned to be a husband. Or was it worse than that? Had he not yet learned to be a man? He ground his teeth, furious with himself, with Leana, with Rose, with anyone who wanted something from him when he had nothing left to give.

Leana lowered her head and stepped back, preparing to leave. "This is your child. Where he will be born is your decision to make." She glanced up as she turned, leaving her heart in his hands. "I will always love you, Jamie. It is my calling . . ." Tears shone in her eyes. "And it is my curse." She was gone like the magpies, flying across the wintry landscape.

Let Leana be cursed then.

He had said the words.

Then you brought this on yourself, Jamie.

"Nae!" Jamie snatched up what was left of the sack of grain and flung the contents all over the barnyard, swinging the sack in big arcs, shaking the last seeds loose, setting the whole barnyard into frantic motion. "This is *not* my fault, God! It's *your* fault!" He railed at the heavens, throwing the empty sack at the sky. "'I will never leave you,' aye? Was *that* what you promised me? Then I will leave *you!* Nothing has gone right in my life. *Nothing!*"

"Ye don't mean that, lad."

Jamie whirled around, his eyes struggling to focus, and found Duncan standing behind him. "I *do* mean it!" he shouted at the overseer, not caring if the man flinched at the harshness of his words. "Everything I own and everyone I love has been torn out of my arms. *All* of it! My future has been decided for me. By my mother, by my uncle, by my cousins—"

"And by God. Or have ye forgotten that he's chosen to bless ye?"

"Don't I have a choice?" Jamie screamed the words, loud enough for God and all of Galloway to hear. "I'm sick of it, do you hear me? I'm tired of doing what others expect me to do." He grabbed a shovel and plunged it into the midden for the sheer pleasure of seeing the muck fly. "I'm weary of having no choices of my own."

"Jamie, Jamie." Duncan carefully took the shovel from his hands. "When ye fight God's choices, ye're bound to be miserable. Mebbe yer arms needed to be emptied so they could be filled with something better."

Jamie threw up his hands. "Who or what could possibly be better than Rose McBride?"

Duncan chuckled, not unkindly. "Yer first love, lad. And I dinna mean Leana." He tossed the shovel aside, lowering his voice as he did. "I've watched ye, Jamie. Watched ye put up a meikle fight, tryin' to keep God awa from yer door. To keep love away from yer heart."

"That's not true!" Jamie fumed. "I am more than ready for love." How could a man as wise as Duncan Hastings not see the obvious? "It's *Rose's* love I want. Not God's and not Leana's."

"Och! D'ye think that wee lass has enough love to right all the wrongs in yer life? No woman does, Jamie. Though if I may say so, ye're a fool not to see that Leana's love for ye is grand and wide and much mair than ye deserve. 'Whoso findeth a wife findeth a good thing,' aye? Well, there are few sae good as Leana."

Jamie looked away in shame, fixing his gaze on the flock of magpies who'd circled around for another peck at the scattered grain. He could hardly argue with the plain truth. Leana loved him completely. He saw it in her eyes, heard it in her words, felt it in her touch.

Her voice, whispering his name, haunted him at night. *Jamie.* The whole of their week in Dumfries, he had given her crumbs, and she'd feasted on them as if they were a banquet.

"I ken ye're deep in thought, lad." Duncan pressed a hand on his shoulder. "I'm pleased to see it. From what little I overheard, it seems God has seen fit to make ye a faither. Ye've some growin' to do first. 'Tis a day that'll change ye, Jamie. For the better, if ye're like most men. For the worse, if ye're like Lachlan McBride."

Jamie's hands balled into fists. "I will never treat my son the way Lachlan has treated me."

"Aye." Duncan brushed his hands on his breeches and started toward the house. "Ye might give some thought to how ye treat the babe's mother then. She deserves yer care and attention, Jamie. Now and in the hard months to come. 'Husbands, love your wives,' that's what the Buik commands us to do. Find it in yer heart to love her, lad. She's waitin' for ye to do that verra thing, but no woman can wait forever."

Sixty-Eight

Jealousy is always born together with love.
FRANCOIS, DUC DE LA ROCHEFOUCAULD

Rose bowed her head halfway, so she could still keep an eye on the others. Her father pulled the candle closer to the Buik, working his jaw as though with enough effort he might sound like Reverend Gordon. "Hear the word of the Lord: 'To every thing there is a season, and a time to every purpose under the heaven.'"

She pressed her lips so tightly together she feared she might bruise them, yet if she opened her mouth, she would scream. *Hoot!* 'Twas the worst season of her young life, with no purpose to it whatsoever. Family worship had only begun, and already she was in a sour mood. Supper had been dreadful. Neda had served hotchpotch, a soup thick as porridge and even less appetizing, no matter how much her father praised it. The neck of one of her poor lambs drenched in too many vegetables made an ugsome stew, to Rose's way of thinking.

Her father's voice ground out the words from Scripture like a flesher grinding beef: "A time to be born, and a time to die; a time to plant, and a time to pluck up that which is planted."

Aye, that was the truth of it. Jamie McKie had planted when he should have plucked, and now a babe would be born, but not to *her.* Not at all. To her *sister.* Rose stared at Leana, whose head was bent over her folded hands, her braids gleaming in the candlelight, and felt nothing but hatred toward her. And nothing but love. Her own Leana, dear to her as the mother she'd never known, had stolen the man she adored and carried his child.

Much as she hated to admit it, Rose feared she might be partly to blame. If only she'd set her cap for Jamie to begin with and not pushed him into Leana's arms. If only she'd told Jamie she loved him before she left for Aunt Meg's. If only she'd refused to travel to Twyneholm in unpredictable December weather. If only she'd demanded her father tell the kirk session the truth about her wedding day. And if only this household would treat her like a *woman* instead of like a *child,* her life would be very much nicer indeed!

Rose made up her mind. She would scream. Aye, she *would* and see what they thought of their charming little Rose then. The idea lost appeal when she considered spending the next day reciting the Shorter Catechism as punishment. Though anything would be better than what she'd endured *this* day, listening to the servants sing and laugh as they worked, relieved with the glad tidings. Now they could hold up their heads on market day, knowing things were settled at Auchengray and that they would no longer be whispered about while they picked over soup bones and fresh fish.

When her father read "A time to weep, and a time to laugh," Rose nearly did both at once, choking on the emotions that roiled inside her like an angry sea. How dare Leana capture her beloved Jamie! Was it because she was the older one? The most skilled at running a household? It certainly was *not* because she was the bonniest. Rose glanced at her sister again, shaking her head. If anything, the unseen babe washed the last bit of color out of Leana's cheeks. Jamie would soon grow weary of so bland a face.

Rose rested her chin on her folded hands, hoping her father might not notice her poor posture. Some days she wished that Jamie had never come to Auchengray. Life had been much simpler without him, to be sure. But other days it was not Jamie she wished gone, but her sister, even though Rose had loved her for all of her fifteen years. Alas, the choice was not hers; they were both staying. Jamie and Leana would not leave for Glentrool until August, her sister had confided in her before supper. Perhaps not even then, if Leana could not easily travel.

Her father paused in his reading, frowning in her direction as though he could hear her selfish thoughts. She straightened and meekly bowed her head while he continued. "A time to embrace, and a time to refrain from embracing." Had he meant that for her then? That she and Jamie were not to embrace ever again? *Och!* It was so unfair. He loved her, truly he did. If only she might hide his name in the Valentines Dealing at Susanne Elliot's! Come Saturday afternoon Rose would draw out his name on a tiny slip of paper, and they would exchange gifts, and he would be her valentine for all of 1789. Wouldn't that be grand?

She felt her chest rise and fall in an imaginary sigh. It was no use hoping such things.

Lachlan's voice had fallen into a pounding rhythm. "A time to get, and a time to lose." *A time to lose, Father.* And a time to cast away her dreams.

Lachlan had called her into the spence after she'd come running through the house, calling Jamie's name like a banshee. "Rose, you are not to carry on like a spoiled child," he'd cautioned her, his expression more dour than usual. "You're a young woman of means. I'll find you a proper suitor when the time is right."

"When would that time be, Father?" She'd not meant to sound flippant but couldn't take it back once she'd said it.

"A time of my choosing," was all he'd said. Which meant no time soon, she feared. She'd spent the balance of the day in her room, pretending to read, while Leana was off spinning wool at her wheel, and Jamie stomped about the barnyard, to hear Duncan tell it, angry with God and all of creation. Rose glanced at Jamie, his dark hair tautly knotted at the nape of his neck, his smooth brow facing her. How serious he looked! Not her lighthearted, laughing Jamie at all. But braw as any Scotsman who ever walked the Galloway hills.

He was seated next to Leana. A bit apart from her sister, Rose was gratified to see, though it would not be long before they climbed into the same bed in the room next to hers. Aunt Meg's description of what to expect on her wedding night had been most unsatisfactory. Perhaps it was best not to know. Leana had known, and that knowledge had ruined her life.

No, Rose. It ruined yours.

She gritted her teeth as her father closed the Buik with the last line of the passage. "A time to love, and a time to hate; a time of war, and a time of peace." Rose felt more hate than love and no peace at all. The worst six months of her life loomed before her. If she was doomed to suffer, she would see to it that the entire household suffered with her.

"I chose this passage for a purpose under heaven," Lachlan said, his gaze moving around the room. "'Tis a day in which two lives are truly joined and a third is anticipated." He paused, staring at Leana and Jamie, as they all were. Leana was blushing. Jamie was sullen. "The McKies will remain with us through Lammas. Longer, if I can convince them to make their home at Auchengray for another season."

Another breeding season, he means. Rose saw Jamie's eyes flicker and guessed he was thinking the very same.

"We will have a time of peace in this household," her father said, his meaning clear. "Let us call upon Almighty God and ask his Holy Spirit to reign over us all."

Lachlan prayed, using words like a hammer, driving home sharply pointed truths until no tool could remove them. For a man bent on having his own way, by any crooked means necessary, her father spoke of righteousness and forgiveness with authority. Perhaps he was required to know only how the words were pronounced.

Rose kept her head bowed, proud of herself for doing so, and dutifully prayed for peace. Yet inside her heart, a war was raging. She loved her sister; she hated her sister; she wanted happiness for Leana and Jamie; she wanted Jamie McKie for herself.

Sixty-Nine

The deepest rivers make least din,
The silent soul doth most abound in care.
WILLIAM ALEXANDER, EARL OF STIRLING

Leana waited for Jamie in their darkened bedroom, just as Jamie had waited for her on their wedding night. He, however, had been fast asleep, and she was more awake than she could ever remember, her heart dancing a fiddler's jig.

Odd to be nestled inside the box bed that had changed her life forever. She'd expected him long before this, but poor Jamie had been through a very trying day. Duncan had hinted about a scene in the barnyard after she'd left, and Rose was inconsolable at dinner and supper both, feeling sorry for herself, making everyone miserable. Neda had done what she could, serving Rose's favorite syllabub, patting Leana's shoulder in passing, seasoning the air with grace—all to no avail. Family worship had been blessedly short, for Neda's hotchpotch did not sit on her stomach as well as she'd hoped. They'd all dispersed on the last amen, Rose to her sewing—a task she only faced when she was already in wretched spirits—Jamie to read, and Leana to prepare herself and their bedroom, praying the next part of their married life might begin on a happier note.

The bedding had been aired, fresh candles were lit, and she'd dressed in the same nightgown she'd worn for her bridal week, neatly pressed by Eliza. Hours earlier the quiet, dark-haired servant girl had left behind her life in the scullery to serve as lady's maid to her mistress, according to the terms of Leana's tocher. The babe in her womb had forced her father to acknowledge the marriage at last.

Now Leana waited, almost breathless to see her husband, her hand smoothing over the wooden box bed walls, remembering.

Jamie, come to me!

He did, at last, stepping into the room with a taper in one hand and his book in the other. "Leana?" he whispered. "Are you still awake?"

"Aye." She tried not to laugh. "I am." As though she could sleep after weeks in a tiny hurlie bed, after weeks without Jamie! "Quite awake."

As Jamie undressed in the flickering candlelight, she watched him without apology, letting the sight of him awaken a desire she'd feared might never see daylight again. He was her husband now—not for a day or a week but for the rest of her days. *Jamie, oh my Jamie!* It was good, it was right, for her to love him in every way she could.

He slid beneath the covers and pulled the bed curtains shut behind him, wrapping them in a world without shadows or sound. They simply breathed together for a moment, their bodies warming toward each other.

She'd thought all day about what she would say when she had Jamie to herself, but now the words were gone. There were only feelings, emotions so close to the surface of her skin that if he touched her, she might ignite and burn to ashes.

"Jamie." She loved saying his name. She would begin there. "Jamie, my love."

He touched a finger to her lips. "Leana, don't. Don't ask more of me than I can give you."

She kissed his fingertip, then pressed his hand against her cheek. "You've already given me a child in my womb, and for that I'm grateful. I promise I'll be patient."

When he withdrew his hand, her cheek cooled. The strain in his voice was palpable. "How patient?"

"Very patient, Jamie." She smiled in spite of the tension between them. "It's one of my few virtues, or have you forgotten?"

"I have not forgotten." He turned to lie on his back and folded his hands beneath his head, his jutting elbows holding her at bay. "And you have many virtues, Leana."

"I'm glad," she murmured, longing to know what those qualities might be. But she was not Rose. She would not insist he flatter her and list them. If Jamie had found some good in her, that was enough. "By patient, do you mean that you prefer we not . . ."

He sighed heavily and turned his face toward the bed curtains. "By patient I mean good night."

The night was far from good. She tossed and turned, unaccustomed to Jamie's presence, her stomach queasy, her thoughts troubled. In the wee, dark hours, when she was certain he was well asleep, she drew close to him, curving herself around him like spoons in a drawer, praying he would not awaken and push her away. Warmed by his body, she finally slept, only to wake in the morning and find him gone and his pillow cold.

It was not the beginning she'd hoped for, but it was a beginning nonetheless. She would be patient. And perhaps he would be merciful.

Jamie spent the day in the farm steading, working hard, as always. Her father had accused him of being lax in his labors, but all of Auchengray knew better. When he returned to the house before supper, covered in muck and sweat, his efforts were obvious. Leana greeted him at the back door, where he was discarding his filthy boots for Eliza to tend to. "Jamie, I've had Willie put a pitcher of hot water in our room," she told him. "And there's a clean shirt waiting for you in the clothes press."

He regarded her evenly. "Very thoughtful, Leana."

"Shall I send Hugh to see you? Might you want to be shaved for supper?" *For later?*

Jamie headed for the stair without looking at her again. "Aye, send the man up in a few minutes. The melting snow has made a muddy mess of the sheepfolds and of me as well." Leana would never tell him that she found him every bit as handsome fresh from the fields as she did fresh from a bath.

He came to the table at seven looking the part of a country gentleman again, taking his seat next to her and offering her a perfunctory nod. His mood was sober all through their meal of roasted snipe, his attention taken with picking through the bird's tiny bones. She feared they would spend another cold night together, and she was not wrong. *Patience,* she told herself, watching him sleep, pulling the bedcovers closer to keep her warm.

Saturday brought the first clear sky in many days. "In honor of Saint Valentine, I ken," Neda said at breakfast. "Will Jessie be bringin' wee Annie round for sweets?" The fourteenth of each February the neighborhood children came knocking on doors, begging for sweets or money or fruit. At Lachlan McBride's door, it would never be coins they took home in their pockets. Meanwhile Rose was already off to the Elliots' house in Newabbey, where the young people of the parish were celebrating the day in the traditional way, with much merriment capped off with a Valentines Dealing. Leana prayed some young man might draw Rose's name from the hat and draw her eye away from Jamie. A selfish prayer, she knew, but a prudent one.

Leana ate her porridge quickly, wondering in which corner of the cellar she'd hidden her best apples. "I suspect we'll have quite a bit of company with the weather so fair. Suppose I wash and polish the fruit, Neda, while you keep an eye on the door. Jessie is always up before the sun."

Neda eyed her, a knowing grin on her kind face. "Unlike a certain married woman I ken who's been sleepin' later than usual."

Leana's cheeks heated. "It is not what you think. 'Tis the babe, wearing me down before he even shows himself." She glanced down at her flat stomach, still amazed at the thought of Jamie's son growing inside her. Was he not awed by it as well? If so, his joy was a closely guarded secret, for his face registered none of it. *Patience, Leana.*

Eager to prepare for their small visitors, she poked around in the dank cellar until she found the basket she was looking for and filled her apron with two dozen firm, red-skinned apples. Cold water, a bit of salt, and a vigorous rubbing polished them to a high sheen. "Have we a nice tray to put them on?"

"Aye." Neda produced an oak tray Duncan had fashioned for her years ago. "I think I hear someone knockin' already, and the wag-at-the-wa' not showin' nine o'clock yet!"

Leana laughed, her spirits buoyed by the thought of her red-haired friend come to call. "That would be Jessie." *And Annie, dear Annie.* Both women hurried to the front of the house and swung open the door to find the mistress of Troston Hill standing on their doorstep, her babe on her hip.

Annie squealed the moment she saw Leana, and Jessie's smile was brighter than the winter's sun.

"Have you a treat for my wee one on this Saint Valentine's Day?"

Leana held up the tray of russet apples. "Aye, and a cup of tea for the mother, if she'll join me." Their guests were ushered in and made at home by the hearth, where Jessie lowered Annie to the floor, kissing her soft curls in passing. Leana discarded her tray and pulled off Annie's many wrappings. "I need to see how you've grown, little one, and I cannot tell with you bundled up so. Look at you, standing up all by yourself! And are you walking now and giving your mother's back a rest?"

As though she understood every word, Annie toddled about the room while Leana clapped, fighting tears. How quickly children grew! She could barely wait to see her own son's chubby legs in motion like Annie's. Would he be fair, like her, or have darker hair, like his father? Eyes of sky blue or moss green? If Jamie was not careful, he would miss all the anticipation of becoming a father and all the joy that came with it.

Jessie watched her with Annie, grinning shamelessly. "You've a babe growing inside ye, don't ye, lass?"

Leana stared up at her friend in astonishment. "Jessie, however did you guess?"

"'Twas written all over your face the minute you saw Annie." Jessie tipped her head to the side, eying her closely. "This babe of yours, is he giving you trouble in the morning?"

"Nae." Leana stood, brushing off her skirts. "I've been able to keep my breakfast down."

"And Jamie, is he pleased to wake and find you next to him?"

"Jessie!" Leana shook her head as though that might cool her cheeks. "Is it your red hair that makes you say such braisant things?"

"That's what my Alan tells me nigh to daily." Jessie's expression stilled. "Truly, Leana, we are happy for you. All your neighbors who saw you ride to the kirk on your wedding day have come to think well of this match. 'Twas clear it was the Lord's doing, however it came about, and this bairn he's blessed you with is proof of it."

"May God be praised for it then." Leana bent down to hand Annie a shiny apple and watched the child's eyes grow round with delight, even as she prayed in silence, *And may God look upon my sorrow and change Jamie's heart.*

Seventy

Endure, my heart:
you once endured something even more dreadful.
HOMER

Rose did not return home from her Valentine festivities until after supper, and Leana was grateful. To
have Jamie to herself all evening without wondering
if his gaze was fixed elsewhere was a blessed
relief. She'd taken particular care with her dress
and pinched her cheeks until they hurt. Neda had
twined a red ribbon through her hair, pinning it up in
a becoming twist high on the crown of her head, the
ribbons dangling behind.

Jamie noticed. "You look well tonight."

She looked up from her book and smiled, closing

it around her finger to mark her place. "A bit of color for Valentine's Day," she said, then appraised his smooth knot of hair, tidy cravat, and polished silver buttons. "You look handsome as well." They were seated near the hearth, family worship concluded, and the table cleared and set for the Sabbath. Lachlan had retired early, complaining of a headache, so it was just the two of them spending a pleasant hour reading by the fire. *Heaven.*

Jamie inclined his head, eyeing the spine of her book. "Still working on *Evelina,* I see."

He remembered. "I did not have time to finish it in Dumfries," she murmured, minding her thoughts so they would not show on her face. "Though I tried my best."

"Aye," he said with a hint of a smile. "You did."

Jamie was smiling at her—*smiling!* Leana returned the favor, grinning like a child being handed a toffee. She wet her lips, trying to think of the most clever comment she could make to keep that look on his bonny face, when the door flew open with a bang and Rose came bounding into the room and landed right between them.

"*Och!* Look at you, reading by the fire like two old people."

When Jamie turned his smile on Rose, it felt like the sun going behind a cloud, so quickly did the air around Leana cool. She swallowed her disappointment and slipped her finger from her book. Her sister's arrival had ended her quiet plans for the evening.

Jamie put his book aside as well, giving Rose his

full attention. "I am an ancient man of four-and-twenty years, lass. After a hard day's labor, this is the most my weary bones can manage."

"I don't believe that for a minute." Rose swatted at him with her scarf, unwrapping it from around her neck. "But you *are* very old, not at all like the young lads who fought to pull my name from the cap in the Dealing."

His smile faded slightly. "Did they now?"

"Oo aye! Peter Drummond, the heir of Glensone, was particularly eager to draw my name."

Leana prayed as she asked, "And did he?"

"Nae. Susanne's brother, Neil, picked my name, and I picked his." Rose made a face, scrunching her nose up like a wee pig. "I don't care what the custom is, I'll not have Neil Elliot as my sweetheart for the next year."

An odd look of relief crossed Jamie's features. For a man who fancied his feelings well hidden, Jamie McKie was as easy to read as *Evelina.* He tugged Rose's braid. "So this Neil fellow is not for you, is that it?"

"Hoot! The lad has crooked teeth and more hair than one of our collies."

Leana captured Rose's hand, squeezing it gently. "Now, Rose, don't speak so cruelly of a neighbor. We cannot help the way we look. God loves us as we are, that we might see one another in a kinder light."

Rose arched her eyebrows. "My, aren't you the holy one, speaking of Almighty God as though you knew his thoughts."

"Not his thoughts," Leana murmured. "Only his words."

Rose shrugged and pulled her hand free. "Well, I've promised to have lunch in the Elliots' pew tomorrow. Do you think Neda will mind if I take the last of her mutton pies?" She spun on her heel and took off for the kitchen, the old couple by the fire already forgotten, it seemed.

Jamie glanced at Leana, the easiness between them gone. "It's late," he said.

Too late. "Might you walk me up the stair? I've felt more lightheaded than usual this week."

"Of course." He stood and offered his hand, lifting her to her feet with a manly sort of grace and guiding her toward the stair. Aunt Rowena had trained him well in the ways of a gentleman. Rowena had not taught him how to be a husband though. That responsibility, it seemed, fell to her.

They undressed by the light of a single candle, with nary a word between them, then climbed beneath the bedcovers and closed themselves in from the winter's cold. Leana waited until they were both settled, then gathered enough courage to gently press her body against his, her head just below his chin, her arms wrapped around his neck. *Jamie, please.*

Leana felt him slowly relax, as though he were thawing. "It was a lovely day," she said tentatively, seeing if he was listening. "Jessie and Annie came to visit and the Bell children and Nicholas Copland's little twin brothers and all five of the Taits. We had only one apple left." She lifted her head to whisper in his ear. "I saved it for you. My valentine."

"Thank you." It was an odd acknowledgment, too formal for a husband and wife in their bedclothes. When he spoke again, his voice was lower, with a note of genuine concern. "How are you . . . feeling?"

He meant the baby. "I feel wonderful," she promised him. And she did, for the first time in days. "Please do not be afraid . . ."

"Hush, lass. No need to speak of it."

What she heard in his voice this time was not concern. It was obligation. He turned toward her, pulling her closer. Her skin heated everywhere his body brushed against hers. "Jamie, sweet Jamie," she said with a lengthy sigh. Could she bring herself to confess the truth? "I've missed you."

"And I've missed you." He said it quickly. By rote.

Leana would not listen to his words then, for they broke her heart. She would listen to what was unspoken. "Love me, Jamie," she whispered, just as she had each of their nights together in Dumfries. He slowly moved his hands over the hills and plains of her body, but when she did the same, he was cool to her touch. Something was wrong, terribly wrong.

She had to know. "Is this pleasure, Jamie?" she whispered. "Or is it duty?"

His hands stilled. So did the air around them. "Some duties are more pleasurable than others," he said, but there was no laughter in his voice. He stopped her questions with his mouth, kissing her thoroughly, distracting her, but the question hovered between them, unanswered.

By the time he'd finished with her, she had tears in her eyes. Her prayers had not been answered after all, not the way she'd hoped. Aye, she had Jamie McKie's name, and she had his child. But she did not have Jamie.

When he pressed a kiss on her closed eyelids to say good night, he must have tasted her salty tears. "I'm sorry, lass." She heard the catch in his voice. "I can only give you what I have. It will have to be enough."

But it was not enough.

Jamie fulfilled all the requirements of a dutiful husband except one: He did not love her. It was too much to ask, she told herself. He did not choose her. Why should he be inclined to love her? That she loved him without reservation did not mean that he would return her feelings. In his gaze, in his words, in his touch, Jamie made very clear what his feelings were and were not.

He tolerated her.

It was worse than no love at all.

Seventy-One

No change, no pause, no hope!
Yet I endure.
PERCY BYSSHE SHELLEY

The weeks of winter dragged on, Jamie toiling on the farm from dawn until dusk, Leana watching her body swell with child. She and Neda spent days taking apart her few gowns and stitching them to fit more loosely, easing the waistline higher. Leana did not mind the changes she saw and felt, knowing they were necessary, that for God to create a child inside her, he needed room to work. Headaches came and went, and she could never get enough sleep, stealing away to their bedroom many afternoons, grateful to give her swollen ankles a rest.

As her body grew, so did Jamie's attention to her sister. He watched Rose constantly, found reasons to brush his hand against hers, read aloud from her favorite books, purchased ribbons from a visiting packman and fashioned them into bows, which she wrapped round her black hair, tossing her braid at him with a coy smile. Such things were done in secret, not in public. No one outside the family knew, or they pretended not to know. But Leana did not need her spectacles to see that Rose still loved Jamie, and Jamie still loved Rose.

Her sister came knocking on her bedroom door one gray Tuesday in late April, looking as pretty as one of the miniature oil paintings Leana had admired at the King's Arms Inn. Rose was dressed in her damask gown, the rose-colored one meant for her wedding. It was the first time Leana had seen her wearing it since their fitting with Mr. Armstrong, the tailor, four months past.

Leana could not hide her surprise. "Surely you did not dress in so fine a gown to sit by my bedside?"

"Of course not," Rose answered, her voice as chilly as the damp spring air. "I have been invited to a small dinner party at Maxwell Park."

"I'm thrilled for you, dearie," Leana said, and meant it. Such social gatherings were intended for hothouse blooms like Rose, not wallflowers like herself. "It would seem there are no hurt feelings, then, concerning Father's refusal of a Hogmanay debut for you?"

Her sister giggled, then bent over and whispered,

"Not after I wrote to Lord Maxwell on two occasions and begged his forgiveness."

"Rose!" Leana sat up, her headache forgotten. "You wrote the man letters?"

Her nose pointed in the air. "I have a fine hand. You've said so yourself."

"It's not your handwriting that concerns me, Rose. It's the audacity of a young woman writing to a married gentleman. Such a thing is simply not *done.*"

"But it *was* done and with the desired result." Rose paused before the mirror on the dressing table, adjusting her sleeves. "I am back in Lady Maxwell's good graces and dining in their home this evening."

Leana was not finished fretting. The child had overstepped her bounds and did not seem the least concerned. "Rose, how can you think of going without an escort? The Maxwells' blood is too rich for Peter Drummond or Neil Elliot, yet you cannot go alone."

"Oh, I'm not," she said airily. "I'll be on the arm of a handsome young shepherd."

Leana nearly fainted. "Not Rab Murray?"

"Goodness, no!" Rose's laugh was a throaty trill, like an actress practicing for a scene. "A much more braw lad than that and a gentleman as well." She turned and smiled sweetly. "Jamie will escort me."

Leana felt the heat drain from her head to her toes. "Jamie?"

"Aye. Hugh is seeing to him now. In my room so you wouldn't be disturbed."

"But how can you . . ." Leana was so taken aback she could not continue. What was Rose thinking? What was Rose *doing?*

"Jamie is my cousin, remember. And as a married member of my family, a perfectly suitable escort."

Leana asked faintly, "And he agreed?" *A foolish question.*

"Naturally. Lord Maxwell is sending his carriage. You may see us off if you like." Rose swept from the room as though she were Lady Maxwell herself, her damask gown and silk petticoats rustling in her wake. "Jamie!" she called, knocking on the room next door. "Come, let us have a look at you. The carriage will be here any moment."

Leana slipped on her shoes and hastened to the hall, just as Jamie emerged from the room with Hugh behind him, a guilty stain on the servant's rough cheek. "Jamie," she breathed, stepping back as though he were someone else, as though he were royalty. Freshly combed and clean-shaven, he was impeccably dressed in a heavy satin coat and embroidered waistcoat, silk breeches and stockings, and buckled shoes polished to a high sheen—the very picture of a great Scottish laird. "I've never seen you like this."

He shrugged, as though making light of it. "My mother sent them from Glentrool."

"Did you . . . ask her to?"

Jamie glanced down at Rose, who had stepped close to his side, as though posing for a portrait. "Your sister did. She was certain Mother would have the proper attire for such an occasion, which it seems she did."

Leana stared at Rose, a hard knot growing inside her, close to the baby, near to her heart. "So you wrote Jamie's mother?"

"Indeed I did. Nothing inappropriate about *that,* is there?" Rose cast an appreciative glance at her escort. "You can see what a fine suit of clothes she sent. Doesn't our Jamie look handsome?"

Leana could hardly dispute so obvious a fact. "You look . . . magnificent," she confessed. "Both of you." They seemed pleased, but not surprised, smiling at one another, admiring each other's feathers like two preening birds.

The sound of horses drew them to the long window at the top of the stair. "*Och!* What a grand carriage!" Rose pressed her hand to her chest with dramatic flair. "That's their smaller one, with two horses. When the Maxwells ride to Edinburgh, they prefer their coach-and-four. Gleaming ebony with velvet curtains and brass lanterns. Still, this one is lovely enough, is it not? Shall we be off, Jamie?"

He inclined his head toward the stair. "Start down without me, Rose. I'll follow in a moment." Rose floated off, humming to herself, while Jamie turned back and looked, at last, at her. "Leana, perhaps I should have told you."

Leana tried to contain herself, but her tone gave away her hurt feelings. "Aye, you should have."

"Would you have objected?" His eyes shone greener than usual in the late afternoon light, and his jaw was tight. "Would you have refused to let Rose attend, refused to let me escort her?"

"Not at all. I simply would like to have known."

Jamie exhaled, clearly battle weary. "I apologize for not informing you. I thought Rose had done so."

"Why would she?"

He grimaced. "She does have a habit of doing as she pleases." Voices floated up the stair—the coachman asking for his passengers. "I must go. Don't wait up for us, Leana, for I fear it will be a late evening, and you need your sleep. For the baby."

"Aye. For your son."

Without another word he left her standing in the upstairs hall, wearing her drab gray gown, her hair mussed from napping, and her eyes wet with tears. She watched them from the window, two splendidly dressed people off to dine with his lordship. While she would stay behind and dine on onion soup.

Leana leaned her forehead on the glass. *Why does he hate me so, Lord?* It must be hate, for it was anything but love. He'd said as much, too many times to count. She would not wait up for them, for she could not bear to hear their jubilant report of an evening spent in one another's company. *My sister. My husband.*

She read until her eyes could not bear the strain, then crawled into bed at nine o'clock, trying not to think of what Jamie and Rose would be saying to one another at that moment. Whispering about her perhaps. Shaking their heads with pity. *Poor, plain, pregnant Leana.* Aye, she might be plain, but she was rich with blessings nonetheless. Her health, her home, the baby in her womb, the love of friends, the love of God. It was enough, truly it was. Perhaps when she tucked her babe in Jamie's arms, his feelings would change. "Please, God," she murmured, drifting off to sleep with a prayer on her lips.

The sound of the door unlatching woke her abruptly. A sharp click. *Jamie.* She opened the bed curtains to find him hurriedly undressing, discarding his fine clothes in a heap on the floor. Without a glance in her direction, he closed the window curtains tight and extinguished the remaining candle, blanketing their bedroom in utter darkness.

"Jamie," she whispered when he climbed into bed, adding his shirt to the pile on the floor, "whatever are you doing?"

"Remembering."

Jamie abruptly pulled her toward him and kissed her with abandon. He tasted like rich food and dry wine and potent whisky. And longing. "Hush now, lass. I want everything to be right. To be just like our wedding night." He kissed her again, harder this time, the sharp stubble of his beard burning her cheek, his hands rougher still.

A shiver ran through her. Of anticipation or fear, she wasn't sure which. "Why, Jamie?"

He did not answer her with words, yet soon proved he meant what he'd said. She ignored the taste of whisky on his lips and wept with joy, so grateful to be joined with the bridegroom she remembered—loving, attentive, generous Jamie. He had missed her, then, at Maxwell Park. Regretted leaving her, regretted hurting her. She could think of no better apology than this one. A night like their wedding night, only better. Because he knew the name of the woman he held in his arms. *Leana.* And because she knew he was her husband, the father of her child, the only man she would ever love. *Jamie.*

In the wee hours of the morn, in the curtained shadows, in his moment of passion, he called out her name: "Rose!"

Leana rolled away from him, nearly sick.

"*Och!* Leana . . ." He groaned, reaching his hand out to her. "I'm . . . sorry. I did not mean . . ." But he did mean it. He meant to call out the name of the woman he loved.

In the wretched darkness all came to light. Her words to him were cold, dead. "I see the way of it, Jamie. If the room is black as pitch, you can pretend I am Rose." *And I can pretend you love me.*

Seventy-Two

Could I love less,
I should be happier now.
PHILIP JAMES BAILEY

Please, God, let me love him no longer.

Leana stared out their bedroom window into the dark July night. It was her only hope, the only way to end her pain. If she did not give Jamie her heart, he could not break it over and over. *Please, God, let me love him no longer.*

To even think the words, let alone pray them, frightened her. Loving Jamie was so much a part of her that if she released him and her love for him as well, she might be left with nothing. *Nae.* Leana gazed down at the thin nightgown stretched taut against her round middle and was comforted. She would be left with something glorious: their son. She'd chosen names, hoping they might please Jamie and draw him closer, if not to her, at least to the child she would bear him.

"What of Robert?" she'd offered him one bright May afternoon when she visited her husband in the pasture, looking after the new lambs. "If we name him after a Scottish king, perhaps our son will be famous someday." Jamie had responded with a vague nod, too busy with the lambs to look up as she spoke.

On a rainy morning in June she'd found him in good spirits at the breakfast table and so tried again. "A son named Simon would let our neighbors know that God listened to our prayers. How does that strike you, Jamie?" It had not struck him at all it seemed, for he shrugged and, seeing Rose's irritation, changed the subject.

Last week she'd ventured a third possibility, sure he would respond to a fine name like Lewis. "Such a name would suit a famous warrior who might defend Glentrool from all invaders," she'd said, smiling as she did. But perhaps he thought she meant Evan would be the invader, because Jamie did not smile back nor agree with her choice.

That night, on the eve of Lammas, Leana had chosen a fourth name for their child, a name she would tell no one but God, who always listened.

When no breeze from the Solway came to cool her skin, she left the open window and crawled into bed, careful not to wake her husband who was snoring softly. The babe moved more vigorously at night, robbing her of sleep but giving her the pleasure of watching Jamie without hiding her feelings. She curled a lock of his dark brown hair between her fingers, enjoying the silky feel of it. *Sweet Jamie.* She had known him through four seasons and loved him in every one of them. But it was not enough to love and not be loved in return. A sense of acceptance, of finality, had fallen over her that summer, as light as the kell she wore on their wedding day.

Please, God, let me love him no longer.

She closed her eyes and let the weight of her simple prayer find a resting place in her heart. To be the sort of mother she longed to be for their son, she needed to be at peace with herself and with God and not struggling every hour of her life, longing for something she could never have. If her prayers were answered, she would not have Jamie, but she would have peace. She fell asleep at last, her fingers still tangled in his hair.

Leana woke the next morning to find Jamie dressed and gone to breakfast. With her ungainly figure, she preferred to dress with only Eliza to help her, but she missed having Jamie in the room. Missed his smiling voice as he regaled her with a story, missed his touch on her elbow as he guided her down the stair.

Stop it, Leana. God could not extinguish her love for Jamie if she fanned the flame of it by thinking about him day and night. She would quench her love as surely as she snuffed out a taper that had burned too long, by pinching the lighted wick with her fingers, feeling the pain for an instant, knowing it would soon fade away. *Please, God.*

Leana descended the stair, her resolve strengthening with each step, and joined the family at the table. She glanced at Rose, who was busy buttering her bannocks, and thought how much easier it would be to ask God to take away Jamie's love for her sister. Aye, a tempting thought, that! But she could not change Jamie's heart. Nor Rose's. She could only change her own.

Please, God, let me love him no longer.

Jamie greeted her when she took her seat next to him, his gaze aimed at her forehead rather than her eyes, his smile vacant. "We're discussing our plans for the day's activities. You intended to spend most of it indoors and out of the sun, helping Neda in the kitchen, aye?"

"Aye, with so long a day ahead. And hot as well." The sun had already been up for hours and wouldn't disappear until nine o'clock. "I've a dozen dishes to fix and a certain sweet to prepare for my sister." Leana eyed her across the table, hoping her words sounded sincere, for they were. "Happy birthday, Rose."

"Sixteen," her sister announced, smiling at no one in particular, then patted the three packages next to her plate. "Might I open these now, Father?"

Lachlan grunted his assent, chewing on a rasher of bacon. He was more sullen than usual, Leana knew, because he did not fancy the first of August. The shepherds and laborers quit their work for the day to celebrate Lammas, honoring the coming harvest, which meant Lachlan was paying for labor he did not receive.

Nonetheless, both Lammas and Rose's birthday would be duly honored at Auchengray. The neighborhood had been invited and the entire household put to the tasks of cleaning shelves, mopping floors, and emptying Leana's vegetable garden of its rich harvest. Perhaps the festivities would keep her sister from dwelling on the undeniable truth: If it weren't for the babe in Leana's womb, the first of August would have been Rose's wedding day.

"Go on," Leana urged her sister. "Father's gift first. The cream-colored paper." Leana knew what was inside, since Lachlan had insisted she make the selection. Rose clapped when she unwrapped the tortoiseshell combs, then tucked them in her hair, obviously pleased. "A fine present," Leana commended their father, relieved she'd chosen well. "Now mine."

Her sister carelessly tore off the paper, forgetting they used the same sheets of wrapping paper time and again. "Ah." Her face was expressionless. "A book."

"Not borrowed from a friend," Leana hurried to explain. "Your very own copy."

Rose held it at arm's length and read the title with little enthusiasm. "*Lectures on Female Education and Manners.* Do you mean to tell me I have no manners?"

"Not at all. I simply thought a young lady who dines at Maxwell Park and has plans to attend a private school in Dumfries in January might benefit from such a book." Leana softened her tone. "I meant it only to encourage you."

Rose put the book aside without further comment, then eyed Jamie's small present with obvious glee. "*This* does not look like something dull and practical. Shall we find out?" She did away with the paper, nearly shredding it in her haste, then sighed with delight at the new handkerchief trimmed in lace. "I would never so much as *sneeze* in such a delicate thing! Jamie, wherever did you find it?"

He grinned. "Mr. Fergusson's last . . . ah, shipment. From Brussels."

Rose fluttered it across the table. "Isn't it lovely?"

Leana conceded that it was, then finished her breakfast, longing to seek the sanctuary of the kitchen. On her twenty-first birthday in March, Jamie had given her a handkerchief as well. Without lace. By the time she'd reached the kitchen, her hurt feelings were brushed aside, and her brow was smooth once more. When she no longer loved him, he would not wound her so.

Neda, chopping carrots with a practiced hand, made her welcome. "Ye look peaceful today, lass."

"Aye." Leana tied a fresh apron around her neck, arranging it over her round stomach with a sigh of contentment. "I've made up my mind about something."

Neda's eyes filled with concern. "Have ye talked with God about this decision of yours?"

Leana offered her the gentlest of smiles. "He's the only one who knows."

"I dinna like the sound o' this." Neda wiped her hands on her apron, hastening around the table to grasp her hands. "Surely ye're not thinkin' aboot leavin' Auchengray?"

"Oh, Neda." Leana drew her close and lightly pressed their cheeks together. "Not anytime soon." She released her, giving her hands a parting squeeze. "We'll stay here until the babe is born. The rest is up to Jamie."

Neda made a face, pursing her lips as though she'd bit into something sour. "I'm not sure the lad is capable of makin' the wisest of decisions on that score."

"But he *is* my husband and the father of my child," Leana reminded her. "Didn't a certain housekeeper teach me to submit to my husband, as unto the Lord?"

"Och!" Neda flapped her hand and resumed her chopping. "So I did, and so ye should. Tell me aboot this decision then."

Now that she'd broached the subject, Leana found it hard to put into words. "I'm . . . that is, I'm praying about . . . something." She turned away, her cheeks hot. Neda would think her heartless. But it had to be said. With one eye on the kitchen door, Leana murmured, "I'm praying God will take away my love for Jamie."

Neda's eyes grew round as tea saucers. "What are ye thinkin', lass? We pray tae love others mair, not less."

Leana's spirits sank. "My heart has been broken and mended so many times, Neda. I fear it will never be whole again. What if I don't have enough love for our babe?"

Neda laughed softly, taking her sharp knife to a mound of potatoes. "Ye've no need to worry. Ane glimpse o' that wee son, and yer heart will break and mend a hundred times. As tae Jamie McKie, the lad sorely needs yer love. D'ye ken the truth o' that?"

Leana's busy hands stilled. "But he doesn't *want* my love."

"What we want and what we need are aften not the same. Yer sister loves his braw form and face, but ye love the man himself, with all his flaws."

"I *did* love him," Leana corrected her, not even convincing herself. "Would the Almighty expect me to love another who does not love me?"

Neda peered at her beneath a stray wisp of hair. "Are ye sure ye want an answer?"

Leana shook her head, sorry she'd ever mentioned her prayer. *Please, God, let me love him no longer.* He might choose not to answer, but she would not stop asking.

Seventy-Three

But still I think it can't be long
before I find release.
ALFRED, LORD TENNYSON

Look who's come for Lammas!" Susanne Elliot stood perched on the threshold of the kitchen, her auburn hair pinned up with a sprig of wild thyme, as befitted the day. "My brother Neil is trying to impress Rose on her birthday. Be glad you're missing his sorry attempts at flattery." She looked about the room with its abundance of produce. "Might I be helpful here?"

"You're our guest," Leana protested, putting aside her well-scrubbed radishes to reach for a basket of broad beans that needed cutting.

Susanne laughed. "I'm also the daughter of a grocer and under our housekeeper's feet at every turn. 'Tis my duty to make myself useful in a kitchen." She'd already helped herself to an apron and found a bare spot on the chopping table. "Anyway, I cannot resist the aroma of baking bread."

"Nor can I." Grateful for such cheerful company, Leana went about her work, exchanging neighborhood news while they prepared dishes of stewed turnips, cabbage and carrots in brown sauce, potato fritters, and onions roasted in their skins by the hearth, where grouse stuffed with blaeberries turned on the spit. Neda had finished her baking before dawn, when the kitchen was cooler. Mince pie and almond tart, Rose's favorite, sat hidden under a cloth along with the Lammas bannock, large enough to serve the family. Servants came and went, spreading plaids on the ground for seating, hauling water from the well. By noon the house and lawn were filled with guests, come to feast on the harvest foods and dance with the birthday lass to a fiddler's tune.

Susanne finally shed her apron, eager to join the others. Looking out the door at the whirling couples, she winked at Leana. "Wasn't your sister the canny lass, being born on a Quarter Day?"

Leana nodded, though her smile was faint. Lammas was bittersweet at Auchengray. As Rose was born, so did her mother die. Leana pressed her hand to her babe, silently begging God for the child's safety and hers, comforted when she felt a swift kick. "Go and dance now, Susanne. You've done more than your share here." The lass flew out the door into the merry assembly gathered around the heap of sticks the shepherds had collected all summer for the Lammas bonfire, to be ignited come sunset.

Leana stood in the doorway with Neda, content to watch. "'Tis a worthy effort, this day," she murmured, seeing Rose flirt with lads they'd known since childhood. "Who knows? Perhaps my sister will find a young man who fancies her for a wife."

"Oo aye! I am greatly in favor of that notion," Neda said, shooing her out the door. "Go on with you, lass. Time you behaved yer age. Take a turn round the lawn with yer Jamie, and see that yer sister dances with Peter Drummond 'til the Lammas moon shines bricht in the summer sky."

Leaving her soiled apron in the housekeeper's hands, Leana donned her bonnet and wandered out into the afternoon sun to discover Rab Murray swapping stories with the other shepherds, a knot of wide-eyed children at their feet. "Mistress McKie," he said, politely tugging at his forelock as she passed. She watched a group of older lads challenge one another, seeing who might heft a sack of newly harvested grain the farthest, while all around her swirled the music. Three fiddlers took turns through the day, keeping their neighbors dancing until they fell on the plaids, exhausted and happy. Rose never grew tired and grabbed a different partner for each dance, confounding poor Neil, whose sad expression put his heart on display for all to see.

Her sister was dancing a reel with Jamie now, her skirts and braid flying, her skin pink as willowherb. They made a handsome couple: his long legs guiding her in graceful circles; her dark eyes shining; her smile, not so innocent as it once was, decorating her bonny young face. When the tune finished with a flourish, they bowed to one another amid much clapping, though more than one gaze drifted toward Leana to see what she thought of her husband's spirited turn on the lawn.

It seemed Jamie sensed their subtle reproof as well and sent Rose off to find another partner. "Leana," he called out to her, extending his hand, "dance with me, wife."

She started to protest, but he would not hear of it, pulling her into the circle with the others, his hands callused and rough against hers, the heat from his body radiating like the sun. Suddenly shy at his touch, she ducked her head beneath his chin. "Jamie, I'm so ungraceful."

"You are never ungraceful," he chided softly. "I promise not to spin you about." He was good as his word, turning her only when necessary, and then with great care, through one dance, then another, until a nod at the fiddler produced a slow strathspey. Jamie bent down to whisper in her ear as their pace eased, "A bit more suitable for you and the babe, I think."

"Aye," she said, patting her brow. Much as she tried to guard her heart, her efforts were of no use. His smile was too close, his touch too warm. Even if it was only meant to appease the gossips, dancing with her husband left her breathless with joy. When the strathspey ended, he bowed deeply to her curtsy, then led her to a table where a much-needed cup of punch waited.

"'Tis a festive day," he said between gulps. "You'd never find so many souls at Glentrool on Lammas."

Glentrool. Dare she ask his plans? "Jamie, I know your obligation to my father ends this day." He gazed at her over the rim of his cup but said nothing. "Were you thinking we might remain at Auchengray until Hogmanay perhaps?"

"Your father would have me stay through breeding season." His expression, his tone told her nothing.

"Does that . . . please you?"

His lengthy sigh told her too much. "My pleasure is of no concern to your father. He has offered me an honest wage now that my 'obligation,' as you call it, has been met. Since we must remain until you have delivered our child, it seems we will stay at Auchengray for a season."

"Is your mother not eager to have you return to Glentrool?"

"She is eager, aye. But she is not willing. Her last letter indicated the time was not ripe for my return." He shrugged, clearly disappointed. "Soon, she said." He tossed the dregs of his punch on the ground, then banged the cup on the wooden plank table. "Thank you for dancing with me, Leana. See that you don't tire yourself." He touched her hand, the smallest of gestures, then strode toward the shepherds, who'd embraced him as one of their own.

Oh, Jamie.

Her prayers had not been answered. Her love for him refused to die.

"The lad still carries your heart in his pocket, I see." Lachlan joined her for punch, his gaze trained on Jamie. "But you never managed to capture his heart. Only his babe."

"And that is enough." Leana put down her cup more firmly than she intended. "For if I have his son, I have what matters most to him." She walked away without looking back, proud of herself for being neither rude nor timid. Though her father never spoke of it, she was of age now and married besides. He had no authority over her. She answered to God as her Maker and to Jamie as her husband. Deep inside a corner of her quiet, compliant self, a jubilant cheer arose.

Hours later, when the food was well consumed and the stories all told, Duncan stepped to the tower of wood that would soon fill the night with a crackling light and held aloft two wooden sticks. "The need-fire," he called out, then began rubbing the sticks furiously together. Custom required he not bring fire from the house; it must be a new fire to hold the darkness at bay. When a spark struck the kindling, he waved the fire to life as all stood watch in a circle around it, their gazes following the sparks rising into the black sky above.

A piper had joined the gathering and played with all his might, piping the flames higher as the dancing began in earnest. Across the lawn Leana watched Jamie gather Rose in his arms to dance. It seemed he no longer cared who might see or judge. He had done his duty by his wife. Now he would see to his own pleasure.

Leana stood back from the bonfire, watching them together, remembering the night when she had danced with Jamie beneath a cold Hogmanay sky certain that he loved her and only her. When she could bear it no more, Leana slipped back into the house, knowing she would not be missed. The doors were open to the warm night air, the rooms abandoned, strewn with the remains of the day's celebration. She climbed to the top of the stair and sat down, holding on to the rail for support, though it was another sort of strength she needed now.

Please, God, let me love him no longer.

Silence greeted her request.

Alone in the empty house, Leana buried her head in her skirts, and her heart gave way. Tears poured forth from the broken places that would not mend, as she grieved for the love that would not let go, even after all her prayers.

Seventy-Four

The greatest of faults is to be conscious of none.
THOMAS CARLYLE

It's your fault, Jamie McKie!" Rose stood before him, hands on her hips, her scolding tone like an Aberdeen fishwife's. "Not a soul at Auchengray knew about your birthday. If your mother hadn't written, we might never have known."

"You might have asked," he teased her, folding his mother's letter and tucking it in his pocket. They'd walked to Newabbey village together to enjoy the splendid September weather and had discovered Mr. Elliot had a letter waiting for him, addressed in his mother's sweeping hand. Impatient as ever, Rose had insisted he read it to her immediately, standing there in the street.

When the letter began "To my son on his twenty-fifth birthday," Rose had erupted. "Well! Since you didn't tell us, there will be *no* presents waiting by your plate and no apple tart appearing from the kitchen."

"I've no need of gifts, Rose, and as for Neda's tart, you would eat every bite yourself."

She stuck her tongue out at him. "Aye, that I would, just to spite you."

Rose. A year older and still as childlike as ever. Precious, endearing, but her charm wore a bit thin on days like this one, when he had so much on his mind. The birthday letter from his mother was expected; she wrote him in Edinburgh during the Septembers he was at university. This one was lengthy, filled with news of the flocks at Glentrool and the latest parish blether, along with the usual concerns about his ailing father. It was what she did *not* say that troubled him. No mention of coming home. No mention of Evan at all. Perhaps she was waiting to hear that an heir had been born.

Only a few weeks remained at most. Leana was certain it was a boy, but it could easily be a daughter. He'd have to prepare himself, have a compliment at the ready, should she hand him a wee lass. Not that he minded the idea; young Annie from Troston Hill was enchanting. At the moment, however, two women in his life were enough. Too much, in fact.

Rose tugged on his sleeve, pulling him up the road toward Auchengray. "Lift your feet, lad, or we'll never make it home in time for supper. You've not faced the wrath of Lachlan McBride until you've walked in the door with the meal already on the table."

"You forget, Rose, I've faced the man's anger over much more than being late for supper." He lengthened his stride, soon outpacing her, making her skirts swish to keep up with him. Though the leaves had not started to fall, the trees were edged with gold and red, striking against a sky the color of Scottish bluebells. Unbidden, a vision assailed him. *The bluebells on Leana's nightgown.* She'd worn it often through the spring and summer. Perhaps she'd hoped it would stir some pleasant recollection of their time in Dumfries. All he remembered of their bridal week was waking up morning after morning with the wrong woman beside him.

Nae. That was not fair to Leana. There were moments in Dumfries so tender they frightened him. He chose not to think of them, but they were there nonetheless.

A warm hand slipped through the crook of his elbow. "Now you're walking too fast," she whined, forcing him to match her pace. "Tell me about the day you and Evan were born so very long ago."

"That would be the *days* we were born. Wednesday night before midnight for my brother, and Thursday morning after the twelfth strike of the clock chime for me."

"You were born just after midnight?" Rose stared

up at him, her mouth agape. "*Och!* Jamie, that is very lucky indeed." She gripped his arm and dropped her voice. "I've heard that a child born at that hour can see the Spirit of God. Have . . . have *you?*"

Nae, but I've heard him. He almost said it aloud, then swallowed his words. Rose would never understand, though her sister might. As autumn moved across the land, the memory of his dream was becoming more vivid again, as though the tilt of the sun and the chill in the air recaptured something of that night on the cairn. *I will never leave you.*

Shivering at the thought of it, he gazed at Rose and steered their conversation in a different direction. "You know what the rhyme says?"

" 'Thursday's child has far tae go.' And you *have* traveled far, Jamie. Edinburgh and Glasgow, even *London!*" Her sigh only lacked words to be a song. "I've been to Moffat and Dumfries, which are hardly a long distance. Oh, and Kirkcudbright with Aunt Meg when I was a child."

He hid a smile, patting her hand. So provincial, his Rose. Her innocence was what drew him to her from the first. And now she had plans to attend a school for young ladies. "To put a proper finish on my domestic skills and genteel manners," she'd explained. Rose would depart from Auchengray in January and take the sun with her, leaving him with a meek wife, a new babe, and no Rose.

He gazed down at her, as bonny as a painted porcelain doll, and thought of the year he'd spent loving a lass he could not claim. Four seasons of stolen kisses and holding hands when no one might notice. Valentines in February, dinner at Maxwell Park, dancing at Lammas. His memories with her were as bright as the fireworks he once saw displayed in London exploding over the Thames. Would they fade as quickly, leaving nothing but a black sky?

An elbow struck his ribs. "Jamie McKie, your face is more dour than my father's." Rose spun in a circle before him, dancing like the Gypsies he'd met on his journey to Auchengray, with her head tilted back and her braid begging to be caught like a black rope. "Cheer up, lad! You're not a father yet. No need to be so serious."

He snatched her braid and tugged on it, bringing her spinning to an abrupt halt. "Only you can cheer me, Rose. With a kiss."

Half a mile from home, in the middle of a country road, with sheep bleating and cows lowing and magpies chattering overhead, Jamie kissed her long and well, for once not caring who might come upon them. He released her at last and gathered the stars in her eyes for a keepsake. "Home, Rose," he said softly. "For I will be a father soon, and I must see to my duties."

Leana was waiting for them at the door. If she noticed their hands quickly slipping apart, it did not show in her eyes. "You have minutes to spare," she warned them, though there was no reproach in her voice. "Clean yourselves up and be seated by seven o'clock. I hardly need to tell you why."

As they hastened up the stair and did as they

were told, Jamie realized that Leana would make a fine mother indeed, good at keeping her brood in order. *Brood?* Would there be more than one child? If she gave birth to a girl, there would have to be more. Several perhaps. The thought of so many lives depending on him made him stumble for a moment on his way down the stair.

He was not prepared to be a father. He had yet to learn to be a proper husband. When he reached the landing, he turned and saw her standing at the bottom of the stair. *Leana. My wife.* She smiled up at him, her body full of his child, her face full of love for him. The unspoken power of it struck him afresh, pressing him back against the stair wall.

It was a love he could not begin to comprehend. A love he could not return. And a love he could not live without.

Seventy-Five

In my end is my beginning.
MARY QUEEN OF SCOTS

The longer the Sabbath service lasted, the more uncomfortable Leana became.

She leaned against the hard wooden pew, her back aching, her legs numb from sitting in the same position through the singing of the psalms and the prayers of confession and the reading of Scripture. The babe had found a new hiding place, lower than before, pressing painfully against her when he turned. Leana realized too late that she should not have come to kirk, not that morning. But compelled by a longing to be in God's house, she'd braved the three-mile ride in the chaise, wincing with every jarring bump.

"Not prudent," her father had said at breakfast, eying her with a certain apprehension, when she'd told him her plan to join them that morning. Difficult as it was to admit, Lachlan McBride might have been right.

Cooler weather had coaxed her out of doors as well. The fourth of October had dawned with pale blue skies and a freshening breeze from the Solway, which meant she could worship without patting at her brow all morning. Jamie sat next to her in the pew, though not too close, giving her a bit of room to breathe. When he glanced down at her, his eyes were kinder than usual, and his concerned expression seemed genuine. "Are you feeling well?" he whispered so softly she almost didn't hear him.

Leana nodded, but something in her face must have told him otherwise. He found her hand, tucked beside her skirt, and drew it into his own. The simplest of gestures, yet it sent her heart soaring. *My dear husband.* Nothing had changed between them. Yet being filled with his child also filled her with compassion. He was clearly a man tormented by something he'd done, or not done. If he might love their son, that would be enough, that would be a beginning.

He squeezed her hand in silent support, and she closed her eyes to savor his touch. So taken was she with Jamie's unexpected affection that she missed Reverend Gordon's introduction of his text for the day, opening her eyes and giving him her full attention when he began to read from the Buik.

"There was given to me a thorn in the flesh . . ."

Aye. She knew about thorns. Her roses had pricked her finger many times, each puncture bleeding more profusely than a small wound merited. Leana realized the thorn he spoke about was not from a rose. He meant some painful experience, some debilitating, unwelcome *thing* that would not go away, that hurt without ceasing.

Like loving a man who does not love you.

She held back a tiny gasp.

The minister neither saw nor knew how carefully Leana listened as he continued reading. "For this thing I besought the Lord thrice, that it might depart from me."

Aye, she had. But not three times. Three hundred times. *Please, God, let me love him no longer.* She blinked away a tear that appeared on her lashes unbidden. She had begged and pleaded for release, but God had not answered that prayer. *Jamie, I love you still.*

Reverend Gordon's deep voice rang across the sanctuary. "And he said unto me, My grace is sufficient for thee . . ."

She touched a handkerchief to the corner of her eye as the truth settled inside her. His grace, his mercy, his love, his enduring presence, his faithfulness *were* sufficient.

Jamie had once told her that he could only give her what he had. "It will have to be enough," he'd said. But it was not enough. It would never be enough. Even if Jamie loved her completely, his love would still not begin to fill all the empty places inside her. Places only Almighty God could fill, because he alone was *enough.*

She gripped Jamie's hand without meaning to, so overwhelmed was she by the minister's words. "For my strength is made perfect in weakness."

Aye! She was weakness itself, but in her weakness she'd found God's strength. Jamie's arms were strong, but they could not hold her in the darkest of nights when everything hurt and all was broken. Only God could. *Only God.*

Her tears would not stop now nor would the joy welling up inside her. It must have shown on her face, for Reverend Gordon was looking directly at her with a curious gaze as he read the last words.

"Most gladly therefore will I rather glory in my infirmities, that the power of Christ may rest upon me."

Gladly glory.

Leana let the words sink in, tasting them, swallowing them with her tears. Could she manage such an impossible task? Could she gladly glory in loving Jamie, in bearing the pain of his rejection, if it meant that Christ's love would shine through her? Would his almighty power sustain her through a lifetime of loving yet being unloved?

Then the truth struck her, and her soul leapt with joy.

She was *not* unloved. She was loved completely. God had loved her through it all. Loved her now, loved her still, would love her always.

How had she neglected to see it for so long? Her

love for Jamie, the thorn in her heart, the love that would not stop, was there for a reason. To remind her that it was no longer Leana loving Jamie; it was God himself. God would never stop loving Jamie, nor would she.

"Jamie!" She hadn't meant to say his name aloud in the midst of Reverend Gordon's sermon, in the kirk where every eye turned to see what the outburst was about.

Jamie gripped her hand, his eyes wide, his voice low but urgent. "What, Leana? Is something wrong?"

She turned to him, longing to stand, to shout with joy and abandon, "Nothing is wrong." Her voice was the softest of whispers, yet it was strong, and the words were certain. "Jamie, I love you. I've always loved you."

"Leana, I . . ."

The first contraction seized her, bending her in half, squeezing her in two. She could not breathe; she could not speak. She could only cling to Jamie's hand and God's invisible strength as she tried to stand. *Help me, Jamie!*

Seventy-Six

My God, my Father, and my Friend,
Do not forsake me in the end.
WENTWORTH DILLON

God, help me!" Jamie shouted, gathering Leana in his arms, his heart pounding.

It had begun.

Neda was the next one to clamber to her feet, quickly making her way to his side, assessing the situation with an experienced eye. "The lass will niver make it home." Neda turned and raised her voice above the murmuring congregation. "Reverend Gordon?"

The minister stood transfixed in his lofty pulpit,

his sermon notes forgotten, his jaw drooping. "Mistress Hastings?"

"We've need of the manse, sir, and yer guid wife as well." Neda did not wait for an answer but instead guided Jamie and Leana out of the pew and into the aisle, calling a handful of women by name. "Come, ladies. Ye're needed at once."

Jamie's only concern was Leana, who clung to his arms for support. "Carry me, Jamie," she whispered hoarsely. Without hesitating, he slid one hand behind her back and the other behind her knees and lifted her off the floor, mother with child, as though she weighed nothing, as though the burden were borne by unseen arms. Leana wrapped her arms around his neck and pressed her damp cheek against his chest as he strode toward the doors, held wide open for them.

Help me, God. Help us both.

He carried Leana the short distance to the manse next door, almost running by the time he arrived, a flock of women trailing behind him. Mistress Gordon was already at the front door, waving them in. "There's always water on the fire, and I've plenty of linens. Come, come." Candles were quickly lighted in the spence and fresh sheets thrown over the minister's bed while the women made room for Jamie and the limp woman in his arms.

He lowered Leana onto the mattress with exceeding care, not wanting to hurt her further, for she was clearly in agony.

"Jamie," she sighed, cradling his cheek, "pray for me."

"I will, I will." He gripped her hand as she bent in two again, waiting while the wave of pain crashed over her, then receded, leaving her breathless. "Go, my husband," she said, stifling a moan. "The women will attend to me."

My husband. He released her hand, reluctant to do so. "Are you certain, lass? I will wait outside the door. Praying, just as you asked."

"Good." She nodded, taking a deep breath. "I love you, Jamie."

"Leana, I—"

"That's enough, lad." Neda abruptly yanked the sleeve of his coat. "Ye're more hindrance than help, if ye want to know the truth of it."

Two women escorted him from the room before he could protest. The door closed in his face, gently but firmly, and he was left standing in the dim hall, blinking until his eyes adjusted enough for him to find a chair.

He sat close by the door where he could listen and be available if needed. Except no one in that room needed him, for any reason, not even Leana.

Leana.

His head sank into his hands.

Leana McKie—aye, his wife, though he'd never treated her as such—had carried his child for nine long months without complaining, without asking anything of him but the smallest favors. "Rub my back, Jamie?" And he would do as she asked but no more. "Might you bring some tea?" she would say, her voice hesitant, then thank him profusely for doing such an insignificant task. She suggested names for their son, good names—Robert, Simon, Lewis—but he pretended it didn't matter.

Leana told him she loved him daily.

Leana showed him she loved him by the hour.

And what did he do? He loved Rose. Told her so. Showed her with gifts and heated glances. He was not unfaithful to Leana in body but desperately false in every other way that mattered.

He had ruined Leana's life and broken her heart for naught.

And she had forgiven him, without his even asking for her forgiveness.

Oh, Leana!

From behind the spence door came a groan that sounded as though it were torn from Leana's body. Jamie groaned with her, his own pain only starting.

"Are ye prayin', lad, as ye should be?" Duncan came up behind him and pressed his rough hand around the back of Jamie's neck. "Are ye thinkin' aboot what it means to be a faither?"

Jamie only nodded, not wanting Duncan to know what desperate thoughts were running through his mind.

But Duncan knew him too well. "And are ye thinkin' what it might mean to the child's mither to know that she is loved by her husband?"

"But I don't—"

"Wheesht!" Duncan slapped him on the back, hard. "Enough o' that foolishness, lad." Duncan marched over to an empty chair and yanked it up to the door. "Ye'll listen to what I have to say and mind me as though I were yer ain faither come down from Glentrool." He banged the chair into place across from him and sat down with a decisive thump. "Do I have yer attention, Jamie?"

Jamie was stunned. "Aye." Duncan had never been so forceful.

"Here's the truth of it, lad. And ye ken that I care for ye, and so does me Neda, so don't be gettin' all in a huff when I say what I must." The overseer leaned forward, his eyes kind but his jaw firm. "The fact is, ye've niver known what it means to love someone, lad. Instead ye've worshiped yer mither and hated yer brither and deceived yer faither— aye, I ken all aboot that. There's none at Auchengray who don't. And ye put Rose McBride on a pedestal she niver deserved. But that woman in that room, yer ain Leana—"

Duncan choked on her name, pointing at the door as she cried out in pain. "Leana, yer only wife, who has loved yer miserable self for a lang and thankless year, is in that room layin' down her life for yer son. And what does this guid woman get from her husband?"

Jamie could barely say the word. "Nothing."

"Naught but cold hands and a colder heart and a wanderin' eye. The dear lass has asked nothin' of ye, not ane thing, except that ye let her love ye and that ye love her in return. Ye've only done half that, Jamie. Ye've taken all the love she had to give ye, but ye've given none back." The man's eyes were bright with tears, his voice shaking. "D'ye hear me, lad? D'ye hear *her,* beggin' for mercy from her travail, all to give ye yer firstborn?"

Jamie nodded, his head falling forward, his own tears dripping to the floor. Words would not come. Only pain came, in waves, like Leana's labor, wearing him down, grinding his pride into bits. *Forgive me. Forgive me.* It was all he could think.

His heart felt like a fist, tight in his chest, the pain unbearable.

Forgive me. Please, God. Forgive me.

His sins unrolled like a scroll before him, too many to count, too many to bear. The lies, the deceit, the greed, the selfishness. The shameful ways he'd treated his brother, his father, his wife. *God, forgive me.*

How dare he ask God for forgiveness when he could not forgive himself? When his sins were without number?

O God, in the multitude of thy mercies, hear me.

Duncan rested a hand on his shoulder, saying nothing for a time, only squeezing it now and again. "Your wife's in pain, Jamie, make no mistake. A woman in travail has naught but sorrow, for she kens her hour has come."

As though in answer, Leana moaned loudly, calling his name. "Jamie! Jamie!"

He shot to his feet and pounded on the door. "I'm here, Leana! I'm here."

"Sit ye doon, lad. Ye've no business in there." Duncan tugged him back to his seat, a wry smile on his craggy face. "Just pray she only calls ye Jamie and not somethin' meikle worse, eh?"

"But I have to *do* something, Duncan. *Listen* to

her." He pressed his hand to his mouth, stifling his misery.

"Ye'll wait, Jamie, like every faither has waited since Adam himself. 'Twill be the most helpless hours of yer life, for ye canna do ane thing to help her. But fear not. As soon as she's delivered of the child, she won't remember the pain for the joy that yer son is born. *Yer* son, Jamie. Are ye hearin' what I'm sayin' to ye?"

Jamie dropped into his seat and hunched over, his hands pressed to his head. "You've cut me to the quick, man. I hardly know what to say or do."

Duncan snorted mightily, then laughed a great, rolling laugh that came from his chest. "'Twill be the easiest thing done in this house today. Ye're goin' to beg God for mercy, Jamie. Ye're goin' to pray like ye've niver prayed before. No young man of my acquaintance has ever needed mercy more and deserved it less, but ye'll ask for it, and Almighty God will give it to ye because he can. D'ye believe that, Jamie?"

I will never leave you. Jamie gulped. "I believe it, aye."

"Say the words with me, lad, for ye learned them at yer faither's knee: 'Have mercy upon me, O LORD; for I am weak.'"

Jamie choked out the words. "Have mercy upon me, O LORD, for I am . . . weak."

"Aye, that's the way. Ye are weak, Jamie, but there's not a man who isn't, if he's honest. What ye're doin' now is the strongest thing a body can do." Duncan rested a hand on Jamie's shoulder. "Now ye're going to pray for the courage to love and respect yer wife. Can ye do that, lad? Can ye pray sic a thing and ken that yer words are bein' heard?"

"Aye." Jamie fumbled for his handkerchief. "Aye, Duncan, I can. And I will."

"Guid. I told ye these words afore, the day ye heard aboot the babe. Now ye need tae speak them for yerself, Jamie. Will ye say them after me? 'Husbands, love yer wives.'"

"Husbands . . ." Jamie broke down. Nothing would come but groaning.

Duncan's voice was low but sure. "Take yer time, lad."

Like granite chipped from a Dalbeaty quarry, the truth finally came out. "I am not . . . a husband."

"Aye, but ye are. The law and the Lord say so." Duncan moved closer, stretching his arm across Jamie's shoulders, his own gruff voice strained to the breaking point. "Come, we'll say it together. 'Husbands, love yer wives.'"

"Husbands . . . love your wives." *Forgive me, Leana.*

"Aye, that's good, Jamie. 'Even as Christ also loved the church.'"

"Even as Christ also loved the church."

"And so he did. Now the last of it: 'and gave himself for it.'"

The hardest of all. "And gave himself for it."

"That's how much love Leana deserves, Jamie. All you can gie her." Duncan stood with a grunt, then squeezed Jamie's shoulder with affection. "Ye ken what else needs to be said and done this night. I'll be in by the hearth if ye need me."

Jamie nodded, blowing his nose. He was ashamed of many things but not of his tears. Not now, not with Duncan. Duncan cared about him. It was plain as day on the man's face. Leana loved him too, and that was plainer still.

Left to himself, Jamie bowed his head, pressing his forearms into his knees, and said the only thing left to say. *Hear me, God. Hear me.*

On the other side of the door, his wife called for him again, her voice pleading. "Jamie! Jamie!" *Leana.* She loved him completely. And he needed her love. Desperately.

Please, God, help me love her in return.

Jamie clenched his hands together, determined to keep praying until his prayer was answered. *Please, God, help me love her in return.*

Seventy-Seven

A Man like to me,
Thou shalt love and be loved by, forever.
A Hand like this hand
Shall throw open the gates of new life to thee!
ROBERT BROWNING

He must love you, lass, to stand so close to your door."

Leana looked at Mistress Bell through a sheen of unshed tears. "Who?" she whispered, her throat parched, her lips so dry she feared they might stick together. "Who is close by the door?"

"Your husband, of course. The one you keep calling for."

Jamie.

Leana fell back on the pillows, already exhausted, yet strengthened by the thought of him so near. Jamie, the man she loved and would always love, even if he never loved her in return.

In a corner of the shadowy room she spied her sister, looking forlorn. "Rose," Leana called, holding out a weak hand. "Come closer, dearie." Before Rose could move, another spasm racked Leana's body. Neda's hand clasped hers with a comforting grip while Leana bore the pain as best she could. When Leana opened her eyes, Rose was there, hovering nearby, her eyes wide with fright.

"Leana," she whispered. "Are you . . ."

"She's fine."

Neda spoke too sharply, Leana thought. *Poor Neda.* Always protecting her like the mother she was. Leana reached for her sister's hand. "Rose is worried because . . ."

"Aye, because of yer mither. I should have realized." Neda's features softened as she slid her arm around Rose's waist and pulled her close. "Agness McBride would be proud of ye both tonight, behavin' like sisters, helpin' each other."

A stream of tears started down Rose's cheeks, but she would not let go of Leana's hand to dry them. "Leana, I'm . . . I'm . . . *sorry.*" The word came out on a sob.

"I know you are, dear sister. So am I. Sorry as can be." The pain came again, stronger, more insistent. She could only squeeze the hands that held hers and endure. It finally passed, followed by a short spell of blessed relief.

"Lass, tell me quick." Neda leaned forward, searching her face. "D'ye have yer mither's blue thread on yer person? Always wise to carry it aboot when ye're near the end o' yer time. The fever and all."

"Nae, I . . . nae." Leana struggled to marshal her wits. "When Mother died, Father was beside himself. He . . . he cut off the thread and threw it in the fire."

Neda's eyes widened. "I'd completely forgotten! Och, lass, that does not bode well." The housekeeper turned toward the other women of the parish behind her. They shook their heads, their faces anxious, their whispers tense.

Leana tried to sit up, determined to say what she must before she could say nothing at all. "Neda, you were the one who told me the child was a gift from God, aye?"

"Och! Ye ken verra well that I did."

"Then trust the Almighty to bring this babe into the world." Leana's words faded into a groan. She felt the baby turning, moving, fighting. Seized with a fresh stab of pain, she drew her knees toward her distended belly, groaning through another contraction, then fell back a minute later, grateful for a moment to breathe. They were coming closer. *Soon, soon.*

Neda bent over her, wiping her brow with a cool cloth. "Are ye sayin' ye want to put aside the auld ways, Leana?"

"Aye, that's it." Leana sighed, grateful she understood. Almighty God had no need of rusty nails or fir candles or spoonfuls of salts. "See that the women hold their Bibles over me. And pray."

Neda nodded, then stepped away to tell the others. Leana could hear their agitated murmuring somewhere on the other side of the fog that enveloped her birthing bed. No matter. God alone would see her through.

Day turned into night, and still she labored. She breathed when she could, screamed when she needed to, and prayed without ceasing. The room was a cave, and she was trapped in its black center, clawing the sheets, begging for deliverance. *Help me, Lord.*

Rose stayed close by, her hands clasped, her eyes beseeching. "Don't die, Leana!" she whispered. "Don't die!"

"I'm not dying, Rose," she assured her between gasps. "Pray . . . pray for the baby to come."

A distraught Jamie burst into the room at one point, shocking the poor women senseless. In the darkened room—the candles burned down to stubs, her pain unending now—Leana could barely see him outlined by the flickering light of the hearth. She said his name, though it sounded more like a groan. "Jaaamieee . . ."

"Please, Neda!" His voice was desperate, pleading. "Please, she's calling me. Can't you hear her? I need to see my wife. Just for a moment, please."

But Neda brooked no visitors in a birthing room and hastily pushed him back out the door. "It won't be lang now, lad, and ye'll have her all to yerself. Patience, Mr. McKie."

Leana watched him leave, his broad shoulders sagging. *Poor Jamie.* She prayed for him to be strong and for God to be stronger still. For her sake. For their son's sake. She had no doubt it would be a boy. *Ian.* That would be his name. *Gift from God.* Aye, the perfect name.

Then all conscious thought flew from her head.

The end had come.

"Almost, Leana." *Neda's voice.* "Ye're so close, lass." *Push.* "There's the head. I see it!" *Deep breath.* "Wait now, wait . . . and . . . push!"

The women circled the bed, their heavy family Bibles held high, their voices lifted up as well. "Deliver her, Lord!" When the child came at last, a lusty cry pierced the air, and all joined in the chorus, Leana the loudest among them.

"Yer son is born!" Neda crowed, gathering the slippery bundle into her arms while Leana lay there, exhausted and drenched with tears, able to do little more than open her eyes. She heard Jamie outside the door, banging on the wood, begging to know if she was well, if the babe was well.

"Someone tell Jamie," Leana whispered hoarsely, watching Neda quickly bathe the whimpering infant. At last the babe, wrapped in fresh linen, was tucked into her waiting arms. How snugly he fit, how right he felt!

Neda kissed them both, her eyes brimming with tears. "Well done, lass. Well done."

Leana nodded her thanks and pressed her lips against his tiny head, still wet from the water, still warm from her body. *Ian.* His hair was dark brown and soft as down, like his father's. "Welcome, Ian James McKie," she whispered. "God has given me the gift of you this night, and I will praise his name forever."

"Leana?" Neda leaned over her, brushing her damp hair away from her brow, a smile in her voice. "There's a braw young faither here quite beside himself to have a word with you. Might you gie him a bittie of your time?" Neda stepped back and motioned Jamie forward. "She's all yours, lad."

Leana gazed over Ian's head and watched Jamie move toward the bed while Rose, a hand pressed against her mouth, eased away, disappearing into the shadows. Jamie did not look at Rose or at Neda. He did not even look at their newborn son. He looked at her, his wife. Straight into her eyes, as though stunned at the sight of her.

"Jamie." She tried to wet her lips but could not. "I must look a fright."

He knelt down on one knee beside the bed. "You look like the mother of my son." Placing one trembling hand on hers and the other on their son's head, he bound them together with his touch. Neither of them could speak for all that was in their eyes.

The room grew quiet around them as Neda ushered the neighborhood women gently out the door, sending them home to worried husbands and hungry children. The housekeeper was the last to leave, her face hopeful as she closed the door behind her.

All was silent but the fire in the hearth.

"Leana, will you forgive me?"

"Forgive you?" She thought she had cried all her tears while she labored, but she was wrong. "I will do better than that, Jamie McKie," she whispered. "I will always love you. Always." When his face crumpled and he fell against the bed, she comforted him, smoothing back his hair. "Jamie, sweet Jamie. My love for you gives me the strength to forgive anything."

His words were muffled. "You are more than I deserve, Leana." After a moment he lifted his face to meet her gaze. "You are the blessing of God to me. I know that now."

"And here is another blissin." She nodded at the babe and held him out a bit. "Will you take your son?"

Jamie straightened, wiping a sleeve across his face, then gingerly gathered up his son and peered into his tiny face, awed. "He looks like . . ."

"Aye." She laughed softly. "A twin of you." When the child began to fuss, she held out her arms. "Better let me feed the lad. You'll stay and keep me company?"

Jamie slowly placed the infant back in her arms, then stood to his feet while she attended to the hungry newborn, kindly averting his eyes while she struggled to get the child settled. When she looked up with a small sigh of relief, Jamie was gazing down at her again, his face full of a yearning she'd not seen before. "Leana, would you believe me if I told you that God once spoke to me in a dream?"

She thought before she answered, stroking Ian's

head as she did. It was clear Jamie had given the question a great deal of thought. "Aye, I believe God might speak to you while you are sleeping, Jamie. Heaven knows, I do."

"You do?"

"Aye." She smiled. "When you're snoring beside me, I can say anything I like to you and never be interrupted."

The babe in her arms wriggled, and both of them laughed. "Already this one has found a way to come between us," she teased.

"Nae." Jamie was suddenly serious. "Nothing will come between us again."

She shook her head, the smile gone from her voice. "Please do not make promises you cannot keep."

He did not flinch at her words. "But I mean to keep them, Leana. Will you give me a chance to prove myself to you? To start fresh, from the beginning?"

"You have nothing to prove to me. To yourself, perhaps, and to God. But not to me, Jamie. I love you." She reached up to cup his rough cheek and felt the warmth of him wash all over her. "Aye, we shall begin again. Now then, tell me about your dream."

"So I will." He found a chair and pulled it as close to the bed as he could, keeping his gaze locked with hers as he smoothed the bedcovers around her, patting the nursing babe in passing. "You'll remember me telling you about the first night I left Glentrool, when I slept beneath the stars on a stony cairn."

"I remember," she murmured. "The night you slept among the crushed berries of Jacob's ladder. The night you might have died."

"But I didn't die, Mistress McKie." He leaned over and gently kissed her, his lips still wet with tears. "I dreamed."

Author Notes

I cannot tell how the truth may be;
I say the tale as 'twas said to me.
SIR WALTER SCOTT

One of the more famous paintings of Robert Burns shows a rapt young Walter Scott seated on the floor, holding an open book while staring up at the legendary poet entering Sibbald's Library. With my first historical novel in hand, I feel a bit as Walter must have, humbled and awed by the talents of those who've already traveled this ground. When I read John Buchan or Neil Munro, George MacDonald or Samuel Rutherford Crockett, Robert Louis Stevenson or Sir Walter Scott, I wonder that I have the nerve even to try my hand at eighteenth-century Scottish historical fiction.

Then I remember that the whole notion 'twas not my idea to begin with, and I rest in the divine guidance that brought me here and the kind souls who've walked beside me with their gleaming candles held high, whispering words of encouragement. A special thanks to my editorial team at WaterBrook Press—Laura Barker, Carol Bartley, Rebecca Price, Lisa Tawn Bergren, Dudley Delffs, Paul Hawley, and Danelle McCafferty—and to my cherished early readers, Sara Fortenberry, Diane Noble, and Benny Gillies—and to my eagle-eyed proofreaders, Susan Richardson and Leesa Gagel. Your enthusiastic direction made all the difference.

My fictional journey across Galloway began seven years before *Thorn in My Heart* found its way into print. When Scotland beckoned as a possible setting for my tale about a woman who was neither beautiful nor loved, a visit to bonny Galloway put the question of location to rest. Photo albums began to fill, as did my writing-loft bookshelves. Five research trips to Scotland and two to England followed as the story unfolded. A thousand colorful photographs and five hundred Scottish resource titles later, *Thorn in My Heart* finally saw the light of day.

Except for historical figures mentioned in the text, such as Robert the Bruce, few of the characters in the novel lived and breathed in 1788. The locations, however, are very real indeed. The only placenames plucked from my imagination were Maxwell Park—though Galloway is thick with

Maxwells—and the farm in Kirkbean called Nether-carse. I simply couldn't bear to think of sullying some fine Galloway farm by having that ugsome Fergus McDougal live there. As to the rest of the major characters, if their stories feel a wee bit famil-iar, that's by intent. You'll find a parallel tale in the Bible, specifically in Genesis 25:19-34 and Genesis 27–29. Leah's heart-piercing story cried out to be told, and I could hardly refuse her.

Perhaps this novel has introduced you to some delightful Scottish words. *Pernickitie* is my personal favorite. I consulted the *Concise Scots Dictionary* (1999) for accuracy and Charles Mackay's *A Dictio-nary of Lowland Scotch* (1888) for sheer pleasure. Proper spellings for the clachans and burghs of Galloway varied from map to map and book to book, sometimes differing in the *same* book. Fran-cis Grose's *The Antiquities of Scotland* (1797) shows Threave Castle spelled *Thrive* in the caption beneath the sketch of the castle, then *Thrieve* and *Thrieff* in the text. You'll recall that Jamie passed brooding Threave Castle on his journey east. The image of Threave on the back cover was taken by Allan Wright, a talented Galloway photographer, whose work can be enjoyed at www.LyricalScot-land.co.uk. For consistency, I based the spellings for *Thorn in My Heart* on Sir John Sinclair's *The Statistical Account of Scotland* (1799), the most useful of all my research volumes.

Two contemporary Scottish ministers were exceedingly helpful during my research visits. Rev-erend William Holland, minister of New Abbey

Parish Church (yes, two words now), not only offered generous hospitality in the form of short-bread and tea at the manse but also answered dozens of questions about parish life in the late 1700s. And Reverend Hugh Steele, minister of Monigaff Parish Church (yes, one *N* now), was kind enough to tromp about the kirkyard with me to locate the gravestones of many a McKie, then directed me to the stained-glass windows above the pulpit depicting Jacob and Esau, as well as Rachel. Another serendipity.

Since raising blackface sheep is not one of the skills on my résumé, I am indebted to Mr. and Mrs. Dempster of Castlehill Farm near Lockerbie, who made me most welcome in their kitchen and filled my tape recorder with the wisdom and experience of their years of raising sheep. At East Culkae Farm in Sorbie, Mrs. McMuldroch chatted about farm life while serving the creamiest, sweetest Scottish tablet (a buttery sort of fudge) that I've ever tasted.

The House o' the Hill Inn was infamous among smugglers, appearing on most of the oldest Low-land maps from the 1600s on. On my latest visit to Galloway, I slept and supped at the present House o' the Hill (circa 1800), where the friendly propri-etor, one John Allwood, not only shared his maps and lore with me but gamely escorted me up to the crest of the hill where the *original* House o' the Hill stood. The ruins remain, surrounded by pines. (I'm quite certain I heard Walloch crashing through the trees, its braw rider desperate for lodging, but never did catch a glimpse of them.) Should you care to make a virtual visit to the House o' the Hill, www.houseothehill-hotel.com will take you there.

When Lachlan suggests Leana run off to Gretna Green to marry, he is referring to an infamous spot just inside the Scottish border where couples could be joined in matrimony without the usual waiting period. In Leana's time, this irregular wedding would have been conducted by one George Gordon, the "high priest" of Gretna Green until 1789. An old soldier, not a clergyman, Mr. Gordon reportedly wore a bygone military uniform with a huge cocked hat, a scarlet coat and jackboots, and a ponderous sword swinging from his belt. His "church," such as it was, looked more like a barn, and his "altar" was an ale cask, its only redeeming feature being the open Bible that sat on top of it.

Leana mentions the book *Primitive Physic, or an Easy and Natural Method of Curing Most Diseases.* Written by Reverend John Wesley (1702–1791), the book was in its twenty-first edition by 1785. Very popular in England, some copies of this book of useful remedies made their way north to Scotland as well. Ministers were often the most educated men in the parish and were frequently called upon to give medical advice, turning to books such as *Primitive Physic* for guidance.

For most of the Scottish nonfiction books on my shelves, as well as the custom map at the front of this novel, I have cartographer and antiquarian bookseller Benny Gillies to thank. His tidy bookshop near Castle Douglas in the village of Kirk-patrick Durham—filled with Scottish books, maps, and prints—is a bibliophile's paradise. Should a trip to his shop not be on your calendar this year, do visit him online at www.bennygillies.co.uk.

My heartfelt thanks go to the librarians of Castle Douglas, Dumfries, and Kirkcudbright, who made me feel welcome and guided me through their shelves. In addition to the titles mentioned above, the following dozen were the most helpful:

William Andrews, *Bygone Church Life in Scotland* (1899)

Tess Darwin, *The Scots Herbal: The Plant Lore of Scotland* (1996)

Rev. C. H. Dick, *Highways and Byways in Galloway and Carrick* (1916)

Malcolm Harper, *Rambles in Galloway* (1896)

Marion Lochhead, *The Scots Household in the Eighteenth Century* (1948)

James A. Mackay, *Burns-Lore of Dumfries & Galloway* (1988)

John Mactaggart, *Scottish Gallovidian Encyclopedia* (1824)

Stuart Maxwell and Robin Hutchinson, *Scottish Costume: 1550–1850* (1958)

Andrew McCormick, *The Tinkler-Gypsies of Galloway* (1906)

F. Marian McNeill, *The Scots Kitchen: Its Traditions and Lore with Old-Time Recipes* (1932)

Eunice G. Murray, *Scottish Women in Bygone Days* (1930)

Marjorie Plant, *The Domestic Life of Scotland in the 18th Century* (1952)

For those who enjoy such information, you'll find my full bibliography on my Web site, www.LizCurtisHiggs.com/Fiction, along with photos of some of the locations featured in *Thorn in My Heart,* additional historical notes, diaries from my Scottish trips, reader comments, links to my favorite Scottish sites, recommended Scottish music that inspired me as I wrote, and some delicious Scottish recipes. Should you care to use *Thorn in My Heart* as a springboard for a biblical study of Jacob, Leah, and Rachel, you'll find a guide for that on my site as well.

Kindly contact me directly to request my free newsletter, *The Graceful Heart,* printed and mailed once a year, and any of the following free items that might be of interest to you:

Thorn in My Heart Reader's Guide
Thorn in My Heart Bible Study Guide
Thorn in My Heart Galloway Guide

Here's how to reach me:

Liz Curtis Higgs
P.O. Box 43577
Louisville, KY 40253-0577

And please visit my Web site:

www.LizCurtisHiggs.com/Fiction

Until next time, dear reader, you are a blissin!

Liz Curtis Higgs

Scots Glossary

aboot—about
aften—often
ain—own
ane—one
auld—old
awa—away, distant
bairn—child
bethankit!—God be thanked!
birsie—hairy, hot-tempered
bittie—small piece
blaeberry—whortleberry
blether—babble, gossip
bletherie—talkative
blissin—blessing
bothy—cottage
bowsome—compliant, obedient

brae—hill, slope
braisant—shameless
braw—fine, handsome
bricht—bright
brither—brother
brose—oatmeal pudding
brownie—domestic sprite
Buik, the—the Bible
burn—brook, stream
by-pit—makeshift, substitute
byre—cowshed
cantie—contented
cantrip—charm, magic, trick, mischief
carse—low-lying land by a river
chauvies—children (Gypsy cant)

clachan—village, hamlet

cliver—clever

close—passageway, court-yard

collieshangle—disturbance, dogfight

creel—a deep wicker basket

creelin—custom for a newly married man that involves carrying a creel full of rocks

cryin siller—coins required for the marriage banns to be read

dashelt—battered

deid—dead

de'il—devil

donsie—wretched

douce—amiable, sweet

dout—doubt

doocot—dovecote

doon—down

drap—drop

dreich—bleak, dismal

dry stane dyke—stone fence without mortar

dwale—nightshade (Chaucer)

faither—father

fankle—entanglement

fash—vexed, annoyed

fause—counterfeit, false

fee—engage, hire as a servant

ferlie—superb, wonderful

fey—close to death, doomed

flindrikine—flirtatious

flit—transport, move one's household

flooers—flowers

fouterie—trivial, paltry

frichtsome—frightening

fu'—full

gaberlunzies—beggars

gavelock—crowbar

gentrice—gentry

Geographiae Scotiae—an atlas of Scotland (1749)

gie—give

gouden—golden

granbairn—grandchild

granmither—grandmother

green—young, youthful

grye—horse (Gypsy cant)

guid—good

gustie—savory, tasty

hae—have

halie—holy

hatesome—hateful

hauflin—adolescent boy, young farm worker

heidie—headstrong, rebellious

heirship—inheritance

heiven—heaven

het—hot

hizzie—hussy

hochmagandy—fornication

horners—those who make spoons, etc. from horns

hoose—house

hoot!—pshaw!

howdie—midwife

howre—whore

hurlie—trundle, move about on wheels

ill-deedie—mischievous, undisciplined

ill-fashioned—ill mannered

ill-paid—regretful

jalouse—imagine, presume

kell—headdress worn by a young, unmarried woman

kenspeckle—conspicuous, familiar

kintra—of the country, rustic

kirkin—a ceremonial attendance at church after a wedding

kist—chest

kittlie—itchy, sensitive

lang—long

lat—let, allow, permit

lickspit—a toady, a fawning subordinate

lingtow—a coil of rope

lingtowmen—men who smuggled goods across land

losh!—lord!

loosome—lovely

luckenbooths—locked stalls

luver—lover

mair—more

mart—an ox, slaughtered and salted for winter

mebbe—maybe, perhaps

meikle—great, much

mither—mother

mony—many

morn's morn—tomorrow morning

neeps—turnips

nicht—night

niver—never

och!—oh!

oo aye!—yes! (from the French *oui*)

orraman—odd-jobs man

oot—out

pernickitie—cantankerous, touchy

pit the brain asteep—meditate

pu'd—pulled

puir—poor

ramstam—rashly, rudely

reested—smoke-cured meat

reive—raid, rob, pillage

ricklie—ramshackle

roarie—noisy

rubbage—rubbish

sae—so

saicre—secret

sair—sorely, vehemently

sark—shirt

scuil—school

shilpit—emaciated, skinny

shooglie—shaky, wobbly

sit—such

simmer—summer

slitterie—messy, sloppy

smeddum—drive, energy, liveliness

sonsie—substantial, appealing

speeritie—energetic, spirited, vivacious

spendrif—extravagant

stane—stone

staw—stole

stayed lass—an old maid

strods—boots (Gypsy cant)

sully—silly

swicked—swindled, deceived

swickerie—trickery

tae—to

taigled—confused, hampered

tairt—tart

tattie-bogle—ragamuffin

tatties—potatoes

thar—there

thocht—thought, believed

thrifite—money box

tickler—problem, puzzle

timorsome—timid, fearful, nervous

tocher—dowry

twa—two

tup—a ram

ugsome—gruesome, horrible

unchancie—unlucky

unco—eccentric, odd, strange

vennel—alley

verra—very

wabbit—exhausted, weary

waddin—wedding

wag-at-the-wa'—unencased pendulum clock

walloch—vigorous dance; Highland fling

wark—work

weatherful—stormy

whan—when

whase—whose

whatsomever—whatever

whaur—where

wheesht!—hush!

wi'—with

widdershins—counterclockwise

wull—will

wutch—witch

yestreen—yesterday, last night

yestermorn—yesterday morning